Devil's Gambit

A Soylent Publications release

Cover art by Steve Archer
Cover design by Jhada Rogue Addams
Cover model: Donna Hirsch

ISBN: 978-0-9893761-0-5

Devils Gambit

Book Two of The Vengeance Cycle

JHADA ROGUE ADDAMS

:: *Does it truly bother you so much to know that women are also capable of such things?* ::

:: *I don't know. I guess I wanted to think that only men did this kinda thing.* ::

:: *Did he not deserve the justice you rendered?* ::

:: *Oh yeah.* :: Jilah nodded as the landscape wooshed by. :: *He completely deserved it – what he endured, as awful as it was, doesn't excuse going out and putting other people through it.* ::

She paused for a moment, then added, :: *It just puts me in a grey area that I'm not entirely comfortable with.* ::

:: *Humans say that their Justice is blind, do they not?* ::

Jilah replied with a halfhearted chuckle, :: *Yeah, but she's not stupid.* ::

:: *Few things in life are ever simply black and white, beloved,* ::

:: *I know. It just makes me...* ::

Argent softly answered. :: *Because of this, you doubt the righteousness of your duty.* ::

Jilah felt her stomach drop, and her mouth was instantly dry. He was right. He usually was, damn him.

:: *Being an instrument of karma is rarely easy, beloved.* ::

Jilah reached the bike, plucking a skullcap from the handlebars.

:: *What it comes down to is – if I don't do this, who will? And as it is, I can only do so much. How many others are out there? How many other women and children are enduring horrors beyond imagining?* ::

She straddled the motorcycle and started it, then set her jaw.

:: *I may not like it, but it needs doing.* ::

This book is dedicated to all my fans who have been patiently waiting for the next book in this series. It's taken me a LONG time to get it done, but it's finally here.

Thanks guys. You all rock the hell out.

I want to thank Kim Turner for her extensive feedback, which helped to change the initial focus of the story entirely, but only made me work harder to make it a better tale. I'm far happier with this version. I also want to thank Lucie Le Blanc, my 'Canadian connection' for maple syrup goodies, for her feedback and help, and my kickass editor, Sue Baiman.

Devil's Gambit

Chapter 1
NO REST FOR THE WICKED

"You are all so deliciously fragile."

A beautiful, nude woman stepped up to a man who appeared to be in his thirties, beneath all the cuts and bruises. Her lips curved into a sharp smile as she leaned in and purred, "It is fortunate for us that you never learned to truly fear the darkness and everything in it."

The man let out a pained groan as the woman took a long, lazy puff off her cigarette, the cherry on the end glowing bright red. She pushed it into his eye and he screamed, pulling at the restraints that held his arms up against the cement wall, above his head. The woman laughed, and as she turned, Jilah couldn't help but notice the strap-on covered in blood and other fluids that jutted obscenely from her pubis.

Oh god. Jilah took a step back as bile rose in her throat.

Hearing the noise, the woman spun to face her, then smiled. A wave of blonde hair spilled over a shoulder, almost covering a nipple.

"Another toy – and a pretty one at that. How lovely."

Jilah shuddered at the sound of that voice, so smooth and smoky. A pleasurable shiver raced up her spine and she shook it off, discomfited with her own response to it.

"Who are you, pretty?

The woman took a step towards Jilah, her eyes sweeping up the avatar's frame. "Or, should I ask, what are you?"

Jilah let the illusion that hid her horns and tail drop, surprised when the woman's smile widened.

"Ah! Now I can see you. Come sister, share his torment with us," the woman purred.

Sister? Jilah frowned and growled, "I'm not your fuckin' sister, lady."

The woman pursed her lips, cocking her hips as another woman who could have been her twin moved into view, all smiles. She was naked as well.

The cruel woman frowned for a moment, peering back at Jilah with an intensely curious expression.

"You are a daughter of Lilith, are you not, sssister?"

Jilah shivered as the woman hissed out the last word. She opened the connection to Argent, readying herself for a possible attack, but so far, the pair only seemed intent on having her join in the torture. She didn't know what would happen if she turned them down, but it probably wouldn't be good. Whatever these women were, they definitely didn't smell human.

Cold anger echoed through the connection as Argent replied, :: *They are Succubi, beloved, be wary. As I've mentioned before, demons can be remarkably strong. I will be by your side as soon as I can.* ::

Halfway between being honestly curious and trying to play for time, Jilah asked, "Daughter of Lilith?"

The woman with the strap-on smiled, her image shimmering and shifting. Jilah was suddenly looking back at a creature with large, black horns and a thick red tail as her human illusion dropped away. Her voice remained the same seductive purr, though, which seemed odd coming through a mouthful of razor sharp teeth.

"Do you truly not know what you are? How can that be?"

The man chained to the wall took one look at this new, horrifying apparition and started screaming, his throat already hoarse and raw. It sounded awful. He was definitely still alive, but he wouldn't be for long if the two bitches in front of her kept at him. The demon's companion, still in her attractive human meatsuit form, moved to hit him in the jaw and the man slumped in the restraints, now silent.

Jilah could still hear a heartbeat coming from the body as she took a deep breath and quietly replied, "I don't know what I am."

Distraction is key. If I'm going to be able to help him at all, I need to divert their attention until reinforcements can get here.

The demoness with the grotesque, soiled strap-on walked towards her, sniffing the air and closing her eyes in pleasure. Jilah desperately hoped that the creature didn't brush up against her. The stench coming from the filthy appliance was repellent, and she was pretty certain that she wouldn't be able to hold her temper if touched.

"You are different, but you still smell of me and mine."

That is so totally not what I wanted to hear right now, Jilah groaned internally.

The creature reached out to her, close enough to brush a claw against her cheek, but pulled her hand away just short of doing so. The demoness pulled her hand back to sniff, then lick her fingers; her eyes heated. It then looked back at her, eying Jilah's body and letting out a sensual sigh.

God, is this what I look like to my targets? I think I'm going to be sick.

Jilah blinked and asked, "What are you?"

The demon's ersatz twin walked over to join her companion and they both laughed as they placed their arms around each other's waists. They spoke as one.

"We are the children of desire, need, and want, dear one."

"What the hell do any of those things have to do with what you're doing to him?" she blurted.

The woman shrugged and replied, "The desire was his." They both looked at each other and chuckled.

Jilah stammered, unable to help herself.

"Wait... he actually *wanted* you to do this to him?"

The demoness smiled and nodded.

"It was once his fondest wish."

Turning back to face him, she crowed, "He doesn't like it too much now that he's in it, though. Pity."

She turned to her sister and they both laughed like it was the funniest thing they'd ever heard.

Jilah shook her head, trying to understand, but failing miserably.

"Wanting something doesn't necessarily mean that it is at all good for you."

Her sister replied, "But you still want it."

3

Jilah's stomach turned as the woman's hand slid down her companion's hip.

"Crave it."

"And that is where we come in," both women explained.

Jilah thought about it for a moment, then frowned. "But, if he no longer wants it, why are you continuing to torment him?"

"It is our calling, sister – our blood. A wish requested is a contract to be fulfilled."

Yep. Definitely much happier when I was human and didn't know that any of this shit existed, Jilah muttered internally.

"So – you'll continue until he's dead," she replied.

They both looked back at her as if she was an idiot.

"Of course."

:: *Their kind are not known for breaking a contract, love.* :: Argent explained.

:: *Where are you?* :: Jilah asked, feeling more than a little nauseated.

:: *Close. Mira is with me.* ::

Jilah nodded and said, "Ah. Gotcha."

The demoness took a step towards her, sniffing at the air between them. Her eyes glittered as she asked, "You truly don't understand, do you?"

Jilah blinked and blurted, "No. I don't."

"She is displeased by our actions, sister. I can taste it on her."

The demoness' blonde companion curled her lip in disgust. Her expression soured as she spat, "There is the stink of... *cooperation* on her. A pact with meat."

A zing jittered along Jilah's nerves as the sisters separated and began to circle her slowly in separate directions. She backed away, trying to keep them both in view. The demoness hissed, "Perhaps it is a *prison* for her, this shell. Perhaps we should *free* her."

Jilah was startled to feel a gentle pressure in her head as an alien voice echoed from her throat, "All have their work to conduct on this plane, sister."

The Succubi stopped in their tracks as the voice continued, "We have our appointed task, as you have yours."

The demoness took a deep breath, her eyes fluttering as she took a step back and nodded. "Agreed."

A mild frown marred her features as she purred, "Your host does not seem as understanding or as... *accommodating.*"

Jilah heard herself respond, "We have no choice in this matter. We are not allowed to exact vengeance upon women – even those with only the seeming appearance of such."

Whoa. That's something I didn't know, Jilah thought to herself, terrified now. *It was a hell of a way to find out about such a limitation. What the hell's going on?*

The woman nodded and stepped back beside her sister, placated.

"As long as you abide by our code and do not keep us from completing the terms of our contract with this one," she waved a claw to indicate the chained man, "we will allow you to pass with no violence offered."

"You have our word on it," Jilah heard herself reply. Suddenly, she was back in control and quaking with anger.

"The fuck I won't intervene," she muttered.

:: Jilah! ::

She turned to see Argent and Mira walking towards her calmly, as if nothing completely horrific was happening off to the side.

:: Good! Reinforcements. ::

Argent walked past her, greeting the demoness with a smile, dropping into a dialect that sounded completely alien. The creature preened, smiling, and greeted him with a nod.

:: What the hell are you doing? ::

He quickly explained, *:: They're right. They have a given job to do – just as you do. ::*

:: You're joking, right? They're torturing that poor man. :: Who was now gibbering to himself. When had he woken up? Jilah watched as he popped a thumb into his mouth.

:: This is the nature of our world. They are not human, beloved. ::

:: But... :: she stammered, disgusted as he continued to converse with the two creatures blithely, as if they were meeting at a party. *:: What they're doing, it's... ::*

:: Wrong? :: Argent responded.

:: Well, yes – for fuck sakes, look at him. He's a wreck! ::

The sanguine's amusement echoed through the connection. *:: And how do you suppose your prey looks after you're done with it? ::*

Jilah blinked, thrown off balance for a moment. *:: That's different. ::*

:: *They are creatures of the Nightside, beloved. Light cannot exist without darkness. They have a valid place in this world – when they are called into it.* ::
That brought her up short. :: *Wait. What are you saying?* ::
:: *This idiot summoned them. He asked for this. Begged for it. He thought himself the ultimate masochist.* :: Argent chuckled softly in her thoughts as he said, :: *He was, of course, incorrect.* ::
:: *So, because he made a mistake, this has to happen to him?* ::
Argent smiled as the two creatures sauntered away from him, hips swaying seductively as they walked back over to the man who was now screeching in a keening wail that hurt Jilah's ears.

The sanguine walked back over to her, his court mask still well in place as he explained, :: *He consciously chose to call them forth, which is no easy task. Minor demons only gain access to this plane when some idiot thinks himself strong and smart enough to actually call them to his side from the Black Rift. He signed a contract with them. Foolishness must have consequences or else this place would be overrun with their kind.* ::

Jilah stared at him, stunned. So, they hadn't lied to her. It was completely incomprehensible that anybody would actually ask for this sort of thing. It also hadn't occurred to her that summoning demons actually worked.

:: *Come, beloved. Leave them to their work,* :: Argent murmured softly, slipping a hand around her waist. He gave Mira a brief nod, and the diminutive woman blurred out of the room.

:: *I'm not OK with this.* :: Jilah trembled at his touch. :: *Not at all.* ::
:: *You don't have to be. But it is the way of things. Someday you will understand.* ::
Jilah shuddered and quietly replied, :: *Don't take this the wrong way, but I don't think I ever want to.* ::

Argent suddenly became very still and Jilah frowned.
:: *What?* ::
Argent held up a hand, then leaned forward, eyes narrowing. :: *It would appear that we are being watched.* ::
A flicker of movement caught his eye and he turned to track it. Jilah followed his gaze, but could see nothing out of the ordinary. She looked back at him, wondering what he'd seen. Whatever it was, it had obviously unsettled him, and she found herself surprised at an

erratic train of thought that whipped through his mind. She couldn't quite understand it, though.

The Sanguine shook his head and took a step back. :: *It is nothing,* :: he assured her. :: *It has been a long night, and...* ::

Jilah shook her head, irritated now. :: *No. It's not nothing. Something spooked you.* ::

Argent looked back at her, uneasy. :: *Simply memories – bad ones. I thought I saw... someone from long ago.* :: He sighed, and shook his head. :: *They are best left in the past, beloved.* ::

Unsure if she wanted to press him, Jilah simply nodded. Perhaps he was right. After all, everybody had their demons to conquer. In this case, some of them were literal. It discomfited her that he didn't want to talk to her about it, but it was getting late, and she was damn near running on fumes.

She gently took his hand and pulled him along.

:: *I think that's enough for one night's work. Let's get going.* ::

He smiled back at her, but she couldn't help noticing a tightness in his expression that hadn't been there before. :: *I could not agree more. The work will still be here when the sun dips below the horizon tomorrow.* ::

Jilah nodded, feeling more tired than she had five minutes ago.

As they turned and began making their way back to the Convent, her mind kept going back over the confrontation with the Succubi. The things they'd said..

She shivered as she murmured, :: *They called me their sister.* ::

Argent nodded. :: *The reality is that you are now apparently half daemon, for good or ill. They were simply referring to the blood kinship they sensed within you.* ::

Jilah took a deep breath, her voice shaking a little. :: *And that voice in me. How could it just take over and talk like that?* ::

This was beginning to scare the crap out of her.

:: *We are in territory now that I am entirely unfamiliar with. I could not say.* ::

Jilah frowned and looked down at her own hands.

:: *The more I find out about what I might be, the more frightened I get.* ::

Argent gently touched her shoulder. :: *Try to see the strength in what you are now.* ::

7

:: Am I a monster? :: she asked softly.

:: We are all capable of being monstrous, beloved. It depends on what side of the definition you stand. ::

Jilah looked up at him, confused.

:: Your chosen targets, your prey, are the things they do not monstrous in your eyes? ::

Jilah's eyes hardened as she nodded. *:: Oh yeah. ::*

:: And do you not suppose that they see you as monstrous in return? ::

Jilah looked away for a moment, unsure. *:: I never really thought about it, I guess. ::*

:: The monstrous has its place, beloved – as does beauty and love and all other things fair and comforting. :: He smiled and brushed her cheek gently with cool knuckles.

Jilah closed her eyes and leaned into his touch. *:: Your logic is remarkably uncomfortable. ::*

Argent chuckled softly. *:: If there were a way to soften the blow of this new world against you, I would, but doing so would be doing you a disservice. ::*

She sighed and nodded, *:: I know. Still sucks, though. ::*

:: At times, yes. It does. Home now? ::

:: Yeah. ::

Argent captured her hand with his and pulled her gently to him. *:: Let us spend the rest of the night together – just the two of us. ::*

:: Really? ::

Over a week had passed since the big undead hootenanny outside the Ursuline Convent had gone down. Argent and Aurelian had been busy working to unruffle all the local and international diplomatic feathers that had been stomped on during the ordeal. Meanwhile, Jilah had gone back to business as usual. During that time, the two of them hadn't really had much in the way of unbroken time to spend together, and it was starting to grate on her nerves. She could tell that it bothered him as well.

Argent nodded, then said, *:: I'll have Aurelian clear my schedule. You've had quite enough of the monstrous tonight. ::*

:: I'd really like that. :: she smiled. *:: A Date night. ::*

The idea was strangely energizing. She could feel herself perking back up the more she thought about it.

:: Where should we go first? :: she asked, grinning now.

Argent chuckled softly. *:: Can we try... sushi? The idea of raw fish is intriguing. I'm wondering if it is as delicious as I've heard. ::*

Jilah nodded and kissed him. *:: Anything you want. ::*

Devil's Gambit

Chapter 2
OUT ON THE TOWN

:: I do love watching you eat. ::
Jilah smiled and popped a bite of yellowtail roll into her mouth, enjoying the zing of the wasabi on her tongue. *It may not nourish me, but at least it still tastes amazing,* she thought to herself as she closed her eyes and savored the taste. Argent had been able to get the owner and the chef to stay up late to serve them. He seemed to be doing his best to spoil her utterly.

:: I thought you found it nauseating to watch people chew, :: she replied, making a happy yummy sound.

Argent chuckled softly. *:: Bah. ::*

Jilah swallowed and reached for another section of roll with her chopsticks.

:: You, sir, are dangerously smitten if you're willing to watch me do something that grosses you out and enjoy it. ::

Argent leaned back in his seat and murmured, *:: With others, I can't share the experience. ::* She watched his eyes flutter closed as the combination of flavors danced along her tongue, and consequently his as well. *:: It's been centuries since I was last able to enjoy the taste of food. I find that I have missed it immensely. ::*

:: Is that why you're taking me to every restaurant in town lately? :: Jilah asked, grinning. Not that she was complaining; she was enjoying his reactions to the food as well. It added an extra dimension to the meal that was quite pleasant indeed. Although feeling truly mixed

emotions and sensations was still taking a little getting used to, it definitely had it's perks.

:: *Now some of the unagi..?* :: Argent asked, hopeful.

Jilah laughed softly and dipped a piece of Eel Nigiri into a small pool of soy sauce. For some reason, she was reminded of the crawfish heads he'd had her dining on the other night. They'd been surprisingly delicious, even though they were completely creepy looking. The idea of sucking out the heads was nauseating at first, but the damn things ended up being quite tasty.

She looked over at him and popped the eel into her mouth.

:: *Thank you for this.* ::

:: *There is nowhere else I would rather be, and we are both due a night together after everything that has happened.* :: Argent smiled, almost drooling at the taste of the eel.

She thought about it for a moment and replied, :: *Well, I've heard a lot about New Orleans nightlife, but haven't really gotten to experience much of it since we arrived..* ::

Argent looked at her with a wry grin and teased, :: *Didn't you have that night out with the ladies?* ::

Jilah bumped her toe into his shin beneath the table. :: *You know what I mean.* ::

Argent laughed and shifted in his seat, raising an eyebrow.

:: *Then, clearly, this is a situation that needs to be rectified.* ::

She laughed and then popped a bit of salmon into her mouth.

:: *So, where do we go after this?* ::

He grinned. :: *Shall we dance?* ::

Watching Argent dance? Oh yeah. That's something she definitely wanted to see. Soon.

She gave him a heated smile and a slow nod.

:: *You always have the best ideas.* ::

The driving rhythm of the music made her senses tingle as they stepped inside the club, and she was briefly reminded of the first time they'd met. Jilah smiled at the memory. God, he'd been sex on wheels, then. Hell, he still was. Initially uncomfortable with the open interest in the eyes of the women, and some of the men, around them, she finally relaxed when she realized that he wasn't really looking at any of them. They all treated him with deference, moving politely out of his way; some of them, while making a strange, subtle hand gesture. *They know who he is here,* she thought to herself. Everybody seemed to want to do something for him – for them, but they weren't overly fawning or gaudy. It was a little heady.

:: *Wow. Moved immediately to the head of the line, and everybody's making room for you to pass through. It's kinda cool.* :: Jilah chuckled, tightening her grip on his hand.

He shrugged and replied, :: *Royalty of a sort has its privileges.* :: He sighed and added, :: *It can also be an enormous pain in the ass at times.* ::

Jilah gently jostled him. :: *Now, now. Tonight's not the night for dwelling on bad stuff.* ::

Argent looked over at her, then smiled, the heat in his eyes intense as he looked her over. :: *Indeed, it is not. There are much more compelling things to focus on at the moment.* ::

He guided her out onto the dance floor with a sly grin, sliding his hand down her waist.

:: *Why do I get the feeling that you're going to be so much better at this than I am?* :: she asked, suddenly nervous.

Argent chuckled and pulled her close, and for the first time in her life she understood how important it was to have a partner that knew how to lead well. His body seemed made for this kind of activity, fluid and graceful as they moved together with the sensual beat of the music around them. The man seemed to pull joy itself from the air and feed it to her as they danced. They'd engaged in another, more lurid, private dance between the sheets before, but there was something about being so completely in each other's space in front of a crowd, even if most of them were focused on their own movements or partners.

She briefly wondered how many people were watching them, and began blushing. Argent shifted against her, driving all thought from her mind, and fire blazed through her body, lighting her up and making her tremble.

:: *Do not sell yourself short, beloved.* :: His voice was low and heated, as he spun her around, catching her hand, then pulling her close, gently touching his lips to hers as they began moving again. :: *You follow wonderfully.* ::

Jilah smiled, giddy and completely turned on, allowing herself to simply enjoy the moment.

:: *As sappy as it sounds, it's everything I wanted it to be, dancing with you.* ::

Argent smiled and quietly replied, :: *I feel the same, beloved.* ::

Chapter 3
SACRELIGE

Jilah squeezed his hand as they walked quickly back through the stone passages leading towards the throne room.

:: *I really enjoyed our date tonight, but if we don't get to the bedroom right now.. ::*

Argent quickly turned and pushed her up against the wall with a savage grin.

:: *Who says we need a bed? ::*

An electric pulse shot through her as he pressed his body against hers with a groan. She dropped her head to his shoulder to muffle her cry as she wrapped her arms around him, clutching at his back.

:: *You're lucky I didn't take you in an alleyway, or on the dance floor. ::*

Jilah shivered and whispered, :: *God, what you do to me.. ::*

Argent pressed his lips to her neck, pulling her hips against his as he growled, :: *I assure you, it is entirely mutual. ::*

Her head rocked back as he nipped at her throat, then Argent went still at the sound of someone yelling.

He pulled away from her as he murmured, :: *Roane and Ariane seem to have cut their trip short. ::*

:: *They're back? ::*

Jilah's heart leapt, after the initial disappointment at having to stop. They could – *would* pick this up later. She had missed her friends and hoped that they'd had a good time on their vacation. Roane had been a wreck after 'the event', as she'd come to call it, and Argent had suggested that the couple head out to Iceland to recover. They had gladly taken him up on it, and had left as quickly as they could get their things packed.

:: *I wonder what brought them back early?* :: she asked as they uncoupled and adjusted their clothes before walking towards the source of the disturbance.

"It's a *sacrilege*."

Roane turned and scowled at Jilah and Argent as they walked into the throne room. Jilah could feel the anger rolling off the necromancer in waves.

"We leave for a week of R and R, and all of a sudden these assholes want to dig everything up and..."

Roane shook her head, wincing.

Argent quietly explained, "It's hardly 'all of a sudden'. Most of the regions throughout the country are experiencing the same issue – the living are running out of room."

Aurelian shifted on his feet, looking distinctly uncomfortable.

"It's bullshit, is what it is," Roane grated, "and disrespectful as hell. The meatpuppets just don't like being reminded of their own mortality. It's WEAK."

Argent murmured, "Do you truly think that this is my choosing?"

He turned away, frowning, "By doing this, our court loses a substantial block of power to stand against the Council themselves. They are well aware that once the dead are relocated that you become nullified as a protector of this region."

Roane scowled, her lips pursing as she thought it over.

"As distasteful as it is, the decision has been taken out of our hands. The human governance has made its decision, and is moving forward with their plans for relocation."

Ariane, who had been standing silently watching the exchange finally stepped forward and placed a hand on Roane's shoulder. "I know how you feel about them, baby, Lord knows I do," she paused, then frowned as she looked over at Argent.

"You know we'll have to relocate."

Argent blinked and Jilah felt a shock roll through him as Ariane continued, "This may be my home, but they are her... people. It would only be fitting to have her near them."

Argent became very still as he replied, "I may not like it, but will respect your decision."

Roane looked over at her lover, stunned. She shook her head and waved her off. "I need to get out of here. I gotta think."

Roane quickly walked out of the room and Ariane looked at Argent, anger in her eyes.

"The humans involved in this decision will regret this," Ariane smiled and Jilah felt a chill in the air as she purred, "And they will deserve everything that comes upon them from this."

Ariane nodded respectfully to Argent before she strode out.

"What was all that about?" Jilah asked, frowning.

Argent began walking to the small alcove office and Jilah followed as he explained, "For some time, there have been rumblings in the human governance about exhuming the bodies from their resting places in the larger cities and relocating them in an area central to the rest of the country so that the numbers and caretaking are more manageable." He sighed and sat down on a sofa, shaking his head. "I never thought they'd actually go through with it."

"But why? Why do it at all?" she asked, baffled.

"A very good question." Aurelian replied as he took a seat across from the Sanguine. "The money needed for a project of this scale is going to be astronomical, not to mention the political squabbles that will take place from state to state over this. If they didn't consider it necessary, it wouldn't be at all realistic."

Argent looked up at her and elaborated. "For years, the New Orleans province has been called 'the City of the Dead' for the very fact that more cemeteries have established plots of land throughout the city than the living themselves. Their population is quickly overflowing its urban sprawls. There are a finite supply of resources available in any given area, and since humans don't see the dead as needing any of them..."

"They're the 'odd man out' and they get shifted." Jilah thought about this for a moment, then asked, "So – where are they going to put everybody?"

"They're moving forward with plans to re-inter everybody out in an area of Ellsworth, Kansas. The committee is choosing to rename the area the Internment Grounds of the States."

Ugh. What a cold, impersonal name.

Jilah shivered at the idea, then asked, "When are they planning on starting this... project?"

Aurelian's expression was one of distaste as he replied, "They're already breaking ground. The current residents of Ellsworth are being paid to begin the process of constructing the cairn facility and the government will soon begin special runs on the high speed railroad system that runs throughout the country to all the major cities."

Argent took a deep breath, then looked up at Aurelian. "Who are the current regents within the borders of Kansas?"

Aurelian took a quick look through the notes in the binder on his lap and replied, "Ellis Jakoby is Prime of Topeka."

Argent crooked an eyebrow and asked, "Only one for the entire state?"

"Ellis has petitioned for additional help out in Hays, but has been denied by the council several times."

Argent steepled his fingers, then looked over at Aurelian.

"Then we may be in a position to help him out, given the rather delicate nature of this situation, don't you think?"

Aurelian sat back in his seat and frowned. "She's too young to rule, Strigaisha."

Argent blinked slowly, then quietly replied. "With the added 'population' Ellis will soon be receiving, she will be in a remarkably potent position; one that could possibly keep the council at bay when she and her lover leave this court."

"They won't allow it." Aurelian shook his head.

"Still, I think it's time that I met Prime Jakoby and extended an offer of... *assistance* with his current situation."

Jilah watched the two of them, not liking the fact that her new friends would be leaving so soon after she'd gotten here. Her fondness for Roane and Ariane had grown quicker than she'd expected. Not being one to make friends all that easily in the past, she was uncomfortable with the idea that the pair were no longer going to be around.

Argent replied, knocking her out of the train of thought, "Set it up."

Aurelian nodded, and began making notes.

Argent looked over at her and sent, :: *The council will be all too eager to send their own emissary to command the city once Roane has left, unless provisions have been made to protect those of us left behind. I like it no more than you do.* ::

:: *It's... well, I just met them.* :: she sighed softly.

:: *I know, love. I know.* ::

She turned and looked over at him, an ache in her heart. How quickly the emotions of the night had turned. It was a little exhausting.

:: *I want to talk to Roane.* ::

Argent placed a gentle hand on her arm, squeezing and replying, :: *Give her time, beloved. She has a great deal to think about.* ::

Jilah nodded, then sighed. The ardor from earlier had cooled significantly, and now she just wanted to sleep.

:: *You're right, and it's late anyway. I'll turn in. You coming?* ::

Argent gently pulled her up and circled his hands around her waist. :: *I'll follow shortly - there is something I need to take care of, then I'll be right there.* ::

Jilah stared back at him, her voice firm as she said, :: *We need to do this date night thing more often.* ::

Argent nodded and leaned in to kiss her. :: *We will* ::

He pulled away and Jilah caught his hand, squeezing it briefly before turning to go, calling out, "Try and stay out of trouble, you two."

Aurelian's voice trailed out, answering, "Yeah, yeah."

Argent stilled as he spotted the bouquet of flowers on his desk; a collection of tuberoses and rosa canina surrounding a single black rose in the middle. How had he missed them before? His stomach dropped as he looked them over.

Well, it would appear that the game is finally afoot.

The tuberoses signified dangerous pleasures, the rosa canina - pleasured mixed with pain, and the black rose - hate, the icing on the cake of this particular message. It was definitely her style, speaking through flowers.

Gwendolyne.

Not daring to look at Aurelian, he quietly asked, "The flowers. Who placed them here?"

The selkie looked over at him, frowning.

"The chatelaine? Why?"

"I believe I am being followed."

He moved to collect the vase, dumping it into the trash.

Aurelian blinked, frowning.

"By who?"

"My sire."

Argent's expression became bland as he sat down on the sofa, hands clasped as he sat forward.

"You're kidding."

Aurelian stared back at the Sanguine. The selkie didn't know the details; Argent hadn't really shared much of his past with anybody up to this point. Still, he knew it was rare enough for a sire to track their get down after so many years apart.

"Unfortunately, no."

Argent pursed his lips, deep in thought. *After all this time - if it is her, why show herself now? What does she hope to gain from this game?*

He looked over at the Selkie, eyes sharp and hard. He had only shared a portion of his past with his former lover, never feeling entirely comfortable with trusting anybody as thoroughly as he had once trusted his sire. That had come back to bite him in a way that had taken him far too long to recover.

"Any idea what she's doing out here?" Aurelian asked.

Argent shook his head, at a loss. He had only partially known what truly motivated the woman a century and a half ago. But now? It was anyone's guess. A cruel, sadistic woman - she had been his perfect match back then. Shifting back against the couch, he realized how much he'd changed from the utter blackguard bastard he used to be. Once again, he checked the connection between himself and Jilah to insure that it was as tightly shut as he could make it. It would only add unwanted complications if she was able to sense any of this. He needed to figure out what the cruel beauty who had turned him, then shunned him outright, now had planned.

He hadn't felt her presence since the night she'd left him, a fledgling barely a night old, to fend for himself.

"Think she'll do anything?"

Argent quietly replied, "She has already sent the message she wished for me to see."

Aurelian blinked, then looked over at the trashcan.

"Does this mean she's going to come out swinging?"

Argent shook his head, taking a deep breath.

"Unless she's changed her tactics, she'll stay in the shadows, waiting to see how her move affects me before she steps out and directly confronts me."

Aurelian let out a nervous laugh. "Well, let's hope it stays that way. The last thing we need in this prefecture is a Sanguine pissing contest. The Council would have a field day with it."

"Indeed."

Argent met the selkie's eyes, then said, "See if you can find anything. I doubt that she will have been lax enough to leave evidence of her presence other than the message itself, but...still. Get back to me with anything you hear, no matter how insignificant it seems."

Aurelian nodded and Argent stood up.

"It has been quite a night. I believe I will retire early and start again fresh tomorrow night."

Chapter 4

ALL TARGETS ARE NOT CREATED EQUAL

Hell of a place to pick up a target.

It was the first hunt that had taken her so far from New Orleans. Jilah tracked him as he walked out of the facility, her gaze quickly flicking back to the guards and cameras while he made his way out to his car. Jilah ground her teeth as the man fingered the keys on his belt and smiled, his expression smug and self-satisfied. A red haze swirled around him, drifting around his body in lazy coils. He'd likely just sated his need with one of the inmates inside.

Tall and wide, the man had to scrunch down to fit his enormous frame into the car. Was there a make and model of car that such a large man could fit into comfortably? A Hummer perhaps. The car started, and she watched as her target pulled out of the space and made his way out onto the road. The stars glittered brightly in the night sky, the moon just a sliver in the dark canopy, a sharpened weapon of light.

Turned out that her prey didn't live far from the women's correctional facility, and Jilah wondered how many off the clock visits the asshole had made to the prison in pursuit of his extra-curricular activities. She followed on foot, easily keeping up with him. The huge man finally pulled into the driveway of a small house and got out of the car, stretching and briefly scratching his balls before closing the door.

Ugh, she thought, wincing.

Although this display, coupled with the visions in her head, made him completely abhorrent to her, she had to admit that he wasn't physically unattractive. Jilah didn't understand why good looking men felt the need to force themselves on women.

She grumbled as she crept around the back of the house. Although she'd defeated creatures much scarier than her current prey, she had to admit that his size was a little daunting. He was almost as big as one of those professional wrestlers. Wanting to share one of her 'guilty pleasures' with her new friend, Gigi had parked Jilah in front of the television in her room one night and had her watch a 'best of' DVD featuring some of the first-rate wrestling matches throughout the years. Jilah had thought it all fairly hokey at the time, but it helped to provide an odd frame of reference for moments like this.

At the back door, Jilah peered inside to see where the man had gone. *How to play it..*, she mused, pursing her lips. *Do I seduce him or do I just go for broke on that enormous forehead of his?*

It wasn't enough to simply dispense justice without 'playing with her food' a little, as Argent was so fond of saying. She wanted to keep it interesting. It was important to enjoy one's work. The man walked into the kitchen and she stepped back into the shadows, continuing to watch him from the relative darkness outside, as he began moving around and making dinner.

Jilah took a deep breath, then cat-footed up to the front of the house. As she stepped onto the front porch, she started going through various excuses in her head before finally taking a breath and rapping on the door. The man's footsteps echoed as he made his way into the foyer, and Jilah tried her best to look doe eyed and lost as he opened the door. There was an edge of irritation in his gaze as he peered down at her, but it softened slightly as he checked her out.

"Can I help you?" he asked, his tone brusque.

"Oh god, I hope so. I'm..ah..well, my car broke down and I totally left my cellphone back at home by accident, so I can't call Triple A, and..."

He cut her off and grunted, "So – what? You're askin' to use my phone?"

Jilah nodded and quickly replied, "Yes, please. That's if it's not too big of a..."

He thought about it for a moment, then muttered, "Come on in."

Apparently he wasn't very fond of chatty women. It was probably easier to let her in than to close the door on her and invite more knocking.

"Thank you so much!"

Jilah smiled and stepped inside, looking around for the phone.

"It's over there."

He pointed to an old, no-frills phone.

She walked over and picked up the receiver, smiling as he looked over at her, nonplussed.

Probably doesn't like unexpected visitors.

Jilah turned back to the phone bringing it up to her ear as she looked around. Thick curtains covered the windows and a shotgun was propped up in the corner across the room. If it was loaded and he was able to get to it before she could subdue him, things could get ugly. She was pretty certain that she didn't want to find out how getting shot felt.

Jilah began patting her pockets, acting embarrassed as she looked over at him and said, "Oh crap, I left the card in the car."

She moved to place the phone back on the cradle and turned to face him. She pointed towards the door and asked, "Do you mind if I...?"

He took a deep breath as his gaze swept over her, assessing her. He shook his head, his eyes sharp and his tone empty. "Nah. I don't think I'm ready for you to leave yet."

Jilah's stomach lurched at the ugly leer on the man's face and she took a step away from him.

"Mister... I... I just need to use your phone. I don't want any trouble," she stammered, doing her best to try to shy away from him as he advanced on her.

"No trouble at all. Just gimme what I want and you can use my phone as much as you like."

She shook her head, blinking quickly.

"I don't think so," she quietly replied. "Look, I'll just go.."

One of his big ham hands darted out to snatch at her and she evaded effortlessly. He cocked his head and blinked, not entirely sure of what he'd just seen.

"Quick little minx, aren't ya?" he hissed, "Doesn't matter. Only need to grab you once – and then you're done."

"You so sure of that?" she asked, her tone mocking now.

His face flushed and he paused, eyes narrowing before he lunged toward her and tried to grab her again. This time, she dropped all pretense and blurred across the room.

The man blinked quickly, starting to frown. Something was puttering around in his little reptilian brain, but it wasn't quite getting through.

How the fuck did she do that? Jilah heard him mutter in his head. *Nah – impossible. I'm just tired. Seein' things.*

He moved to catch her again and she sped behind him, reaching out to tap his shoulder before blurring back down the hallway, well out of reach. She watched him shiver as he whirled on her, beads of sweat beginning to appear on his forehead. The man paled and his lower lip began to quiver, but he still didn't seem to be getting it. His body was, though. Something in his psyche was having a very primal response to the darkness and all that lived in it. A forgotten childhood memory. It haunted him.

She fairly crowed with laughter at the realization. He was terrified and was too stupid to realize it.

"...the *fuck* are you?" he spat, fists clenching, tightening as his knuckles turned white.

"What, you can't figure it out? Big strong man like you?" she mocked him, placing a hand on her hip, her lips curling into a sharp, hungry grin.

"No...," he whispered, blinking rapidly. His eyes were welling up with tears and one trailed down his cheek.

Oh, this is almost too easy. She slowly started walking towards him.

A stray thought in his head brought her up short and she stopped, staring back at him as a vicious memory of his flashed through her mind.

Pain, sharp and brutal – a sharp voice in the darkness, "Don't you dare tell anybody about this, you little fucker. I'll cut your goddamned balls off and jam 'em down your throat."

It was a woman's voice. The realization hit her like a sharp slap. *Whoa.* Jilah blinked, completely thrown off balance. She cleared her throat and quietly asked, "How long? How many times?"

Her target grew even more pale, which Jilah wasn't even sure was possible without him actually passing out. He hissed, "W-what the fuck are you talking about?"

She couldn't be sure who his attacker had been, but the voice had definitely been female. *What kind of woman molests a child and talks to them like that?* She boggled, diverted from her hunt for the moment. Jilah couldn't wrap her head around it. A female rapist?

Jilah opened her connection to Argent and he quickly responded, :: *It is a human condition, beloved - not simply one exhibited by males of their species.* ::

She looked over towards the man and murmured, "The woman who... molested you."

His expression became immediately cold and angry. "Fuck you, bitch. I do the taking, I'm in control. No *woman* could..."

He spat the word 'woman' out as if he was trying to expel it forcefully from his vocabulary - as if the very word itself was poisonous.

She sighed softly.

"So that's why you do it," she replied, the fleeting connection with his tragedy and the sadness she'd felt for that little boy quickly passing.

Doesn't make it right, she growled to herself.

"Do what, bitch? Who are you, and what the fuck are you really doing in my house?" he snapped, trying to regain the upper hand.

She could feel the strong desire in him to step forward and hit her, but he was still scared and wary.

Smart move, she thought to herself. He was angry, but wasn't going to give completely in to it and leave himself open to whatever she might do to him.

:: *Are you going to be able to handle him by yourself?* :: she heard Argent ask through the connection.

:: *It'll be a little rough, but I should be able to take him down.* :: she replied, wanting to try something new. A test.

She looked back at the enormous man, catching his gaze and snaring him with her own. The man's jaw dropped, and his hands tightened back into fists as the memories of all the female inmates that he'd raped and mutilated rushed from her thoughts into his mind. They stabbed at his psyche as he hissed and slumped to the floor, seizing, his feet jittering as his hips bucked over and over. A choked, gurgling cry escaped his lips and Jilah walked up to him, peering down at his face.

His face twisted in a grimace of horror and pain, and she winced as a guilty stab of conscience brought back the vicious memory of his molestation. As a child, he had been a victim as surely as the numerous women he'd attacked had been. Where had his justice been before his psyche had twisted into that of the sexual predator at her feet? Had anybody tried to help him? Had he even ever told anybody? It was unlikely that he would have shared this with anyone.

Jilah crouched and watched the man's enormous body twitch as his eyes became crazed. That brief spark of sadness returned as she thought about the horror he must have endured, how alone he must have felt.

:: *And yet he was able to put others in the same position – without regret, my daughter. Do not forget this.* :: The voice of her patroness whispered through her thoughts, not really making her feel any better this time. :: *His own choices brought him directly to death's door. His victims have been avenged and he will not be alive to do this thing again to others.* ::

True enough, Jilah frowned. It still didn't feel right.

:: *Beloved, worry not. Come home.* ::

Argent's worry echoed through the connection.

Jilah nodded and sighed as she pulled a cellphone out of her back pocket. She dialed the number that Mira had given her and provided the address of the house and the size of the 'carpet'. The cleanup crew would now do the rest.

:: *At least there's that.* :: she replied sourly.

No more rush body disposal. With access to an outfit dedicated to removing the evidence of such things, she only needed to focus on the tracking – the kill. It seemed somehow disconnected. Like eating meat from the supermarket without knowing the origin and process of it. Packaged and wrapped, it seemed sanitized and somehow empty. She walked past the body of the man at her feet, feeling a sadness that chilled her.

She shook her head to clear it as she walked out the door, closing it gently behind her.

:: *Does it truly bother you so much to know that women are also capable of such things?* :: Argent asked quietly.

Jilah started to run back to a motorcycle she'd borrowed from Aurelian earlier, and had parked a few miles away from the detention facility.

: *I don't know.* :: She frowned as she sped up. :: *I guess I wanted to think that only men did this kinda thing.* ::

:: *Did he not deserve the justice you rendered?* ::

:: *Oh yeah.* :: Jilah nodded as the landscape wooshed by. :: *He completely deserved it – what he endured, as awful as it was, doesn't excuse going out and putting other people through it.* ::

She paused for a moment, then added, :: *It just puts me in a grey area that I'm not entirely comfortable with.* ::

:: *Humans say that their Justice is blind, do they not?* :: he asked.

Jilah replied with a halfhearted chuckle, :: *Yeah, but she's not stupid.* ::

:: *Few things in life are ever simply black and white, beloved,* ::

Jilah sighed and replied, :: *I know. It just makes me...* :: She shook her head again, not really sure what she was trying to say.

Argent softly answered. :: *Because of this, you doubt the righteousness of your duty.* ::

Jilah felt her stomach drop, and her mouth was instantly dry. He was right. He usually was, damn him.

Sensing her distress, he added, :: *Being an instrument of karma is rarely easy, beloved.* ::

Jilah reached the bike, plucking a skullcap from the handlebars.

:: *What it comes down to is – if I don't do this, who will? And as it is, I can only do so much. How many others are out there? How many other women and children are enduring horrors beyond imagining?* ::

She straddled the motorcycle and started it, then set her jaw.

:: *I may not like it, but it needs doing.* ::

She could feel Argent smile through the connection.

:: *And there you have your answer.* ::

Jilah let herself smile a little, her heart warming as he added, :: *I will begin drawing a bath for us. It will be ready when you arrive.* ::

:: *Best boyfriend ever.* :: she smiled. :: *Thank you.* ::

:: For you, my love? Anything. See you soon. ::

While the bath had been relaxing, Jilah was still bothered about Roane and Ariane's situation and their impending departure. She wondered how Gigi was taking it. Not well, she supposed. The three of them seemed to be a fairly close knit bunch. Jilah rapped on the door, hoping that her friend was okay. Roane peeked out, then smiled, opening the door wide and Jilah stepped in to hug her tightly. She was surprised at the realization of how much she was going to miss them.

"You going to be alright?" she asked.

Roane shrugged, then waved her in.

"Don't have much of a choice, really. I gotta be."

Ariane clucked and moved around the room, collecting items and putting them into a canvas bag. "Ain't nothin' so precious it can't be ruined by idiots with money who think they know better."

Roane nodded, closing the door.

Jilah walked over to the couch and sat down, asking, "You guys heading anywhere special tonight?"

Roane flopped down beside Jilah on the couch, kicking up her feet on the coffeetable and watching as her partner continued packing. "Ariane's heading out to the cemetery – says she's got some 'splainin' to do."

Immensely curious, Jilah frowned, then asked, "Can I come with you?"

Ariane nodded quietly.

Roane looked over at her.

"Got any white clothes?"

"Uh, not really."

Jilah looked over at Ariane, wishing that there were something she could to to make it better.

Roane chuckled. "Don't worry. We'll find you something."

Jilah watched as Ariane bowed her head and began speaking quietly to herself and Roane looked out at the city of white concrete houses within the walls of St. Louis Cemetery #1.

She didn't want to be impolite, but had so many questions. Jilah turned to her friend and tentatively asked, :: *Argent says that she talks to what he calls Voodoo spirits – I forget what they're called. Is she talking to them now?* ::

Roane looked back over at her partner, her expression tight. Sea green pigtails bobbed as the necromancer nodded and replied, :: *She prays to Baron Samedi and Maman Brigitte, asking for their blessing – and their forgiveness.* ::

Jilah blinked. :: *Forgiveness?* ::

Roane shook her head, closing her eyes.

:: *People say the dead don't feel, but they do. It's not the same for them once they pass, but they still see, still feel for what they once had. They still watch over us.* ::

The necromancer's expression darkened as she growled, :: *This is wrong – but Ariane says good will come out of it, although I'm damned if I know how.* ::

Roane sighed, then turned to Jilah, explaining, :: *She sees a lot more than I do, even though I can feel them in my soul when I call them.* ::

Jilah looked over at Ariane as the mambo began rocking back and forth, her lips moving quickly.

Roane scuffed her boot on the ground and the look in her eyes softened as she turned to watch her partner. The muscles in her jaw tightened and she looked away, her expression pinched with bitterness. :: *I don't know what this is going to do to her... leaving her people like this.* ::

Jilah's chest tightened at the pain in her friend's voice.

:: *Her 'people'?* ::

:: *Mambo Annalise Danticat of Les Enfants du Cimetière is Ariane's direct descendant.* :: Roane explained.

:: *Le what?* ::

Roane chuckled softly, then replied, :: *You remember – the people in white that showed up with the guys that were painted like skeletons?* ::

Oh. Them.

Yeah, that wasn't something she'd be forgetting anytime soon. Just the mention of it conjured up vivid images of well muscled, ebony skinned men painted like death, the outline of skeletons rippling on their torsos as they danced like they were fucking the air in celebration. A chill coursed along Jilah's skin. She swore she could hear the echo of drums again before she pushed the image away. Something about it made her blood rush, embarrassing and exciting her at the same time.

:: Whoa. ::

Roane grinned and nodded, :: Yeah. Some folks think they're a little scary, but they're good people. They're just a little more... intense than most. Anyway, Ariane keeps watch over the congregation and makes sure they're provided for; taken care of. ::

Jilah thought about this for a moment, then asked, :: Does it bother them that she doesn't age? ::

Roane shook her head, frowning. :: She doesn't let them see her. Mambo Annalise is the only one that she has direct contact with, and even that's brief. Voudouisants don't take too kindly to those who traffic with the 'dead who walk'. :: She paused for a moment, then added, :: Still, Mambo Annalise - their head priestess, trusts her, even knowing what she is. ::

:: And what is she? :: Jilah asked, unable to help herself.

Roane met her eyes. :: She's my..ghoul. ::

Jilah blinked in startlement at the term.

:: Ghoul? ::

:: Damn. I keep forgetting how much of this life you're not aware of. And just so we're clear, she doesn't eat the meat of the dead, like all the folkloric books say. She's a different kind of ghoul. :: Roane took a deep breath, then explained, :: So, long time ago, she got really sick - like, close to death sick. I had to feed her a great deal of my blood to keep her around. The problem with this is that she now needs to drink from me every night, or she'll die. ::

It wasn't necessarily a decision Jilah would have chosen for herself, but then her own lot was far from perfect, she had to admit.

She asked, :: How did she take it? ::

Roane grimaced. :: At first? Not well. ::

She looked back over at her girlfriend and her expression warmed. :: But she came around. ::

It sounded like there was a great deal more behind the story, but Jilah didn't want to push it. She was already asking enough invasive questions. She hoped that Roane would trust her enough to talk to her about it someday.

Jilah quietly said, :: *Her people - they didn't look like much scares them.* ::

The way they had arrived that night, dancing with such joyous abandon, wild eyes and... that powerful singing. It still haunted her, but not in a negative way. No, they didn't look like much frightened them at all.

Roane chuckled, then replied, :: *It's not so much fear of us, but - well, we're outside their finite existence. We don't end unless we choose to. It's something they consider completely unnatural, and it doesn't sit well with them.* ::

Jilah nodded, pursing her lips.

:: *I guess I can understand that.* ::

Roane looked over at her partner, eyes filled with frustration.

:: *I hate this.* ::

She took a deep breath, then huffed it out. :: *I can't make this better for her.* :: She shook her head, squeezing her eyes shut. :: *She was born here. Her lineage has been a part of this place for a good, long time - and now it's like a large chunk of her is becoming physically wounded.* ::

Jilah frowned, wishing desperately that there was something she could do to help. She felt the pain radiating from her friend and reached out to gently take her hand.

Roane looked back at her, eyes glittering with unshed tears. Her hand tightened around Jilah's and she whispered, "Thank you."

Jilah replied with a sad smile, :: *Anything you guys need that I can help with, you just ask. OK?* ::

Roane nodded and replied, :: *Well, we'll need help packing at some point..* ::

:: *I'll be there. Do you know how soon you'll be leaving?* ::

Roane brought a hand up to the back of her neck, cupping it.

:: *Hard to say. Aurelian's checking around to see how soon they'll start emptying the graveyards out down here. I think other places are taking priority at the moment - New York City, Chicago, bigger cities.* :: Roane's expression closed down as she added, :: *but they'll be starting here soon enough.* ::

:: *Do the... do Ariane's people know that this is happening?* ::

Roane nodded, running her fingers through her bangs before she replied, :: *Damndest thing. It's like they knew before we did.* :: She let out a sarcastic laugh, :: *Would've been nice to get more of a heads up about it, though.* ::

She sighed and dropped her hand to her waist, continuing, :: *It's kinda odd. It's like they're not really upset about it. Like they know something we don't. Even Ariane doesn't seem that shaken by it - she's more torn up by the fact that we have to move away from her home.* ::

As if in response, Jilah heard Ariane break out in an eerie full throated laugh that sent a chill down her spine.

Roane shivered and muttered, :: *Hate it when she does that.* ::

:: *What's it mean?* ::

Jilah looked back at Ariane, almost taking a step back when she saw the unsettling grin on the woman's face.

Roane eyed her partner and shrugged, :: *Damned if I know. She's keeping it all under her hat for now. It's a little irritating, but if it keeps her from becoming a wreck over all this, I'm all for letting her keep it to herself until she feels like sharing.* ::

Jilah could understand. They stayed in the graveyard, keeping a silent vigil as they watched Ariane pray to the spirits of the dead – leaving only when it was time to get back before the sun rose.

On the walk back, Ariane kept behind them, keeping her own counsel. Jilah and Roane walked in silence, neither of them wanting to disturb her.

A firetruck approached them, lights flickering and siren blaring. The world slowed to a liquid crawl as Jilah spotted something on top of the vehicle's ladder. When she tried to get a better look at it, she was startled to see long trailing streams of sea green, light and dark blue hair waving gracefully with the currents of the air around the head of a teal skinned female creature that gripped the ladder tightly, grinning into the wind. Dark bluish tiger stripes decorated its arms and torso. Its facial features were smooth, liquid – with two enormous black eyes that overpowered the rest of its face. Greenish spined fins rested back along its forearms, coming to sharp, vicious points at the elbows.

"Whoa. What's that?" Jilah asked, fascinated.

As if it could hear her, the creature turned its head towards her, baring needle sharp teeth as the fins along its arms flared out. Time sped back up as the firetruck raced by. Jilah turned to see the creature dip down to become a vague outline against the ladder.

"Jengu – African water spirit." Roane replied.

Jilah looked over at her friend. "Aren't water spirits supposed to live in bodies of water?"

Broken out of her reverie, Ariane moved to walk beside them and explained. "Jariah's an odd one; she likes fires. She rides with fire truck crews throughout the city for sport."

She paused for a moment, then watched the truck as it turned a corner, siren still blaring. "She followed her people across the sea during the Middle Passage. Jariah made Lake Pontchartrain her home long ago. Lots of... others were transported along with the human cargo of the slave trade."

The mambo paused with a thoughtful look.

"The more... primal ones – the ones that don't play well with others, they stayed back in Africa. Some of them came, only to fade away when their people stopped believing in them; others wandered off to different parts of the country. A lot of them stay in the wilderness, away from people. It's better that way."

Jilah shivered and rubbed her hands along her arms. "Why'd she react that way when she saw me?"

Ariane shrugged, her tone noncommittal as she replied, "We all see the predator in each other. That, and I think your blue hair might've set her on edge."

Jilah looked over to see the ghost of a smile playing along Ariane's lips. The mambo shrugged, adding, "Could also be Mami Wata on a tear."

Roane gently jostled her lover with a shoulder. "Mami Wata don't look anything like that."

Ariane looked affronted and brought herself up, sliding into patois, "What a white girl like you be knowin' bout Mami Wata?"

Roane laughed and poked Ariane in the side, "Only what you tell me, Vodou woman."

Ariane shook her head, chuckling. "Ghede child" Ariane spat, still smiling.

"The dead do have the best parties." Roane replied, shrugging. "I should know."

Jilah chuckled, relieved at the exchange.

They were going to be just fine.

Chapter 5
SAY WHAT?

"I'm sorry, could you repeat that?"

A tall, dark skinned woman stood before Jilah, her silver toned hair sweeping up from her face into a ponytail of long dreads that flowed down her back. Copper bangles decorated her left wrist, and the fingers of both hands were full of shiny copper rings. There was even a smooth, soothing tone to her voice that Jilah found reassuring.

The woman replied, "As an avatar of Duregayeh, I dispense justice to those who would would force themselves on women and..."

Jilah cut the woman off with a wave of her hand. "So, essentially, you're saying that you do the same thing I do, right?"

The woman blinked, her brows knitting in brief confusion before she replied, "Yes."

She then frowned and asked, "This surprises you?"

Jilah eyed her suspiciously, not really comfortable with facing the fact that there were now more than one of – well, whatever it was she happened to be. Whoever or *whatever* this woman was, she certainly didn't look the part. Brown baggy pants, an olive green top and sports sandals didn't seem like suitable clothes in which to be out kicking ass and sucking down dinner. She looked more like a sham astrological consultant than an avenging warrior.

Jilah had dispatched her first target of the night when the woman had appeared on the scene and formally introduced herself. Jilah's prey still lay at the end of the alleyway in a heap where he'd slumped over, his hand twitching as he slowly expired.

Jilah's voice cracked a little as she replied, "Yeah, it tweaks me. I mean, if you're really like me, don't you remember what it was like when you were starting out?"

The woman peered at her strangely, pausing for a moment before answering. "It was quite a long time ago, and the memories of that first year have faded with time."

Jilah looked the woman over. Even with the silver hair, the woman before her didn't look a day over thirty five.

"How old *are* you?"

"This year I will be seventy three. Why do you ask?"

Jilah stammered, "Seventy three?? Are you kidding?"

Smiling and nodding, the woman answered, "Not at all. We age much slower after becoming vessels for our patroness. But surely you haven't forgotten this already?"

"Actually, no. I don't seem to remember that particular bit being part of the brochure." Jilah snapped sourly.

"The brochure?" The woman blinked, confused.

"Never mind, it doesn't matter," Jilah waved the woman's question away in frustration, asking, "What was your name again?"

"In this incarnation, I am called Zolah. It is the name I assumed when the mantle of my patroness was placed on my shoulders so many years ago."

Jilah found it strange that the woman's demeanor was so calm, so peaceful. Where did it come from, this reservoir of tranquility? Was there a way to make peace with the darker side of herself so that it didn't feel so *alien* inside her? She was actually beginning to feel a little guilty for being such a grouch. Zolah seemed like a genuinely nice lady.

"I'm sorry. I get just a little on edge when people throw me off like this. Especially when it keeps happens repeatedly within a really short period of time."

Zolah nodded politely, still smiling. Jilah admired her patience.

"You are still so young, but very strong. You are doing a fine job."

Jilah frowned, then asked, "How do you know that I'm young?"

Zolah made a gentle flourish in the air with a hand as she responded, "Your scent. Your demeanor." She paused for a moment, her gaze becoming intense as she continued, "Your scent also seems familiar. Was your demon perhaps hosted in another woman about ten years ago?"

Jilah blinked quickly, taken aback. She was not at all comfortable discussing this so casually with a stranger. She was glad that she still had her shields cranked up so that her appearance was more human, but was mystified as to how the woman knew about it. If Zolah was who she said she was, did she have a demon inside her as well?

Best to play dumb, she thought to herself. *Maybe she can shed a little light on this whole 'host for a demon' thing.*

"Demon?"

Zolah placed her hands on her hips and frowned, as if she were dealing with a particularly thick child.

"We are all host to a demon, child. It's what gives us the abilities our patroness can utilize to work her will on this plane of existence. Were you told nothing at inception?"

Jilah stared at her, open-mouthed. Inception? What the hell was this woman going on about? She quickly recovered and grated, "Actually, no. I wasn't exactly given a guided tour. It's been more like one of those seat-of-your-pants kind of learning experiences."

It was now Zolah's turn to stare as Jilah continued, asking, "And what do you mean by *inception*? What, did everybody else get a memo or something? Was there a class I missed?" She was getting angry now.

Zolah's expression became guarded, and her voice softened as she murmured, "When was your incept date, child? The day you were born into this new life?"

"A little over six months ago," Jilah replied, grumpily.

Zolah's expression went slack as she shook her head.

"No, no. That cannot be right. I thought perhaps that you were ten or twenty years into your service, but less than a year? That is impossible."

At this, Jilah raised an eyebrow, putting a little attitude into her tone as she replied, "Oh, I'm here to tellya that it's been just a little over half a year. Trust me."

Something in the woman's demeanor changed. She seemed to draw into herself and she started mumbling something in a language that Jilah couldn't recognize. A rush of wind swept along Jilah's skin and the hairs on the back of her neck stood straight up as she felt a wave of power press against her, flowing around her before fading out. Before she had time to react, it had stopped, leaving her shivering slightly. Zolah leapt away from her like a cat, her expression stony as she stood in a defensive stance.

Her voice was flat and toneless as she asked, "You are not of me and mine. What *are* you?"

Jilah scowled, wondering what the hell had spooked the woman so badly. "Wait a minute – what the hell are you talking about? One minute we're all friendly and the next you're wigging out on me. What'd I do?"

"I see your true face now, devil. If you are truly of the sisterhood, why do you sport wicked attributes?" Zolah spat her words out angrily, glaring back at her. "I ask again, *what are you?*"

Jilah took a deep breath before grating her teeth and growling.

"Look, lady. *You* approached *me*, remember? We both run around at night doing the same thing; bringing assholes to justice, right? And wicked attributes? What's that all about?"

Zolah frowned, taking a tentative step forward. She tilted her head back as if tasting the wind. Her brows knit as she asked, "Why then do you hide your inhuman features, unless you are a dark soul?"

"What? Inhuman...what the?" It took a moment before Jilah realized that the woman must have penetrated her shields and was now seeing her added *bonuses*. She winced and quietly responded, "Oh. That."

The silver haired woman nodded, waiting for an explanation.

Jilah's voice quavered as she replied, "They ah... just kinda popped up."

The extra bits were still a bit of a touchy subject with her. She still winced when she went by mirrors, catching a glimpse of her reflection. Applying makeup had become its own special kind of torment. She frowned as something occurred to her.

"Wait, you're over seventy, and this hasn't happened to you? I just assumed that it was part of the package deal."

"As far as I know, none of us have sported such darkly altered features. It is as if what you host inside you is being reflected in your very being." She whispered, now seeming a great deal more subdued. "I cannot deny the fact that you smell very much like one of us.

There is a subtle difference to you, but your scent and your resonance – they are unmistakable. How can this be?"

Jilah slumped, suddenly tired. She had held out a hope that she'd finally met somebody that could explain her condition – what kind of creature she had become on that fateful night; and just as it was looking as if she'd found the answers, they were snatched away again. Jilah sighed and rested back against a tree, her tail gently slapping against the bark at its base.

Better than against my legs this time, she thought to herself. The damn thing seemed to have a mind of its own at times. She let out a weak laugh, answering, "Damned if I know. I've been hoping that somebody could explain it to me."

Zolah took another tentative step forward, a hand extended as if to reach out to reassure her.

"Are you all right, child?"

She wasn't particularly happy being referred to as a child, but for a woman who supposedly had her by almost forty years, she just went with it. Jilah nodded, taking a deep breath and letting it out as she met Zolah's gaze.

"It's just that, well, it really hasn't been the most positive experience, so far."

Jilah pushed herself away from the tree, continuing, "Nobody ever sat me down and explained this, or wrote anything down for me."

She wasn't sure why she was confiding so much in a complete stranger, but talking about it seemed to be helping. Sure, Argent could listen to her, but had no ideas as to her origin. They hadn't really discussed how he came to be sanguine, so for all she knew he could have been handed the Cliff Notes version on the sanguine lifestyle as well as having been tutored. She made a mental note to ask him about it when she got the chance.

Zolah's expression grew sad as she listened, watching Jilah gesticulate angrily as she continued, "And now you're telling me that there's a whole pack of us out there? What, did they all get training of some sort? 'cause if so, I'm gonna call bullshit on this whole gig."

"You were truly never initiated? Never tutored before choosing this life?" Zolah looked back at her, stunned.

"Choosing?!?" Jilah took a step away from the tree.

"How about *this* for *choosing*." Her tone grew venomous as she continued. "While some dickhead was slapping me around and..." she winced and shook her head, continuing, "*raping* me, I get this voice in my head that asks me if I want help. My head is ringing and I'm pretty sure that the guy is going to kill me after he's finished with me, so what the hell was I supposed to say? No?" Jilah was practically yelling now as she continued, "And for going out practically every goddamned night after that, I get run into the ground and laughed at by whatever turned me into what I am. Not to mention the fact that she's vague as hell about almost everything."

Zolah stared back at her. "How could such a thing have happened? This is not the way it happens with us."

Jilah let out a harsh laugh, grating, "Well that's the way it happened for me, *sister*. Just count yourself lucky that you got a primer and that you had an actual *choice*." She leaned back against the tree again, arms crossed now.

"How is it that you have been able to continue her work without going insane?"

The woman was curious, and obviously flustered.

Jilah realized that while her road had been painful, vivid and somewhat apocalyptic at points, she had made it through relatively unscathed, always bouncing back from whatever she'd been thrown into. Yes, she'd gotten the crap knocked out of her several times, but so far she hadn't been on the receiving end of any permanent damage. Was she supposed to have gone crazy without a mentor? If she hadn't run into Argent, would she eventually have gone down that road? The distinct possibility gave her pause.

"I've had a little external help. He's kept me sane." Jilah replied, her voice soft.

The woman was staring at her as if she'd gone mad. With a hushed whisper she asked, "You've MATED already? Less than a year in?"

Jilah cocked an eyebrow as she wondered what was so extraordinary about her finding a partner.

"Yeah – what of it?"

Zolah stepped up to Jilah and touched the side of her face. Jilah winced and quickly jerked away as the woman explained, "It usually takes a fledgling sister two to five years in the field before she's mentally and emotionally capable of dealing with both her given task and the possibility that there is love in the world for her to claim. It's unheard of for anybody within their first year to do so. Our calling shows us the worst in men, which makes it difficult to move past that and into a healthy union with one. Over time, a great many of our number find that they much prefer the company of other women instead."

Well, I guess that would make sense, Jilah thought to herself. She smiled as she recalled the night that Argent had cured her of her initial timidity about physical contact, among other things. "He was very... *convincing.*" She flushed briefly at the memory of that night.

Zolah was now peering at her as if she'd just encountered a new species of bug or animal. Jilah watched the woman carefully, her blue tail whipping quickly back and forth in irritation. The silver haired woman pressed a thoughtful finger to her lips, her copper bangles and rings glittering as they caught the light from the streetlamps.

"What now?" Jilah snapped, placing her hands on her hips. "I'm the one that should be pissed here, seeing as how I seem to have gotten cheated out of the training basics that you were lucky enough to know to stand in line for."

Zolah held her hands up in a placating gesture.

"No, child, I am not angry. I'm wondering what comes next. You are the only one of us who has ever survived completely out on her own, with no previous training or contact before the bonding. We have no mention of anything like you in our entire recorded history, which is quite extensive and thorough."

Jilah frowned at the implication, wondering what it meant. *Nothing good,* she figured.

The woman continued, "This is most interesting, and is something that was not at all expected when I was sent out to meet you."

Jilah backed up, curling her hands into fists. "Whoa, hold the phone. How long have you guys been watching me?"

Zolah blinked and clasped her hands at her waist, her voice gentle as she responded, "We were made aware of your presence after you arrived in New Orleans. When you tracked and killed the monster Saulnier in the swamp."

"Wait – you mean the psycho molester with the kids in those cages?"

Zolah responded with a single nod and Jilah growled, "If you knew about him, then why the hell didn't you guys deal with him earlier? What kind of people are you, letting children suffer like that? Do you know what I had to do to them after I killed him?" She shuddered and took a shaky breath. "What it *did* to me? Do you have *any idea*?" She was shouting again, advancing on the silver haired woman.

Zolah took a deep breath and held up a steady hand. "We have watchers, but they cannot be everywhere at once. There are also many deserving targets that we as a collective force are sent out to track and bring down, night after night. We cannot possibly deal with them all quickly, but we do what we can. Our ranks stay constant due to the limited number of demons and qualified hosts that respond to the call of our patroness. The demons that help us in our fight have agreed to do so until they pass beyond this realm."

"And what does this have to do with me?" Jilah snapped. "I mean, I'm happy to fight the good fight, and to get it done, but..."

Zolah cut her off, replying, "You are a fledgeling hunter; one who never formally joined our ranks. And from what you've told me, you were never approached, never petitioned. When I was sent to find you, to meet with you, our Synod had no idea who you were. Your origin is a mystery to us; one that we wish to speak with you about at length. I have been sent by the Synod as plenipotentiary to make our presence known, and to encourage you to return with me so that we may learn more about you."

Jilah gaped at her, rocking back on a heel.

"Are you off your nut? I just got here! Where the hell do you get off..."

"Please," Zolah pleaded, "this association would be as beneficial to you as it would be for the Synod itself. There are many things that we can teach you – as much as we can learn from you, I would imagine."

The idea of learning more about herself and her abilities appealed to Jilah, but she was understandably wary. How much could they really teach her if she was as alien as Zolah seemed to think she was?

Was she even the same kind of creature? Some of the things that the woman spoke about seemed to ring true, but – leaving New Orleans so soon after arriving here? There was a great deal to be done, but most of it would end up being handled directly by Argent and Aurelian anyway. The only thing she had to do was to put in appearances, put on the show of being Striaga – but in reality there wasn't much else for her to do, for which she was grateful. Most of her time was taken up with her nightly appointed rounds.

She jumped a little as Argent's voice echoed through her thoughts.

:: *Beloved, you are late. Did we not have a date?* ::

God, the man's voice was enough to make her legs weak when he purred like that. His tone was husky and heated, and she silently berated herself for forgetting. She had promised to come right back after disposing of tonight's target. Getting distracted in conversation hadn't been on the agenda, and consequently the date had completely slipped her mind. She could tell that he was concerned, but was also teasing her with the promise of what would happen when she finally arrived back at the convent.

:: *Uh, oops.* :: Jilah replied, wincing.

:: *Is everything alright?* ::

Her head swam a little at the disorientation of feeling him sit bolt upright as she stood her ground.

She looked over at Zolah who was now frowning at her and asking, "Is anything wrong?"

Jilah held up a hand and closed her eyes, placing the fingers of her other hand on the bridge of her nose, trying to reorient herself as she replied, "Gimme a sec, okay?"

:: *Having a conversation on two fronts is difficult.* :: She paused, feeling Argent's confusion through the link as she continued, :: *Okay, it's like this. I'm apparently not the only one doing this kinda job. I just ran into this chick who says that she shares my job description, but she's freaked over the horns and the tail. She says that she wants me to come with her to talk to her Synod, whatever the hell that is. They're apparently all curious about me because I shouldn't exist the way I do. She's also offered to teach me about what I am, and what I can do. It was enough to make me entirely forget my promise to you earlier tonight. I'm a little scattered right now, but...* ::

Jilah felt a flood of warmth and reassurance from her lover as he interrupted her.

:: *I'm on my way. Where are you?* ::

She let out a little sigh of relief as she opened her eyes and looked around for an obvious landmark that he could use for reference.

Argent sent, :: *I will be by your side in moments, love. Wait for me before going anywhere with this woman.* ::

Jilah nodded as the connection dimmed, opening her eyes and looking over at Zolah who was now watching her expectantly. Jilah leaned back against a tree and explained, "I just get these... headaches sometimes, y'know?"

She didn't want this woman knowing more than she'd already told her and wasn't entirely certain that it was wise to tip her hand about Argent's presence, but she knew damn well that he wouldn't have stayed away if she'd told him to. Having him here would help her think clearly as well. A surprisingly large part of her wanted to go with this woman, to hear her out and to find out what she could, but she wasn't sure that was prudent.

Zolah gave her a strange look, one that said that she didn't entirely believe her.

"So," Jilah continued. "Let's say that I choose to go with you. How long would I be away from New Orleans?"

Zolah smoothed the front of her pants as she replied, "It is possible that you would spend up to a month speaking with the Synod. It is the only way that we can be reasonably certain that we are able to learn all we can about your condition, as well as passing on the knowledge that you should have received at the time of your inception."

"And what exactly is a Synod?" Jilah asked, her curiosity growing by the minute.

"The Synod is our governing body. They ensure that we are all properly trained and monitored so that we function as efficiently as possible. Burnout happens more quickly with certain hosts, and in each successive jump to a new host, they have to take time to adapt to their new environment. To bond with the host in a fashion that is well suited to both the host and the demon."

Zolah's eyes narrowed and she leapt away from Jilah. The avatar felt Argent's hands on her hips as he pulled her close.

:: *Don't mind her.* :: Jilah murmured to him. :: *She scares easy.* ::

:: *I see that.* ::

Jilah smiled as she heard him chuckle softly.

She turned to Zolah and leaned back against Argent's chest. "It's okay. He's here for me."

Zolah blinked rapidly as she looked back and forth between the two of them and stammered, "The mate you spoke of – he's one of the *bloodchildren?*"

Jilah cocked her head and frowned, asking, "How did you know what he was?"

Zolah gave her an admonishing glare and replied, "You do not get to be my age without knowing a thing or two about his kind, child."

"Fair enough." Jilah placed her hands over Argent's as he rested his chin on her shoulder and peered at the silver haired woman as if she was a particularly tasty snack.

Zolah's eyes narrowed again, and the woman shook a finger at him, chiding, "Do not even think about it. You would not be able to catch me."

:: *Lover man, play nice. Tweaking her is only going to provoke her, and she's not really doing anything that would hurt me.* ::

Argent smiled and placed a gentle kiss on the side of her neck, his eyes never leaving the woman before them. :: *Oh, but I'd like to run her down, just to see if she's as good as her word.* ::

Jilah poked her elbow gently into his ribcage and he gave a halfhearted wince, then chuckled. "Zolah here says that if I go..." she turned to address the woman directly, asking, "Where would we be going again?"

Zolah shook her head slowly, having a difficult time believing what she was seeing as she numbly replied, "Washington D.C."

Jilah turned back to address Argent, continuing, "So, if I chose to go to Washington D.C., to hang out with her Synod, I'll be gone for about a month." Sure, she could've had the conversation silently with him, but she wanted Zolah to know that he was an integral part of her decision process.

Argent stepped out from behind her and directly addressed Zolah, his voice pleasant as he asked, "And why is it that you come into my prefecture unannounced? Does your Synod not respect the governance of the cities it sends people into?"

Zolah blinked, sputtering, "We were not aware that we needed to appeal to a governing body in order to enter New Orleans. Have things changed so much? The last time we visited, there were no such rules in place."

Argent smiled, now wrapping a possessive arm around Jilah's waist.

"Things have most definitely shifted since I have taken the mantle of Strigaisha. New rules are in place and are being enforced heavily now. You would do well to inform your Synod of the change."

Zolah visibly blanched and bowed her head, her voice taking on an entirely different tone as she replied, "Our apologies, Strigaisha. No offense was meant. We were unaware of this new change. We were also unaware of your direct connection to our sister."

The Sanguine watched as the woman looked back up at him, bewildered. She looked shaken.

Jilah swatted at him, pulling away as she snapped, "Play *nice*, dammit. You're scaring the crap out of her."

Zolah clasped her hands before her tightly, trying to master herself. Something was definitely spooking her, and Jilah wasn't entirely sure that it was her lover's fault. She moved forward, trying to defuse the situation.

"Hey, are you alright? I know he can be a little scary when he gets all dominant, but..."

The woman shook her head sharply, cutting her off. "No. It is not him that has me at odds." Her voice was a hushed whisper as she glared over at Argent. "It has been a great many years since my demon has spoken through me. It is she who recognizes what he is, she who knows of what he speaks. It is disorienting and uncomfortable, but it is a part of who we are. I had almost forgotten what it felt like."

Now it was Jilah's turn to tweak a little. Her *occupant* had spoken through her as well recently, so she could relate.

Been there, done that. She thought to herself.

After Argent's sister had fused Jilah with the strange force inside her that helped her to dispatch her prey, it seemed to be easier to interact with it. Before, it would slide in and force her to a purely spectator position, taking control of her and getting the job done on its own. Now, it came easily, and was *much* stronger. It no longer felt like a secondary force – something separate. Her need to hunt was also getting more pronounced, and she noted that she was becoming more vicious, more bloodthirsty. It was unnerving, but when she considered her prey – no, they deserved no mercy. What was it to Jilah that she was now playing with them as a cat would a mouse while she exacted the price for their crimes from them? They had done as much to the women and children they forced themselves on.

No, that particular moral dilemma had been tended to. Vengeance. An act for an act.

She jumped slightly at the touch of Argent's hand on her shoulder.

:: *What's wrong?* ::

She gave Zolah a sympathetic look before turning to him with a sad smile.

:: *She's just bringing up some stuff that I hadn't thought about before. Things I think I need to face, to figure out.* ::

:: *Do you believe that she and her kind can explain the changes taking place within you? That they can expound upon your origins?* :: He leaned into her, gently squeezing her shoulder.

She ventured another look to find Zolah watching her interactions with her lover intently.

:: *Honestly? Yeah. I kinda do. I don't think they can tell me everything, but I think they can help me flesh some of this out – give me a little more to go on.* ::

With a soft sigh of resignation, he murmured, :: *You should follow your instincts, beloved. Keeping you here in ignorance will only frustrate you, and I want you to be content with me. With this life.* ::

Jilah looked back at him, taking his hand and squeezing it.

:: *I wish you could come with me. I want you with me.* ::

Argent smiled, raising her hand and gently pressing soft lips to her knuckles. :: *As I want you with me – need you beside me. But this sounds as if it is something that you need to come to a resolution on. And that is entirely your own journey. I only hope that it will not take you so far from me for too long. ::*

Jilah smiled and kissed him, then lightly cuffed him on the arm. *:: You'd just better miss me, dammit. ::*

:: I can assure you that missing you will not be a problem. ::

She turned to find Zolah staring at them with a look of confusion. She was trying to figure the situation out, and was apparently having difficulty. There seemed to be a lot of that going on tonight. Jilah took a step forward, still holding Argent's hand as she announced, "OK. I'll come back with you. But not tonight. I have some things I need to take care of before I kick on out of town."

The woman nodded, clearing her throat as she ran deft fingers along one of her necklaces. "This is definitely going to be one of the more interesting field reports that I have ever had to deliver. It has been..." she paused for a moment, searching for the right wording, "*enlightening* to meet you, Jilah. When would you like me to come for you?"

"Tomorrow night would be good. I'll have time to get myself together before then." Her grip on Argent's hand tightened and he gently pulled her back into his embrace.

Zolah met the Sanguine's eyes and gave him a slight nod. "Strigaisha, was it?"

Argent nodded, his voice smooth and cultured as he answered, "It is."

"As plenipotentiary of the Synod of the eastern corridor I now take my leave to come back here one night from now. In the future, we assure you that we will announce all scheduled visits to your prefecture ahead of time."

She looked back at Jilah, her expression softening as she smiled and added, "I will see you tomorrow night, sister. Thank you."

Jilah presented her with a smile and nodded gamely, "Yep. Lookin' forward to it. Tell the folks I said hi."

Shaking her head in confusion, Zolah turned and disappeared in a swirl of light.

"So," Argent asked her as he started walking back in the direction of the convent. "Do you think I could've taken her?"

Jilah let out a full throated laugh as she let him pull her along.

"Possibly. But then I would have learned nothing further from her, and wouldn't have a chance at figuring out what it is that I'm supposed to be."

He waved her statement away, casually responding, "Details. You're quite fixated on them, you know."

She socked him in the arm, then presented him with a wicked grin.

"Race you back?"

At this he laughed and said, "You're on."

Jilah dropped her head down to her lover's shoulder with a sated smile. The covers were rumpled, barely covering either of them as she curled up beside him.

Argent sighed and pressed a cheek to her forehead. It wasn't exactly the best time to mention it, but it needed to be said. :: *I am going to need to assign somebody to accompany you while you travel.* ::

Jilah frowned, moving to look back at him.

:: *Is this one of those things you're doing because you don't think that I can take care of myself?* ::

Argent shook his head and placed a gentle kiss on her forehead. :: *I am quite aware of your capability to defend yourself, love. This is more a function of the court. Due to your position, you need to be provided with an escort.* ::

Resignation rang through the connection as Jilah sighed and rested her head back on his shoulder.

:: *This is something that I can't get out of, isn't it?* ::

Argent pulled her closer, shaking his head slowly, hating that he had to say it.

:: *Yes. It is part of the politics.* ::

:: *Who were you planning on sending with me?* :: Jilah asked, letting her fingertips play along his chest.

Argent remained silent for a few moments, enjoying the feel of her touch, before answering.

:: *I will speak with Cynette and Alain tonight. Because they are the court enforcers, you will need to be accompanied by a member of their Pack.* ::

Jilah pushed up on an elbow and looked down at him.

:: *Do you really think that's a wise decision? After what I did?* ::

Argent looked over at her, knowing that the very idea made her uneasy. :: *It is the only decision to make. If I do not send Pack with you, it is an insult to their position in the court power structure. They are both well aware of your loyalties, if a little distressed about your capabilities.* ::

It's not their pack I'm worried about, she thought to herself as she brought her hand back to rest on his chest. *It's my ass.* The Alphas were still very unhappy about the packmate that she'd destroyed shortly after arriving.

He covered her hand with his own, squeezing gently.

:: *Do not worry about vendettas, love. They understand the new order of things and will stand within it. You need not fear reprisal.* ::

Her eyes narrowed as she looked back at him. :: *How can you be so certain?* ::

Argent sobered, his tone becoming serious.

:: *Trust me on this. The Tribe of the Savage Moon will not wish to cast its lot against a ruler with access to a power that can raise an army of zombies.* ::

Jilah winced, sucking in air. :: *Good point.* ::

:: *Indeed.* :: he murmured.

:: *We don't have to get up and moving on this anytime soon, do we?* :: she asked, pouting her lower lip out slightly.

Argent smiled, chuckling softly as he pulled her into a kiss.

:: *Are you kidding? If I'm not to see you for the next month, we will stay in this bed as long as time allows. Preferably until the very last minute.* ::

Jilah let out a delighted whoop and grabbed the covers, pulling them over their heads.

"Ha!" she crowed. "Totally sinkin' your battleship!"

:: *I believe that I am starting to become used to your unusual euphemisms. I think I actually understood that.* :: He laughed as she straddled him and slid back against him.

:: *Oh yes.* :: He murmured as he pressed into her, gripping her hips tightly and groaning. :: *That is most definitely what I thought you meant.* ::

:: *Does this mean that I'm becoming less of a mystery?* :: she asked, her smile growing sharp and wicked as she moved against him.

:: *Less talking. More sinking.* :: His voice growled through her thoughts as he clutched at her hips, losing himself in her.

Chapter 6
THE SYNOD

Argent carefully assessed the young man that stood before them in the throne room and Jilah couldn't help notice that the man was fairly attractive; his brown hair slightly tousled as if he'd just woken up. Sharp eyebrows framed crystal blue eyes in a face with soft, almost feminine features. He hardly looked like a guardian of any sort.

:: *He's awfully...young. He looks like a model. Are you sure?* ::
Jilah stood beside her lover, unsure of how she felt about the man's dispassionate manner, as if he was used to being displayed for critical assessment. Maybe therianthropes were used to it? Argent silently looked over at Alain, who nodded back at him.

:: *Looks are usually deceiving. If Alain is sure of him, then I trust him. If he does anything to displease his Alpha, he will be disciplined severely. And this pup well knows it.* ::
Argent took a step forward and addressed the young man with a formal tone.

"As the Tribe of the Savage Moon's given escort, you will accompany my Striaga to her intended destination, standing watch until it is her time to return."

The young man nodded almost imperceptibly, his voice soft and lilting. "As my Strigaisha commands, I shall."

He then looked over at Jilah and nodded to her as well, the smile curving his lips not quite reaching his eyes. She blinked and nodded in response, unable to quite figure out the strange feeling that seemed to be emanating from the man.

She then looked over at Cynette and Alain, giving them a nod as well before saying, "I accept the due of the court from its enforcers, vowing to return him to his Pack in one month's time."

Argent had coached her on her responses beforehand, and she always had access to that enormous encyclopedic data dump that he'd pushed into her grey matter. Even with this, she still felt a little unsteady when it came to interacting formally with other court members. She always worried about saying the wrong thing or giving unintended offense.

:: It seems that your collector has arrived, love. ::

Argent turned to see Zolah stepping into the throne room, her gaze moving for a moment over the intricate tapestries hanging along the walls. Jilah steeled her nerve and hefted a large black rucksack onto her shoulder as she walked over to meet the woman.

:: Did you really need to pack so much? :: Argent asked, already knowing the answer. His amusement echoed through the connection.

:: You know me. I'm leaving for a month, and I'm a clotheshorse. Did you expect any different? :: she chided playfully as Zolah stepped up to greet her.

"It is good to see you, sister." Zolah smiled, then blinked as she noticed the pack that Jilah was hefting. "Do you usually travel this heavily?"

Argent chuckled and Jilah glared back at him.

"Let's just say that I like to be prepared for any clothing eventuality." She turned and grinned back at Zolah.

Jilah felt the young man's presence almost intruding into her space as he stepped up beside her and Zolah looked over at him, frowning.

"Oh. He's my, ah, escort."

Zolah looked back at her, an eyebrow crooking up.

Jilah quickly added, "Unfortunately, that's part of the deal. If he can't come with me, I can't go."

Zolah paused for a moment, then turned to Argent, who was watching her expectantly.

"This is unprecedented and unusual, but not unworkable. The Synod extends its invitation to you both, but the escort will have to understand that there are certain parts of the facility that are barred from any outside of the sisterhood."

She and Argent had discussed this earlier, knowing that this would likely be the case. He had explained that the escort was to be both a representative of the court and backup in case she ran into trouble. Jilah wasn't comfortable with the idea of needing fallback help, but if something did happen to come along that she couldn't handle, she had to admit that it would be good to have a wolf handy to back her up. Besides, it was part of this odd job now, as Striaga of the court of New Orleans. She'd roll with it.

Zolah added, "There is also the possiblity that his presence will make some of the other sisters uneasy. The newer hosts are not usually comfortable around men that aren't targets."

Jilah blinked, frowning. :: *I hadn't thought of that.* ::

She turned to Argent and asked, :: *Is there a female in the pack that could... ?* ::

Argent shook his head, his expression firm.

:: *It would not be wise to turn down the pack's choice in this matter. Trust needs to be restored at this point, and that would be a bad way to go about it.* ::

Yeah. After Gregor, she guessed she could understand. It was a pretty huge move on their part, trusting someone who'd destroyed a former pack member with another one of their own to keep watch over her.

Jilah looked back over at Zolah.

"I understand. He'll hang back when he needs to."

Zolah trailed deft fingers along the collection of necklaces at her throat, asking, "Are you ready?"

"As ready as I'll ever... "

Jilah's words trailed off as the world around her warped with a horrible wrenching feeling that was nauseatingly familiar. Jilah heard her rucksack hit the floor as she slapped both palms down on marble tiling. She knelt and retched loudly, a crimson splash marring the pristine whiteness of the marble beneath her. "...be." she croaked as she spit and tried to stop the rest of the contents of her stomach from dumping out on the floor.

"Ayafeh! I do sincerely apologize." Zolah stammered and moved to help her up, dabbing at Jilah's mouth with a handkerchief. "I had no idea that your reaction to the translocation would be so violent."

Jilah looked up at her, and snapped. "Why is it that people constantly do that before telling me? Man..."

:: Beloved! Are you alright? ::

Argent's presence flared in her mind, startled. She winced and coughed before answering him.

:: I'm fine. She just gated us somewhere before warning me and I threw up some of my dinner. If it's any consolation, she seems to feel really bad about the fact that it made me sick. ::

Jilah felt him relax and she slowly dampened the connection as she looked over to see her escort peering down at her with a strange expression. He didn't seem affected in the least. *What, am I the only one that upchucks when that happens?* she grumbled to herself.

"Where are we?" Jilah croaked.

"We have arrived at the Synod locus, our effective general headquarters. You have my apologies that the trip affected you the way it did. Are you okay?"

Zolah looked really worried, and Jilah found herself wondering how bad she looked to her new companion.

"It's alright. I'm fine."

She echoed the same sentiments mentally to Argent as she waved the concern off, picked up her rucksack and hefted it back onto a shoulder.

"Just don't do that again without telling me."

Zolah responded with a quick nod. "Of course."

Jilah squared her shoulders, then asked, "Is there somewhere I can put this?"

"You can leave it with our office assistant. I will then present you to the Synod governing body."

Zolah turned to go, and Jilah followed the silver haired woman through the large white room. It was a foyer of sorts, but there were no distinguishing decorations or details. A hallway led back into a featureless corridor. Other than the main entrance, the facility looked like the inside of an innocuous federal building, very bland

and well worn. They made their way up to a large plywood door with a black plastic sign on it that read 'Applicants Only'.

Zolah turned the handle and the door opened into a receptionist area. The office itself was a little shabbier than the one Jilah used to work at before her life turned upside down. An older woman at the desk smiled and waved them inside, her manner warm and inviting.

"Come on in, honey. Just make sure you close the door behind you." She spoke with a strong southern accent.

Jilah looked around, wondering when the weirdness would start. Would the walls change? Would the geometry of the office suddenly appear in angles that induced nausea? The woman stood and walked around the desk, peering over steel grey glasses to meet the avatar's eyes.

"You look as if you're waiting for something."

Jilah blinked and looked back at her, her train of thought sidetracked.

"Nah. I'm good."

The woman smiled and extended a hand.

"I'm Josette. It's very exciting to meet you!"

Really? Jilah wondered if she said this to all the new girls as she took the woman's hand, shaking it and stammering, "It's, ah, nice to meet you too."

"You can leave your bag with me."

Josette directed her to a door to her left. "The Synod is waiting for you. I'm afraid that the young gentleman will have to wait here though."

Jilah turned to look back at her companion. He just stepped over to a bank of seats along the wall and sat down, not bothering with the stack of magazines on the table beside him.

What, is he just going to sit here the entire time with nothing to do?

She didn't even know his name. Jilah felt somewhat bad about that. Perhaps she'd get it out of him afterward. She slid the rucksack off of her shoulder and set it down beside the desk before turning to follow Zolah through the door. Jilah cast a quick, curious glance back at her escort who flashed her an empty smile, then looked away from her.

Strange guy, she mused to herself as she quickly moved to catch up with Zolah.

The hallway deposited them into a large meeting room. A group of thirteen women of varying ages sat along one side of an enormous, oblong, ebony table surrounded by comfortable looking black leather chairs. Zolah directed her to sit at one of the two chairs positioned on the other side of the table. Jilah nervously moved to take a seat, her gaze moving quickly from person to person, wondering if there was anything specific that she should say. She squeezed the leather arms of the chair, wondering for a moment how much the furniture had cost them. It was a very comfortable chair and she relaxed back into it and waited for them to make the first move.

The woman seated at the center of the table was the spitting image of a British actress that Jilah really liked. Short silver hair in a playful cut framed a soft, square shaped face that was aging remarkably well. The woman's eyes seemed almost lavender in this lighting. It was highly unlikely that this was actually her, however. The reassuring familiarity of the woman's face put her a little more at ease, for some reason.

"Welcome, huntress. My name is Thea. We have many questions for you, but don't want you to feel as if you're at an inquisition. Perhaps it would put you more at ease if you asked us the question that is most present in your mind."

Jilah was surprised to find that the woman had a British accent as well. It suited her. She blinked and readjusted her position in the seat, clearing her throat before asking, "OK. I guess the biggest question that I have is who and what is the Dark Lady?"

The women on the other side of the table looked at each other as Thea repeated, "The dark lady?"

Jilah frowned, assuming that they already knew. *Guess not.* What did the patronesses for these women look like? Did she appear differently to everybody else that served her? Was there more than one?

"Yeah – you know, the lady with the slithery voice that sounds like dried leaves rustling who is currently parked in my grey matter. She's the one who gave me, ah, the job I currently have."

Well, *gave* was being a little generous. Forced was more like it.

The sounds of hushed whispers filled the air as the other women talked in quiet, insistent tones amongst themselves. Thea silenced them with a look and asked, "What exactly does this dark lady look like?"

"Black skin; so dark that light doesn't seem to reflect off it. Sharp teeth, long forked tongue and a necklace of really nasty looking intestines.."

Thea's eyes narrowed and Jilah trailed off. Was she pissing them off already?

Thea took a slow breath, then said, "Child, Zolah spoke to us of your inception, but more details will help us to see things clearly. Can you please walk us through the events of that night?"

Jilah leaned forward, recalling the memory.

"I can do better than that, if you'll give me your hand."

This prompted more hushed comments among the gathered women. Thea's expression grew wary and she paused for a moment before slowly extending a hand across the table. Jilah clasped the woman's hand in hers and sent her the images, the feelings, the resonance of that night. Thea's eyes widened in shock and Jilah's body jerked; the woman pulled her hand away as if burned. Thea looked back at her and wiped her hand along her thigh, giving her head a quick shake. Several of the women stood up, anger in their eyes as they stared back at Jilah.

"I am quite alright." The women slowly sat back down, but now watched Jilah with a guarded expression. Thea continued, asking, "How did you do that?"

Jilah shrugged, really hoping that she hadn't hurt her. She seemed nice enough.

"I don't know, really. I just push the memory through the connection. I figured that you guys could do the same thing."

Thea shook her head, her tone grave as she answered, "None of us are able to do this unless it is directly in the course of performing our duties, even those who have been around for hundreds of years."

Jilah paused to let the woman's words sink in as Thea continued, "Your patroness is dark, malevolent. She destroys without mercy and would have you do the same."

Jilah blinked. *Well, duh.* She almost laughed.

"Are you telling me that when your people go after your targets they're merciful about it?"

Thea frowned back at her, affronted. Her voice strained as she replied, "We are as merciful as those in our calling are allowed to be."

Jilah gave the woman a look of utter disbelief.

"And what exactly is that supposed to mean?"

Zolah leaned towards her, answering, "We run our prey to ground and dispatch them after they realize the true horror of what they've done. When we see the understanding in their eyes, when they are truly repentant, we then feed off of and send them to the next life."

Jilah peered back at her, hesitant as she asked, "And how, exactly, do you get them to come to this realization?"

Thea's voice was soft and quiet as she replied, "We had assumed that our methods were the same, but now we are coming to understand that this is not the case. How do you achieve this when you run your targets down?"

Jilah straightened in her seat, her voice clear and matter-of-fact as she answered, "I gather the collected memories of their victims and force them back through the psyches of their killers in a loop. It drives them insane pretty quickly. I imagine that repeatedly experiencing the attack through the eyes of the women and children they destroy enlightens them to a degree. I can only hope that it hurts a great deal more than it appears to before they finally kick off."

A hush fell over the table and Jilah watched Zolah's eyes grow wide. Thea became rigid, her fingers splaying out on the table. Jilah looked at the faces of the women around her. They were all in shock.

"Was it something I said?" she laughed weakly, feeling a growing pit in her stomach. This did not bode well.

Thea slowly blinked her eyes, recovering. "This is unheard of. What you are speaking of is defilement."

At this Jilah let out a short, sharp bark of laughter.

"Are you kidding me? What the hell do you think those assholes are doing out there? Just racking up notches on their bloody bedposts?" She leaned forward, angry now as her words grew sharp. "This ain't exactly a tea party ladies. This is no less than they deserve."

In fact, I wish it were a lot worse, she thought to herself as she watched Thea's eyes change color. They'd gone from lavender to ice blue in a matter of seconds.

Ah! The weirdness begins.

Jilah quickly backed off her anger, then stammered, "I-I thought that's why you brought me here. Because we had the same goals, and did the same things."

"Young lady", Thea began, mastering her own emotions as she continued, "It is my belief that you have been tainted and sent on a wicked errand. It would explain the serious discrepancies in our methodology. And you say you have run across no others such as yourself since you first crossed over into this life?"

Jilah gaped back at her, wondering why the hell she'd come here now. They couldn't help her; only accuse and judge her. It was the last thing she needed. Her anger flared back up as she growled, "Look, lady, I may not be the nicest of people when it comes to tracking down my prey, but trust me when I say that they get what's coming to them."

The light touch of Zolah's fingers on her arm caused her to jump a little.

"Jilah, please listen. Lady Thea isn't sitting in judgment of who you are."

Could've fooled me, she muttered internally as she turned to meet Thea's gaze. The woman's irises were slowly bleeding back to lavender.

"She is correct, huntress. We ache for you."

The emotion in the room suddenly shifted, the heat from the anger receding as she continued, "We grieve that you were taken in such a poisonous fashion, not given a true choice. You had no idea what you were agreeing to when your patroness offered her help. And we fear that you are headed down a very dark and dangerous path, for both you and your prey."

Jilah took a deep breath, trying to figure out what to do. Although the idea that Thea might be correct about this was very uncomfortable, the woman sounded reasonable. Perhaps she had a valid point. It might be worth it to listen to what she had to say.

"Please explain what you mean." Jilah asked, placing her hands in her lap and calming herself. Getting more agitated wouldn't do her any good at this point.

Thea extended a hand across the table again. The woman's fingers trembled slightly as she did so. It was costing her a great deal to offer her hand so soon after the last experience.

"I feel that until I am able to witness you in the execution of your duties that I cannot properly judge the situation. Would you allow me to know this of you?"

Jilah nodded and reached out to take the woman's hand, searching for the memory of the cabin in the swamp. Before their fingers touched, she warned, "I'm going to show you the worst thing I've witnessed, the worst thing I've had to do."

Thea nodded, taking a slow, steady breath and bracing herself as Jilah's hand connected with hers. The woman took it remarkably well this time. There weren't any dramatic gestures on her part, and Jilah wondered how she managed it as the last of the memory of that night cycled through.

When she broke the connection, Thea let out a sigh as a tear rolled down her cheek. The woman's voice was shaky as she asked, "How on earth were you able to bear the burden of this without training? Without a community to share, to purge the horror?"

Jilah's expression tightened as she placed her hand back in her lap. She wasn't sure that she wanted to tell them the entire story.

"I did have a little help... recently."

Thea looked over at Zolah, who nodded back to her. Thea's voice was soft and understanding as she murmured, "The bloodchild. Your mate."

The tension in her fingers release a little.

"Yes."

"Child, I am truly sorry. For both what you have experienced, and for what I now have to tell you."

Thea's expression was so very sad and Jilah felt something skittering just at the edge of her thoughts. It was angry, but it stayed in the background, listening. Waiting. The woman paused for a moment, and Jilah felt a significant energy shift in the room as she spoke.

"It is as I initially thought." She took a deep breath, then explained, "When you do this thing, when you break their minds, you break their souls as well."

Jilah's eyes narrowed as she considered the implications of what Thea was saying.

"Please tell me exactly what you mean by that. I want to be completely clear."

Thea nodded, and added, "When their minds shatter under your assault, their soul does as well. They are well and truly lost, and are unable to go back to the source of themselves to start over again, to take with them what they've learned to the next part of their journey in the life after this one. For them, the journey is over, and they are simply... no more."

Jilah wasn't entirely sure that she understood the problem here.

"And? Explain to me how this is a bad thing. These men rip the souls of their victims apart with their actions and get off on it. For most of them, it's their entire existence. It's what they live for, the one thing that truly brings their own souls joy. Shouldn't animals like that be put down? It's obvious that they don't want to stop. Eliminating them is the only way to handle it. It's elemental, really, no more rapist, no more rape."

Thea placed her hands in her lap and cleared her throat, her expression one of infinite patience.

"You are not hearing me, child. We are all in agreement that these men must be punished for their actions. None of us takes issue with that. It is, after all, what we are here to do – to be the vessels of judgment and punishment for our patroness. *But,* this lifestream is but one in a sea of possibilities. We are not judge, jury and executioner for every reality, and that is, in effect, what you have become. You are cutting off the possibility for these beings to learn from what they've done."

The woman leaned forward, her tone becoming grave as she continued, "Did you honestly think that the only reason you were given this gift was to make others simply suffer? We force our targets to face what they've done, so that they may see the horror in it and learn from it. In this, there is a great deal of suffering for them, yes, but that is hardly the entire reason for our task. The end result is not the same. Our targets are able to move on after they cross into the next life, to pay for their crimes then move beyond them."

Her voice became hushed, her eyes haunted.

"Yours simply end. Forever."

The ramifications of the woman's statement began to sink in and Jilah felt her limbs go numb. A familiar chittering laughter rang out in her thoughts and her skin grew cold, gooseflesh chasing along her arms as she looked back at Thea.

:: *This is what you do, beautiful daughter. Cherished weapon. You are justice without end. You are my hand, working my will in the world, and it is glorious.* ::

Something in Jilah wrenched sharply and she cried out, clutching at a sudden stabbing pain in her stomach. The laughter became nasty and the voice of her dark patroness grew cold and dangerous.

:: *We have an unbreakable accord, weapon. You would do well to remember this.* ::

The room began spinning and before her vision winked out she heard Argent's echoing cry, but couldn't quite make out what he was saying.

Argent reclined on an elegant crimson chaise lounge in his office as he flipped through the collection of papers in his lap. It was taking longer than he liked to go through the multitude of reports that had been waiting on his desk. He tossed them down on the table beside him in irritation. How he loathed these seemingly endless piles of paperwork. Granted, he had people to sift through most of it, but the more important issues always ended up on his table.

He didn't trust these sorts of documents to anybody but himself. Judiana's replacement had made quite a mess of things. It was taking a rather overwhelming amount of work to set everything right.

There was a gentle rapping at the door and he turned to find Aurelian standing there, watching him. Argent smiled and waved the man over, happy to have a momentary distraction from duty.

"You're too tense."

Aurelian sat in a chair across from him, his tone seductive as he smiled and began drumming his fingers slowly on one of the hand rests. The selkie crossed his legs and the smile became wicked.

Argent chuckled, his voice low as he watched Aurelian bite his lower lip.

"And you are too obvious."

Aurelian laughed and tossed a paperclip at him.

"She's been gone for less than a couple of hours and you're already snappy."

"Bah." The sanguine croaked, batting the tiny missile away and readjusting himself on the chaise lounge. "It's the paperwork."

Aurelian uncrossed his legs and leaned forward, resting his elbows on his knees, his hands clasped before him.

"Bullshit."

Argent darted a mildly annoyed look at him, which only caused Aurelian to laugh again.

"You're so cute when you're all piney."

Argent frowned and narrowed his eyes back at the selkie.

"I am hardly pining for anyone."

Argent indicated the piles of paperwork before him with a sweeping motion of his hand. "I am simply irritated by the processes necessary to run an efficient system of government. Especially one that was so completely screwed up by the last tenant of this office."

He flicked a finger at the topmost paper, knocking it off the stack. They both watched as it quietly floated to the ground.

"It is one of the reasons that I left in the first place."

Aurelian let his hands rest in his lap as he leaned back into the chair.

"Anything I can do to help?" he asked with a hopeful expression.

He really shouldn't let himself get so easily distracted by this. There was far too much to do. The memory of the selkie's warm, bronze skin beneath his fingers flared in his mind, calling forth other more involved remembrances, sending a shiver through him. Both excited and irritated with himself that he found it so hard to resist Aurelian when he became so set on seduction, the sanguine gave in and raised an eyebrow, sitting up a little straighter.

"Perhaps."

"Ah, I like it when you get all coy."

The selkie grinned playfully.

It was Argent's turn to laugh now as Aurelian uncoiled from his seat and began crawling towards him on all fours. The blonde moved with a liquid grace that sent a gentle thrum through Argent, lighting up all his erogenous zones. The sanguine shifted in his seat, jolts of quicksilver racing through his veins as the man crept closer.

Argent murmured, "She really is right, you know. You are a complete and total slut."

Not that he minded, really.

Aurelian shrugged as he moved closer.

"If the shoe fits."

Argent's eyes dilated as the selkie placed a hand on the cushion at his side, grabbing it and gently sliding it away from him. The sanguine raised an eyebrow and chided, "Now, now. I just spent all last night otherwise engaged. I really must get some of this work finished."

It was a weak excuse, really, and not at all believable. Aurelian responded with a playful rumble that sent a shiver through him. The man really was incorrigible. And insufferable. And delightful. He chuckled as Aurelian settled himself between his legs, then let out a soft, resigned sigh and watched Aurelian's lips curl into a wicked grin.

"Well, best to just go along with it then, I guess." Argent murmured, holding back a groan as Aurelian began sliding those thick warm hands up his legs, squeezing when they reached his hips.

"You're not going to close your eyes and think of England now, are you?"

The selkie leaned in and ran his thumbs down along the inseam of Argent's leather pants, digging his fingers into the tops of the sanguine's thighs.

Argent grinned, then sighed as Aurelian's lips brushed his own.

"Hardly."

The sanguine pulled him close, capturing the blonde's lips with his own. Aurelian growled as Argent started pulling the selkie's shirt out of his pants, cool fingers sliding under and up along the planes of his back. Aurelian quickly pulled it off and tossed it to the side, breathing heavily now. The selkie grabbed Argent's hips, pulling him against the tight line of his body, and Argent groaned, rocking against blazing heat. Aurelian's fingers twined in Argent's thick black hair before offering the sanguine his neck. Argent pressed cool lips against heated skin, nipping softly at the hot red rush running just beneath the surface, just waiting to be released.

"God, do it." Aurelian groaned, shuddering as Argent bit a little harder, without breaking the skin, teasing. After all, turnabout was only fair play.

Something plucked along the connection to Jilah and Argent frowned, pressing a hand against the selkie's shoulder as he opened the connection up.

"Wait."

Jilah's thoughts rushed into his mind in a terrified jumble. Argent was immediately standing and screaming down the line to her, but he'd already lost her.

"SHIT!" he roared, glaring down at Aurelian who was now looking up at him with a startled expression. Argent worked to control his breathing, his hands tightly fisted at his sides.

"Our girl get herself in trouble?" Aurelian asked, instantly focused as he stood up, his voice full of concern.

"It is difficult to tell. She has apparently passed out, but it remains a mystery as to why."

Argent mastered himself and growled, "I had a bad feeling about sending her in the first place."

"So when do we go get her?" Aurelian looked like he was ready to hit something. He'd become very protective of her over the last few weeks.

Argent's expression hardened as he pulled his black leather jacket on.

"We don't even know where she is."

Without the connection to lead him to her, there was little he could do until she woke up.

Suddenly, muffled music started playing from somewhere, startling them both. Argent crooked an eyebrow up and Aurelian quickly reached into his back pocket, pulling out a cell phone and answering it. Apparently, there was now a rather emphatic visitor asking for Argent in the throne room.

Aurelian turned to look at him and nodded, "Go. I'll wrap up here."

Argent blurred out of the room and into the main chamber. He breathed a silent sigh of relief as he recognized the silver haired woman from earlier.

"Is she okay? What happened?" he asked, his manner gruff as he strode up to her.

Zolah quickly explained, "We don't know. Since you are her mate, we figured that your presence would help her with whatever seems to be happening."

Argent frowned, rocking back on a heel. And they hadn't brought her back because she'd gotten sick on the first trip out. He wanted to be angry with the woman before him, but making Jilah sick a second time wasn't the wisest thing to do.

Aurelian stalked into the room with a worried expression.

"Is she okay?" he asked as he walked up to them.

Argent looked back at the selkie, unsure what to tell him.

"It sounds as if she simply passed out, but they do not know why. I am going to return with this woman to insure that my Striaga is safe. Once I am reasonably sure that she is, I will return."

"But..." Aurelian stepped forward, reminding him, "an escort."

Argent frowned, shaking his head and sending, :: *I've been alone in the world for many years until now. The court needs to look strong so soon after the recent conflict and power play for the city. Make excuses, reroute requests and visits. Just make sure that nobody knows I'm gone.* ::

Although it would look bad if he went alone, it would be worse if he hobbled the court by taking any more essential people with him.

Aurelian let out a weak laugh as he pointed over to Brigliadoro who was now padding over to them.

"Won't he notice?"

Argent sighed and nodded. :: *Let the inner circle know, but nobody else can be aware of my departure. It is too soon for me to be leaving the city for any length of time. I will return as quick as I can.* ::

Brigliadoro stepped up to him and Argent explained, "My mate has found her way into some trouble. I must go to insure that she is in otherwise good health." The enormous gargoyle nodded once and turned to stalk back to his place in the shadows.

Argent clasped Aurelian's hand tightly. :: *Call me if anything happens that demands my immediate and direct attention.* ::

He turned and walked back over to the silver haired lady who was waiting patiently towards the front of the room.

"At least you carry a damned cellphone now!" Aurelian yelled after him as the pair winked out of existence.

Chapter 7
THE EDGES OF A SHOW OF FORCE

Jilah's eyes slowly fluttered open and Argent's face swam into view. She frowned as she realized that she was now lying down.

"Where..? What happened?" she croaked, trying to sit up before he pushed her gently back down into the bed. *Bed?* She looked around, finding herself in a room with furniture and fixtures that looked like they were in high conservative fashion during the Nixon era.

:: What is the last thing you remember? Let me see. ::

Argent's voice was soft and reassuring, and she nodded as she opened the connection up a little more to let him in. It would be easier than explaining it all to him, anyway. She felt him recoil slightly at her memory of the conversation she'd had with the Synod. With a start, she realized that he'd suspected she was destroying souls when she performed her given task.

He quickly explained, *:: I wasn't clear that you were doing it to everybody that you hunted. We were only certain of the fate of Alain's packmate. He said that Gregor had entered what they call the dreaming, the time after death for them, broken and unaware of itself. ::*

Jilah shifted uncomfortably in the bed, then groaned, "Oh god." She backed away from him, scooting up against the headboard.

:: Oh god! And they sent a packmate to guard me? After knowing this? ::

Jilah looked over to find her escort peering over at her from across the room. His arms were crossed, his expression distressed.

"Is the Striaga going to be alright? Have I failed to protect her?" he asked, clearly upset.

Argent turned to address him, his tone gentle. "This is something that you could not have protected her from. You are absolved of blame for this."

Jilah's escort relaxed, running his palms along the length of jean clad thighs as he leaned back against the wall. She could tell that he still wasn't happy about it.

Zolah walked in and Jilah almost teared up at the expression on the woman's face. Such sad sympathy. She wasn't sure if she deserved it. Jilah had always wondered if there was a possibility of life after death, and for some reason that made it easier for her to conduct her duties for her patroness. In the beginning, it was all very black and white, taking hateful beings directly out of the equation. One less predator in the flock to destroy the sheep. She had never bothered spending time thinking about what happened to her targets after she finished with them. It never really occurred to her to do so. Now she was being confronted with the harsh reality that something akin to reincarnation did exist, providing an opportunity for people to change and to learn from their savage, unforgivable behavior in this world.

Knowing that she was actively cutting people off from that possibility caused an uncomfortable struggle within her. In her mind rapists and child molesters deserved to burn, to suffer as much as humanly possible. All of the horror, loss and grief they sowed in the world – it was the very least they deserved.

But gone forever? That somehow seemed a hell of a lot less palatable. It also occurred to her that the last few times that she'd gone out to conduct her work, she had reveled in the suffering of her targets more than usual. After all, it was always sweeter to be on the side of a righteous cause, having the surety of purpose that the suffering she caused was for a good reason. It presented her with an almost orgasmic high at times when she delivered justice in the dark lady's name, and it was starting to become addictive. A part of her saw this for what it was; she was slowly becoming like them. With every life she took, all the pain she drank down, in a way, she was gaining the same kind of power and self-satisfaction that her prey did. Causing the suffering and madness that she spread in the minds of her... *victims* was beginning to become necessary. She was starting to crave it.

Her stomach churned at the very thought. Jilah blinked back tears.

:: *They're right. I'm just as bad as the people I'm hunting.* ::

Argent reached out and gave her a brief shake, forcing her to look up at him.

:: *Stop this. There was no way you could have known.* ::

She frowned at him, scared now.

:: *They said that I was tainted. That I'd been sent on a wicked errand. I'm beginning to think that they're right.* ::

Argent gathered her into his arms and kissed her forehead gently. She leaned into him, gripping the lapel of his jacket.

:: *How do I fix this? Can I fix this?* ::

:: *I don't know, love. But I will do what I can to help you find out.* :: he murmured, gently stroking her cheek.

She pulled away and looked up at him, frightened. :: *I don't know if the Dark Lady living in my head wants me to fix it. I think she'll fight it.* ::

Argent stiffened, then quickly mastered himself.

:: *We will figure something out, beloved. Fear not.* ::

Zolah cleared her throat softly, asking, "Are you in physical pain, still?"

Jilah shook her head and quietly replied, "No. No *physical* pain."

There was a light rap on the door frame and Thea poked her head into the room.

"I apologize if my words were the cause of your distress."

Jilah sat up, resting her head on Argent's shoulder.

"No, it's okay. It's something I needed to hear. Needed to know."

Thea nodded and stepped into the room.

"When you're feeling up to it, we'd like to give you a tour of the facilities – but now, I'll leave you so that you have time to convalesce."

She smiled and turned to go, but Jilah held up a hand.

"Wait. I'm okay to go now."

Argent turned to stare at her.

:: *Are you sure? Shouldn't you rest?* ::

She waved him away, shaking her head.

:: *The only way that I'm going to figure any of this out is if I get to it. Staying here and resting will only ensure that I make myself crazy by over thinking everything.* ::

Argent sighed and let her stand up, turning towards Thea as the woman asked, "Are you quite certain?"

"I need to learn as much as I can, as quickly as possible." Jilah paused for a moment, uneasy. "At least before I get sent out on another job."

"I understand completely."

Thea nodded and addressed Argent. "One of our sisters can escort you back to your prefecture, if you'd like, Strigaisha."

Argent inclined his head and smiled. "That would be much appreciated. And thank you again for bringing me to her as quickly as you did."

He turned to glare at Jilah, his voice halfheartedly chiding. "And you. Stay out of trouble."

She nodded quickly. :: *Oh yeah. I'll do my best.* ::

He took her hand, squeezing it gently.

:: *Do not run yourself into the ground with this, love. Find out what you need to know, then come home.* ::

She gave him a brief hug and replied, :: *I will.* ::

Argent turned and walked to the door, his tone smooth and lilting. "Ladies, it has been enlightening."

Jilah jumped as her young escort stepped beside her. She looked over at him, frowning.

"What?"

The young man set his jaw, his posture practically radiating Alpha now.

"I'm not letting you out of my sight."

Jilah wheeled on him, irritated. Before she could say anything, Zolah politely broke in, saying, "It is alright. Given the circumstances, we will work around his presence."

She still didn't like the idea of having a babysitter. It wasn't as if he could do anything if her patroness decided to take another chunk out of her in some fashion. This was an internal battle that only she would be able to fight. Jilah hoped that these women would be able to find a way to keep the 'soul destroying' part of her job from happening before she was called into service again. She looked back over at her escort and something familiar tugged at her memory. She tried to chase the thread of thought, but it was elusive and was quickly gone. She shook her head to clear it and walked toward Zolah.

"Might as well get started now. Where to first?"

Zolah showed her the rest of the floor, which didn't seem very big. In her opinion, it was also somewhat raggedy. As she looked off to the left, Jilah noted a patch of carpet over by a pair of thin metal, windowed doors that reached up to the ceiling. It had what looked like very old, greenish black mold spreading within the fibers. She grimaced and looked outside, seeing a hotel across the way through the windows. Somebody had apparently pulled the lock out of the housing of one of the doors and taped it shut for some reason, and both doors were completely taped over with what looked like cardboard that had gotten doused in a fair amount of water. The cardboard scalloped in places, the ridges of the inner lining showing through.

Strange..., she thought to herself. *What, are they government funded or something?*

It was odd that there didn't seem to be any other office workers. The low-walled cubicle farms were deserted. 'Temp pools', she'd referred to them when she used to work in the same environment. Not everybody who had worked at her company had been a temp, including herself, but the cubicles always gave you a sense that your boss could be lurking around any corner, taking nefarious notes to ensure your quick dismissal. The entire space was oppressive almost by default, as most office buildings seemed to be. There were no personal touches anywhere that she could see, but at least there were none of those wretched 'motivational posters', with skiing men jumping over volcanoes simply because they could, in sight.

Zolah led them towards a door, and Jilah asked, "So - did you guys run out of money a while back, or what?"

Her companion smiled, reaching for the door and gently pushing it open.

"Everybody says that when they see the façade."

Jilah blinked, taking a quick look around again before following Zolah into a stairwell. The walls were painted with the same, base, nonthreatening beige she'd seen in her own building. Jilah padded over to look down the stairwell, through the five inch gap that spiraled down into darkness. They started their descent, and she realized that she couldn't see the bottom of the stairwell through the gap. As they reached the second landing, the scenery began to shift. The slick, painted cinder blocks in the stairwell slowly morphed into craggy stone, starting to look like cave walls. The stairs were carved out of chunks of the same substance. Jilah looked over to see her escort and Zolah watching her with a patient expression. She provided them with a sheepish grin, then followed as Zolah began heading down the first set of stairs.

As they descended, Jilah noticed that this part of the building continued to utilize electrical lighting. Thick, industrial wiring ran across the ceiling, snaking up through holes drilled in the rock. The air was a little colder and slightly damp about two floors down from their original perch on the stairs above. The doorways on the landings were now large apertures carved into the rock, leading to corridors that went further into cave-like tunnels. On the next floor down, the stairwell was lit with gas lanterns only. Flickering orange flame danced behind the glass, throwing jittering shadows against the walls around it.

Guess it gets a little too wet to keep electricity reliable down here, she mused to herself as Zolah walked into the aperture for this floor. Although the flames in the lanterns were small, they did a decent job of lighting the way. Zolah instructed her escort to keep his eyes averted as they walked past a small room on the left.

"It is imperative that you not meet their eyes," she whispered.

Her escort nodded and kept his eyes on the floor, but Jilah could tell that it rankled him more than he let on. Just inside the room were two young women doing their best to fight one another. An instructor watched the pair, nodding and writing notes down on a clipboard. Two other women sat on a stone outcropping off to the side, watching the scene before them intently. Jilah observed the sparring women and frowned. They moved with strange jerky motions, almost as if they weren't quite used to their bodies yet. The movements and the flow of the sparring partners bodies were slow and forced, as if it was taking a great deal of concentration to stay in focused motion. The expression on one woman's face was a mixture of frustration and determination. Sweat was dripping down her brow and she pooched out her lower lip, blowing a dangling drop of perspiration off the tip of her nose before closing with her sparring partner again.

Jilah blinked. These were the fierce fighting warriors that the Synod was sending out against the world's injustices? Jilah had envisioned classrooms full of women in martial arts uniforms sparring with a variety of weapons: an echo of the spy genre movies that she was so fond of. It was silly, but she had hoped that there might be a glimmer of that to be found here. The reality was almost distressing.

Zolah explained, "They are new arrivals and have recently joined us. It takes a while to get used to the fusion of host and demon, until both are capable of working with each other with little or no effort. Only then can the true talent of the demon come into play."

Jilah remembered her own awkward physical adjustment period and winced. She kept her voice low as she asked, "And the chicks on the bench?"

Zolah looked back at her with a confused expression, replying, "I see no bench."

Jilah blinked, then explained, "The ones sitting it out, up against the wall over there."

"They have yet to go through the process of integration and so can only watch now. We've found that training hosts in the combat arts before inception makes it more difficult for them, because they then have to completely relearn the moves and the pattern of thought needed to react instinctively in a fight."

Jilah frowned, understanding but still curious. "Why such a small group?"

Zolah began walking again as she explained, "As I stated before, our numbers are constant. When a demon is in the process of becoming available for integration, a suitable host is contacted and brought here. It is not a thing that happens often."

"So, there's not an army of you guys running around out there?" Jilah mused, sliding her thumbs into her pockets.

"Hardly." Zolah responded. "We are of a sizable number, but the world is very large, and we can only do so much."

"What's up with that? Why'd it shake out like that?" Jilah asked.

Zolah smiled and replied simply, "It is as it is. This is how it has been for as long as any of us can remember."

"What, and you just go with this? None of you question the reasoning?"

Jilah found that hard to believe. Who wouldn't want to further investigate something like this? She had done everything she could to try to find out who and what she'd become after the change.

Zolah chuckled softly as she answered, "To whom would we voice our questions? The ones who guide us, who speak to us, tell us what we need to know so that we may conduct our duties as effectively as possible."

"Must be nice," Jilah muttered quietly.

Zolah looked over at Jilah, her expression still serene and ever so patient.

"All else is faith that balance is maintained through our actions."

Jilah wanted to know more, uncomfortable with her guide's simplistic, overly trusting reasoning, but realizing that she wouldn't get a more in-depth or direct answer from her. The sounds of gently splashing water echoed off to the right as they came to an alcove with a large hole in the floor. As she stepped closer, she could see a stone archway beyond the hole. Nestled in the middle of the archway was a brilliantly painted image of a bird of fire, the legendary Phoenix. The bird was spreading its wings in fiery flight, its essence trailing out of a blackened, cracked eggshell that was crumbling to ash. Looking down, Jilah saw that the hole masked a set of stairs leading down. She looked back up and the Phoenix thrummed with a quiet resonance, the smaller flames around its wings seeming to almost move in the torchlight.

Jilah blinked and leaned in for a closer look when the sound of Zolah's voice snapped her out of her reverie. "It is the symbol of our duty; we who reanimate the memories of victims to ring out in the minds of their despoilers. We bring them back to extract their taken measure from their attackers."

Jilah looked back at her escort, surprised to find him somewhat mesmerized by the image as well. Zolah pointed down to the stairs in the floor.

"That is where we are headed next. The meditation spire."

Zolah set her foot lightly on the first stair, gesturing for them to follow. A soft light danced along the walls of the stone stairs that went down. The steps looked as if they had been carved out of the stone with crude tools. Jilah was beginning to feel a little caged in as she followed and she worked to control her breathing. These people had treated her well, so far, offering her no harm. She'd grown somewhat used to the tunnels of the Convent. Surely she would get through this momentary hitch of fear as well. The sounds of water flowing and splashing over rock amplified, her boots echoing against the stone steps as they descended.

"This is one of the oldest parts of the complex. It's been here for as long as some of the demons can remember." Zolah's voice was soft and soothing and it resonated through the chamber in a way that put Jilah at ease.

"See now, that's another thing that I have questions about. The whole demon thing. Aren't demons bad?"

Jilah flicked a tiny brown spider off her leg. Her eyes tracked it as it skittered up the wall and into a small crack in the stone. The coloring of the rock was growing warmer now, almost reddish.

"Life is balance, sister. In our way, we are hosts to creatures that could be considered by some as 'evil'. You've no doubt felt your demon's presence within you, talking and acting through you at times of necessity. A great span of time ago, the founders of the Synod came to the realization that darkness best knows the actions of its own. The relationship between host and demon is necessary to maintain balance. With our demon, we are able to perform the feats needed in order to complete our chosen tasks. With us, our demon is able to stay within this plane of existence and subsist on the emotions necessary to sustain it. Without that, they would be sent back to their home domain, which is bereft of that which they need most. Through this connection, we came to realize that the creatures that we hosted were not so much evil as simply having a different moral code. This symbiotic relationship has benefited both our species for thousands of years. It has brought to fruition a broader understanding of each other as well."

Jilah coughed and almost slipped on the stairs.

"Wait, how long?"

Surprisingly strong hands caught her and she turned to find her escort steadying her, trying to right her so that she didn't tip and fall down the stairs. He quickly pulled his hands away from her, but didn't shrink back as he stared back at her, as if daring her to say anything.

Zolah watched this exchange, pausing a moment before nodding and continuing.

"The demons we are host to are very long lived indeed."

They reached the bottom of the stairs and the room opened out into a rust colored cavern. Flickering light from tarnished bronze lanterns cast a warm glow across the walls. It glinted off a cascade of water that ran down one side of the cavern; the falls breaking off into a web of runnels that danced over nodules along the cave wall, almost making the flow look like a small bridal train. It all collected into a large, naturally formed pool in the cave floor. The echo of the flame danced across the surface of the water, sending little ripples of pale light to play across the ceiling. Jilah couldn't tell how deep it was from where she was standing. Simply being in the room, she felt as if she could breathe easier. Jilah took a deep breath and relaxed for the first time since she'd set foot in the Synod.

It was warmer in this room, moreso than in the cavern above. Jilah looked over to the right and spotted another pool; this one had steam rising from it.

"Wow. It's like a spelunking version of ClubMed." she murmured to herself before turning and asking, "So, because of your agreement with these demons, would you say that their wings are figuratively clipped in a way?"

Zolah gave a solemn shake of her head. "Not at all. They simply understand that this is the most efficient way for them to feed without decimating their entire food source."

Jilah blinked, taking a step back. "Now that is entirely too creepy."

She eyed Zolah as she asked, "And you guys are okay with that?"

Zolah gave her a strange look. "It is what it is. Balance must be maintained. Predators have as much a place in the chain as prey does."

Jilah looked over at her escort who was watching their interaction intently.

"You getting all this?" she asked, feeling somewhat snippy. The conversation was leading her back to uncomfortable moral ground, and she didn't like him witnessing it.

The young man held up his hands in a placating gesture and drawled, "Hey. I'm not here to judge. I'm here to escort, remember?"

Curious now, Jilah rocked back on a heel and placed her hands on her hips. "But, if you *were* here to judge?"

He hesitated for a moment before his expression closed down and he took a step back, not taking the bait.

Jilah's eyes narrowed and she frowned. *He's hiding something.* She was pretty sure it was something big. Overwhelmed by curiosity, she dipped into his thoughts and was slapped with enough anger that it sent a chill across her skin. How could someone be so furious, yet look so empty on the surface? Her respect for her escort's sheer willpower doubled. She caught a fleeting image in his thoughts and the familiarity in him suddenly clicked with a horrible realization. She quickly yanked herself out of his head and wrapped her arms around herself, suddenly shivering.

Her escort's eyes now blazed a fiery orange and she could feel a sudden wave of heat rush from him.

Zolah stomped her foot and angrily hissed, "Not in here! You will not defile this place of peace and tranquility with your rage."

As if remembering himself, her escort's eyes slowly reverted back to their initial crystal blue. He turned and walked away from them, his hands opening and closing quickly.

Jilah felt as if she'd been punched in the stomach. Stunned, she whispered, "He was your father. Gregor was your *father*. Oh shit."

The boy slowly turned to face her, doing his best to keep his beast from rising to the surface. Jilah could tell that he was struggling with it, and her respect for him cranked up another few notches. It looked pretty painful. He said nothing, but simply stared back at her.

"And they chose to send you as my escort."

The very idea confused the hell out of her. Why command him to go out in the world to protect the person who had destroyed his father? It seemed terribly sadistic.

Her escort closed his eyes, taking a deep breath before opening them again and slowly walking back towards them. His voice was soft as he explained, "I have chosen this as part of my rite of passage. I felt that it would be a suitable test of my character."

He took another breath, a shaky one, as he jammed his hands in his pockets.

"They told me what he did, and why he had to be condemned. Why he had to die." He walked up to her, his eyes blazing as he spat, "But he didn't deserve *you*. What you did to him. Because of you, I will never be reunited with him after the great run. My father is gone."

He looked away, sounding bleak, blasted.

Jilah trembled, her voice cracking as she responded, "I didn't know... I thought..."

Zolah stepped between them, her eyes glittering as she gazed back at the man, staring him down.

"She speaks the truth."

His expression tightened as he looked away from her. Zolah continued, her voice soft and soothing, "She knew nothing of the finality of her actions until this very day."

"Please," Jilah croaked, moving away from them. "I'm so sorry. If I could fix it I would." The young man watched her as tears began rolling down her cheeks, his expression unreadable.

"Perhaps you should go." Zolah politely entreated, touching his shoulder and pointing him towards the stairs.

"No." His tone was forceful as he stood his ground. "My place is here with my Striaga. My duty."

Jilah looked back at him, her voice shaky as she whispered. "Why?"

His posture straightened and she sensed something strong and regal rise up in him.

"Because you helped save my Pack, my city. Because if what this woman says is true, you only did what you thought was right. And because I chose, of my own free will, to give my bloodbound oath to protect you."

Jilah took a step toward him, her voice quavering slightly as she murmured, "I regret that through my own action I almost caused you to break that oath, and I welcome both your protection and your honor."

Another phrase that seemed to come out of nowhere, but it felt right, and after the tension eased on her escort's face she figured that it was the right thing to have said.

He gave her a polite bow and the ghost of a smile played along his lips. This time, it was reflected in his eyes as well. She stepped up to him and said, "We were never formally introduced. I'm Jilah."

She held her palm out and he looked at it for a moment before tentatively placing his hand in hers.

"I am Maslin. And I am at your service, Striaga." His voice lilted softly as he spoke.

Strange boy, she decided. *Both strong and soft. If he can pull this off without killing me to avenge his father, I'll be really impressed,* she thought to herself.

The tour ended in a small, but impressively well stocked library. Comfortable chairs covered with soft, copper colored fabric sat in several locations throughout the room. An odd looking fireplace warmed the room, giving it a cozy, welcoming feel. Zolah pulled a large, oxblood colored book off one of the shelves and handed it to Jilah.

"This will answer many of your initial questions."

She turned back to the bookshelves, indicating a row of leather bound books. "The rest of these are historical references of the sisterhood. You are welcome to read any of them."

Jilah checked out the cover. The leather had been branded with a strange sigil that she didn't recognize. The pages were thick and old, but still strong. They were warm to the touch. The book felt almost alive in her hands.

Zolah indicated a large chair near the fire and said, "I'll leave you to your research. There's a cord over by the fireplace. Just give it a tug when you need my assistance."

Jilah nodded and curled up in one of the chairs, kicking her boots off and tucking her feet beneath her. Maslin sat across from her, keeping an eye on the open doorway as Jilah cracked the book open, breathing in the strange spicy scent of the pages. There was a light tang of musk, but she couldn't place the other scents. Her eyes scanned the page and rested on the word *Inception* in the table of contents. She quickly located the beginning of the chapter and began her research.

According to the text, before entering the sisterhood, each of the women chosen had been sought out by a presence that was referred to as the Emptor. Each recipient saw the Emptor differently. She had many guises, but her appearance always heralded the same thing: first contact with a new, able bodied soldier to join the fight. After the initial contact by the Emptor, a plenipotentiary of the Synod was then sent forth to visit the woman to see if she was receptive to this particular line of work. This apparently proved to be a somewhat difficult task in some cases, but the individuals who chose to see what the whole sisterhood thing was all about would, when ready, eventually go to the Synod for inception and training.

Those who chose to abstain, well... The Synod didn't worry about these women running off and telling anybody else about their existence. Most people look with a pitying eye on those who tell of odd things that fall outside of the realm of normal human existence.

It stated that inception was the process of bonding the demon to its new host. This was apparently an arduous undertaking that did not always progress as smoothly as it could. Jilah was able to find only slight references to failures in which the combination proved incompatible. Not much was ever said about what happened after that determination had been made, though, which seemed somewhat ominous. She wondered what happened to the hosts after the rejection.

Reading further, she could see that, after the bonding was solid, the new host was instructed through a procession of vigorous repetitive training exercises on how to act in tandem with it in order to be as successful and fluid in combat as possible. The training period apparently lasted anywhere from three to six months. After this, the new vessel was then sent out into the world in a paired attachment – usually with a much older agent that could teach her the ropes in the field, one who could easily extract her from a truly dangerous situation should the host find herself in one on her first few trips out.

Jilah began to understand why Zolah had been so startled at her progress. As she read through the stages of the process, Jilah realized that she had been cast into a writhing, teeming sea of utterly alien experience with little more than a life preserver – and expected to swim flawlessly. Reading about the social bonding and camaraderie that these women shared in the beginning amongst their peers and mentors brought tears to her eyes. There had never been anybody to guide her, to help her directly. She'd had to learn the lion's share of it on her own, all by the seat of her pants. Sure, the dark lady popped in and out at times, to help her out, but it had been shaky and tenuous at best. It was downright frustrating and confusing.

Thinking back, Jilah began to see an edge of malice to it that she hadn't really let herself notice before.

That familiar scratching voice crept through her mind, seductive and smooth, :: *See how much tougher, how much more capable you are. You are worth ten of them! You are much more powerful than they have the capacity to realize.* ::

Jilah let the voice speak. It took a strong effort on her part not to argue with it, not to respond with bitter accusations about how she'd been cheated. As if in response, dark laughter skittered through her thoughts.

:: *You are my knife, my measure of vengeance on the pox of this world. Can you not see the good you do? As if you need these weak willed women to show you what you are. You are power, my will manifest and made flesh, and they will not have you.* ::

Sharp pain stabbed through her head and Jilah cried out, pressing her fingers to her temples. Maslin was immediately at her side, but she held him off, croaking, "No. It's okay. It'll pass."

At least I hope it does, she thought to herself as she jerked in her seat.

Maslin peered curiously at her, his eyes seeming to shimmer as the pain twisted again for a moment, becoming almost unbearable before finally cutting off. Jilah let out a choked sigh and slumped in the chair, covered with a sheen of sweat. Chittering chuckles resonated in her ears and slowly faded, the dark lady's words starting to fade out as she spat, :: *No. They will not have you. You are MINE.* ::

Jilah wiped a hand across her forehead, letting her eyes slide closed. *At least I didn't pass out this time.*

"What happened?" Maslin's voice was low and controlled, almost a growl.

Jilah replied with a weak laugh and wiped her hand off on her pants.

"Bitch is finally showing her hand."

Her escort frowned, confused, "What's that supposed to mean?"

"It means that I'm probably going to be going through this a lot in the next couple of days." she grated, pulling herself up in the chair.

"The thing I don't get? I just don't understand why she waited this long. Why let me come here if it put me at odds with what she wanted from me? It doesn't make sense."

To be honest, she didn't understand the motivation for letting her connect with Argent – to be part of his life, either. If the dark lady had wanted an easily controllable toy, wouldn't it have been better to keep her ignorant and alone?

"I don't understand."

Maslin took a handkerchief out of his back pocket and proceeded to gently pat her face dry.

Jilah looked up at him, suddenly exhausted.

"And I don't know if I could explain."

She slowly stood up, her legs wobbling slightly. Maslin caught her and she cringed. At first, she hadn't wanted a babysitter. It made her feel helpless. But now she was strangely reassured that he was here. It certainly kept her from cracking her head open on something, which was a bonus. He helped her back into the chair.

"Do you want me to call Zolah back?" he asked, worry filling his face.

Jilah shook her head, placing her hand on his arm. "There's nothing anybody can do for this. It's all internal."

She paused for a moment, pondering something.

"No, go ahead and yank the rope. There's something they might be able to help me with after all."

Jhada Rogue Addams

Devil's Gambit

Chapter 8
RETRAINING

The target was walking calmly through a fairly deserted parking garage. It was late and most of the occupants of the building had already left for the night. Perfect hunting grounds. The man in the steel grey suit strode confidently to his car, briefcase in hand, the sound of the heels of his dress shoes hitting the cement echoing through the mostly empty underground space. He pulled out a set of keys and pressed a button on the fob as he pointed it at a black Mercedes. The car responded with a chirp, the lights flashing once as the doors automatically unlocked. She looked around for security cameras, making sure to stay out of all possible tracking shots. So far, she was moving too quickly for them to follow as she blurred from post to post.

The man tossed his briefcase on the backseat, and she let out a quick whistle from behind him. The man swiveled, his eyes widening as she darted forward and forced him into the front seat, moving to straddle him. She grabbed his jaw and forced his gaze to meet hers. The man writhed in her grip, making a horrible choking sound as he tried to escape. The conduit for the memories of the women he'd savaged opened and began to flow freely into his mind.

Jilah had hoped that by experiencing the way the sisterhood themselves hunted, she could figure out how to shut down the process that kept permanently destroying her targets.

It was slightly disorienting as the memories of the blonde woman behind her played in her consciousness, but Jilah struggled to stay with it. The act was almost... gentle, really, which was surprising. It felt like simply tapping into a well of consciousness, then attaching a tether from a given pool of memories to the target. The memories flowed from the source into the man's mind at their own pace.

"If this starts hurting her, pull her out. Immediately."

Maslin's voice echoed in an odd resonance when mixed with the memory. It had a dreamy, ethereal quality, but it was reassuring to knowing that he was on her side with this. Although, she figured that a large part of it had to do with the shame that he'd bring on himself if he failed to successfully protect her.

She waved it off, grating, "Don't pull me out until I say. No matter what happens."

The flow of memories continued at a slow, steady pace. She could now feel the man trying to push her off of him. There was something else she noticed then. Had she just missed it in her previous hunts? She felt a steady pulse that hadn't been there before, a rhythm that was growing louder as the memories sank in, forcing the man to see what he'd done. To experience the hell he'd created for these women.

It was a slow process, far more sluggish than what she was used to. A rather large part of her wanted to rush it, to force it all down the man's synapses in a blistering wave, the way she usually did. She wanted to stab the images and anguish into the man's head like a psionic knife. It helped that this moment was only a memory playback. If it had been happening in realtime, Jilah wasn't certain that she could have controlled herself. The urge to force it, to shatter the psyche of the man beneath her, was overwhelming. She felt herself shaking like a junkie needing a fix.

Being relegated to sit back and watch as it happened in this way felt like being physically restrained. Jilah had never been comfortable with the feeling of helplessness. She gripped the handrests of the chair and the metal groaned under the pressure, deforming beneath her hands before one of them snapped up and away from the chair.

"Striaga..." Maslin cautioned.

Jilah snapped, "NO! I have to see it through."

The steady pulse became louder, quickening now. Jilah had the distinct feeling that she was reaching an edge from which she needed to back off of soon, but she had to hear something specific first. The waiting was almost painful. Closer...closer...THERE. Something snapped in her thoughts and she felt the lock on the man's mind recede. There was a slight coppery taste on her tongue as she felt her mouth fasten to the man's neck. The emotions and sensations were muted, but she could feel herself responding to them. She was suddenly ravenous. She should be *feeding*. This should be nourishing her, but nothing was coming through. It tasted stale and dry, like dust and bones, and something in her raged.

Jilah forced it back down, the pain and the rage, as she shook in the chair, howling now.

The man in the playback was pleading, apologizing and babbling. Begging to be allowed to die quickly. She could feel his remorse, true regret at what he'd done. The pain he'd caused. It was disorienting, but strangely reassuring. She felt his emotions slowly fade away as he passed...

"Not enough. Not ENOUGH!"

Jilah roared as she leapt out of the chair, breaking contact with the blonde avatar behind her. The woman leapt back as if she'd touched something foul. There was a terrible screaming, shrieking noise ringing out through the room and Jilah couldn't figure out where it was coming from. She felt herself being tackled and thrown to the ground, her hands pulled behind her back.

Somebody was yelling something, but she couldn't quite make it out. Jilah was thrashing around on the floor, snapping and snarling as she slowly came to the realization that the horrible caterwauling was coming from her.

Awareness snapped into place as somebody moved beside her. Unable to control herself, Jilah threw off her captors and lunged, clutching eagerly at the warm body, crushing it to her and burying her teeth in its neck.

She was buffeted by a flurry of soft, gentle blows as she fed.

Rapid, high pitched shrieks began ringing through the room and Jilah felt a pair of hands slap firmly down on her shoulders. A strangely calming presence slid into her consciousness. She was slowly coming down, relaxing. The presence gently coaxed her away from her meal and she slowly became rational enough to be horrified at her behavior.

In a flash, she was across the room, scooting up against the wall and clamping a hand over her bloody mouth. Maslin was in the middle of the floor, twitching and gasping for air. She watched as the wounds in his throat began closing up and she started shaking.

:: *Jilah! ANSWER ME!* ::

The words thundered through her head, acting like a hard slap to the face.

She blinked quickly, mentally stammering, :: *Oh shit... Shit... I almost killed him..* ::

Jilah felt her lover crank the connection open and started to cry as she felt his presence wrap around her. She reached out and gripped a warm, strong hand, pulling it to her, around her. She felt arms surround her, holding her tightly as she rocked back and forth, trying to stop the tears. Argent's utter hatred for her patron burned brightly through the connection and Jilah winced at the intensity of it.

She felt Argent struggle to master himself, putting a tight leash on his anger.

:: *You scared the crap out of me. You know that?* ::

Jilah let out a shaky sigh as she rested her head on his chest. She didn't know what to think, what to say. She felt completely awful.

Through the connection she could see Argent slump in the chair he was sitting in, looking at the massive swath of strewn papers all over the floor.

:: *What a mess. If you keep doing this, I'll get no work done at all.* :: he grumbled.

She sighed, now feeling guilty that she'd startled him so badly.

:: *Sorry I ruined your office.* ::

Argent replied with a nervous laugh and Jilah watched as he began sifting through the paperwork on the floor, slowly collating them back into their original piles.

:: *Please tell me that good things are coming out of this, at least?* ::

Jilah winced, wanting to give him good news.

:: *I thought I was on to something, but as you can tell it went... awry. Poor Maslin... I can't believe I...* ::

:: *Hush. It was hardly something that you could control, and young Maslin is far more resilient than most. He will heal. That bitch squatting in your head has a great deal to answer for,* :: he growled, tossing another stack of papers onto the table.

:: For your own sanity, I'm going to crank the connection down as far as I possibly can. I don't know how many more times this is going to happen and only one of us needs to go through it. :: Jilah shifted in his lap.

Wait... somebody's lap.

Who was holding her if Argent was busy cleaning up his office?

Jilah looked up to find herself in Thea's arms. The woman had pulled Jilah into her lap and was holding her and looking back at her with a sad expression.

"God. Maslin... is he?"

She looked over to find her escort eyeing her warily, wiping the blood off his neck and face with a towel somebody had provided him.

Thea remained silent as Jilah gently pulled away from her. The women in the room were watching her very carefully, their expressions guarded as she took a step towards her escort.

"Maslin... I'm so sorry."

Jilah winced and berated herself. Well hell, what exactly were you supposed to say to somebody when you'd just tried to eat them by accident?

Maslin looked as if he was going to move away from her as she knelt down beside him. His voice was gruff but she could hear the tremor in it as he replied, "Don't come any closer. I won't be able to hold it back if you touch me again."

Jilah pulled away, crestfallen.

I really screwed up this time.

:: Beloved, stop this. He knew the risks involved. :: Argent chided softly, sending warmth down the connection to her.

:: That doesn't make it OK, :: she snapped.

Argent remained silent, waiting for her to calm down.

:: Did you know that he's Gregor's son? :: she replied as she stood up and turned away from Maslin.

All emotion over the connection shut off entirely. *Not a good sign.* She quickly added, *:: Before you get all pissed, it was his decision to come with me. He said that doing it was a test of his character. ::*

:: It is not him I am angry with, beloved. Alain should have told me. ::

Oh, he was not happy at all.

:: Please, let it go. For all we know, there might be a perfectly good reason why he didn't. He knows that I didn't mean to... :: she paused to look back

over at Maslin, who was watching her carefully. There was something different in his eyes now that she hadn't seen there before. :: ...do what I did to his father. ::

:: For you, I will drop it. The pup is honor bound to protect you, under pain of bloodhunt should he fail. This is enough for me to trust him. ::

Bloodhunt? They'd kill him? Jilah's jaw dropped and she stammered, :: Are you kidding? What kind of barbaric uber masculine bullshit is that? ::

Amusement echoed through the connection, and she could feel Argent smiling now. :: They are wolves, beloved. It is their nature. ::

:: There are some things I will never understand about your world, I swear, :: she grumbled.

Argent chuckled softly and cranked the connection down.

:: Our world, now, love. Our world. ::

Jilah turned to face the five women who had now dropped back into their seats, but were still watching her with wary eyes. And rightly so, she thought to herself. She had absolutely no idea of what to say after what had just happened.

The women were still staring at her and Jilah frowned and looked behind her.

"What?"

Maslin cocked his head to the side, his eyes mesmerized as they followed something down by her legs.

"I do admit that I like the tail," he murmured.

Her mouth dropped open. She had damn near torn his throat out and he was fascinated with *that*? She gathered her shields around herself and Maslin let out a disappointed sigh. She looked over at him and he shrugged, "You look good in horns and a tail."

Jilah stared at him for a moment, completely befuddled. She then turned back to watch the women relaxing back into their chairs. Thea pressed a linen handkerchief to her forehead as she sat back down in her seat.

"If we decide to try something like this again, we need to have a more adaptable contingency plan in place before things get so completely out of hand." She looked flushed.

"Ya think?" Maslin muttered before getting to his feet. "I'd suggest a cage or a cement room, to start."

Jilah nodded, agreeing with him. They would have to have a way to effectively restrain her in place or something worse might end up happening.

She looked over at Maslin, noticing that he really wasn't looking so good. His face was pale and he was trembling slightly. Because of the damage he'd sustained, he likely needed to eat. And soon. She could feel the hunger coming from him in a thrumming wave.

Jilah looked over at Zolah and softly asked, "You wouldn't happen to have a large, ready source of raw meat available, would you?"

Unfortunately, the solution wasn't that simple. Maslin explained that in his current state, the meat would have to be warm – from a fresh carcass. His resources had been too depleted with everything that had happened. The combination of the cacophonous mess of violent emotions, and then being drained of blood was wearing him more than a little thin. Coupled with the fact that he wasn't being given a chance to recharge through food, this was a recipe for Very Bad Things. He sat beside her in the back of a van, clenching and unclenching his hands as one of the sisters drove them out to a large, local park. Zolah rode silently in the passenger seat, turning back every few minutes to keep an eye on the pair of of them.

"It's late enough that all the tourists will be well gone from the park and the local Pack has a special arrangement with the National Park service to use this land for emergencies, as long as too much of the natural wildlife isn't consumed and the boundaries are contained." Zolah explained, adding, "As long as there are no garish messes left behind, we should be fine."

"'Boundaries are contained'?" Jilah asked, not liking the sound of that.

"The Pack patrols the points along the perimeter of this park because it is adjacent to human settlements. They do this to ensure that their own don't get out of hand." Zolah explained, not liking how Maslin was beginning to shudder. He was rapidly becoming less capable of controlling his shift.

Before they left, Zolah had contacted the Alpha of the Delmarva Tribe to ensure that it was acceptable for Maslin to hunt on their lands, assuring him that once the situation was resolved, they would immediately bring Maslin to him so that proper Pack procedure could be followed. It didn't go over particularly well that he had already been in the area for many hours before announcing his presence to the Pack, but after Zolah explained the unusual situation, the Alpha had relaxed. Crisis averted.

They had been in the car for what seemed like forever, driving along a winding two lane highway that curved through the woods when they finally reached a long access bar across the road. Zolah jumped out of the front seat and pushed the bar up high enough for them to drive under, then dropped it back down across the road and hopped back in. Once they reached the parking area, everybody piled out of the car. Maslin looked out into the forest beyond the picnic area and Jilah watched as a dim shimmer of light flowed over his skin. It was beautiful, almost mesmerizing. Maslin quickly turned to look at her, his eyes now sharp and bright orange.

His voice came out strangled as he croaked, "Run."

Jilah and the women quickly blurred up into the trees, well out of reach. As she watched from her perch in the branches, Maslin collapsed to all fours in a morphing flash. One moment he was a man whose eyes and teeth were going wonky, then the next an enormous brown wolf was darting off into the darkness. His clothes lay in ragged patches where he'd been standing moments before. Taking a moment to look around, to get her bearing, Jilah heard the sound of rushing water a little bit behind them. A waterfall? It sounded huge. There was a rustling in the bushes and the wolf raced back towards them, pausing at the tree she and Zolah occupied, peering up into the canopy of rustling leaves.

The wolf whined briefly, standing on hind legs and pressing its paws to the trunk, then clawing at it. It then darted away, back into the forest. Jilah wondered if she should follow him, to make sure that he was okay, then kicked herself for thinking it.

He's a werewolf. Of course he's going to be okay. What's the most dangerous thing that could live in this place? Deer? There was a baleful howl off in the distance. A second answering howl sent gooseflesh rushing across her skin.

She hissed over to Zolah, "I thought he was supposed to be alone in the park."

"He was." Zolah sounded distinctly irritated.

"Aaron would not have broken his word. He said that none of his pack would be close to the drop point so that your escort could run free and unmolested."

There was a sharp yelp, followed by the sounds of vicious snarling. Fighting with another shifter was the last thing Maslin needed at this point. It was enough to prompt Jilah to action.

"Fuck this."

She darted down, out of the tree, blurring towards the source of the sounds. The enormous brown wolf appeared to be fighting off an equally large red wolf. They were almost as large as ponies. Jilah crept closer, her eyes narrowing as she tried to keep downwind. The pair were really tearing into each other and another frantic yip echoed in the night air. She was fairly sure that you threw water on cats to get them to quit ripping into one another, but wolves? She had no idea. Unsure of what action to take, or how to separate the pair, she decided to try distraction.

She yelled, "Hey assholes! Cut it the hell out before I beat the crap out of both of you."

The distraction certainly had the intended effect. Both wolves paused and whirled to face her, growling.

Ok, genius, now what? How do you reason with a werewolf?

Zolah hissed at her from the trees. "What on earth are you doing?!"

The wolves swiveled, now staring up into the branches of a tree off to the left.

"Hell if I know. I hadn't really planned that far ahead yet."

Both wolves snapped their attention back to her.

"At the moment, it looks like they're confused and don't know what to chase down first."

They seemed to be quickly making up their minds, though.

Prey on ground, prey in tree. What's easier to run down? Duh.

"Oh shit," Jilah yelped as they leapt at her, blurring easily out of their range. The wolves tracked her, turning to intercept her. She heard a stream of what sounded like cursing coming from the upper branches of a tree as she zoomed past it. Maybe she could stay ahead of them long enough to tire them out.

At first, it was kind fun, racing and darting around trees and along pathways, always staying just ahead of them. After several close calls and a rather close encounter with a very sharp set of claws, however, she found that her stamina was beginning to flag. Her earlier 'meal' had hardly been filling and she could feel herself tiring out quicker than usual.

Man, they're quick little buggers.

She darted to the side, avoiding Maslin's gnashing teeth only to slam with jarring force into a thick, but strangely pliable tree that made an 'oof' sound as she collided with it. It hit the ground with a strangely meaty thud.

So this is it..., she thought to herself as the two wolves closed in.

She braced herself for a fight and closed the connection to Argent, slamming it shut as tightly as possible. Jilah wasn't sure that she could take both of them herself. If she was going to die, she figured the least she could do was to spare him the agony of experiencing her death through it.

A piercing howl echoed through the night air and immediately the two wolves whimpered and began backing away, tails between their legs and bodies low to the ground as their ears flattened alongside their heads. Jilah tentatively sat up, then blurred back up into the tree near Zolah, trying to recover her breath.

"That was very stupid." Zolah chided as Jilah watched the wolves cower beneath her.

"OK, so what would you have done?" Jilah asked, irritated.

Zolah simply shook her head, keeping an eye on the interaction on the ground.

"What's going on?"

Zolah replied, "Your extended foolishness gave me a chance to call the Alpha."

Jilah watched an enormous shaggy figure move forward on two legs, its arms outspread as it growled and took another aggressive step forward. The sound chilled her blood.

"So, is that...?"

She looked over in time to see Zolah nodding at her in response.

The Delmarva pack Alpha was a truly frightening vision; an eight foot tall apparition with midnight black fur. He uttered a strange growl and the red wolf immediately slunk over to his side. The enormous bipedal wolf cuffed the red wolf's head roughly, then turned to Maslin. The standing black wolf let out another strange growl and Maslin darted off into the woods. The bipedal wolf shimmered, then dropped to all fours in front of the red wolf who was now pawing quickly at the ground before him. When the change completed, the red wolf darted forward and quickly licked the muzzle of the larger black wolf. Together they headed off in the other direction, and Jilah released a breath that she didn't know she'd been holding.

"Where are they going?" Jilah asked, watching the retreating forms of the wolves as they disappeared into the woods in the other direction.

"They've left so that your escort can hunt in peace." Zolah breathed, shaking her head.

"Your actions were very unwise and could have gotten you seriously injured or killed."

Jilah looked over at her and shrugged, "It worked, didn't it?"

Zolah just gaped at her in disbelief.

Jilah sighed and shook her head. Argent was going to be furious when she shared the memory with him.

Maslin walked out of the woods, naked and dripping wet.

Jilah couldn't help noticing that he had a very nicely toned body and it seemed that the evenings activities had excited him. His rampant nature didn't seem to bother him and he moved with a calm, relaxed confidence as he walked back to them. Jilah's eyes widened as he strode towards her, and she quickly looked down at her feet, embarrassed. She found herself wishing that she'd thought to bring a spare change of clothing for him.

Zolah went over to the van, digging around for something while the other girl, an attractive brunette in jeans and a bare midriff t-shirt, gave him a bold stare with a hungry look in her eyes. The girl shifted from one foot to the other as she watched Maslin step over a downed tree on the pathway.

Oh, ugh. Is that how I look when Argent's around? Jilah wondered, turning and walking back towards the van to help Zolah find what she was looking for. She let out a sigh of relief as the woman held a large beach towel out towards her and glared over at the younger girl.

As if in answer to a question that Jilah hadn't yet asked, Zolah murmured, "She is still new and has a great deal to learn. She has yet to go on her first hunt. To see man at his worst. Otherwise she would not be looking at him as if he were something tasty to eat."

Jilah frowned as Maslin eyed the girl warily and walked around her.

"If she's a man-eater, what's she doing in the sisterhood?"

"Sometimes those who seem the least likely are chosen. She's quick, and very strong, but her bold and cocky demeanor will get her into trouble if she's not careful." Zolah shook her head slowly.

Maslin padded up to Jilah and she offered him the towel, doing her best not to look at him.

"Is there something wrong?" he asked, wrapping the towel around himself and drying off.

Jilah let out a choked laugh and shook her head, turning towards him now that he was covered.

"No. I just... haven't seen many guys naked. It's a little embarrassing."

She felt a flush creep into her cheeks as Maslin cracked a smile, uncovering himself to rub the towel on his head, making his bangs fall over his eyes.

"That's sweet." The lilt was back in his voice again.

Jilah narrowed her eyes at him and growled, "Just get in the van."

He laughed and tied the towel around his waist, climbing in as Jilah made her way around to the other side.

"What time is it?" Jilah asked, looking for, but not seeing, a clock in the dashboard.

"A little after four in the morning." Zolah answered, yawning. "It has been a very long night. We'll head back to the Synod and show you to your room."

"Room? As in singular? One room?" Jilah stammered, casting a nervous glance over at Maslin, who was now watching her with a great deal of amusement.

It looked like an upscale hotel room, maybe a little bigger, with nicer art on the walls. The curtains were the kind that you could draw against the midday sun and never even know it was past daybreak. An enormous king size bed covered by a beige comforter sat across from a television console. There were dark cherry wood tables on either side of the bed, each with their own light. The bathroom was pretty standard, with a slightly larger than normal tub/shower compartment. To Jilah it felt oppressively cramped, even though there was plenty of room to maneuver around the bed. She stared over at it, really not wanting to sleep in a bed with someone that wasn't Argent. There didn't seem to be another suitable sleeping area in this place.

"I do apologize that we only have the one room. We were unaware that you'd be accompanied by a companion, and the other rooms are taken."

"Oh, uh... it's okay."

Jilah fidgeted as she took another step closer to the bed. For a king sized bed it really did seem way too small.

"Are you sure you don't have a rollaway bed or something?"

Zolah shook her head, her expression worried, "I'm afraid not, unfortunately. Will you be alright?"

Jilah nodded a little too quickly and Maslin moved to stand beside her.

"We'll be fine. Thank you very much for your hospitality."

He smiled and the edges of Zolah's mouth quirked as she turned to go.

Jilah watched her close the door behind her as if watching the safety of land drop out of sight. Maslin's voice broke her train of thought, making her jump a little.

"Since you seem to be terrified at the prospect of sleeping in the same bed, I'll take the floor. I'll just need some covers and pillows."

He didn't sound angry at all. His voice was very matter of fact, and somewhat gentle as he moved to grab the topmost sheet.

Jilah held a hand up. "You can't sleep on the floor. It wouldn't be right."

She frowned for a moment, muttering, "Deja vu" under her breath.

Maslin looked back at her, his crystal blue eyes glittering.

"Are you certain? You seem awfully uncomfortable with the idea."

Jilah winced and looked away from him, stammering, "Look, I almost tore your throat out earlier. I damn near killed you. Why are you being so nice to me?"

Maslin looked at her and blinked. "I believe that you truly couldn't control yourself."

He frowned and continued, "There was something really different about you. You just became something... not you."

Jilah let out a weak laugh and replied, "You've known me for less than a day. How could you know it wasn't me just being a supreme asshole?"

Maslin smiled and quietly said, "That would be telling."

Jilah eyed him, then pointed to the bed.

"Just get in. It's the very least I can do considering what happened. Making you sleep on the floor would be an insult."

At least he was wearing pajama bottoms now. While he looked amusing in oversized pink teddy bear pants, they didn't seem to dent his dignity, which she found intriguing. He looked down, then grinned as he looked back at her.

"Oh. Yeah. I really should've stripped down before I shifted. I wasn't thinking."

He chuckled and lifted up the covers, sliding underneath them.

"Trust me. There's been enough lack of foresight for both of us to be in girly frou frou pajamas tonight."

Jilah shuddered as she stepped over to her rucksack and began pulling out her own nightwear.

"I appreciate your trust, Striaga," he murmured, and she turned to look over at him. He was watching her with a thoughtful expression.

Jilah found it difficult to meet his eyes as she replied, "And I appreciate your forgiveness."

Maslin smiled and she asked, "Do me a favor?"

Maslin raised his eyebrows, shifting beneath the covers.

"Sure."

"Just call me Jilah while we're here. Please?"

He smiled and nodded as she padded over to the bathroom.

"OK. Jilah."

She grinned as she closed the bathroom door and quickly changed. Now that sleeping was imminent, she was utterly exhausted. She padded back over to the other side of the bed and slid in, wriggling around to get comfortable.

"I have a question."

Maslin's voice was quiet and she could hear him rustling under the covers.

Jilah looked over at him, relieved that there was space enough for a person and a half between them.

"Shoot."

"Are you afraid of me? Is that why you're hesitant about sleeping in the same bed?"

He had that same thoughtful expression she'd noticed earlier, and he turned towards her, waiting for her answer.

She frowned and shook her head, turning to meet his gaze.

"No, Maslin. I don't think you'll hurt me, even after what happened."

She paused for a moment, wondering how she should word it.

"I just have intimacy issues with guys that aren't Argent."

Well, and now Aurelian. She hated to admit it, but the surfer boy had gotten under her skin and she was growing fond of him against her will. She was feeling uncomfortable enough without adding the idea of somebody else to the mix.

He remained silent and she added, "I like you, Maslin. I have a great deal of respect for what you're doing, what you're putting yourself through. I don't know if I'd have the strength to do it." She kept her voice soft as she regarded him.

He smiled back at her and something changed in his expression.

"You're a lot different than I thought you'd be."

"Is that good or bad?" she asked, eyeing him warily.

His smile broadened as he rolled over and pulled the covers up to his neck.

"Good night, Jilah."

She let out a long sigh and snuggled into the covers, letting her eyes slowly close.

"'night Maslin."

Chapter 9
POISONOUS REVELATIONS

Jilah's eyes flickered open at the sound of the bathroom door closing. Disoriented, she rolled over and looked at the curtains. A faint ribbon of light peeked out from beneath them, and she wondered what time it was. Figuring that Maslin would probably wake her up when he finished taking a shower or whatever it was that he was doing in there, she rolled over and tried to wring some sleep out of the next few minutes.

As she drifted back to sleep, she was suddenly sitting in a small, dark room with a single chair. She frowned as she looked around, seeing nothing particularly remarkable about the room. The vision of a young woman dressed in an outfit that was very out of date slowly came into focus. Her skirts were muddied and covered with brown, rusty looking splatters. She held her hands clasped tightly before her, knuckles white with tension. A thick, brown syrupy substance dripped down the front of her skirt like molasses. There was a ragged hole in the woman's chest, framed by the tattered remains of her blouse. The soiled garment was covered with so much of the rust color that it looked as if it had been dyed that way.

The woman's face came into sharp focus; her jaw slack and open. That same foul, dark, syrupy substance was now drooling out of one corner of her mouth, down her cheek and onto her chest. Her eyes were a brilliant cornflower blue, and they seemed so out of place in that ghastly, haunted face. They blinked once, slowly, and a different version of Argent swam into view.

His features seemed to have a great deal more color to them than she remembered as he presented the woman with a nasty, smug grin. He squeezed a shiny chunk of wet, red meat between his fingers. The doppleganger's voice was harsh and ugly. It cut through her thoughts as he purred, "Well, pretty thing – you wanted to give me your heart." He laughed, a sound that sent the wind up Jilah's back as he continued, "And now I have it."

The sound of a woman's sharp, mocking laughter rang through Jilah's head as he presented the dripping trophy to a platinum haired beauty kneeling beside him. The woman leaned into him, smiling as she took a bite out of it, then smeared his cheek with a ruby kiss.

"And I must say, I do believe my lady has found it to be delicious."

They both began laughing as Jilah watched the ruined body slump to the floor.

The scene shifted, and now the lady was struggling furiously beneath Argent's rough, vicious hands as he forced himself on her.

The image seared through Jilah's slumbering brain and she bolted upright in bed, shaking and clutching the covers so tightly that her fingers ached.

What the hell?

Jilah shook her head to clear it, blinking quickly. *Nightmare. Gotta be. But where the hell did it come from?*

Another scene, equally foul, crawled through the fabric of her psyche, and she pressed fists against her temples, willing it away.

:: *Think what you like, daughter of mine, but this is the reality. This is what he was, oh so many years ago. This is what he is still capable of.* ::

The voice of her patroness cackled in her thoughts, and Jilah kept her hands pressed tightly to the sides of her head.

:: *There's no way that's him. You're lying!* ::

She jumped as she felt a hand on her arm, leaping out of bed and coming up in a defensive posture with an angry snarl.

"Whoa! Jilah, calm down! It's just me."

Maslin stayed on the bed, his hands held out in a placating gesture.

"Okay? It's just me. I'm not going to hurt you."

Jilah frowned, shaking her head again to try to clear the ugly, obviously fabricated memories before looking back at him. It took her a moment to realize that he was naked and dripping wet. Again. She had probably startled the hell out of him and it looked as if he had leapt directly out of the shower to see what was wrong. She quickly turned away, clenching her hands into fists as she worked to control herself.

"I'm OK." She took a deep breath, slowly letting it out. Her voice was quiet as she murmured, "Just... please put some clothes on."

Maslin blinked, then seemed to realize his state of undress.

"Ah – sorry. I'll be right back." He darted quickly back into the bathroom.

Jilah backed up to the bed and sat down, resting her hands on the mattress as she let out a shaky breath. She wanted to contact Argent, to talk to him about it, but she also didn't want to keep interrupting him. He had plenty of work to do and she didn't want to add to it. Maslin was at her side again, now back in the pink pajama bottoms, his expression concerned as he crouched down and looked up at her.

"What happened?"

Jilah met his gaze and eased back into the mattress a little more, her right hand absently plucking at the sheets.

"The queen bitch just came up with something horrible, *unbelievable*, to screw with my head."

Maslin peered at her curiously, his voice soft and gentle as he asked, "What was it?"

She shook her head firmly, her brow knitting as she answered, "It's not important. I think she's scared, though; otherwise she wouldn't be pulling such an obvious stunt."

There was no way that could have been him. No way whatsoever, she thought to herself. The Dark Lady *had* to be lying – trying to distract her from further research. Yes, surely that's what it was.

"Are you finished with the shower?" she asked.

Maslin frowned, then nodded. "Yeah, I'm done."

"Good. I'm just going to take a minute to scrub up, then we can track down Zolah."

Jilah ducked into the bathroom, quickly closing the door behind her, not wanting to remember the false vision that her patroness had presented to her. She leaned over to turn the water on, testing the temperature. By the time it felt comfortable, she realized that she was shaking against the edge of the wall. *Ah, crap,* she hissed to herself as she gave herself a one armed hug as she leaned against the bathroom wall. *How am I going to maintain with this going on?*

She took a slow, shaky breath and stepped into the shower, keeping her thoughts on what she was doing in an attempt to keep from freaking out any further. Unfortunately, it wasn't working very well. She started at the sound of gentle rapping on the door.

She stood stock still, her voice quavering as she answered, "Yes?"

"I just wanted to let you know that Zolah was just here. She says that breakfast is ready." Maslin's voice was muffled and it sounded like he was still worried about her.

That makes two of us, Jilah mused as she began soaping up.

"I'll be out in a sec."

Food sounded really good at this point.

Then, all at once, the realization of the folly of her initial bargain with the Dark Lady hit her like a ton of bricks. She had allowed something dark and ravenous to take up residence in her head, and it likely wasn't going to leave without a fight. This last vision was pretty strong proof of that. As she finished washing up and rinsing off, Jilah found herself repeating the same couplet that she'd run through her head when she felt that somebody was trying to probe her mentally.

Mary had a little lamb, its fleece was white as snow. And everywhere that Mary went, the little lamb was sure to go. Mary had...

Perhaps filling her thoughts with white noise would give her time away from her patroness, a chance to figure out what her next course of action needed to be.

Zolah explained that they would be breaking their fast with Aaron this morning so that Maslin would have a chance to properly introduce himself to the Delmarva tribe Alpha. They stepped into the room, and Jilah's eyes widened as they met Aaron's steel grey gaze. He was an enormous man who definitely had a commanding presence. Most of his long, raven-black hair was tied back in a leather thong. He wasn't necessarily attractive by conventional standards; his face had a large scar that slashed down the side of his cheek and it looked as if he had three days growth of stubble. He looked like a big, shaggy biker who hadn't had time to wash the dirt of the road from his clothes.

Aaron stood up and walked over to them, eyeing Maslin curiously. His voice was a rough, husky rumble, as if he'd popped out of the womb with a cigar in one hand and a bottle of Jack Daniels in the other.

"Well, pup – you find what you needed at the falls?"

Maslin nodded, his voice strong and firm as he replied, "I did. My thanks to you and your tribe for your hospitality. And I extend my apologies for not announcing my presence before entering your territories."

Aaron looked him over for a moment, then gave a gruff nod.

"The reasons were explained to me and I accept your humility as good faith that you meant no disrespect or harm to me and mine."

He looked over at Zolah and smiled, his eyes twinkling with warmth before he turned and sat back down. Jilah was surprised to see her smile demurely before leading them to their seats. The spread before them was very generous, but Jilah didn't feel like eating. Maslin sat next to Aaron, and the two men talked quietly amongst themselves as Jilah leaned over to Zolah and quietly told her about the taunting, hurtful vision from her patroness, but didn't go into damning detail. She saw no reason for the woman to know exactly who the vision had been about.

Zolah nodded, keeping her tone low as she replied, "We were afraid that this would happen once we learned of the details of your inception."

Jilah took a slow breath as the woman continued, "This entity who speaks to you – it is likely that she is just now understanding that you are no longer comfortable with her presence. If she is truly malevolent, as Thea believes, she will turn against you and try to destroy you with the 'gift' that she feels she has presented you with."

Zolah gently placed her hand over Jilah's, her voice fierce but calm.

"My sister, we will do everything possible to free you from this creature. Please believe this."

"But how can you if you don't even know what it is?" Jilah's answering whisper was small and shaky as she looked down at the woman's hand. *How the hell do you run from something that lives in your consciousness?*

"The Synod is discussing the possibilities amongst themselves. I am sure that they will come up with something." Zolah offered softly.

Jilah looked up to see Maslin watching her with a curious expression. Aaron turned to look over at her as well, eyes glittering as he sniffed the air and frowned.

A wrenching pain suddenly blazed in her chest and Jilah cried out.

Argent's green eyes glittered and he laughed as the woman beneath him shrieked. He mounted her roughly as a soft, delicate hand trailed over his shoulder. Another woman's face came into view. She was an icy beauty with crystal blue eyes and long platinum hair that looked as if it had been matted with blood in places.

"Choke her, my love. There is not yet enough fear in her."

The woman smiled, as if doting on a child that was performing particularly well.

Argent obeyed, placing his hand on the woman's neck and pushing down as he began to squeeze. The woman started choking and bucking beneath him as she tried to get away from what was happening to her.

"You're right, beloved. It does make the ride more invigorating this way." Argent quipped, laughing as he roughly entered her.

Argent's smile was joyous as the blonde beauty leaned down and began to drink from her. The vicious exultation and satisfaction in Argent's expression was enough to make Jilah sick.

MARY HAD A LITTLE LAMB, Jilah tried her best to fight it, but the onslaught of the vision was too much. The laughter of her patroness skittered through her mind.

:: *You will go after him, weapon. You must. You will judge him and find him guilty. And with the amount of crimes that he's committed, he will suffer so very sweetly before he dies. He will provide us with a most excellent meal.* ::

Jilah raged, unable to control herself as she forced the connection between her and her lover wide.

Argent was walking into the office when the connection slammed into him with the force of a freight train. His knees buckled at the onslaught and he heard the sharp, ringing laughter of the dark, cancerous bitch that squatted in his lover's grey matter.

:: *She comes for you now, dog. This betrayal will break the last ties of trust she has to you or anything but her work. Without you, there will be no more distraction. She will once again hunt pure and true.* ::

With a start, he watched as parts of his tainted past crawled through his lover's mind. He winced at the pain and betrayal that echoed down through the connection from her. Jilah was cracking under the strain of it, trying to fight against the vision. Tears pooled in his eyes when he realized that she was so very certain that her patroness was lying; that this was some sort of devious trick to turn her against him.

It broke his heart that she wasn't correct – and that through the connection, Jilah now knew this as well. Her despair stabbed at him as Jilah then tried to pull away from everything: her patroness, the connection to him. She was shutting down, closing down with a finality that chilled him. And soon, he was sure, she'd hunt him. The entity in her mind would give her no other choice.

So many lifetimes ago, and still there was no redemption from his past. Oh, he'd been that person – and done all the things that she'd seen, and worse. Much, much worse. He'd been a rakish, charismatic animal before he was turned by the one woman that he thought truly understood the dark hunger inside him. The things they'd shared, before the turning; the nightmares of the years spent with her still plagued him. A hundred years of suffering and anguish wasn't nearly enough of a price to pay. Seeing his sire again through his lover's vision, catching a glimpse of that glowing, perfect face tore him apart. Losing her and walking the world alone and broken for a century hadn't been enough, it seemed. Now he was going to lose the woman he saw as his only salvation as well.

He was on the floor staring off into space when Aurelian found him, curled up next to the door frame. He was vaguely aware of the large man picking him up and asking him something. He couldn't quite make out the words.

"Argent, goddamnit!" the selkie bellowed, giving him a rough shake.

"Snap the fuck out of it!"

Argent blinked and looked up at him. His voice came out in a hushed croak that scared him, "My sister."

Aurelian looked back at him, confused. "Your sister? What about your sister? What the fuck just happened?"

Aurelian paced back and forth in front of the bed, badly shaken. In the entire time he'd known the sanguine, he'd never seen Argent go catatonic. The Strigaisha simply lay in the bed, staring up at the ceiling. Aurelian had no idea what he was going to tell the court about this development. How long was this going to last? Several hours had passed already. He could only keep this under wraps for so long before people would eventually demand an audience.

He ran a hand through his hair in frustration, then turned at the sound of a woman's voice.

"We have heard your call and we are here, brother."

The sanguine's red headed sister was standing in the doorway, her expression unreadable.

"We will take him now." Her voice echoed strangely, sounding as if several people were speaking at once through her vocal cords.

"He can't leave. He.."

Aurelian started towards her and she presented him with a sad smile and explained, "He will not rouse from this without our help."

Aurelian's heart stuttered and he stumbled back against the bed. "You know what this is?" he asked.

Argent's sister nodded, replying, "It is as it was before. We will tend to him. Mend his wounds."

As she stepped forward, Aurelian stood.

"What, that's it? No explanation? You just take him?"

She looked up at him and said, "It is our way. He knows of this."

She moved to collect Argent, then turned to go, but Aurelian stopped her with a gentle hand on her shoulder.

"Will he be okay?" his voice quavered as she looked back at him.

"Only our brother can answer that for himself. For now, we must go."

Aurelian watched her go, stunned into inaction for a few moments himself.

"What the fuck do I do now?"

He then shook himself and pulled his cellphone out, dialing Mira's number. Maybe with her help, he'd be able to keep this from turning into a political disaster.

Maslin sat by the side of the enormous bed, dabbing at Jilah's forehead with a cool cloth. She was clutching the sheets, her knuckles white with tension and her face tight from anguish. Her eyelids remained closed, and Maslin could see her eyes zooming around beneath them. Whatever dream she was having, it was ugly.

"There is not much else we can do."

Zolah patted him on the shoulder gently, her expression sad. "This is an internal struggle that we cannot help her with."

Maslin sighed as he continued the vigil. Two days had passed since her initial collapse.

Chapter 10
D**A**MN**A**TION

Argent sat on the bed in their chamber while Jilah railed at him, shrieking. She had every right to be angry and he would sit here and take it if that was the only way to keep her here. As long as she didn't leave. He didn't think he could bear it if she truly left. She was so upset that he could no longer make sense of what she was saying. Her eyes flashed as she snapped at him, her expression ugly and hateful; her emotions battering at him like physical blows. The last words she spat rang out clearly in the room.

"...NEVER FORGIVE YOU!"

Jilah's mouth tightened in a hard line as she growled, "Now run. And god help you when I run you to ground."

Argent blinked, unsure if he had heard her correctly. He gave her one last pleading look and she turned from him, her expression cold and empty. Every sense of self preservation he had was screaming at him to flee, and although he wanted so badly to stay - to have her near his side, his instincts took over and he bolted from the room. He blurred through the corridors and out of the convent, wondering how far he'd be able to get before she tagged him.

It didn't take long.

He'd gotten just out of the city limits when she slammed into him, knocking him to the ground. There was a loud snapping sound as he felt ribs crack, and he winced in pain as he rolled to a stop. His body began quickly healing the damage, but it burned and itched like mad as the bones fused themselves back together. He groaned and rolled over, looking up into his lover's face.

Her expression was harrowing. Jilah's lips were curled back in a ghoulish grin as she cooed down at him.

"Lover man."

She kicked him squarely in the face, breaking his nose with the toe of her boot.

Argent tried to blur away from her next kick, but it connected soundly with his side, cracking his healing ribs again, along with several others. He huffed in pain, cradling his side with his hand as she pushed him over onto his back with a booted foot. Jilah's voice was warm and soft, mocking as she slowly straddled him.

"Did you enjoy this body?"

She gave her breasts a squeeze, laughing.

"Was it good for you, while you used it?"

She rocked into him, bending down to breathe softly into his ear.

"Did you laugh to yourself while you fucked me? Knowing that you were mocking everything I was with your actions?"

Argent's throat closed and his voice came out in a strangled gasp.

"God no. I never..."

He saw stars as she cracked the back of her hand against his face. The bones in his cheek shattered and he blinked quickly as she grabbed his jaw and wrenched his head back to look at her. She let out a dark chuckle, letting her fingers play along the planes of his chest as she purred, "You're awfully durable, lover man. Perhaps I should make this last as long as possible for you; chew on you like a cat toy before I break you."

"Jilah, please..." he croaked, any urge to fight back leaving him.

He screamed as she snapped the bones in his wrist.

"No," she growled. "You don't get to talk, lover."

She squeezed the broken shards in his wrist, twisting her hand slowly and reveling at the painful grinding sound of his bones as he shifted beneath her in pain.

"Oh, that's much better."

She cocked her head to the side and sighed, sounding disappointed as she added, "Although since you seem to want to try to reason with me, I guess it'd be easier if I just got this over with."

Jilah smiled and Argent saw something flicker in the depths of her eyes. Something inside her pupils opened and quickly closed, like the iris of a camera.

"There, there, lover." Her tone was softer now, almost loving. "Just look at me."

Her pupils dilated and both her eyes flashed to black. Strange dancing lights beckoned in the depths of her eyes and Argent found himself inexplicably drawn into them. One, in particular, came forward slowly. He frowned as the shape swam into a recognizable form, then his mind reeled as he was suddenly wrenched out of his body. He was now looking up at a younger reflection of himself, watching his own expression become venomous as a sharp pain blossomed between his legs. The sanguine's consciousness, realizing what was happening, tried to scrabble away from what was happening, but he stayed fixed, unable to move as his replica above violated him, viciously tearing the body of the woman he occupied asunder.

His doppelganger's expression was ugly and vicious, and Argent found a part of himself breaking, just a little, as it roughly attacked him. The feelings of utter pain, helplessness and humiliation were excruciating, and there was nowhere to run. No way to escape. The sound of his own screams were drowned out by the nasty, lilting laughter of the indigo haired goddess astride him, her talons pulling ribbons of flesh out of his shoulders.

Argent sat bolt upright in bed, screaming, his throat ragged and painful. He blinked rapidly and looked around, his body drenched in a sheen of sweat.

A dream. He let out a shaky breath as he placed a hand to his forehead. His brow was sopping wet, and he wiped his hand on the dark purple sheets at his waist. *Just a dream.*

He winced at a sudden pain in his side and face, looking down to find a light bruising coloring his skin. Bringing his hand tentatively up to his nose, he winced in pain when he touched it. His shoulders began to burn and ache. *Okay, not a dream.*

He shuddered and the pain in his ribs and shoulders was suddenly searing. He slumped back to the bed as S'llethe stepped into the room.

"Brother, be still. We cannot heal you if you insist on being so active."

Argent frowned, grimacing at the pain it caused in his nose when he looked over at her. She regarded him with a sad expression and she sat in a chair beside the bed. Argent was surprised to realize that several other members of his long lost family were in attendance as well. They were all watching him with weary, sad expressions as they moved to stand around the bed.

"What...?" he croaked, clutching at the sheets from the pain in his throat. Everything hurt. He felt ragged and exhausted.

S'llethe shook her head gently, her voice a gentle murmur as she replied, "Mindspeak. Save your vocal cords. You have been overusing them."

A lithe man with strongly feminine features that Argent didn't recognize leaned over to pour him a glass of red liquid.

:: *Where am I?* :: he asked, looking around at dark, clay colored cave walls. Several wall sconces provided a low, comfortable light. It felt very familiar, but he was having a hard time placing it.

"You are home, brother. Do you not recognize your old room?"

:: *Home?* ::

He shifted beneath the covers, groaning at the sharp pain in his ribs.

:: *What of the court? My mate?* ::

S'llethe gently placed her hand on his wrist and Argent hissed. The bones were still knitting themselves back together, and the combination of pain and itching was maddening.

"She hunts you now, brother. Even though she is not yet aware of it. Soon, she will come."

Argent felt himself go numb at her words.

:: *So – no dream then?* ::

S'llethe nodded, her tone low and sad.

"No dream, brother. She has made her choice and only she can choose to stop."

His sense of loss was overwhelming and he closed his eyes to try to regain some measure of composure.

"She means to destroy you, brother. To bring balance."

S'llethe and the others looked down at him and the compassion he saw in their faces as he opened his eyes was almost too difficult to deal with. They were all too familiar with the trauma he had already endured due to his past transgressions.

:: *Will this balance ease her heart?* :: he asked, taking in a slow, shaky breath.

S'llethe shook her head. "No. It will destroy her and turn her into a mindless tool for the force that governs her. It will present this force with everything it desires."

Argent felt the first stirrings of anger.

:: How do I stop this? How do I help her? ::

"Take the measure of the balance, brother." His sister gently kissed his brow. "Take it and show her that you've learned from it."

Argent trembled slightly, his inner voice shaky. *:: I don't know if I can. There's so much... so much that I've done. So much to answer for. ::*

S'llethe smiled beatifically down at him, smoothing a wet patch of hair from his forehead.

"Oh yes, brother. But you have already paid an enormous price for your past. More so than you think."

He frowned up at her, not sure if he understood her clearly. He knew, though, that he couldn't expect a further explanation. She leaned forward, gently touching her hand to his shoulder. His muscles barked out in pain, but he grit his teeth against it and forced himself to listen as she continued, "It is in this that the entity resting in your mate has made its mistake."

:: What do you mean? I don't understand. ::

"You will, brother." S'llethe smiled down at him, her expression becoming triumphant. "You will."

Chapter 11
PURSUIT

Jilah snapped to awareness, drenched in sweat. She clutched the sheets to her chest as she spotted Maslin at the edge of the bed. Her escort was watching her with a very guarded expression. Everything grated – it all hurt, like the feel of a cat's tongue running roughly over a patch of skin that it had slowly licked raw. It all tightened into a white hot ball of anguish that came to one focal pinpoint. In that moment, everything became clear. Jilah felt her soul go cold – hardening into something that could feel no pity, no appreciation – no joy. Just a hard, frozen edge that would crack and tear anything she chose to direct it at.

Her eyes narrowed and she pushed Maslin's hand away from her forehead.

"Don't," she growled.

She spotted Zolah standing in the doorway. The woman's expression was one of confusion as she explained, "He is only trying to help."

Was she kidding? Didn't she know better at this point? The taste of bile was overwhelming – the ultimate betrayal of her heart making her lash out at the nearest target available. Jilah laughed back at her, a nasty, bitter sound as she snapped, "You should know by now, *sister*, that they only do what benefits them most in the moment."

Zolah's jaw dropped as Maslin gently placed the moist cloth on the table at the side of the bed and stood up. He quietly left the room without a word, his posture stiff.

"What on earth are you talking about, child?" Zolah stepped into the room, hands on her hips. "He has been sitting with you night and day for the last three days, taking care of you. I would hardly consider that something that's benefited him in the moment."

Jilah tossed the covers back, her lip curling at the ripe scent of her moist bedclothes. A sickly combination of sweet and sour scents flooded her nostrils. Had she purged poison out through her pores while she slept? It certainly smelled that way. What a stench. She quickly stood up and walked to the bathroom.

"He's taken an oath to do so. More fool him."

Zolah stepped in front of her, blocking her way. It was the first time that Jilah had ever seen the woman angry.

"You act without honor, behaving in this manner. What the hell has gotten into you?"

Beyond caring now and simply wanting to lash out to hurt anyone around her as badly as she'd been wounded, Jilah gave the woman an appreciative nod, her tone amused as she replied, "Cursing now, eh? That's interesting. Did you pick that up while I was out?"

She wanted to take a shower. It was well past time to get out of these wretched clothes so that she could track her lover down. The need to watch him suffer sang in her soul.

Zolah's expression darkened and Jilah watched as the woman's hands clenched into fists. Zolah's voice was shaking with anger as she replied, "I do not know what has transpired to bring this out in you, but you will show me and your escort the respect we deserve or you will leave. Now."

Jilah chuckled, rocking back on a heel.

"HA! I knew you had a pair on you somewhere."

She placed a hand on the woman's shoulder and shoved her hard, tossing her into the wall.

"Too bad it's far too little, too late. I'll just wash off in your shower, then I'll be on my merry way. Until then, fuck off and stay out of my way, lady."

Jilah turned to walk into the bathroom and spotted Maslin in the doorway.

Nosy little fucker, she grumbled to herself as she eyed him. He was trembling, and his eyes were quickly bleeding to orange.

"Oh good," she jeered. "The pup finally wants to come out and play. You ready to get a taste of what your father got?"

Maslin stood his ground.

"Kick my ass later, but hear what I have to say."

Jilah crossed her arms, giving him an insouciant smile.

"Fine. Speak, Lassie, speak."

The boy's eyes glittered as he growled, "Zolah tried to track the Strigaisha down and was unable to find him. He's gone missing. Nobody's telling us anything."

Jilah paused, frowning. He'd disappeared? No matter. The Dark Lady would lead her right to him. She shrugged, narrowing her eyes, her tone dead and cold as she muttered, "I'll find him soon enough – and then won't he be sorry?"

Maslin leaned closer to her, scenting the air. He looked back at her strangely, frowning as he took a step away from her.

"What are you?"

Jilah placed a finger to her lips, thinking about it for a moment.

"Hmm. That's a really good question."

Her eyes flashed as she grinned and grabbed his shirt, jerking him close, until their faces were almost touching. She dipped into his mind, digging around for something, anything that she could latch onto, that she could force memories into – but there was nothing. This boy had never committed a crime that she could punish him for. Disgusted, she pushed him away from her.

"Fuckin' Boy scout," she growled under her breath.

With a dramatic roll of her eyes, she began stripping out of her clothing.

"Fuck the shower. I'm outta here."

She was losing precious time if Argent was running already. But then again, did she really expect him to just stay still while she exacted his payment for his crimes? It would definitely have made her job easier, but having to chase him would be more entertaining: it presented her with a challenge that offered a hell of a bang at the end. She quickly pulled on a pair of black BDU pants and a black tanktop. Maslin stood silently in the doorway, watching her.

"Enjoying the show?" she growled as she slid her feet into a pair of tanker boots.

His expression softened as he shook his head and moved to check on Zolah. The woman was groaning and holding her head as he helped her up. Zolah frowned, her expression so sad as she met Jilah's gaze. The sympathy in the woman's eyes sickened her and she found herself wanting to claw them out to be free of it.

Perhaps later, she thought to herself as she slid her arms into a black leather jacket and looked back at the pair of them, curling her lip in disgust.

Maslin quietly asked, "Where will you go?"

Jilah presented him with a bright grin as she zipped up the jacket.

"As it so happens, my *precious Strighaisha* is next on my list."

She walked over to the door, her eyes bright as she added, "And time, she's a-wastin.'"

Maslin glared at her and she could see a strange, shimmering field slowly begin to swirl around him, but he stayed put.

Jilah growled, "Good dog," as she walked out of the room.

Zolah looked over at Maslin, her expression so very tired as she let him lead her over to the bed.

"A great deal of time has passed since I've been in a physical altercation with another being that matched my own strength. I forgot how much I could hurt."

Maslin picked her up and gently placed her down on the bed, hoping help would arrive soon.

"Pick up the phone and dial star star one. That will get you to the emergency team. Just tell them that we're in the guest suite."

Maslin nodded and began dialing. He passed on the information to the answering attendant and shortly after, Thea and Aaron strode into the room.

Aaron was at Zolah's side in a flash, holding her hand as she addressed Thea.

"It has happened."

The older woman pursed her lips, then let out a heavy sigh.

"Has she selected a target?"

Thea stood at the foot of the bed, her expression unreadable.

Zolah tightened her grip on Aaron's hand as she answered, "She now tracks her mate, if what she says is to be believed at this point."

Thea's lips thinned into a grim moue.

"This is not entirely unexpected. Perhaps her patroness believes that if she excises him from Jilah's life with such finality, it will shatter her; make her malleable enough to use again. I can't imagine that what we've told her host while she was here pleased her."

Maslin looked back at Thea, his body shaking slightly as he murmured, "How can I help?"

Thea assessed him for a moment before asking, "Can you track her? Keep an eye on her?"

Maslin nodded, the timbre of his voice becoming stronger as he replied, "I'm one of the best trackers that our pack has."

Aaron turned to him, pressing an odd looking phone into his hand. It had a small leather lanyard attached that had teethmark indentations in it.

"Stay in touch on this. It's a GeoSat phone; you should be able to get signal wherever she leads you. The first number in the call list comes directly to me. Let us know where she goes."

Maslin took the phone, responding with a grim nod. Thea laid a gentle hand on his shoulder and murmured, "Go lightly, wolf. As you're now well aware, she is no longer herself. She will not be swayed from her course and if you get in her way there is a very strong chance that she will not hesitate to kill you. Do not present yourself as a target."

She then kissed him on the cheek.

"Go now. Follow her. We will work here to find a solution, to save her from the entity that drives her to her own destruction."

"Still no word?"

Mira's tone was clipped and irritated.

Aurelian shook his head, running a hand through his hair.

"Nothing."

His eyes tracked her as she paced back and forth, the intensity in her expression sending a chill up his spine.

She paused, deep in thought, then asked, "Do you think Gigi could whip up a shade that could act in the Strigaisha's stead while he's... otherwise occupied?"

Aurelian shook his head.

"I doubt she'd be able to get his scent exactly right. It'd be easier to explain an actual absence than the possible discovery and subsequent betrayal of putting a puppet into play."

He stared down at his phone, willing it to ring. With a frustrated sigh, he muttered, "We're not going to be able to keep this from the others for much longer."

Mira's eyes flashed as she glared back at him.

"Give it a few more days. Between the two of us, we can keep things going – hopefully without anybody having to know."

The Selkie nodded as she added, "He'd better have a spectacular fucking explanation about this when he returns, or I'm kicking his high holy ass."

Aurelian let out a weak laugh as she turned on her heel and walked out of the room.

Quite the clusterfuck you've created here, boss. Where the fuck are you, Argent?

Jilah stepped out into the night air, tentatively working to crank the connection with her lover open just enough to get a feel for his location. She blinked as she realized that she could no longer sense him. She then threw the connection wide open, still finding nothing. What had happened to the link? And why wasn't her patroness showing her where he was? Irritated, she looked around; she was standing in front of an innocuous office building on an almost deserted street. A man was walking quickly along the sidewalk on the other side of the street. A familiar red aura slowly curled around him in lazy circles and Jilah smiled to herself.

Dinner's on. Time to power up, she thought to herself as she blurred across the street, forcing him to lock gazes with her, then locked her teeth into his jugular. She took as much of the red stuff from him as she could, leaving him barely enough to suffer for a short period of time, but there were other tasks to tend to tonight. She'd need all the food she could get.

I wonder if I put the speed on, how long it would take me to get to New Orleans?

She could probably track the trail from there. Only one way to find out.

"Okay, lady. What the hell is going on here?"

Jilah raised an eyebrow and spun around to find the source of the voice. Jilah's eyes narrowed as she spotted a cop heading towards her. She then laughed and blurred down the street. Let the flatfoot figure it out without her. As the buildings whipped and whooshed by, Jilah wondered if she should perhaps hunt down a map – and a compass. Since she didn't have to stick to the highways, she could make it as straight a shot as possible. With the connection between them dead, the only chance she had of finding him was to start from the last place she'd seen him.

A twisting sensation in her gut stopped her in her tracks. Her head was suddenly filled with a string of successive images. Argent was in a place that looked almost like an enormous rabbit warren of tunnels. Bile rose in her throat as she watched a young woman tending to his wounds. Somebody had definitely fucked him up pretty bad. She cocked her head as she wondered how he'd gotten injured. Had somebody else gotten to him first? He wasn't looking at the woman, but instead staring up at the ceiling, glassy eyed. He wasn't moving.

Aww, poor baby. Momma will be there soon. And she's gonna make it all better.

Jilah smiled as she realized how close he was. *Momma's gonna make you choke on it.*

She laughed as she sped off towards the Blue Ridge Mountains of Virginia.

Maslin trailed behind her, moving as fast as four legs would take him. Jilah was moving at an astounding rate and he found himself wondering if she was going to run all the way back to Louisiana at this rate. If so, he was going to have to take a fair amount of hunting breaks in between to keep up his energy. He damn sure hoped that Thea and the women of the Synod would be able to do something. He'd really come to like Jilah in the short time that they'd gotten to know each other, and didn't want the utter bitch who had subsumed her personality to take her place.

At least her trail stayed strong. The combination of her natural scent, coupled with the intense emotions coursing through her were practically leaving a glowing neon arrow indicating where she'd passed through.

Maslin stopped for a moment, confused by a patch of ground that held a jumble of scents from his quarry, then shook his head to reorient himself. There – she'd deviated from her course and was now heading further inland. He took a moment to clear his nose of the confusing mess of smells, then bounded back onto the trail.

How long will it take her to run out of energy? When will she have to stop and refuel? he thought to himself.

He was already starting to feel the strain of pushing himself to speed after her. He was barely keeping up at this point, and would likely have to eat something soon.

Jilah had just passed through Shenandoah National Park when she felt a marked decrease in speed. Her legs started getting a little shaky and she immediately stopped. She had to eat. She had been covering a lot of ground at an obscene speed, and it was now taking its toll on her. Her strength was flagging and any kind of blood would do at this point. She quickly spotted a doe and downed it, drinking her fill. The liquid didn't taste the same, and she found that she definitely didn't like having to pick fur out of her teeth. Something plucked at the edge of her consciousness, something that she couldn't quite fully remember. She brushed it aside as she walked away from the carcass, not caring what happened to it. Again came that curious feeling. It was almost as if something in her felt sympathy for the animal.

Jilah let out a sharp bark of laughter, quashing the thought.

Bitch, please. We got work to do. Don't start up with that, now. she growled angrily at the sensation as she pressed ahead, blurring across a set of railroad tracks.

Argent flinched at the sound of his sister's voice.

"She comes, brother. We will not let her physically lay hands on you."

She presented him with a sad smile as she added, "But we cannot stop her from other forms of attack."

Argent nodded silently as he did his best to prepare himself for anything that his lover might throw at him. He had barely made it through the loss of his beloved Gwen. Her image burned bright in his mind now, a blinding flicker of the memory that the bitch squatting in his lover's head had forced to the surface before the connection closed off. He had never been a saint, this was true; in fact, there were uncountable times when he'd been an outright monster. Especially before he'd been turned. But then, that had been the beginning of the end, hadn't it? The memory rose up to push out all other thoughts, as clear as if it had happened yesterday.

Gwendolyne's ice blue eyes glittered as she looked down at him, her lower lip trembling. His lover's smooth platinum locks flowed over her shoulders like frothing water and he wanted so badly to run his fingers through them, to comfort her. The pain in his gut was slowly fading, and he could feel the trickling wetness at his back as he lay on the floor, clutching at his stomach. In hindsight, he really should have known better than to trust such men, but he found it difficult to give up his fondness for intrigues and deceit. His betrayer sat crumpled and inert in the corner of the room across from them, eyes glassy. After the man had driven the blade into his stomach, everything had become a blur. He could see that the man's two associates had suffered a similar fate.

Her presence was reassuring. After all this time, he was finally going to be with her in the capacity that she needed; that he'd been so desperately wanting. He felt a painful pulling in his chest as she leaned over him, whispering something in her native Germanic as she dipped down to trail her tongue along the side of his neck. So many times they'd played this game, but she'd never taken it to the point that he'd asked her – begged her to. And now, she had no choice. Surely she would turn him, rather than be in a world without him. When he felt her teeth sink in, he hissed in pain. For some reason, her kiss was sharp and rough instead of the langorous, pleasant sensation that it had been in the past.

He could feel his fingers and toes slowly growing cold as she drank from him, wondering if she would stop in time. His lips were starting to turn blue and he was shivering by the time she finally pulled back and pressed him to her bosom; to the trail of crimson trickling down into her bodice. In his first sweet taste, he knew he was lost. His body latched onto her as she shared with him this most precious gift. Her life. Her love. He moaned and his teeth tore the cut open wider. He knew he was hurting her, but she kept her arms around him in an iron grip.

Too soon, it was over and he felt a strange swirling pain in his gut as she pushed him away, back to the floor. The pain quickly became an unbearable tide of agony that crashed against him as he arched against the floor crying out. He felt a hand across his mouth and had a moment to wonder what she was doing before he started screaming.

After what seemed like hours, he found himself back in their bed with a mountain of covers piled on top of him. The pain was gone, but he found himself wondering how he'd gotten there. Had she carried him all the way across town? He quickly sat up, tossing the covers on the floor and frowning when his beloved was nowhere to be seen.

"Gwen?" he called out, his chest tightening as he saw a single, dark crimson rose on her dressing table, her signifier of mourning. He quickly leapt out of bed and swept through the house, looking for her, but she was nowhere to be found. He was filled with a cold foreboding as he made his way back to the bedroom, scanning the room for any signs she might have left behind for him. A small scrap of paper over on her writing desk caught his eye. He slowly crept up on it, not really wanting to read what it said.

She's gone, he thought to himself, his hand trembling as he reached down to collect it.

Beloved. The thing you most sought from me has now been given – but at great cost. I find that I am unable to see you through the new life that now opens before you. How do I make you see that when I turned you, I also killed the one in my heart I loved most? I cannot explain further and will not *return for you. Make your way in the world as you see fit, my fledgling, and fare ye well.*

The letter fluttered to the ground as he stumbled backwards, tripping and collapsing to the floor, his entire body going numb.

She's gone - oh god.

Argent cried out and sat upright in the bed, and S'llethe was there, gently squeezing his leg.

"Brother, it is time for you to eat."

He looked over at her, his eyes wild and still disoriented from the vivid memory. He spotted the glass in her hand, and winced.

"You must gather your strength, brother - or you will both be lost." she murmured, handing him the glass of warm, crimson fluid.

Argent took it from her hand, offhandedly wondering how they managed to keep it so warm in such a thin glass container. He supposed it didn't really matter as he took a deep breath, then downed it as quickly as he could. God only knows what they put in it. It tasted appalling. Still, it seemed to do the trick. He could feel his body responding to the nutrients in the blood, and whatever else happened to be mixed in with it.

"I think that, perhaps, I am a very great fool," he murmured as he handed the glass back to her and slumped back against the mattress.

S'lllethe smiled at him warmly and murmured, "You are simply linear, brother. And singular. It is like this with your kin, and others of your origin."

He wasn't really sure if that was supposed to be reassuring, but she had said similar things over the many years that they'd known each other, and rather than sounding condescending it had always sounded warm and comforting. He sighed and let her pull the covers up to his shoulders as he forced himself to stare at the ceiling, no longer willing to hold court with the painful memories of the past.

After another quick snack, Maslin leapt back into pursuit of his quarry. The mountains were proving to be rough terrain and were consequently taking a great deal out of him. He hoped that the grueling pace that Jilah was setting for herself was slowing her down a little as well.

At least there was plenty of game to keep him well fed, and at night he didn't have to worry so much about steering clear of hunters. Besides, in his overly sensitive nose's experience, most of the people in mountain territory either reeked of natural stink, or wore 'scent free' suits that were anything but, which made it easy to steer clear of trouble.

Although he had only been briefly introduced to the Strigaisha, he still felt a duty to the pack to protect him, as well as the crazed indigo haired demoness that was now bearing down on Argent's location; wherever that ended up being.

Chapter 12
ALL HELL BREAKS LOOSE

Jilah growled as she blurred through the woods, annoyed at the fact that she had to stop and eat yet again. Did he have to hole up somewhere on the friggin' Appalachian Trail?

She could tell that she was getting close, and was eager to take her frustration out on him in person. Oh, to hear the wretched music that his bones would make as they shattered.

THERE.

She stopped, her back ramrod straight as she tracked it. The trail was faint, but unmistakable. An image flashed in her mind of where she could find the entrance, and she quickly spun around to find – a jagged collection of rock that went straight up.

Jilah blinked, unsure if her eyes were fooling her. She stepped over and placed her hand tentatively on the rock face, letting her fingers skim along its surface. Cold..cold...warm. She tapped at the warm spot, and the wall began bowing inward with a strange, grinding sound. Within moments, a round passageway had opened and Jilah peered inside, seeing no light whatsoever. She frowned, unsure now how to proceed. If the rock was creating the tunnel, couldn't it just as easily collapse once she'd taken a step inside and crush her? She wasn't entirely certain that she wanted to take the chance. With a start, she realized that she was now seeing a dim flicker at what looked like the far end of the tunnel.

"You are welcome here, Destroyer. We bid you enter of your own free will, and assure you that safe passage is guaranteed."

Jilah quickly leapt away from the source of the voice, startled to find her lover's sister standing to the side of the tunnel.

Now extremely wary, she replied, "And why, exactly, would you help me hurt someone who you refer to as your 'brother'."

S'llethe simply responded with that same, maddening warm smile.

"Because you are his balance. And he is yours."

Jilah's eyes narrowed as she growled, "Yeah, right. Whatever that means."

S'llethe maintained her smile, inclining her head toward the tunnel.

"We will not stand in the way of justice, but do not be too disappointed in what you unearth in pursuit of your given duty this night."

She then bowed and stepped out of the way.

Jilah's jaw dropped as she gaped back at the woman.

"Are you saying that you *knew* what he'd done?? And still you stood by his side and called him *brother*?" She was stunned.

The woman responded with a polite incline of her head, her tone soft as she said, "We are well aware of our brother's past weaknesses. It is not our place to punish him for his transgressions."

In Jilah's mind, this was just as bad as openly condoning his actions. She cocked her head to the side, then rushed the woman, reaching out to grab her only to be thrown back hard against the rock surface. She felt several ribs snap on impact. As she crumpled to the ground, S'llethe's voice had an edge to it now.

"No. You will be allowed to harm none other than your intended quarry in this place, Destroyer."

Well, I guess that was a stupid idea, Jilah grumbled to herself as she stood up and began dusting herself off. Although, it would seem that the woman was telling the truth and this eased her doubt. If S'llethe could wield that kind of power, what would have kept Argent's sister from killing her already? The knitting of her bones itched vaguely, but she barely felt it. She regarded the woman with a wry expression and nodded to her.

"As long as I get what I came for, I'll be a happy girl."

"You will find much more, but that will reveal itself in the fullness of time."

The woman was smiling again. It was maddening.

What the hell is that supposed to mean?

S'llethe was an annoyance with her cryptic speech patterns, and Jilah itched to kill her, but it would be a futile and frustrating endeavor. Besides – the occupant inside her had let her know that women weren't 'on the menu', so to speak.

Best to just progress with the duty ahead and worry about the rest later.

Maslin watched Jilah enter the cave and pulled the cellphone from the collar around his neck. When the call connected, the gruff voice of the Delmarva tribe Alpha rumbled in his ear.

"Speak."

Maslin leapt almost a full foot in the air as he felt the light touch of a hand on his shoulder. He clamped his hand over his mouth to keep from yelping out loud. The woman standing before him was a beauty of a category that he had no description for. There was something about her that looked and smelled familiar, but he couldn't quite place it. She was smiling gently at him and nodded towards his phone, murmuring, "Tell them where you are, then come with me. There is apparently a part you must play in this as well."

Maslin's jaw dropped before he heard Aaron's menacing growl on the other side of the line, "What the hell's going on?"

"Uh," he began, collecting his thoughts. "I've run her to ground. We're in the middle of nowhere – I think in West Virginia somewhere, but it's hard to tell. They don't put many signs in the mountains that indicate when you've crossed state lines when you're running through forests."

Aaron remained silent and Maslin continued. "I'm not really sure what's going on, but I don't think she's going anywhere else for the moment."

"Leave the phone on. The GPS will track your location. We'll be there as soon as we can."

The line clicked off abruptly and Maslin looked back at the phone, frowning.

"Well, I guess that's that."

He looked over at the woman, who was now gently taking him by the hand.

"You wouldn't be able to explain exactly what's going on, or what my part in it is, would you?"

The woman shook her head, still smiling. "We can only take you where you need to be. The rest is up to you." There was something about her voice, something about the timbre. She didn't smell human, but the scent wasn't one that he could reference.

Maslin walked with her to the cave entrance, his tone strained as he asked, "You sure you couldn't be just a little more vague?"

The woman laughed, and pulled him gently into the mouth of the cave. He grinned and dropped the phone outside the cave, enjoying the sound of her laugh.

"Fair enough. Just say when."

There was a strange sensation of disorientation as Jilah made her way toward the source of the light. She feltlightheaded and a little giddy. Jilah frowned, realizing that the last meal that she'd had was now miles away. Unless somebody was being entirely too proactive and way ahead of her in the game, there was no way that any sort of drug could have been administered. Nobody had touched her, to place anything on her skin, but she was definitely starting to feel the effects of something. She stopped and stumbled into a wall, leaping away from it when her hand touched it. The surface of the rock was warm and had pulsed under her fingertips. She moved in for a closer look and was startled to find the shape of the surface moving slowly. It was as if there was an undercurrent of something just beneath the surface.

She looked back the way she'd come and her throat closed with a loud click when she saw that she was now cut off from the surface.

"Shit," she breathed, her voice sounding strained and almost external to her – as if the word had been uttered by somebody else. Jilah felt something in her shift and looked down at her arm. Something pressed up from beneath her skin as if it was trying to get out. Something scaly.

Her skin then smoothed out, as if nothing had happened. She poked at it, running her fingers along her forearm and feeling nothing but her own flesh and bone. Something in her psyche faltered, and she felt a chill go up her back at the sound of her patroness' voice.

:: He is close, daughter. What you feel now, it is temporary and it is nothing. Remember your quarry, weapon. Remember your given task. ::

Another memory flash assailed her, and an image of Argent's cruel laughing face sprang to life in her thoughts. She rallied, pulling her righteous anger around her like a defensive cloak.

Better. That's better. Now to track the prick down and teach him the error of his ways.

Suddenly, the oppressive atmosphere of the tunnel vanished and she was able to see the light again. It was closer now. There was a room, just a little bit further down the tunnel. She could almost taste the presence of her lover; bitter gall dripping on her tongue. A part of her still felt something for him, but that part only served to stoke the fire of her fury higher. The betrayal and pain fueled her rage as she began walking slowly and purposefully down the tunnel towards the light.

"Soon it ends, my love," she spat, the sound from the heels of her boots echoing off the walls of rock that surrounded her.

Argent's eyes flickered open at the sound of someone coming towards the room. It was time.

He let out a shaky sigh and steeled himself, wondering if she'd make it quick, or if she would draw it out as long as possible. If she knew it all, if his deeds had truly been laid bare, he imagined that the entity that drove her would ensure that he'd suffer as much as he was physically and mentally able. Argent pulled himself upright, sitting back against the wall behind the bed as she stepped into the room. For a moment, he felt a painful thump in his chest as he looked back at her. She was almost majestic when she was this angry, this sure of herself.

"Hello, lover." Jilah trilled as she slowly stalked closer to him, eyeing the bandages and smiling. "What, did somebody else get to you before I did?"

Argent looked back at her, confused. His voice was gruff as he answered, "You decided to warm up on me several days ago. Do you not remember?"

He could feel her uncertainty as she looked back at him. Something nagged at the back of her mind, but he felt her push it away as she stepped up to the foot of the bed, peering more closely at his dressed wounds.

"How is that possible? And even if that were the case, why are you still trussed up? Shouldn't you be fully healed by now?"

Argent frowned as he pulled himself straighter up against the wall.

"You are... different," he murmured.

He saw no reason to explain the reason for his slow recuperation. As cliche as it sounded, he was losing the will to live, and his body's processes were responding in kind, going into a sort of hibernation healing mode of sorts. Everything was slowing down.

Jilah's teeth flashed, sharp and white as she purred, "And you are the same. The very same as everybody else I've ever tracked down."

Argent felt his heart twist, unable to look away from her as she slowly advanced. His voice was quiet and grey as he responded, "I was, once. A lifetime ago. And you have every right to..."

Jilah cut him off with a snarl, "To what? To take your heart, like you did that poor girl's? How many others did you rape, mutilate, and torture, you sadistic prick? How many lives did you and your ice princess destroy to have your fun?"

Her voice remained calm and level as she spat at him. "You and everyone in the world like you sicken me. You spend your lives soul-killing the ones that you touch, taking their lives and tossing them away as if you had every right to do whatever you pleased with them."

She grabbed his injured wrist, tightening her grip and watching him wince in pain as she grated, "A creature such as yourself has no capacity for anything but inflicting mayhem and despair on all those you touch. It's all a fucking game to you."

Argent clenched his jaw, straining to keep from crying out. He could feel the initial fissures in his bones from the original split begin to separate and pain sang along his nerve endings. Beads of sweat peppered his brow as he croaked, "I love you – and forgive you for what you must do."

Jilah leapt away from him as if burned. She clutched her hand and glared back at him.

"You forgive ME?" she roared.

He could feel her anger building, a palpable force that filled the room as he looked up at her with silent resignation. She watched him, as if waiting for him to say something; becoming even angrier when he didn't respond.

"Haven't you been keeping score, pal? YOU are the one that fucked up. It was your bright idea to start victimizing the women around you – that was a path you chose, asshole. You forgive me?!? Are you fucking KIDDING me? Just who the hell do you think you are, anyway?"

Argent watched her for a moment before taking a deep breath and replying, "You are correct in your assessment of my character. I have done many unspeakable, horrible things, yes. A great many of them, I enjoyed to the fullest extent possible at the time. This I do not in any way deny."

Jilah blinked. She stood there, staring at him, mouth agape as he continued.

"You ask who I think I am. I am one who has gambled and lost all. One who has searched for redemption, a way to atone for my past, and has found only the cold reassurance of the grave. I have lost my soul," he murmured, his eyes bright. "And now you, my heart, have come to collect a debt that I thought paid long ago. I urge you to take your measure, to finish this. I will not stop you."

White sparks flashed across his vision as she backhanded him and his head rocked back, cracking painfully against the wall.

And so it ends... his thoughts trailed off as his mind was suddenly awash in agony under the full force of her attack. It was so much worse than he'd imagined, and it just kept going.

He remained true to his word as she savaged him, ripping and tearing his flesh – his soul, long past the point when he wished he could feel no more.

Maslin dabbed at the avatar's forehead with a damp cloth as he watched the spectral scene play out before them. It was highly distressing to see both the solid images of his Strigaisha and Striaga in bed, side by side; along with the ghostly image of her tossing him around the room like an overly playful cat with a very wounded mouse. Maslin's hand shook at the sound of each blow, each tear and the woman on the other side of the bed placed a gentle hand on his arm, her voice soothing and reassuring.

"It is the only way for the debt to be collected in a manner that will keep the balance."

Maslin winced as Jilah tossed the sanguine across the room, the body colliding against the cave wall with a sickening, meaty thud before sliding to the floor. He was horrified to watch new cuts and bruises appearing on the body beside his charge, hoping that his Strigaisha would be able to heal his injuries. At least they weren't anywhere near as bad as the damage that his spectral avatar seemed to be taking. It was very much like watching a car wreck happening in slow motion. He knew what was coming, and had an idea of how bad it would get, but he couldn't look away.

The woman beside him was applying a strange smelling balm to Argent's injuries as fast as she could. Soon, they were joined by three other individuals who began helping her. Maslin watched her lean over to whisper something in the sanguine's ear. The body on the bed bucked and cried out in a keening wail that sent a chill through Maslin's heart. The therianthrope cringed at the sound. He never wanted to hear anything like it again in his lifetime. The spectral action in the room suddenly went from vigorous to a standstill as he watched a ghostly outline of Jilah pull Argent's face close to hers.

The avatar had an almost reverent expression on her face as she looked down at her lover, who was now looking back at her, his jaw now open in a silent scream.

The utter horror of it shook him to his bones and he felt the wind go up his back as he looked away, unable to watch further.

His voice was haunted as he murmured, "Please tell me that this isn't her. That this isn't what she wants."

The woman looked over at him, her expression sympathetic as she patted at the brow of her patient.

"In a very base way, it is. This is what she was born into, and now this is what she does."

Maslin gaped at her with astonishment.

"Then why do you want to help her?"

The woman smiled, her voice taking on a musical lilt as she responded, "Because at the moment, she is out of balance, due to the presence of the rider within her."

Maslin shook his head, not understanding as he looked back over at the spectral pair. His Strigaisha's ghostly form was on the floor, body bowing upwards in a way that looked excruciating. Argent grimaced in pain as his fingers clawed at the air. Jilah had taken a step back from him and was now looking as if she was warring with something inside herself. Was she uncertain about what she'd done?

"She begins to see the truth now, wolf. And this is where she must choose."

Maslin looked back at her, frowning.

"Choose what?"

Jilah looked over at the body of her lover, his tormented shrieks slowly dying out as she backed away from him. Again, she had the feeling that something was very wrong here, but it was becoming stronger now. She felt the presence of her patroness in her thoughts, sated and pleased with herself. There was a smugness to it that Jilah couldn't remember feeling before. Usually, at this point she would leave, or take her prey somewhere in order to bury it, but this was most definitely a special case. After a few minutes had passed, she began to feel as if she'd done something... *off*. The feeling plucked at the back of her mind as she watched Argent's body continue to twitch. Something tickled her cheek and she brought up a hand to brush it away, startled when her fingers came away wet.

Tears? Am I crying?

She frowned and wiped at the other cheek; it was wet as well. Her body shook as she was suddenly consumed with grief.

Oh my god. What have I done?

She collapsed numbly to the floor, her legs splaying out beneath her. She couldn't look away from him.

The memory of Thea's voice echoed through her mind as she heard herself begin to cry out in anguish.

"When their minds shatter under your assault, their soul does as well. They are well and truly lost, and are unable to go back to the source of themselves to start over again, to take with them what they've learned to the next part of their journey. For them, the journey is over, and they are no more."

A strange, keening wail rang out in the room. She moved towards Argent and a sharp pain rang out in her mind.

:: *Daughter. Most precious weapon. He is an animal, and has been judged as such. You do yourself a disservice by mourning him.* ::

"He deserves to learn from his mistakes!" she shouted, "They all do!"

:: *They all deserve oblivion, child. Do you honestly think that the man who attacked you that first night had the capacity to ever learn from what he was doing?* ::

Jilah crept closer to the body of her lover, her tears darkening the red clay of the floor where they hit as she touched his ankle.

"I still love him.

The moment she said it, she reeled in shock. The voice of her patroness called to her, doing its best to be comforting, reassuring; but it sounded all wrong.

:: *He never loved you, child. He doesn't have the capacity to. You have done what is right, and must leave this place. There is so much more for you to do in my service.* ::

Jilah pulled Argent's body into her lap then, cradling him as she rocked back and forth, still keening. The words of her patroness sparked an anger inside her as she stroked her lover's hair, unsure what to do next. She wished that she could take it all back, make it all better. Suddenly Argent's body went slack in her arms, and Jilah stiffened. His head lolled back against her shoulder, his body so very cold to the touch. Colder than she'd ever remembered him being.

Every fiber of her being screamed at her to do something, to move, and yet she was paralyzed. Gone. Even after everything he'd done, all his odious crimes, she still felt a pit form in her chest.

Was he redeemable? Was it possible that such a man could ever be?

Something tightened in her and she crushed his body to hers, her knuckles going white as she began weeping silently. The possibility was off the table now. She would never know.

He's gone. I did this.

I made him gone.

Maslin recoiled as the beautiful woman dipped her fingers into Argent's chest. The Strigaisha's skin remained unbroken, but her fingers seemed to dance just below the surface of his skin.

"What on earth are you doing?" he asked in a horrified whisper.

"She has chosen. He needs to know that he cannot leave."

The small room was suddenly full of people, their hands joining in quick succession as they formed what looked like a labyrinth around the bed. Maslin reeled as he watched the hands of all the individuals in the chain meld together. A strange series of bioluminescent colors and sounds started circulating through the surrounding bodies, ending at the woman across from him. The lights inside their bodies looked similar to those he'd seen within some of the deep sea creatures on a television program he'd seen when he was a kid. He watched as the light flowed in pulses down the woman's arm and into Argent's chest. It was easily the most bizarre and beautiful thing he'd ever witnessed, but hoped furiously that it worked. Several moments passed as the lightshow continued, and Maslin found himself dazzled by the event unfolding around him. Tears started rolling down his cheeks, and he felt his heart thrum strongly in his chest as the woman looked back up at him. With a gasp, Argent's eyes flickered open and he looked around, bewildered. He looked over at his sister with a horrified expression, trying to push her away from him.

"NO!" he screamed, his voice full of despair as he tried to get away.

"Hold him, wolf. He will fight it, and he cannot be allowed to."

Her voice was firm, but she was smiling as she looked down at the struggling sanguine.

Argent redoubled his efforts, but was too weak to have any real affect. Maslin's heart went out to the sanguine as he heard his Strigaisha's voice break.

"Please! I cannot go through this again! Let me go!"

"You must, dear brother. It is part of the price to be paid." She brushed her other hand tenderly across his jawline. "We would take this from you, if we could; but only in this way will your debt be paid in full."

Argent scrabbled against the bed, trying to find purchase, trying to find a way to get away.

"ENOUGH!" he roared, tossing Maslin off him. S'llethe gently outmaneuvered him, stepping aside as he tried to grab her.

Her voice was stern and chiding.

"There will be no violence in this place. You of all people should know this."

He looked up at her and let out a anguished huff.

"Cease fighting this, and it will go much smoother for you. Do you not remember last time?"

Maslin pulled himself off of Jilah's inert body and gaped at her.

"Last time? Wait, you've done this to him before??"

S'llethe looked over at him, her expression mildly irritated. "He can be a stubborn creature."

Maslin looked down at Argent who was now frowning up at her. Some of the misery had faded from his expression as Maslin saw him struggle to ease out the lines of his face, to a point where he looked almost bland.

"Do not forget to mention linear."

At this, she smiled and sat beside him on the bed.

"You submit then, brother?"

Argent nodded, then took a deep breath, letting out a heavy sigh. "It would appear that I have little choice."

Maslin shook his head, his ice blue eyes flashing as he asked, "Are you all crazy?"

Argent now looked over at him, seeming to truly see him for the first time. He then looked over to see the sleeping form of his lover beside him, and his expression wilted, his eyes glittering.

"She will hate me, when she rises," he whispered, closing his eyes. "I have lost her."

Maslin found himself wanting to ask exactly what the sanguine had done to earn her wrath, but realized that it would likely be better if he said nothing. There was such pain in Argent's voice, and the anguish was now back in his expression.

"How can I help?" he asked, lamely. Argent looked wracked with grief.

S'llethe gently brushed a wisp of hair away from the sanguine's forehead.

"She is who she is, brother. You knew this from the beginning."

Argent's expression hardened, his voice shaky as he answered, "Yes. I did."

"You were unprepared for how strongly she felt about it. It is understandable."

Maslin stared at the woman, stunned that she could say such things to anybody in such a desperate state.

"Surely you don't need to be so painfully blunt with him after what he's just gone through?"

S'llethe looked up at him, smiling. "We tell him this, because it is our way. He understands."

"Please," Argent groaned. "Allow me some time alone."

"Of course, brother."

S'llethe moved to stand and Maslin noticed that the room was no longer crowded with people. Where had they all gone? He hadn't heard them leave.

"Come, wolf. There is much game in these woods, and you would do well to eat something after all that has transpired."

Maslin shook his head, not understanding anything that was going on; and not entirely sure that he wanted to.

"Give her time, brother." S'llethe called back over her shoulder before walking out of the room.

Maslin took a quick look at the pair on the bed, then darted out after her. Perhaps things would look a little different after he'd gotten a little food in his belly.

Jilah sat, still rocking Argent's body in her arms. So alone. She felt so utterly alone. The presence of her patroness rustled quietly in her consciousness, and she grimaced.

"This is what you wanted, isn't it? From the beginning. A puppet that you could maneuver any way you liked."

Her voice came out in a hushed whisper. As she placed her cheek to her lover's cold forehead, she frowned.

"It was all a trick. From the very beginning, wasn't it?"

Now hoarse from crying, the broken sound of her voice made her shudder slightly.

"If it wasn't me, it would've been somebody else."

:: *You were unique, daughter. And you were receptive. And, you needed my help, did you not?* ::

Jilah let out a bitter laugh.

:: *And I was clear about my services demanding a strenuous payment, was I not?* ::

Jilah spat, "If I had known that this was anything close to what you had meant I would have told you to go fuck yourself."

:: *And that is the nature of bargaining with my kind, daughter. As your people are so fond of saying, in for a penny, in for a pound? Your own actions have led you to this point, precious daughter. This, you need to remember.* ::

"I see." Jilah growled, a cold anger shaking through her now. She gently lay Argent's body down and stood up, dusting herself off and squaring her shoulders.

"I'm done. No more. Find another patsy."

Light, chittering laughter echoed through her mind, sending a chill up her spine. :: *Oh, I think that we are just getting started, you and I. Perhaps sending you on another run will cure you of this stubborn insolence.* ::

Bright, sharp pain flared through Jilah's head and she clutched at her temples, screaming. :: *This one will be long and hard, but you will learn to appreciate my gift in the end.* ::

Images of guerilla soldiers holding down women and brutally taking them, one after the other while the rest of the company stood around to wait their turn flashed through her head. There were so many of them. Too many.

A warzone?

The images intensified, becoming other camps, other areas. Scene after scene the same horrific thing played out in her mind, over and over.

:: *This should keep you busy for a good, long while. Besides, my beautiful weapon, your task here was simply honing you for the job ahead. And there is so much to be done. So much pain to be reaped.* ::

Sharp laughter rang out in her ears, and Jilah cried out as everything quickly faded to black.

Argent turned to look over at his lover as she groaned and twitched beside him. Knowing that he was the source of so much pain for her caused an unpleasant twisting sensation in his chest. If not for that damned squatting demon in her psyche, things might have turned out very differently. But then again, if not for her, the woman beside him would not have drawn his initial notice. The irony would have been amusing if he were twenty years down the road, looking back at this moment. Now it cut at his heart and he grimaced as she shifted against the bed, gripping the sheet tightly in fisted hands. He wanted to gently pluck the thread of connection between them, knowing that if he did he would remove the dampener that S'llethe had placed on it to keep her from causing far worse damage between them.

Not knowing what was happening to her was far worse. It was obvious that she was suffering, but there was no way that he could assist her. And with everything that had now passed between them, he was unsure if she would ever welcome his presence again, much less his help. He reached out a tentative hand, gently resting it on her shoulder and she shuddered at his touch; but didn't pull away. His expression was pained as he murmured, "I do not know if it helps, or even if you can hear me – but I am here."

At the sound of his voice, Jilah relaxed. She still whimpered and jerked slightly, but it was much less pronounced now.

He gripped her shoulder a little tighter, his tone strained as he whispered, "Fight it, beloved. Know that I am with you."

Chapter 13
A DEMON UNLEASHED

Maslin headed back into the tunnels, feeling much better after a full run and hunt. As he pulled a shirt over his shoulders he heard a familiar voice ahead.

"Your friends are here, wolf. They come to help our brother's mate."

S'llethe smiled at him and turned to walk beside him as they made their way through the network of tunnels that wound throughout the mountain.

"They arrived shortly after you went off in search of nourishment," she explained as they rounded a corner and entered a large open section of cavern. Aaron gave him a quick nod of respect, his arm possessively draped around Zolah's waist. She was looking a little better now, Maslin noticed. Thea walked up to him, her face lined with concern, and he gave them a quick run down of the events as they'd happened.

Thea paled.

"She has destroyed her mate?" she asked in a hushed whisper. "Our hostess, while hospitable, hasn't been exactly forthcoming with decipherable information."

Maslin looked over at S'llethe and replied, "Yeah. That seems to be their 'way', as they put it. Jilah hasn't killed him, but she thinks she has. I'm eager to go back and check on them though, just to make sure that the situation hasn't changed. Would that be okay?"

He looked over at S'llethe who smiled and extended a hand out to him.

"We will escort you back to our brother and his mate. The tunnels can be somewhat disorienting if you are not in the company of one of us," she trilled, her voice bringing a smile to his lips.

There was something about the sound that brought him a strange sort of peace.

Argent roused at the sound of somebody entering the room, his hand never leaving his lover's shoulder he met his sister's gaze.

"How can I help her?" he asked.

S'llethe moved towards him, gently dropping Maslin's hand.

"This is her own battle. She will not see you until she finishes it."

Argent frowned back at her.

"What exactly do you mean when you say that she will not see me?"

S'llethe knelt down beside him, her arm lightly touching his wrist.

"You must go back to your duties, brother. You have a Prefecture to tend to, and you cannot be here when she wakes."

At this Argent fairly exploded from the bed, baring his teeth."I will *not* return without her."

S'llethe chuckled softly, shocking Maslin and the others.

"It is as it is, brother. If you push this, you truly will lose her."

Argent's lips tightened in a thin line as he paused to consider what she was saying.

:: *Then there is a chance...* :: he sent to her, his body beginning to tremble.

"You must let her go for now. Only after she has worked the burden of her promise off will she be able to see you again."

"But what...?" Argent began, but S'llethe cut him off with a wave of her hand.

"This we know, and this we tell you. There is but a chance if you go now."

Argent stiffened, then gave her a stiff nod, his expression empty.

Maslin stepped forward, spluttering, "Wait, you're just going to send him away? No resolution, no guarantee?"

Argent looked over at the young wolf, his tone hollow as he replied, "It is as it is."

Maslin opened his mouth to respond, but Argent continued, "We need to return to court."

Maslin, still stunned at the turn of events, shook his head and stood his ground.

"I said I'd protect her, stay with her."

Argent took a step towards him and sighed. "It's not Jilah anymore, Maslin. She would kill you if she saw you again."

"It doesn't matter."

Maslin frowned, determined to see his task through to the end.

"We can do more good for her – and ourselves, by staying out of her way."

:: ...and I will explain to Cynette and Alain.. ::

Maslin sighed, then quietly nodded.

Argent then turned to Zolah and Thea, presenting them with a formal bow.

"Ladies, I thank you for your intervention, and dearly hope that you will be able to attend to and help my Striaga if she needs you."

Thea responded with a slow, graceful nod, her hands trembling slightly as she replied, "We are distraught that our sister has been torn from you and will do all in our power to keep watch over her."

Argent responded with a wan smile, then stepped forward and addressed Aaron.

"You do me great honor by allowing a member of the Tribe of the Savage Moon to visit and hunt on your grounds. I am most appreciative."

The Alpha gave a gruff nod. "It was a light infraction and no harm was done. I'm guessing that you'll show me the same courtesy if me or mine ever find ourselves down your way?"

Argent replied, "We welcome the visit."

Maslin looked over at Zolah. "Keep her as safe as you can, okay?"

Zolah looked back at him, her tone warm as she assured him, "We will do everything we can for her."

Maslin stepped over by Argent who was now beginning to waver a little bit on his feet. He quickly reached under and placed the sanguine's arm behind his shoulders and held him up. Argent let out a hiss, then quietly thanked him.

"I fear that I am not entirely at peak proficiency at the moment."

He looked over at Thea, noting that Zolah had moved closer to Aaron. The Alpha had placed his arm back around her waist.

"May I impose upon you for a return trip?"

Thea smiled and stepped towards him.

"Of course. I will see you safely back to your prefecture."

"Did you even bother checking your fucking messages?"

Aurelian was barreling towards them, furious. It was the angriest the sanguine had ever seen him. Argent took a stumbling step towards him and Maslin quickly moved to grab his arm, putting it around his shoulders. Argent looked up to see Aurelian stop dead in his tracks, turning ashen as he got a good look at the array of injuries he'd collected while he was away.

Argent tried to stand on his own and swayed, then murmured, "Please... just get me to the bed."

He'd never handled helplessness at all well. It brought up too many painful memories. It also made him fairly crabby.

"What the hell happened to him?" Aurelian's voice was a pained whisper as he moved forward and picked the sanguine up, easily hefting Argent in his arms.

Thea quietly took a step back, saying, "I must return. If there is anything you need... "

Argent looked over at her and winced. Even turning his head hurt. He'd been doing his best to put on a stoic face, but it was exhausting, and he was running out of energy.

"I'll let you know. Just go. Help her."

Aurelian frowned as he looked down at his lover, completely confused, "Wait, what? What the..?"

Argent snapped, "I will explain everything if you just get me to the damned bed and let me rest for awhile."

Aurelian turned to Maslin and said, "I've got it from here."

The therianthrope frowned, then gave a quick nod and quickly walked out of the room, shaking his head.

Argent could feel the tight rein the man was keeping on his anger as Aurelian carried him carefully back to the bedroom.

His tone was clipped, irritated. "You need to eat."

Argent waved it off, wincing, and Aurelian growled. "You *will* fucking eat. This is *not* an option."

Argent sighed, knowing that he didn't have the energy to argue, and he had to admit that fresh blood would help him recover more quickly.

"Eat. Rest. Then explain, dammit."

They reached the bed and Aurelian gently placed Argent on the bed, settling the pillow and covers around him.

"I am not a child." Argent snapped, his own temper rising now.

Aurelian settled beside him and nicked his wrist, presenting it to the sanguine. The two of them glared back at one another for a few moments as spatters of bright blood dotted the sheets. Argent nodded and Aurelian gently pressed the redness to the sanguine's mouth, watching him carefully as he drank. The selkie's blood was fire in his veins compared to the liquid that S'llethe had been feeding him. Argent groaned as the pain in his body flared, then smoothed out, easing down. Argent gripped Aurelian's wrist then, pressing it tightly to his mouth as he fed, drinking greedily. He was both relieved and guilty that he could still take pleasure in something so simple.

Aurelian groaned, then swayed, and Argent pulled back before taking too much. When Aurelian moved to touch him, Argent flinched and the selkie pulled away, frowning. Argent could feel the hurt echoing from the selkie, but there was damn little he could do about it. He was doing everything he could do to deal with his own pain at this point. Aurelian took a deep breath, looked away, then said, "I'll go and let you rest, but when I come back, we're talkin' this shit out."

He then stood up and left the room.

Argent watched him go and sighed as the door closed behind him. Aurelian's hot, healing blood shot through his veins, restoring him; which only added to his guilt. He wasn't looking forward to having to discuss any of what had happened, but he owed his court at least that.

Jilah woke with a start, sitting straight up, confused to find herself in a bed. Had somebody moved her? She quickly checked herself for bruising or damage, already knowing that she would find nothing. Her body seemed to heal much more quickly now. She looked over to where she'd left Argent's body, but it was no longer there. Her heart thumped painfully as she leapt out of bed, wondering if he'd dragged himself off. The possibility that she hadn't ended him quickened her pulse as she tore around the room, and out the door, searching for him.

:: *He is gone, daughter, and there are much more suitable tasks that you should be setting your mind to.* ::

Jilah snarled at the voice as she pounded through a corridor off to the right.

"Fuck you, bitch. We're quits."

A chittering chuckle rang out in her thoughts as a sharp pain stabbed into her mind.

:: *I will only tolerate your insolence for so long, vessel. Do you wish me to cripple you temporarily to bring you to heel?* ::

Jilah cried out as she dropped to the ground, her fingers lengthening into claws that ripped jagged furrows into the red clay of the cave floor. She slapped a palm to her head, and hissed. Instantly the pain stopped and Jilah slumped, groaning.

:: *You are intensely stubborn, weapon. The blood child is dead and gone – and you still have the matter of my debt to repay. You only waste time by engaging in this foolish rebelliousness.* ::

Jilah growled, "Oh, I'm sorry. Am I inconveniencing you? Wait a minute while I cry over that one. Fuck off!"

The pain returned, more intense than before. The dark lady sounded almost bored now as she replied, :: *Since you will not learn to heel without fighting it, I will have to train you another way, no?* ::

The pain doubled and Jilah began screaming.

:: *What you feel now, of course, is only a mental projection. I would not want to cause physical harm to such a useful vessel. The more you fight me, the more I shall have to show you that your manner of behavior is not appreciated. ::*

Jilah's throat closed up convulsively and she passed out.

Zolah watched as her friend's body twitched, then dropped. She winced and sucked the wind between her teeth, cursing the entity that would do such a thing. It was an abomination and it took every bit of willpower she had to keep from going over to help her friend up.

Only observe, sister - and help when it would not be apparent that the assistance came from us. The entity in her head must suspect nothing.

Thea's words rang in her memory. The head of the Synod was certain that if the entity was eager enough to send Jilah to utterly destroy somebody that its host truly cared about, it would think nothing of sending her against anybody else who happened to get in the way of her agenda now. They would be of no use to her dead, so it was decided that it was best to simply observe and report back for the moment.

Zolah stayed vigilant as she watched Jilah continue to writhe in agony in between bouts of unconsciousness. She could only imagine what the ebony skinned witch in her friend's head was putting her through. After what seemed like hours, Jilah slowly got to her feet, stumbling along the passageway as she headed towards the exit.

She makes her way to her next target, Zolah thought to herself, warring with the need to stop her friend so that Jilah would send no other people to oblivion and the need to let this run its course. It didn't sit at all well with her that they had to allow her to run free, knowing what she was capable of, but short of killing her outright, there seemed to be little choice. Since they weren't entirely certain that they could imprison her without losing other members of the sisterhood, their only option was to simply witness events as they unfolded.

Argent looked over at the selkie laying beside him, watching him with a wary eye. Aurelian had continued reacting poorly to his condition, and after the initial flurry of questions about his whereabouts, it had taken Argent an hour to reassure him that he was, in fact, as well as could be expected after what had happened. He'd left out the fact that Jilah had been the one that had beaten the holy hell out of him. There was no reason for anybody else to know, and it had been, after all, entirely out of her hands. She hadn't been herself, and in many ways, he had completely deserved it.

"Did they tell you when she'd be back?" the selkie asked, his tone hopeful.

"They did not."

Argent let his head fall back to the pillow, his thoughts going to a dark place as he looked away from Aurelian. Aside from his own anguish at the loss of his mate, there were too many questions that he wasn't able to answer, and although Aurelian had finally stopped demanding information, it was clear that he wasn't at all happy about it. Argent could tell that some of the selkie's frustration came from the fact that he now had nothing to present to the members of the court that had inquired about his disappearance. He'd been gone too long for Aurelian to effectively hide it, and the selkie had dodged most of the questions, but it had really bothered him that Argent hadn't at least called to tell him what was going on; or at the very least where he was. There was only so much he could do with no information.

The fact that Argent had been back for two days now and hadn't really moved from the bed wasn't putting Aurelian at ease, either. Argent was actively distancing himself, both emotionally and physically, since his return and he could tell that Aurelian was discomfited by it, unsure of what to think. He'd begged off on any kind of intimate contact, explaining that he wasn't ready to be touched again yet. The mixture of humiliation and disgust he still felt from the collected memories of the women that he had brutally attacked centuries ago still haunted him. He had never felt so helpless, even after Gwen had left him. He took it as his due, closing his eyes and letting out a pained sigh.

The bed felt enormous and alien without Jilah and he turned away from his friend, their other lover. He wanted more time to mourn, but he knew better. Argent hadn't given Aurelian the chance to give him the rundown on everything that had happened during his absence. The selkie had been too shocked to do much more than simply try to make the sanguine feel better. Argent turned to look up at the ceiling, frowning as he tried to stem the tide of poisonous, ancient memories that assailed his mind, making it almost impossible to focus on anything else.

And yet, he was already tired of inactivity. Physically, he was well enough to get up and tend to the work that had piled up in his absence. He couldn't stay in this bed forever. He'd already gone underground once, and wasn't ready to do it again. If he stayed here, the spiralling horror show in his head would only get worse. He needed to get up and do something.

Argent took a deep breath, then sat up and scrubbed at his face. A shower suddenly seemed like an excellent idea. He heard Aurelian shift in the bed behind him when he stood up.

"Give me a half an hour and I'll meet you in the office," he called back as he walked into the bathroom, closing the door.

Jilah stared over at the decrepit house; the place she once called home. It seemed that a lifetime had passed since she'd left with Argent, heading down to New Orleans, to her new life. She pursed her lips as she stood in the driveway and tried to remember where she had placed an extra stash of money. All else was forgotten as she went to collect the shovel from the shed in the back and began digging through a rancid pile of old garbage. The reek was wretched and she forced her breathing through her mouth as she slowly unearthed a small metal box. She quickly pulled the box free, opening it.

She muttered angrily to herself as she jammed the bills into a black backpack at her side.

Her next stop? The Democratic Republic of the Congo. Not exactly a prime tourist destination, especially for women. She would've thought that getting into the country itself would be impossible, if it weren't for her ability to cloud the minds of others. Jilah had no passport, no papers. No matter which way she figured it, this was set to be an intensely discomfiting trip, if the images in her head were anything to go by. She didn't quite know how to prepare herself for what she was going to encounter, so she'd done her best to just go with it and see what happened.

After all, as the reigning high bitch queen of the universe was so fond of saying, *It is not as if you have a choice.*

Jilah zipped the backpack closed, taking one last look back at the house behind her.

So much started in this house, and now I'm leaving it again - although nothing pleasant is waiting for me at my destination this time.

The thought was sobering as she stood up and walked into the kitchen. She was happy that she'd left a small portion of her copious clothing collection behind, now, although much of it needed adjustment for her new form. She had no desire to go back to New Orleans and explain to the court that she'd killed their Regent. God only knows what they'd do to her if they knew. She had already done her grieving about the new circle of friends that she would be leaving behind. Jilah already missed Gigi's sarcastic, light banter. Even Aurelian's lack of presence was just beginning to be felt.

No, it was best to steer clear of NOLA entirely. There was nothing left in that city for her now, anyway.

Jilah pulled her motorcycle into the airport parking lot, wondering when she'd be coming back to it. God only knew how long she'd be out of the country on this particular errand. She had changed into a pair of black canvas utility shorts, knee high black grinders and a white GWAR – Scumdogs of the Universe t-shirt. She'd had to cut a hole in the shorts to accommodate the tail, which left a slight breeze in the back, but she was going for functionality rather than form. It wasn't as if she had to play dress-up anymore, now that she could force people to see what she wanted them to see. It was going to be almost unbearably hot being that close to the equator. She was somewhat thankful that she would be doing most of her job at night.

The rumble of the motorcycle was reassuring and familiar as she made her way through the parking structure, checking for a good place to park the bike for awhile. She had enough money to cover any parking fees that she would incur while she was gone, and she wasn't even sure if she'd be coming back at all. She wasn't certain she wanted to, either.

Jilah frowned and rocked the bike up onto its stand, then locked the helmet onto the saddlebag. She felt the flickering presence of something and stiffened for a moment as she tried to track it. By the time she'd dismounted and looked around, the feeling was gone.

With a deep breath, she refocused and headed towards the elevator.

"Trample the weak, hurtle the dead," she muttered to herself as she pulled her shields around herself, tightening them up.

Back at the paperwork again, Argent looked up to see Maslin standing in the doorway, watching him. He set down the stack of papers he'd been reading through and waved the young man in.

Maslin stepped inside, clearly nervous. Argent cocked an eyebrow at him, his tone light as he said, "I promise not to bite."

Maslin started, then a small smile curved his lips. "Apologies, Strigaisha. I wasn't sure how my presence would be received."

Argent leaned back in his chair, pausing for a moment before replying, "There was nothing you could have done. I cast no blame on you."

Maslin let out a sigh of relief. He'd kept his distance from Argent since they'd gotten back and still blamed himself for the events that had unfolded. Although, he had no idea what he could have done to change the end result. He was glad to have been any help at all, even if it hadn't seemed like help at the time.

"Sit, young Maslin, please."

Argent indicated the chair across from him and Maslin perched on the edge of the seat, his hands clasped before him.

Argent chuckled softly, crossing his feet. "My sister tells me that you were of great assistance to her during..."

Maslin quickly stammered, "It wasn't so much, Strigaisha. I only wish that I had been able to do more."

"You do yourself a disservice by demeaning the role you played. I am grateful to you." Argent's voice was quiet and soft as he regarded the young man before him.

Maslin relaxed now, taking a deep breath before replying, "Thank you, Strigaisha. That means a great deal."

Argent peered at the boy curiously.

"Are you content with your current position in the pack?"

Maslin looked back at him with a wary expression.

"Why do you ask?"

Argent's emerald eyes glittered as he replied, "I am in need of what Aurelian calls a personal assistant."

Maslin frowned, unsure of how to respond.

Argent continued, "I am pleased with how you conducted yourself in your duties for the court, Maslin. I would have you fill that position. I have spoken with Alain on this and he agrees that you would be perfect for it."

Maslin shifted in his chair uneasily. This was the last thing he expected; a job offer. Still, it was a lucrative placement, and would give him opportunities that his current status within the pack structure would not otherwise provide. His father would have been proud of him if he were to accept such an offer.

His voice quavered a little as he looked back at Argent and asked, "May I have time to think about it?"

Argent smiled back at the young wolf, his voice warm as he replied, "Of course."

The officials at N'Djili International Airport in Kinshasa had been most accommodating. Jilah had converted some of the cash she'd brought along into Central African Francs, even though she would easily be able to fool anybody into thinking it was whatever she wanted it to be. Sometimes, economy of energy was the smarter move. Besides, she was going to be stirring up enough trouble in this region without attracting more attention to herself. It took a little getting used to, being able to communicate mentally to the people she ran across who didn't know a stitch of English. Most of the time, she'd run into what sounded like strangely accented French, which, although she had a passing familiarity with it now, she didn't know enough of to engage in a real conversation of any sort. Intent and imagery were key in both understanding and making herself understood.

Jilah hefted her backpack high on her shoulders then stepped out of the airport into the sweltering night. The air was muggy and heavy on her skin, a physical presence that was uncomfortably thick and moist. She felt a palpable need to scrape her skin clean as she took in her surroundings.

Palm trees rustled in the slight breeze and Jilah noticed that the night sounded entirely different here. The nocturnal animals smelled different as well.

She'd taken several steps out of the airport when a flood of images assaulted her, almost knocking her over. They stopped with a sickening jolt and Jilah doubled over, spitting blood out onto her boots. As she looked up, wiping her mouth with the back of her hand, she noticed several people walking quickly towards her. She frowned and blanked their minds before blurring off towards her intended destination. Questions weren't something she had the time to deal with.

She had a job to do.

Zolah watched, eyes wide, as Jilah proceeded to conduct wholesale slaughter on a small detachment of soldiers. The woman had almost lost track of her when Jilah began racing towards the western provinces shortly after walking out of the airport.

Jilah was exceptionally fast, but Zolah was able to scent her trail easily. A cold anger chilled the very air around her as the avatar tore headlong through the forest. For this, Zolah was grateful. Otherwise, she would've lost Jilah within minutes. It was difficult to know how long the chase had taken. Zolah had expended a great deal of energy in just keeping up, wondering where the hell they were headed.

Shortly after crossing the border into the Sud-Kivu provinces, Jilah tore into her duties with an almost fundamental fervor. As soon as the attacks began, all sounds of indigenous nightlife had come to a complete halt. It was as if the very land itself knew that something utterly unnatural hunted tonight. Its inhabitants were laying low to insure that they didn't become its next target.

Uncontrolled militias left over from the Second Congo War and the Rwandan conflict continued to move unchecked throughout the country, frequently looting, murdering and raping damn near anybody they stumbled upon.

Zolah found it ironic how the Hutus had been disgusted and filled with utter loathing for the Tutsis, but when it came down to satisfying their base urges nobody seemed much to care about raping a member of what they deemed an 'inferior race'. Her lip curled in revulsion. Some of them actually thought that they were doing these women a favor by touching them, inflicting themselves upon them. Racists of every stripe carried the same sick justification in them; that they were 'in the right' – so therefore anything they did, any horror they inflicted, was ordained by some higher power that approved of their actions.

Some of these soldiers were barely old enough to have reached puberty, but they were felled just as mercilessly as grown men, their bodies bucking and twitching, foam flecking their screaming mouths as the memories of their victims ripped through their synapses. The very idea that children could be trained to treat women in such a way sickened Zolah to her core. The women that they had all been taking turns with when Jilah had shown up were now cowering in the dirt outside a tent with rusty, ruddy splotches in the fabric. Zolah winced as she realized that copious amounts of blood must have been shed inside in order to decorate the fabric in such a gruesome manner. She didn't want to think about it.

The men had apparently rounded up the women, keeping them in a separate tent so that they could be used until there was nothing left to bother with. Several rigid bodies with bloated, distended bellies lay in a nearby ditch, and Zolah shivered at the sight.

Flickering torches lit the appalling scene before her, throwing jittery shadows along the ground and walls of the tents. It reminded her of some of the campier depictions of hell presented in old black and white silent movies, but the horror here was very real.

The women kept screaming the same word over and over again, their expressions full of terror. One woman's eyes were rolling in their sockets like a spooked horse and she made guttural, heart wrenching sounds as she tugged at her shirt with a savage grip. It was as if she were trying to tear herself apart. Zolah had to dip into their minds in order to find out what they were saying.

Devil! DEVIL!!

Another woman convulsed on the ground, apparently unable to come to terms with what was happening before her. Although utterly incomprehensible and repugnant, being repeatedly gang-raped by soulless militant thugs was a very harsh reality that the women in this area had come to terms with by now; as much as any person can become used to such a thing being a common occurence. It was something that they simply did their best to evade, if at all possible.

Coming face to face with the supernatural in such a vivid, violent way, however, was quite another thing entirely. Especially when their liberator happened be a large blue queen demoness who had no compunctions about literally ripping people to pieces before their eyes.

Zolah wanted to help them, but it was essential that she not break cover. The soldiers dropped one by one, screaming and clawing at their eyes and Zolah was crystal clear that she had absolutely no desire to become a target. Although she had no dark past to haunt her – no reason to loose vengeance's sword against her, Zolah wasn't entirely sure if Jilah's patroness would destroy her soul out of spite or not. Losing her soul permanently would help none of these women and would not help her friend when, or if, she eventually began to see reason again.

The soldiers were effortlessly reduced to twitching body parts that would draw clouds of flies when the noonday sun was high overhead tomorrow. The smell was overpowering. Already the stench of vomit, urine and perforated bowel permeated the air and it hit the back of her throat in a sour wave. She closed her nose and breathed through her mouth to keep from gagging. Jilah had torn directly into the guts of her first few targets, spilling crimson spattered fleshy coils of entrails into the dust. At least there was a mild breeze to carry some of the repellent stench away.

Killing fields were never pleasant. Zolah had been on her fair share of them. She shuddered at unbidden and unwelcome memories that tried to come forward, forcing them back. Now was definitely not the time to revisit them.

Jilah maneuvered with a vicious intensity, seemingly unstoppable. Zolah noticed that Jilah's physical appearance was changing with each successive massacre as well. She had dropped her appearance shields entirely and her horns were now much larger than they'd been back at the airport. Her tail was becoming thicker as well, longer and more prehensile as she now used it to toss people around the campsite. She was also developing a distinctly blueish tinge to her skin.

No wonder the women were gibbering. Perhaps they thought that they were now in hell.

And as quickly as it started, all sounds of conflict stopped. The only sounds remaining were the screams and wails of those still trying to dig their eyes out of their sockets to free themselves of the loop of horror that they'd started by viciously raping these women, along with countless others, in other villages throughout the countryside. Jilah paused momentarily, her chin and chest looking as though she had dumped a bucket of bloody gore over herself; the white t-shirt was now a slick, dark red.

She scented the wind, peered over at the cowering women, and growled before blurring off into the night.

Zolah moved over to them then, doing her best to put them at ease with mental signals and imagery. It was highly unlikely that help would come for them in this godforsaken place. Nobody truly seemed to care what happened here in this corner of the world, or others like it, and it was very likely that these women would die anyway if it was up to government intervention, even if she did help them.

It had been her experience that in the poorer locations of the world, where a small, privileged few owned all the wealth by crushing it out of the people and the land around them, that life was indeed very cheap. And imminently expendable. Other countries, those who considered themselves civilized, would simply see this as a woeful but entertaining little horror show and thank whatever deity they chose to report to that it wasn't happening to them. That this hell was not their 'lot in life'.

Many flowery speeches would be made, tearful recountings of true stories would be aired briefly. Collegiate movements would come and go. Woeful marketing paraphernalia would be tossed around like confetti on New Year's Eve as everybody busied themselves patting each other on the back for 'getting involved' – and then the world would quickly forget that anything horrible ever really happened, as it so often did.

After all, the reality was that nobody liked being presented with a problem that didn't have a quick fix. Or an easy sell.

Disgusted, she quickly dialed up the Synod and gave her report, hoping that she'd be able to at least bring some viable help to the immediate situation.

Everything was pure instinct at this point. Somewhere along the way, Jilah's previous moral quandaries about utter soul destruction had died off. After witnessing the wretched victims of countless savage attacks – all the 'comfort women' that the soldiers were using in every way possible, she had completely shed any sense of guilt for the end result of her actions.

It was all so much more horrific than she could have ever imagined. These men were no better than rabid, plague-ridden dogs, and deserved to be utterly destroyed, by any means necessary.

"And I'm the dogcatcher, motherfucker," she growled, the resonance of the words in her chest thrumming as she stalked among the bodies to insure that the amount of suffering meted out far outshone the initial crime. In her eyes there wasn't enough pain and anguish that could ever pay for what they'd done.

At first, she had questioned her patroness' forced decision, sending her here. Now, she once again found herself swooning with an unwavering loyalty to her given cause. She stood between life and death here, sanity and madness; fighting a tide of violence and utter disregard for human life that she only hoped she could keep up with. No matter how many men fell – and at some point she'd stopped counting because there were just too many, there always seemed to be clutches of other patrols, other squads and platoons roaming around that were more than eager to force themselves on the various women and children in the area. Rape was a recreational activity to them and they took greedy advantage of their victims every chance that presented itself.

They cut a swathe of horror and disease through the countryside, not caring what they spread, or how they transmitted it. Sickness was very likely the last thing on these mens' minds. Jilah could smell the stench of plague on some of her targets; at times she almost gagged on it.

It helped that her targets also proved to be very handy fuel rechargers. Just how much blood had she choked down in the last three hours? Whether their blood was teeming with illness or not, it still nourished her the same. It didn't matter. She would keep going until her body needed to rest; then she would simply pick up where she left off after recuperating.

She hardly noticed that her skin was now a dark indigo color, her fingers curving into permanent, blue-black claws as she bore down on her next target, sighing with pleasure at the sound of his gibbering shrieks.

This, she thought as she bit into his neck, roughly sucking down the crimson life that pumped out of it, *is true glory.*

Her patroness' response was a smooth, liquid purr.

:: Yes, my daughter. My most beloved weapon. It is. ::

Jhada Rogue Addams

Chapter 14

THE CHANGING OF THE GUARD

The sun was just starting to creep over the mountains and Zolah was startled to realize that she was relieved that these men were now gone – their souls permanently destroyed; and this troubled her. How people could behave towards one another in such a brutal, selfish, hateful fashion was so completely repugnant to her that she almost cheered Jilah on.

The avatar was apparently now bedding down for the day to recover from the overabundance of activity that she had forced her body through during the course of the night. Zolah watched the slow rise and fall of Jilah's chest as she shifted in her sleep. The avatar's horns and tail were now so large that she was relegated to sleeping on her side. Her friend clutched her indigo claws close to her chest, nuzzling her nose into her knuckles, the rest of her body curled into a fetal position. Her appearance had only grown more fearful as the night, and her seemingly relentless duties, had progressed. The squatter in her psyche meant to run her into the ground, it seemed.

Jilah's entire body was now a deep indigo color, her hair still pulled back in a long braid that was soaked with blood and covered in bits of gore and bone, the white stripe long ago turned crimson where it threaded in and out of the braid. Her clothes were caked with blood, bone, and ragged strips of skin. She looked every bit the ideal of a folkloric demon now.

Zolah shook herself, feeling soiled just looking at her. The strong urge to bathe was overwhelming. She had no idea how long the woman would be out, but if she was to get clean, she'd have to take her opportunity now. She was dripping with sweat. The sound of running water was fairly close; a nearby river. Zolah blurred over to the banks, wanting to get clean before the oppressive heat of the day burned into her bones. She waded into the water, clothes and all. She sighed as she moved through the refreshing current, quietly singing a brief song and giving a silent prayer to her guardian spirit before submerging herself, reveling in the sensation, wanting to live only in this moment. It was the only way that she knew of to truly take a break from what she had witnessed.

Afterward, she collected the solar GPS phone from the backpack she'd left at her hiding spot on the shoreline and dialed the Synod. After giving Thea a rundown on everything that she had seen, Zolah shared her discomfort over how she was beginning to feel about the men that Jilah was destroying. There was a pregnant pause on the other end of the line before Thea responded.

"It sounds as if you are personalizing the situation too acutely to continue to observe free of bias, sister. You must remember that the creature that Jilah serves is not doing this out of any altruistic desire or need. It very likely consumes the souls that she harvests for it."

The very idea was enough to send a cold shudder through her.

"Why wasn't this voiced earlier?"

"We have had a great deal of time to ponder and research this matter since she first came to us. And even if we had known this beforehand, do you honestly think it would have helped her to hear it? She was already warring within herself about her true nature without adding this wrinkle."

"Very truly stated." Zolah agreed, wondering if Thea was right.

"It is our feeling that you are now being negatively swayed by what you are seeing, perhaps in a way that might prove to be permanent should you continue to stay for much longer. We will send a relief replacement so that you may take time to rest and process all that you have borne witness to."

Zolah nodded, now knowing that Thea was correct in her assessment. Already she could feel herself sympathizing with Jilah, moving closer into agreement with the method of utter destruction that her dark patroness was forcing on her victims. It was time to go home and bring somebody fresh in to bear witness.

"When may I expect my replacement?" she asked, keeping an eye out for anything that might try to catch her unawares.

"We will have somebody at your side as soon as possible. We've already selected a suitable candidate and are preparing her for departure now."

Zolah breathed a sigh of relief. She hadn't realized what a toll this watch was taking on her until she had time to think about it, and discuss it. Now it weighed heavily on her. It was good that she was going to be able to go home soon.

"Thank you, Thea. Both for your clarity and your wisdom in guiding this situation," she replied, terminating the connection.

She looked back over at Jilah. The avatar looked effectively dead to the world, only twitching slightly while she slept.

My friend, how sad I am that I have to leave you, she thought to herself, wishing that she could say the words – wishing that the blue skinned demoness that once was her friend could hear them without killing her.

Aurelian stepped into Argent's office with a frown as he moved to sit across from the sanguine, handing him a report.

"There has apparently been a bit of a kerfuffel going on in the République Démocratique du Congo lately."

Argent peered at him curiously, his tone curt as he replied, "And this kerfuffel that you speak of – it has what to do with our Prefecture, exactly?"

"Just read it."

Aurelian's expression grew serious and Argent looked down at the papers. His eyes narrowed as he scanned the text.

Strikezone: Democratic Republic of the Congo
Preliminary Investigative Findings of Questionable Preternatural Activity in the Eastern DRC Region
Threat Assessment: Medium to High

Province: Sud-Kivu

Argent began quickly flipping through the report, wondering what was now drawing the rather intent interest of the council to this particular region. According to the report, something was apparently butchering guerrilla soldiers in the South Kivu territories at a distressing rate – more-so than would usually happen in a military skirmish. The locals interviewed seemed to believe that this was all the work of what they referred to as a 'blue demoness' who moved almost quicker than the eye could track. This was, of course, understandable cause for alarm within the ranks of the council.

Throughout a large portion of the African continent, the given prefectures were not always as strict about their policies of enforcing complete invisibility of the preternatural denizens from the population. There were still enormous stretches of forest and jungle in which many creatures could live happily without ever encountering a human being.

Sometimes the more playful types liked to play tricks or let themselves be glimpsed briefly by villagers that were far removed from any real connection to the outside world. For the most part, this was considered harmless entertainment. It was one of the reasons that certain mythological stories still ran very strong in certain places in Africa. The council had pretty much realized as a given that this sort of activity would be tolerated to an extent, but definitely not encouraged.

Now, it seemed that something in the Eastern Congo region was getting out of hand. Hundreds were now dead and it was pretty obvious to anybody that had shown up after the mayhem was over that the victims had not been killed by other people, or animals. Carnivores didn't hunt like this, leaving so much rotting meat just laying around. The scavengers, however, were having a field day with the overwhelming bounty of remains that were being placed at their disposal.

Whatever this creature was, teeth and claws were making marks that nobody had recorded before. Throats were pulled out, bellies slashed – parts of the report read like the inside of an abattoir; the only connecting pattern was that a great many of the bodies appeared to have tried to dig their eyes out of their heads. It was also noted that a fair amount of them succeeded.

It was the personal account of a sighting, however, that caused Argent's chest to tighten as he read.

Translator states: He says that she has sharp claws, horns and a tail, all black. Everything else on her is blue, her skin, hair, everything. She is a water demon, he says. There has not been rain in many months, and he says that God has sent a blue demon to feed the earth with their blood instead of water because of their wickedness.

He quickly looked up at Aurelian, who gave a solemn nod.

Argent took a deep breath, no longer wanting to read any more. The body count seemed to indicate that she was being pushed for an almost insane kill count. Had Jilah slept at all since she'd gotten into the country? He knew she was quick and effective, but even he tired after constant motion, constant conflict; and anybody, supernatural or not, would fall eventually if they ended up having enough bullets pumped into them. Had she been shot? Injured?

The sanguine angrily spat, "How soon until she can take no more? How long will it be before that squatting whore finally lets her rest?"

He felt sick. He could only imagine the hellish nightmare that his beloved was now being pushed through. He only hoped that she'd found a way to shut out any pain that her patroness was causing her. Helpless frustration and anger ate at him as he tossed the report down onto the table. Apparently it wasn't enough that the bitch had pushed her to destroy him.

His sister had explained to him the suffering that his lover had endured when she thought she had truly ended him. It had eased him, to hear how strongly his death had affected her, but it bothered him a great deal that there was nothing that he could directly do to ameliorate her current situation. What she was being forced to endure was unforgivable. This was an enemy that he could not fight, and knowing that there was nothing that he could do to rectify the situation filled him with impotent fury.

Raging, he looked over at Aurelian and growled, "Enough."

Aurelian crooked an eyebrow at him, wondering if he was now thinking of boarding the next international flight to Kinshasa. Ill advised as it may be, he knew how heated the sanguine's passion could get and knew that it would be folly to stand in his way.

"You wanna go get her?" he ventured, startled as Argent responded with a harsh laugh.

"Hardly. I have no desire to endure such an attack again, and that is exactly what the end result would be until she is free of that foul squatting thing."

He paused for a moment before continuing, "No, I must be patient and trust that things will work out as they should; no matter how much my own frustration plagues me."

"Wait, are you saying that *Jilah*...?" Argent watched as a slow, dawning horror filled Aurelian's expression.

Argent waved the selkie's inquiry away with a gesture and quietly murmured, "It is of little importance, and I have no wish to speak about it. I have paid for my past. I will suffer no more for it. It does me no good to brood over a thing I have no influence over."

He stood and said, "The meet with the Prime of Witchita. Set it up. I will visit with him as quickly as he is able."

Aurelian blinked and asked, "You sure?"

Argent gave him a bland look and Aurelian quickly nodded and wrote something down in his notebook.

"I shall go tell Roane that we have a visit to conduct."

Breathing a sigh of relief, Jilah lowered herself into the river, busily scrubbing caked dirt and gore from her skin. She was glad that she hadn't chosen leather attire for this trip. She could only imagine how nasty that would have gotten. She frowned as she ran her claws along the curved length of one of her horns. It was about two inches wide at the base now, and possibly eight inches in length as it curved out and up from her forehead. The other one matched it. At least they didn't seem to be heavy. She wondered if they were hollow inside, like cow horns.

She took a moment to stare down at her clawed hands, the tips of her fingers permanently curled into black razored points now. *All the better to cut 'em up,* she mused silently as she continued to scrape at the grime and nastiness covering her. Appreciative that she was receiving a break in order to tend to her own overly soiled condition, she looked up into the darkening twilight sky. The stars here seemed different, clearer. More real.

The land felt feral and clean at heart, at least in this part of it. There was no pressing need to become something you weren't while you were here. Here under the glittering swirl of stars, listening to the multitude of night creatures rustling around, you simply existed as you were; no pretense, no obfuscation. It was strangely soothing and relaxing. The rhythm of life here was so very different than back home. And with such a target rich environment, she'd be able to nurse herself on a steady diet of corrupt blood for years. She could lose herself here. She *was* losing herself here.

And she was just fine with that.

Zolah kept watch from the treeline, wrapping her shields tightly around herself to avoid being noticed. Her replacement, one of the sitting members of the Synod itself, had arrived about half an hour ago. After filling the sister in on the events of the past twenty four hours, she realized that she wanted to say her goodbyes, in a way, before she made her long journey back home. She smiled, relieved that her friend was finally taking the time to clean herself off. The very idea of walking around, of doing anything while covered in a thick layer of offal repulsed her, and she didn't know how Jilah had endured it until now. At least the avatar seemed to be taking time to relax for the first time since they'd arrived. From time to time, a glimmer of the friend she knew would show on her features. It reassured her. She thought that Jilah looked strangely at peace as she took another dunk underwater.

Her replacement gently tapped her shoulder and Zolah knew that it was time to head back to the airport. She was eager to eat real food again. Her demon had kept her subsistence levels up through various feedings on some of the animals that she'd encountered, but she had long ago lost her taste for fresh human blood. Her demon still needed it from time to time, but she now much preferred an almost exclusively vegetarian diet. This was usually a signal that the last stage between the host and symbiote was beginning. Soon, it would be time to allow the demon to pass to another younger woman, one whose blood quickened at the idea of the hunt. Zolah would then be able to live out the rest of her life as a human woman. The merging with the demon slowed down the aging process for the duration of the pairing, but it would resume at regular speed once the two were no longer joined.

This was also another reason that Thea wanted her back home, so the transition could be more natural. She knew it was coming soon as well. Zolah's glory days of the chase and battle were long over and it was time for her to move on. She would stay connected to the Synod in an ancillary capacity, never wanting for another job, but she greatly desired a break to spend some time alone with Aaron before she made any big decisions. She cast a final glance back at her friend, silently wished her well, then started off in the direction of the airport.

Maslin boggled as Argent shared the contents of the report with him. He had decided to take the position, and as part of his first day, the sanguine had apparently chosen to knock him on his ass with the sheer volume of information that he had to deal with on a daily basis. Argent watched the young man's reactions, surprised at the emotions and thoughts he found in the forefront of the wolf's mind.

Maslin worried about her safety, truly cared for her. Argent smiled at the sweet innocence of it and Maslin peered at him curiously.

"What?" he asked, confused.

Argent collected the report from him, his smile vanishing as he placed it on a stack of papers off to the side.

"There is a very real likelihood that the council will intervene directly if she continues in this fashion for much longer."

Maslin gaped, angry now and momentarily forgetting who he was addressing.

"Are you kidding? The current situation in parts of the DNC is one of the worst atrocities on record to date. Rwanda wasn't exactly a cakewalk in comparison, but nobody ever acts to help when anything on this scale occurs anyplace that isn't considered a 'mecca of civilization'. Don't even get me started on Darfur; and now the council wants to step in to stop the one thing that's actually starting to making a difference down there?"

Argent steepled his fingers, his expression mild as he leaned back into the chaise.

"Have you forgotten the council's purpose entirely?"

Maslin blushed, remembering himself.

"My apologies Strigaisha, I have spoken too boldly."

Argent's tone was gentle as he replied, "No, Maslin. It is for this reason, and your rather formidable education, that I chose you for this position."

Maslin blinked as the Strigaisha continued, "I desire counsel that is free of pandering or calculation in an effort to gain my respect. Always speak your mind with me, especially when it comes to matters on which you feel we will not agree."

Maslin nodded, feeling somewhat relieved but curious now as he asked, "Isn't there anybody that you can talk with about matters like these? Aurelian?"

Argent shook his head slowly.

"Aurelian is too close. I need somebody that doesn't remember me as I was so many years ago."

"Understood, Strigaisha. And thank you."

Maslin leaned forward in his chair, his tone serious. "What's going to be done if she gets herself into a scrape with the council directly?"

"That is the entirety of my concern. For the moment, she seems to have stayed well outside of the limits of any major populated areas, but I have the feeling that once the creature that drives her exhausts her supply in the rural territories, she will then direct her to the cities. Once that happens, the council will act swiftly and without mercy to preserve its interests."

Maslin suppressed a shudder, not wanting to think about it. Even though he was not entirely familiar with the inner workings of the council, he was aware of their position and their creed. He also remembered the old stories that circulated from when he was a pup. The shifter Tribes liked to think that they were an entity unto themselves, but they were realistic enough to realize that the council keeping the law of the land ensured that their kind wasn't discovered and consequently persecuted and slaughtered.

The sanguine looked bleak as he brought his hand to his face, gently pinching the bridge of his nose.

"And I was worried about the trouble she would cause here with her given duty. I never in all my decades expected her to draw the direct attention of the council proper."

He took a long, slow breath, then closed his eyes.

"I can only hope that this runs its course before intervention occurs. If the council steps in to stop her, there is very little action I can take, I fear."

Roane popped her head in, asking, "'m I disturbing anything?"

Argent shook his head and stood.

"Thank you, Maslin – for your input."

Maslin nodded and got to his feet, smiled at Roane, then replied, "I am pleased that I can contribute, Strigaisha."

Roane grinned at Maslin as he walked out.

"He's a cutie – he stayin'?"

Argent presented her with a wry smile and nodded, "Yes. He will be staying."

"Zing! More eye candy. Sweet."

Argent shook his head and chuckled.

"How is it that you always manage to stay so ebullient?" he asked, mystified.

She shrugged and replied, "That's easy – I just try to keep my head out of my ass about stuff. Take things as they come, you know..."

She sobered a little, sighing. "It's not always easy."

"Come. Let us see what we can do about making the best of your situation."

He placed a gentle hand on her shoulder as they walked out of the room.

"Thank you...for this," she murmured. "It hadn't even occurred to me."

They walked through the corridor, towards Gigi's room.

"It is still not, as they say, a 'done deal', but we will certainly do what we can to see that it becomes so."

Roane smiled and gently nudged him, asking, "So, how's our girl handling herself at school?"

Argent forced a smile and replied, "She fares well and is gaining a very broad... education."

Roane was glad to hear it. She missed her friend and hoped that she would be returning soon.

"So... Ellsworth. What're they going to do about the human correctional facility out there?" she wondered.

"Aurelian says that the prisoners are already being distributed to other facilities throughout Kansas. Apparently they are refitting Leavenworth to accommodate."

Roane shook her head. It was insane logic.

"And the residents – they're just going to pack up and go? They're ok with this?"

"None of the humans in Kansas are pleased that their state is set to become a dumping ground for..."

He trailed off, seeing that Roane's jaw was tightening.

"My apologies for not phrasing that more... politely."

Argent frowned.

"There has been an uproar about this for quite some time, but the people that want to push this through are determined to see their own vision of the future."

"I just... I never thought it'd happen. I never thought that anybody would dare." Roane's hands curled into fists.

"What we need to focus on now is how best to adapt."

Roane nodded. "So, what is this Ellis Jacoby anyway? Is he like us?"

Argent looked over at her, curious.

"How much did Judiana tell you about the other prefectures?"

"Not much, really. She kept a lot of stuff close to her chest."

He frowned and asked, "I don't imagine that you've ever heard of Pecos Bill?"

"Nope."

Argent explained, "Ellis is what you'd call a direct inspiration for one of the more colorful entries in American Folklore. He's a coyote."

Roane blinked. "A shifter?"

"He is capable of changing forms, but coyote was his initial shape. He chooses to keep his human shape because it entertains him."

"Then this has the possibility of being a very interesting meeting," Roane replied, smiling.

"Prime Jacoby."

Argent gave a small bow from the waist as the man before him nodded with approval. A gleam of amusement glittered in the Prime's eyes. Argent had only met him a couple of times, but he'd always looked as if he was just waiting for the punchline of a joke that happened a few minutes ago.

"Regent Argent."

The prime nodded, then chuckled. "Y'know, I never could get over how weird that sounds together. Take a load off."

]He waved towards the sofa. "You guys want anything? We got..." he turned around, as if looking for something, then yelled, "SARAH! What we got?"

Argent winced and looked over at Roane who was doing her best not to laugh.

:: *Is he usually like this?* :: she asked.

:: *He's very... energetic. I had forgotten how much.* :: Argent replied.

Roane grinned and sat down on the edge of a couch.

"We got pickles! And jam!" a woman's voice shouted back.

"What, that's it?" the Prime shouted.

"Oh, and a can of Pringles! I think they're expired, though."

Argent sat beside Roane, waiting for the drama to play itself out. It had been an uncomfortable lesson years ago, learning that Ellis would only act in his own time. If pushed, it would only get worse.

The Prime turned back to them, frowning.

"Sorry we aren't better stocked."

Argent smiled and waved it off, "It is quite alright. We refreshed ourselves before the trip so as not to burden our host with having to provide..."

"Horseshit."

Ellis narrowed his eyes.

Argent blinked. "I beg your pardon?"

"You got pain in your eyes, son. I know when I see hungry. Don't bullshit a bullshitter."

The Prime sat on the edge of a large mahogany desk in the middle of his living room..

Argent blanched, uncomfortable and unable to hide it. He'd forgotten that about Jacoby too. If you could be sure of one thing around the coyote – all masks came down around him. It made him an effective, if unorthodox mediator.

Not that anybody really utilized him as such. Ellis was a bit much to take for most people.

"There is a matter unrelated to this that is... distracting. My apologies for not keeping it better hidden. It is of no consequence."

Jacoby stared at him for a minute, then took a deep breath. "We haven't known each other all that well, so I'm not gonna press you on it."

Argent breathed an internal sigh of relief, then nodded, "I appreciate that, Prime Jacoby."

"Fuck that, call me Ellis. If we're gonna be workin' this closely together, I'm gonna get tired of hearin' that honorific shit all the time."

It was not always easy to remember that not everybody who ruled stood on ceremony. In this case, Argent was actually relieved.

"Ellis, this is Roane."

The sea green haired necromancer stood up and Ellis looked her over.

"She don't look all that scary," he cocked his head, then grinned, "I like it. It'll throw people off. Fuck with their heads."

:: *Oh, I like him.* :: Roane sent, returning the coyote's smile.

Argent was very grateful that at least something was going smoothly.

Argent had been pleased at how quickly Roane had taken over the brunt of the negotiations. After all, he had only been there to act as intermediary to the meeting itself. She had exceeded his expectations and he was certain that she would be capable of handling the new territory. By the time they were done, she had the Prime agreeing to set aside a respectable portion of his state's allotment for the creation of a house set to her specifications in Ellsworth proper. She hadn't asked for anything enormous, or over the top, which was likely why he was so ready to accommodate the request.

It was understood that she would remain with the court in New Orleans until the project workers got around to relocating/ evacuating all the cemeteries within the city limits. It still remained to be seen how long it would take for the exhumation crews to get around to Louisiana. Ellis had his people currently prepping things for the arrival of the first bodies from New York City.

According to the plans that the Prime had shown them, the cities with the highest population counts were first on the list for evacuation. From what he was hearing, a very vocal section of the population was horrified by the idea. There had already been an enormous protest in Washington D.C.

Unsurprising, he thought to himself. Argent found the very idea repellent, but then, rarely did sanguines comfortably tolerate the presence of truly dead things of any kind. He couldn't begin to imagine the stench of opening all of those graves.

The desire of the majority of humans to remove themselves from engaging with the process of their own natural end had always fascinated Argent. People were growing less and less tolerant of reminders of their mortality. Science had always intervened when nature would have otherwise taken her due, presenting humans with a longer life span now than ever before. Major metropolitan areas were densely packed sprawls that went well out into where the suburbs used to exist.

Perhaps they consider it the next logical step in their own evolution, this... shunting off of their dead to a manufactured wasteland that no-one will ever visit. It seemed a fool's errand to him as he leaned back against the couch in his office, letting out a sigh.

There was a knock at his door and he looked up to see Aurelian standing in the doorway.

"Did you need anything before I head off to bed?"

They'd been sleeping together less frequently of late – Argent hadn't allowed any other intimacies between then since his return, and the sanguine was surprised to find that it bothered him this night. Aurelian had gotten better at hiding his feelings about it, but from time to time, they'd come to the surface. Tonight it was easy to see that he was hoping that the strigaisha would extend an invitation. Argent scooted over and placed a hand on the cushion beside him and Aurelian's eyes widened with surprise.

Argent spotted Aurelian's nervous smile before the selkie settled next to him, asking, "What's up?"

Argent simply placed a hand on Aurelian's knee, giving it a squeeze before letting it slide down his thigh. He was surprised at how good the warmth beneath the man's jeans felt. It had been too long since he'd actually reached out and just touched anybody like this. He found that he'd missed the contact greatly.

Aurelian's breath hitched and Argent looked over, meeting his now heated, but hesitant, gaze.

"I need..." Argent looked down, the words wouldn't come as he let his hand slide down a little further.

The large man trembled beside him, his hand closing over Argent's cool fingers. His voice was breathy as he asked, "You sure?"

Argent moved his hand to thread his fingers with Aurelian's as he murmured, "Oh yes. Very."

He admired Aurelian's restraint as the selkie stood and pulled him up into a slow, tightening hug.

"You scared the shit out of me." Aurelian muttered, dipping his head down to drop against Argent's shoulder.

"I am... sorry," Argent murmured as he gently pulled out of the hug and tightened his hand around Aurelian's.

The selkie smiled then and the tight tension between them eased as he pulled Argent along as he made his way to the door.

"You realize you're going to have to make it up to me, right?"

And with that, Argent smiled, and it healed something in him. "Of that, I have no doubt."

Chapter 15

THE GAME COMES TO A HEAD

Someone was calling her name.

Jilah let the ruined body of her most recent target crumple to the ground. Frowning, she spun around to see the shimmering form of a familiar woman standing behind her.

How the woman had been able to wade through the veritable sea of gore around them without getting a spot of blood on her, was only slightly less mysterious than how she happened to be here in the first place. Eyes narrowing to slits, Jilah growled at the intruder, her expression twisted in a grimace of rage. The interloper looked exactly like her dead lover's 'sister'.

Jilah's voice came out in a guttural rumble as she spoke, her claws quickly clutching and flexing in a nervous repeated tic

"I thought we were done. What the fuck are you doing here?"

S'llethe regarded her with a critical eye, her expression empty as she replied, "This is enough. You tear at the very balance itself now, tipping the scales too far in pursuit of your game."

Jilah gaped back at the woman, her tail thrashing around her legs in the dirt, kicking up blood and dust. Low, harsh laughter rang out of her throat and her voice took on a menacing unearthly tone as her patroness spoke through her.

"And so the watcher becomes the guardian of balance now?"

It sounded like the hissing of a multitude of snakes – something so utterly wrong to be issuing forth from a human mouth.

"You have no say in this matter, glittering shapechild. The collection of my debt from this girl and this world are far from paid off."

At this, S'llethe smiled and took a measured step forward.

"Are you so certain that this continues to be true, dark mother?" She laughed softly and it sounded both soothing and terrifying.

A chill went up Jilah's spine at the sound. She felt her patroness withdraw as she faltered and stumbled to her knees. She looked over at her dead lover's 'sister', momentarily cut off from the driving, burning presence of the dark creature in her psyche.

Taking advantage of the silence, Jilah looked around at the devastation she'd wrought. What corrugated tin shacks and cinder block buildings were still standing were covered in slick inky splashes and stains that reflected black under the moonlight. These men had never seen her coming and she'd taken full advantage of it. Apparently at some point, she had arranged the heads of the men into a gruesome pyramid, resting them against one of the walls of a concrete dwelling across the street. Strange sigils had been drawn in the dirt at the base of the spectacle, eldritch symbols scratched in the clay. Her claws themselves were caked with bloody mud. Looking at the display before her, she felt her stomach wrench and she threw up onto the collection of dismembered bodies that lay scattered at her feet.

S'llethe's voice was gentle as she stepped up to Jilah and murmured, "She plays with the fabric of all that is, to call something far worse forth into the world."

Jilah looked up at her, horrified.

"WORSE? Than this?"

S'llethe nodded, her expression solemn.

"It is what she is; what she does. She is the destroyer without the controlling force of the creator within. Her only purpose is to devour the world."

Jilah reeled back as if slapped.

"And you locked her in here with me? Lady, what the fuck were you THINKING??"

S'llethe chided her gently, "We have our reasons, child – and to be clear it was you who agreed to the initial bargain. The debt had to be cleared before we could truly act. We are the Watcher, the one who bears witness; and in cases such as these, when balance needs restoration, we are the Guardian."

Jilah stammered, wondering when her patroness' presence would roar through her again. It was disconcerting that the DarkLady had been so distracted by a simple question for this long.

S'llethe, sensing her distress, explained, "She measures her odds now, sister."

Frowning, Jilah felt like a very small pawn in a much larger game, the scope of which she was incapable of comprehending. She was just at the edge of truly realizing the extent of what she'd done, driven by the entity who had so fiercely clutched the reins of her psyche in an iron grip. The presence came back in a sudden rush, flooding her senses. Jilah grimaced as control of her body was again violently wrenched from her.

The voice that issued forth from her lips sounded muted, somehow, less commanding.

"It would appear that you are correct, shapechild guardian." she spat the words out, making them into a damning curse. "Although it nauseates me to admit it, I find that I cannot deny that this one has paid the debt I called upon her and then some."

She sounded disappointed, but still defiant. Jilah could feel an eager smile play along her own lips as the queen bitch crowed, "No matter. I now rescind my gift and leave this empty vessel to the rest of her wretched existence."

Jilah could barely believe what she was hearing as a violent physical wrench pulled an agonized scream from her throat. She dropped to the ground, shaking. The feeling of disbelief echoed in the presence inside her, then rage cracked through her synapses like a whip as her dark rider tried to collect the portion of its imbued essence once gifted back into itself. Several more attempts were made, each more appalling in both sensation and pain, until S'llethe's voice rang in her ears.

"This child will maintain her gift, dark mother, and all else that you have given her. This is to be your consequence for collecting such a grievous toll from her through obfuscation and manipulation."

Jilah heard her patroness' roar as it shook through the treeline of the jungle around them.

S'llethe laughed, and Jilah thought that she detected a hint of taunt in her tone as she continued, "If you had not chosen to force her hand in the slaughter of her soultwin, perhaps we would have been lenient; but you became greedy. Your own actions decided the price."

S'llethe paused for a moment, then her smile became almost cruel.

"And to ensure that you do not send your next intended host after this one in the future, we bind you from taking such action again. This child and those who stand with her are to be left alone, to change the fabric of this timestream as they will."

Jilah felt the entity's cold fury whip through her as she spat something in an alien language that she couldn't understand.

Suddenly, it felt as if her body were splitting, physically and psychically trying to separate into two distinct halves. An unnatural howling raged through the air, tearing at it and everything around her. The pain was unbearable, sending white hot ribbons of agony shooting through her synapses. It quickly shorted them out and the world began to go grey around her. She sent a last final call out, a flood of images and feelings, certain that she was now dying.

Although he was beyond hearing her at this point, he was her last thought as the darkness consumed her.

:: Argent... ::

The sanguine snapped awake and sat up, startled at the sound of his lover's voice in his thoughts.

Spurred on by the intense feeling that she was in imminent danger, Argent immediately got up and began going around the room, pulling clothes on, his only thought focused on getting to her side as quickly as possible. As he zipped up a pair of black jeans and pulled on a white tank top, he became vaguely aware of somebody yelling at him.

When he turned to look, he found Aurelian staring at him, open mouthed, naked, and white as a sheet.

Argent frowned back at the selkie, wondering what had him so spooked? He was surprised at how calm he sounded as he said, "Come now. Surely you've seen me get out of bed before."

Aurelian shook his head briefly then pointed at the digital clock across the room. It was two o'clock in the afternoon.

Argent sagged back against the bed in shock. In the entire time since his rebirth, he had never risen during the day. Already, he could feel the oppressive weight of it bearing down on him. Strange that he hadn't noticed only moments ago. He shivered, shaking his head as he tried not to think about it.

Aurelian slid a hand around his waist, his voice soft, "What happened?"

A violent tremor shook the sanguine's body and Argent's voice dropped to a whisper as he replied, "Jilah. She's in trouble. She thinks she's dying. She regrets... killing me," he murmured, hardly able to believe it as he clutched the back of Aurelian's hand.

"...killing you?"

Argent sighed and closed his eyes, his tone weary as he finally explained himself. Until now, Maslin was the only other person in his court who had known the truth of what had transpired during his absence. It was something he had not wanted to discuss and hadn't desired to share it with anybody when he returned.

"Didn't you trust me?"

The selkie sounded hurt and Argent turned to face him.

"It was not so much an issue of trust. Had you found yourself in a similar position, would you have readily talked about it so soon after?"

He was frowning now, somewhat irritated that Aurelian was taking this personally.

Aurelian dropped his eyes and replied. "You're right."

He looked back up into the emerald eyes of his lover, his tone firm as he asked, "So, what now? D'we go get our girl?"

Argent frowned for a moment and Aurelian saw his expression go neutral, the way he usually looked when he was talking head to head with somebody. After a few moments the sanguine shook his head, calming now.

"My initial fear was that the council had taken action against her. It appears that a rather unusual intervention has taken place."

He flinched, then murmured, "However, it may be awhile before she comes back."

"What's that supposed to mean?" Aurelian asked.

"I assume it is something that will be explained when the messenger arrives in person."

Relieved that Jilah was now safe, but irritated that he now had to wait for an explanation, he stood up and continued dressing.

"How can you be so calm about this?" Aurelian asked, baffled.

"I have little choice in the matter," he explained, not liking it at all, but understanding that Jilah might need time before seeing him again. He wasn't quite sure how the shock of the realization that he still lived would be received.

There was a brief knock on the bedroom door. Argent blurred over and opened it to find Gigi standing in the doorway in mid preen. The enormous beehive wig perched on her head was a veritable tower of emerald, and her body was covered in a tight fitting, flesh-toned leotard that had strategic patches of ivy and green glitter winding across it, covering just enough to be on the edge of scandalous. She looked as if she belonged on a float celebrating the rites of spring, standing next to a prancing satyr.

Unable to help himself, Argent chuckled, asking, "Where on earth are you going dressed like that?"

Gigi tutted, patting gently at the wig, her tone haughty as she replied, "A rather elegant, eligible and – more importantly – interested individual has decided to invite me to a Bacchanalian faerie feast, not that you'd know of such things being cooped up in this sweaty, sordid little bedroom."

She eyed the pair of them generously, pursing her lips and puckering them.

"And the reason as to why you're here disturbing us?"

"Actually, I was looking for Aurelian. Mira said he'd be in here. There's.." As her words trailed off, Gigi's eyes narrowed for a moment, then quickly widened as she whispered, "Wait a minute... What are you doing awake?!?"

She looked past him to Aurelian and raised an eyebrow in query, but the selkie simply shrugged and offered a noncommittal grunt.

"Thanks, mister 'helpful as always'," she snapped.

Aurelian spluttered, "What, like I know? He just popped awake! Neither of us knows how."

Gigi crooked an eyebrow imperiously and looked back over at Argent.

"Well, I'm sure you'll both put your rather considerable talents to the task of figuring this particular mystery out, but in the meantime there's a delightful woman in your throne room who desires your presence."

She gave them a quick flourished courtsey, then in a cheery tone said, "Now that my message has been delivered, I do believe I'm off to be the belle of the ball. Don't wait up, boys."

She then sashayed down the hall, humming When the Saints Go Marching In to herself.

Argent blinked, shaking his head and laughing now. He was surprised that he was actually somewhat happy for the first time since his return. The time spent with Aurelian last night had gone a long way towards healing much of the pain of being separated from Jilah. He still missed her greatly, but was now able to think about her without that bone wearying ache in his chest. He looked back at Aurelian, feeling a bit of the old fire surge back into him. His beloved lived. He wouldn't see her today, maybe not for quite some time, but it was enough, for the moment, that she still lived.

"Are you coming or not?" he asked, his tone not entirely curt.

Aurelian stood up and pulled on a pair of faded blue jeans with frayed holes in the knees.

"Yeah, why not. I mean, seeing how this sort of thing is my job, and all."

His tone was playfully noncommittal as he zipped up and ran fingers through his platinum blonde locks, smoothing out some of the bed head tangles.

Argent stepped into the corridor, asking, "Remind me again why I keep you around?"

"Mind blowing sex?"

The selkie grinned and waggled his eyebrows as he caught up to him.

Argent chuckled and shook his head as they began making their way to the throne room.

"Surely there must be some other viable reason."

Aurelian laughed then, low and throaty.

"Ha! You wish."

Zolah watched as Argent entered the throne room, a large blonde man following closely behind him. A very shirtless, attractive blonde man with a broad expanse of nicely tanned chest. She had seen him before, but he'd had more clothes on then. Both men were dressed very casually, as if they'd just pulled themselves out of bed. For a moment it threw her.

Without meaning to, she blurted out, "We lost her."

Argent cocked his head to the side, asking, "You... lost her?"

Zolah took a deep breath and began slowly, "One of the women from the Synod itself was sent to follow Jilah as she tended to her given duty."

Surprised at the dedication and endurance it must have taken to keep up with his mate, he was impressed that they'd stayed on her for this long. Not wanting to keep the poor woman hanging in distress, he quickly stepped forward and replied, "I know where she is. She's safe, and being tended to at the moment – by my sister and her kin."

Zolah let out a sigh of relief and Argent watched as the tension melted from the woman's posture. She said something under her breath in a language that he couldn't understand, then looked back at him.

"When did you receive this news?"

"Only moments ago, as it happens. Most unusual that."

Argent's expression was wry as his thoughts pondered what could have pulled him awake midday. Strange that his sister hadn't thought it odd, either. She sounded as if she'd expected him to be up.

Zolah frowned, asking, "Unusual?"

Argent slid his thumbs in the pockets of his jeans and responded with another question, "Exactly how familiar are you with my kind?"

The woman eyed him thoughtfully for a moment before responding, "I have met only one other such as you in my lifetime, but I have known about the stories and mythology surrounding the bloodchildren for many years."

"And in all that time, over all the research done and stories read, had you ever heard of one who could walk during the daylight hours?"

Zolah was now looking at him very strangely. "Never. There have been no such recorded creatures."

Argent arched an eyebrow, amused.

"And yet with the deadly blazing orb high in the noonday sky, here I stand, animate."

Zolah blinked, then frowned. "Was there anything significant that brought this about, or have you always been..?"

Argent let out a soft laugh and rocked back on a heel.

"I am as mystified as anyone else by my current condition. Until I woke, shortly before your arrival, the day had always been closed off to me; my body, for all intents and purposes, dead and unaware from sunrise to twilight."

Zolah eyed him, her tone shrewd as she asked, "I feel that you are likely missing something crucial. Was there a particularly significant event...?"

Argent became very still, cutting her off as he whispered, "Jilah reached out to me. With what she felt was her dying breath, she reached out to me."

"Dying breath?"

Zolah almost choked. Her throat made a distinct clicking noise as it closed up.

Argent quickly reassured her, "She was mistaken, of course. But still – she called out, and found me. I could not resist her call, and here I stand."

Aurelian let out a breath. "Whoa."

Argent nodded gravely.

"Indeed."

Would he find himself able to walk in the daylight again? The idea was both heady and terrifying. Although intrigued, he was not quite foolhardy enough to test it anytime soon. He had no idea what kind of shock his body would endure when confronted with the sun again after so many years in darkness, and wasn't eager to find out.

The selkie frowned and looked over at him, "So, whaddya think this means?"

"Damned if I know."

Argent paused for a moment, hearing the whisper-thought of his sister in his mind as she and Thea stepped into the throne room. His smile was tight as he turned to greet them.

S'llethe walked over to him, her voice soft and low as she murmured, "We cannot say when she will rise, brother – only that she will."

Thea stepped up to them and explained, "It is difficult to say how she'll react to your presence at this point – and considering what she's already been through, we believe that it is in her best interest to stay with us until she's recovered to a point where she's ready to hear that you still live."

Argent looked over at S'llethe, eyes narrowing as he asked, "And your opinion on this?"

S'llethe smiled and nodded once.

"We are in agreement, brother."

Argent's posture stiffened as his hands curled into fists. His eyes narrowed briefly before he regained his composure and drew a deep breath.

"We understand that this is difficult for you, brother, but your mate needs to let things reveal themselves in their own time." S'llethe's expression changed as she stepped forward and wrapped her arms around Argent, her tone soft as she murmured, "We are with you, and we watch over you both. Things will right themselves. You must trust in this."

Argent nodded, his expression rigid and formal as he gently pulled away.

"I shall wait to hear from you both as her condition progresses, then."

Argent looked over at his sister, asking, "Would you perhaps be privy to the cause of my current condition?"

S'llethe smiled, laughter in her eyes.

"A gift, dear brother. A restraint loosened."

Argent stilled, his mind full of questions. Although he knew he'd likely never receive a full explanation about the origin of this gift, he couldn't help asking.

"Why?"

"Perhaps the Source feels that it is enough to have endured all that has presented itself to you in your long life."

S'llethe brushed his cheek with a gentle hand.

Argent closed his eyes, trembling. Freedom from the oppressive fear of the sun? He shook his head.

"I am not..."

S'llethe didn't let him finish, placing a finger against his lips.

"Those she hunts are cyclical. They have separate times in the liferhythm, different incarnations, to learn the lesson of how they should comport themselves. You do not. Your kind only have this linear progression to grow, to learn – and you have. More than you allow yourself to realize. You are worthy of this."

It was the first time he'd ever seen anything close to anger in her expression. She was pissed that he didn't think that he was worthy of the gift. A sense of shock rang through him at her words.

"How odd, to realize that they can claim true immortality." He replied softly. "How ironic."

S'llethe nodded, looking back at him now with infinite grace and patience.

"I will end, someday. I don't think I was fully expecting that," he explained, frowning. "Why didn't you...?"

S'llethe's tone was soft and warm as she replied, "It was not for you to know until now."

Aurelian quietly stepped into the office and S'llethe moved to kiss Argent on the cheek.

Looking very discomfited at having been privy to such an intimate moment, Thea murmured, "We will provide you with regular updates about your Striaga."

"Thank you both," he replied.

The women departed and Argent looked over at the selkie. Aurelian was peering at him strangely, as if trying to figure something out.

"You okay?" he asked.

"Say what you need to say."

Argent slid his hands into the pockets of his black jeans.

"Alain wishes to speak to you."

Argent nodded, not wanting to have this conversation with the Alpha, but knowing that it had to happen eventually. He was actually grateful that the Alpha had given it this long. Alain had trusted him and he now wanted that trust repaid.

"He's in the throne room," the selkie murmured.

Maslin's expression was grave as he stood beside his Alpha. Alain simply looked mild as he waited for an explanation.

"It was a test that she had to endure entirely on her own." Argent's chest tightened as he thought about it.

Alain eyed him, frowning. "This thing you have done, it has sown mistrust in the pack against Gregor's cub."

"Would you have him countermand a directive from his Strigaisha?" Argent asked.

The alpha stilled, his expression unchanging.

"There must be a price paid for this in order for Maslin to clear this from his name in the pack."

Argent nodded, frustrated that Maslin was now caught in the middle, having no fault in the situation of his own. He'd done everything he could to protect Jilah. Still, there was nothing to be done for it, and Maslin knew it. Argent could see it in the man's face.

Maslin stepped forward and bowed his head to his alpha, his tone somber as he said, "I accept the punishment for neglecting my charge. It is mine to bear and mine alone."

Argent winced inwardly as Alain, sighed, then quietly replied, "You are banished from hearth and howl for a sixmoon and are stripped of your title."

It was a harsh sentence. Years of hard work would have gone into the place he'd earned within the ranks of the pack – and now it would all have been for nothing. Maslin would have to start over again, at the bottom. Argent felt for the boy, but there was nothing he could do to intervene when it came to pack law.

Maslin nodded, his voice breaking a little as he replied, "Am I allowed access to collect my things?"

Alain took a step back and shook his head, his expression somber. "No, Maslin."

Argent spoke up then, asking, "May I collect them for him?"

Alain's features tightened as he frowned and replied, "The Strigaisha is always welcome on pack lands."

It was clear that the Alpha didn't like the idea, but the fact that Argent had asked had obliged him to honor the request.

Argent nodded, then turned to Maslin.

"You are welcome to stay at the court for as long as you need. It owes you a debt that it cannot possibly hope to repay."

Maslin looked over at the sanguine, eyes just shy of brimming with tears. He was both grief stricken with the loss of his title and deeply touched by the Strigaisha's generous offer. He nodded, then looked away.

Argent then looked back up at Alain. The Alpha nodded, then quietly turned and walked off.

Argent sighed as Maslin strode off in the other direction. He resolved to do everything he could to try to make the young man's situation bearable.

For the moment, however, there was something else to which he needed to attended.

Chapter 16
RECOVERY

Pain flared in her mind as a quick rush of images flooded her grey matter.

Dark angry eyes. The slash of a vicious grin. A dappling spray of blood against brick.

This didn't feel old, like the others; this was happening now. Jilah jerked awake, twisting the sheets in a fisted hand. She looked over to find Argent dormant beside her. For a brief moment, something tugged at the corner of her mind, but she brushed it away. She had to get to the girl in time.

Sun's gotta be up already, she groaned to herself. No rest for the wicked.

An indigo braid threaded with a stripe of white thumped against her back as she quickly got out of bed and yanked a black tanktop over her head.

"Shit...", she muttered, disoriented. She always hated the day runs. At least they were rare.

Jilah hopped on one foot as she tried to pull a pair of black BDU cutoffs on, then moved over to her boots.

"How close - how close?" she grated and landmarks for the location flickered in her mind's eye.

Live scenarios didn't happen all that often and Jilah wanted to get there as quickly as possible to stop her target from killing his current plaything.

She wouldn't be as strong as she would've been under the cloak of night, but she'd found that she was still able to easily outmaneuver and overpower damn near anybody she ran up against - as long as they were human.

Casting a quick glance back at her lover, she took off for the door at top speed, nearly bowling over Aurelian as she raced through the corridors. The blonde flattened against a wall, calling out, "Go get 'em, slugger!"

Another mental tug was brushed away and Jilah shot him the finger as she darted around a corner and rapped on Gigi's door, cutting short the muffled conversation that was taking place inside.

"Who is it?" a singsong voice called out from behind the door.

"Gigi, darling – I love you, and I'm really sorry to bug you but I need you to get your ass in gear. I got a live one and I need to get there quick."

Jilah felt her stomach turn as she waited for the sorceress to answer the door. As much as she hated the nausea that flooded her system after gating, it was a necessary evil in this instance. A strange ache started in her chest as she thought about it, and she frowned. Maybe I won't throw up so much this time, she thought to herself, crossing mental fingers.

Gigi opened the door and stepped into the hallway, wrapping a silk floral print kimono around herself.

"Where?" she asked, all business.

Jilah grabbed the woman's hand, pushing the memory to her as gently as possible. Gigi quickly pulled away, rubbing at her hand as if she wanted to wash it off. The sorceress shuddered and murmured, "Oh god. Are we going to get there in time?"

Jilah frowned.

"No way of knowing."

Gigi made a quick gesture that looked awfully familiar and then Jilah was blinking quickly, choking back almost overwhelming nausea. At least it hadn't been as bad this time. Perhaps knowing about it ahead of time...?

Suddenly, a girl was screaming; the high pitched wail of someone dancing along the edge of passing out from pain. Jilah immediately locked onto the sound, blurring into a room with a medical examination table. A young girl who couldn't have been more than fifteen was strapped to the table, flailing out at her attacker, an average looking man with sandy blonde hair and blue eyes. The girl's eyes widened in surprise as Jilah kicked out and down at the side of the man's knee. Her target crumpled, shrieking in pain as he crashed into a tray full of knives and saws. They clattered around him, some of them cutting or sticking into him as they fell.

"Oh god, oh god, oh god!" the girl kept screaming as Jilah quickly moved to snap the man's arms and legs.

With her target effectively immobilized, she stood up and looked down at the girl. The poor thing was a mass of cuts and bruises. At least the wounds were fairly shallow and nothing appeared broken. Physically, she'd be alright. Emotionally and mentally – that would take a great deal longer, if ever, to heal.

Gigi came into the room, her voice soft and soothing, "Hey darlin' – we're gonna get you outta here, OK?"

Gigi's hand made an undulating gesture as she walked up to the table and the girl relaxed, breathing slowly.

"She'll be okay – I think he was just getting started on her."

New meat, Jilah thought to herself, shuddering.

"Does he have anybody else down here?" Gigi asked as Jilah pushed the sandy haired man over onto his back with a booted foot. Her target's eyes blazed with a hatred that seemed to writhe within them, poisonous and dark. It was somewhat unsettling.

The avatar took a look around the room and winced. It was full of medical equipment, but the room was far from surgically sterile. He had likely been doing this for a good, long time before finally getting caught at it.

"Pens... he keeps us in the pens until he's ready... t-to..." the girl dissolved into quiet tears, covering her face.

Jilah's eyes narrowed as she looked back down at the man at her feet. She moved to pick him up, looking over at Gigi as she explained, "She shouldn't have to see this. She's been through enough."

Gigi nodded and Jilah walked out, looking for a suitable place to conduct her business. She dropped the target into a dark corner, her eyes fluttering as the memories tore at his psyche. She left him gibbering to himself, then pulled out the cellphone that Mira had given her.

The voice on the other end of the line simply asked, "What and where?"

After providing brief details, the line clicked and went dead. Jilah then made her way back to the makeshift operating room.

"I'm sorry you had to see all this."

Gigi frowned, shaking her head. "All this time in a supernatural court – I thought I'd seen some rough shit, girl, especially with Gregor – but this?" She shivered.

They found one of the girls dead in her pen, a filthy enclosure that looked more like one of the cages that prisoners of war were placed in during the

Vietnam war. The other girl kept babbling and giggling, scratching at painful looking rashy patches all over her skin.

Jilah frowned, crossing her arms.

"The live runs are the hardest."

Relieving the teenager of the harshest memories of her time here hadn't been easy. Jilah was finding that extended exposure seemed to prove more difficult to remove them from a victim's psyche. The other girl was too far gone. There was nothing Jilah could do for her and a feeling of impotence gnawed at her gut.

Gigi placed a gentle hand on her shoulder, her voice soft. "You did everything you could, honey."

They reached a set of stairs that led up to what looked like a trapdoor in the ceiling. Jilah looked up at it, frowning as Gigi asked, "Is it like this all the time?"

Jilah looked back at her, pursing her lips as she thought about it. "It's always bad, but it's never as 'in your face' as it is with the live ones. Their memories are painful, but they're easier, in a way. I know the dead rest – I can feel it once they come through me and..." she shook her head and turned to the stairs. "But these girls? Yeah, they're alive, but they're not going to really rest again for a while."

A heavy weight settled on her shoulders as she pushed up the trapdoor, peering out through the crack as she raised it. It opened out into a room filled with bright, colorful paintings and plants. The riot of color was jarring after seeing the horror that lived beneath them.

Definitely a woman's touch. Is she still home? Jilah wondered to herself.

She turned, holding a finger up to her lips as she looked back at Gigi. The sorceress nodded, stepping lightly.

Upstairs, Jilah heard a floorboard creak. She grated her teeth as she stepped up into the room, holding the door up for Gigi. Dammit. The cleaning crew was already on its way.

A woman's voice trailed down the stairs. "John! If you're done fucking around in the basement with that stupid project, I need you to come up here and hang something for me."

Jilah's eyes narrowed. Had the woman known what was going on in her own home? Gigi stepped into the room and Jilah lowered the door, catfooting into the dining room. Everything was immaculate. There was actually plastic on the furniture and a plastic runner along the carpet.

Who actually lives like this? *Jilah thought to herself. Was it a show house?*

"John, dammit - get up here."

The woman's voice again, more insistent this time.

Jilah looked back at Gigi and whispered, "Mira's day team is going to be here any minute. Can you put a whammy on her or something?"

Gigi hissed, "Can I beat the holy hell out of her if she knew what that asshole was doing in her basement?"

Jilah looked back at her companion for a moment.

"I thought you didn't like violence."

Gigi shook her head and trilled, "Not like what's down there, but knockin' a bitch out? Gigi ain't a stranger to fights, darlin'."

Jilah chuckled softly. "You're full of surprises."

They made their way through the eerie, nicely decorated living room, towards the stairs. Not a thing was out of place. Maybe the happy couple spent most of their time upstairs?

Jilah felt a hand on her shoulder and quickly spun, finding nothing there. She frowned as she realized that someone was calling her name - but it sounded as if it was coming from very far away.

The features of the room began to fade and a chill went through her body as the voice became louder.

Everything faded out.

When Jilah next opened her eyes, Zolah was looking down at her, eyes wide with startlement.

Thea stood behind her, looking so very sad.

"Where... what happened?" Jilah blinked.

All at once, it came rushing in - emotion slammed into her like a freight train. Unbidden, a cathartic scream tore from her throat and the others in the room moved to hold her down to keep her from hurting herself.

Jilah woke to the sound of a familiar voice. Groggy, she shifted on the bed and opened her eyes. Her eyelids felt thick and heavy. Everything seemed to be happening in slow motion around her. She watched as Zolah turned to smile down at her.

"Back from the dead, I see," the woman chuckled. "How do you feel?"

Jilah's tongue felt thick and mushy in her mouth as she croaked, "Like I got hit by a bus. Maybe a couple of them."

She tried to sit up and a symphony of pain crashed through her head, bringing tears to her eyes.

"Oh god," she groaned. "What the fuck?"

Zolah gently pushed her back down to the bed, her tone soft as she said, "You must rest, sister. You have much to heal."

Jilah looked around, trying to block the pain out as she tried desperately to figure out where she was. The bed itself was very comfortable, but it didn't really seem to belong in this room, this... cave. Flickering shapes danced on bare, clay walls from a lantern on a small table next to the bed.

"Where am I?"

"One of the recuperative suites at the Synod." Zolah explained. "Try to focus on the sound of the water. It will help."

Jilah frowned, wondering what the hell the woman was talking about. After a few moments, the sounds of a burbling fountain broke through her disorientation. Almost immediately, she started to relax as the water splashes echoed in the room, taking away some of her initial fear. She sighed and felt herself sink back into the mattress, relieved as the pain started to recede.

"Let it take you where you need to go, sister." Zolah murmured.

The sensation of falling was overwhelming as Jilah's eyes slid shut. Her stomach flopped, and she began feeling a little queasy. A riot of colors swirled around her as she opened her eyes and the sound of rushing water was now coming up quick from beneath her. She turned to look down to see a large, dark blue colored pool rushing up to meet her. Hues of teal and green rimmed the edges of the shoreline. She spotted a waterfall cascading into it from a cliff high above, thick with vibrant green foliage.

Fear shook through her as she plunged feet first into the dark blue depths. Sound became muddled and bubbles drifted around her as she struggled to breathe. A full minute passed before Jilah realized that she wasn't drowning. The sense of oppression immediately abated and Jilah began looking around as her descent slowed. Light from above reflected in jagged patterns that danced along her skin. The lake was crystal clear around her and Jilah's eyes tracked a large dark shape as it moved through the water, off in the distance.

:: *Be not afraid, young avatar. None will cause harm to you in this place.* ::
A woman's voice, gentle and soothing, brushed against her awareness. A sense of tranquility settled into her bones, a very welcome feeling compared to the jangled sensation of waking in a foreign place.

A ribbon of mixed hues of indigo and green cut its way gracefully through the water, then another one appeared.

:: *What are you?* :: Jilah asked, transfixed by the delicate aquatic dance of color before her. The ribbons chased each other as she watched them spiral their way to parts above, to the surface.

:: *I am to be your guide now, little one. I will help you to repair that which has been sundered,* :: the voice explained.

Jilah frowned, trying to find the source of the voice. A dark shape was moving towards her and Jilah squinted to try to make sense of what she was seeing. As it came closer, she realized that it had a woman's shape.

:: *Is that you?* :: she asked, startled as she spotted a long, ornate tail connected to the lower half of the woman's torso. It started at the woman's hips, blue-green scales glittering along the thick, powerful tail as the light from above played against them.

Soft laughter echoed in her thoughts and the voice replied, :: *Tell me what you see.* ::

Well, hell, she'd seen weirder things at this point

:: *It looks like a mermaid.* ::

Jilah felt curious amusement as the voice responded, :: *Intriguing. I am consistently surprised and pleased by the variety of forms that your kind sees in me.* ::

As the mermaid drew closer, Jilah could see that the human appearing portion of her torso had a bluish tinge to its skin. Swirls of luminescent scales decorated her body, accentuating her curves. Thin, filmy fins that started just under her ribcage flared out from her sides, rippling in the water like the material of a delicate, flowing evening gown. The face was a bit flatter than a normal human face, but no less beautiful because of it. Thin membranes quickly blinked over enormous tilted eyes as the mermaid peered back at her.

A mane of seaweed green hair flowed like liquid around her head and shoulders, swaying gently with her movements.

:: *Are you the Emptor?* :: Jilah asked, remembering what she'd read a lifetime ago.

The mermaid shook her head and smiled as it positioned itself before her, reaching an inquisitive hand out to gently brush her temple. Each of the creature's fingers had thin webbing between them.

:: *Your true face – it is different from the others.* ::

The mermaid looked puzzled, peering at her with the naked curiosity of a child.

Jilah looked embarrassed and quickly explained, :: *Oh, yeah... uh... I was kinda merged with the... ::*

The mermaid looked startled and blinked as it pulled away from her to look her over.

:: *Yes. I see now. Little one, this is no cause for shame.* ::

The mermaid moved to hold her hand, aqua, jewel-toned eyes peering back at her with sympathy.

:: *You are the child of the destroyer.* ::

Jilah winced, uncomfortable of the reminder.

The mermaid nodded, and the dark green mass of hair around her head flowed around her face with the movement.

:: *Much unbalance has been wrought, and much must be made right.* ::

:: *You're talking about the people she... consumed through me.* :: Jilah replied, looking down and willing herself not to think about Argent. Of all the things she'd done, that was the sorest point of regret. :: *How do I make it right? I don't know of a way to bring them back.* ::

:: *There is nothing to be done about the flow that was disrupted in the lives you presented to the one who consumes. They are gone from the stream and will not re-enter it.* ::

A pain pierced Jilah's heart, reopening the wound she thought she'd closed back in Africa. The mermaid placed a gentle hand on Jilah's chest, peering into her eyes.

:: *It is this you must fix. Here lies the imbalance that must be resolved. All else will take care of itself.* ::

Despair crept in, wrapping around her psyche. :: *I don't know if I can.* ::

:: *There was a life in you before this...* :: the mermaid explained.

Jilah looked back at her, feeling hollow and nauseous from the inside out. :: *That was shit. My existence before all this was shit. I was nothing and nobody, and this – HE helped me... LIVE instead of simply existing.* ::

The mermaid peered back at her and replied. :: *The source of this strength is not external. It in you then, little one, even if you did not see it. It is why she chose you.* ::

Jilah shook her head, angry.

:: *She suckered me. I was just an easy mark.* ::

:: *Are you so sure of that?* ::

Jilah looked away, becoming less comfortable with the conversation. A pressure started building in her head and the embers of her anger began burning brighter.

:: *I ended the only person that ever really mattered to me – by HER command, and then ran off to do anything else she told me to.* ::

She wrapped her arms around herself, her anger chilling her to the bone. :: *I'm weak and don't deserve...* ::

Eminently patient, the mermaid replied, :: *You twist yourself up with sorrow, cutting yourself with it in the belief that you now have no worth.* ::

:: *What, so you're a shrink now?* :: Jilah snapped, irritated.

:: *Misdirected anger will not help you resolve the rending of your spirit. It will only lead you further from it.* ::

:: *Please... just... let me grieve.* ::

And there it was.

Jilah felt the pain in her heart swell up, almost choking her until it finally spilled out and away from her in an inky, black cloud.

The mermaid pulled her into an embrace and Jilah wept.

"Don't try to move, I'll get it for you."

Jilah opened her eyes to see Zolah reaching out to hand her a glass of water with a straw in it. Jilah laughed and it came out as a dry croak. *Water, water, everywhere...* she thought to herself. Her lips felt tight as she smiled at the irony.

The cool liquid was a blessing to her parched throat. Zolah had to stop her from gulping it all down a couple of times, but Jilah finally started pacing herself, drinking more slowly. When she'd finally had her fill, she looked over at Zolah and handed the empty glass back to her. Her friend smiled at her, a question in her eyes.

Jilah answered, describing all that she could remember as Zolah's expression lit up, joyous.

"The Water Mother! This is a wonderful sign!"

Jilah shifted in the bed, coughing. Her throat was still a little rough, but the water had helped, as had the time spent with this Water Mother than Zolah spoke of. Her heart, while still heavy, felt a little lighter now. The oppressive weight of misery and loss was slowly starting to ease down.

Jilah still wasn't sure if this was a good thing or not, but she supposed that it was at least progress.

"How long was I out?"

Zolah gently patted her arm and explained, "It has been a week since you last opened your eyes."

Jilah boggled.

"A week??"

Zolah nodded. "Time passes very differently with the Water Mother. Still, this is the longest that one of our own has been catatonic during a visit with her."

Jilah tried to sit up and winced at a pain in her groin.

Zolah's expression was apologetic as she explained, "We had to catheterize you, otherwise... "

Jilah held a hand up, stopping her.

"I get it. Ugh, it aches."

"Did the Water Mother say that you would be seeing her again?" Zolah asked, leaning towards her a little.

Jilah nodded, groaning at the pain it caused in her head. At least it wasn't as wretched as the last time she'd woken.

"In a roundabout way, yeah."

Zolah nodded, then replied, "Then we will need to leave it in for when she next takes you away. The visits will not be far apart, from what others have said in the past."

Jilah shifted again, trying to find a comfortable position.

"Do you see her differently? I mean – how does she look to you?"

Zolah smiled and leaned back in her chair.

"She comes to me in the wind, a fierce ebony skinned warrioress with many swords and knives. There is always a storm rumbling in the background when she speaks, and the air itself is alive with movement."

Jilah pondered that for a moment, then asked, "Why do you think her appearance alters so much from person to person?"

Zolah shrugged. "I cannot say why she chooses to show herself in different ways. It is possible that it is not she who projects the image to us, but we who project what we need most for her to be onto her."

"I gotta say I'm not entirely comfortable with trusting anything all that much at this point," Jilah replied bitterly.

Zolah nodded patiently. "Given what you have endured, I can understand your hesitation."

Jilah took a deep breath, then frowned, asking, "Where do I go from here? I mean, once I'm up and around again?"

The sense of loss and disorientation was beginning to come back. The overwhelming feeling of having to deal with everything at once shook her, and she fisted her hands at her sides, willing herself to stay calm.

Zolah leaned back in her seat and replied, "We understand that it is early in the process for you, but Thea wanted you to know that you are most welcome to stay with us; to continue the fight."

Jilah tried to laugh, and winced at a sudden pain in her side.

"Yeah. Let me get back to you on that."

Argent sat on the roof of the convent, dread rising in him as the horizon slowly became lighter.

"You sure you want to do this?" Aurelian sat beside him, jostling him gently with a shoulder.

Argent nodded, taking a deep breath. "I need to know."

"It's just... this seems a bit extreme."

Argent's lips curved in a wry smile as he replied, "You are familiar with the saying 'Nothing ventured, nothing gained'?"

Aurelian chuckled, then leaned back to rest on his palms, holding himself up as he muttered, "This isn't exactly like dipping a toe in."

Argent looked over at the large, person sized, black matte finish metal box beside them, locked into place on the roof. A heavy, black wool blanket also lay on top of Argent's legs.

"It is not as if I haven't taken precautions," he explained.

"But Judiana..."

"Judiana was a great deal younger."

He then turned to the selkie with a fond grin.

"And you are here to cover me, should anything untoward happen."

The first fingers of dawn began peeking over the horizon and Argent shivered. Aurelian turned towards him, his golden eyes glittering.

"At the first sign of trouble..."

"Yes, yes – you really are turning into quite the mother hen, you know?"

Argent waved him off, mesmerized by the coming of the sun.

At the first bright sign of the edge of the orb itself, Argent steadied himself, wondering when the pain would hit. So far, he couldn't detect any. Aside from the fear that things might go horribly wrong, he had to admit that the scene before them was magnificent. Nothing could have prepared him for the overwhelming emotion that shook through him as he witnessed his first sunrise in almost three hundred years.

"Does it hurt?"

There were no words for this experience.

"Oh god. I had forgotten how much I missed it," he murmured, shaking his head. "No – there is no pain."

The colors of their surroundings grew bright and bold as the sun slowly rose into the sky, almost blinding him.

"I thought I would never again see the world bathed in light."

His eyes brimmed with tears. "She was right. This truly is a gift."

After a few minutes had passed, Aurelian murmured, "It also changes things…"

Argent looked over at him, frowning.

"Yes – of course. It changes everything."

Argent stood up, letting the blanket fall to his feet. He moved to the edge of the building to peer down at the street below.

"I feel absolutely no ill effects – no pain, no nausea."

He paused for a moment, wondering about something before he asked, "Come here."

The selkie moved toward him and Argent grabbed his wrist, holding it up and sniffing it. His tongue darted out to taste the selkie's skin and Aurelian shivered as Argent bit down. The zing his body gained from the blood was still the same as he remembered. The man was still as delicious as ever.

He looked up at Aurelian, his lips curling in a blood colored smile. "Apparently, I am still sanguine."

Aurelian chuckled softly, "And apparently, I still taste good."

"Always." Argent grinned, licking his lips before looking back towards the sun. He took a deep breath, sobering.

"Even if this is the only thing that has changed, it is a sizeable power shift." He frowned. "I cannot see the Council being comfortable with this."

Aurelian thought about it for a moment, then replied, "We don't have to tell them."

Argent shook his head, unsure.

"Perhaps it will be enough that Roane is leaving the city – otherwise, this would be seen as a rather egregious power grab."

He looked back at the selkie and added, "There was already concern enough with a sanguine that can command armies of the dead. With her relocating…"

Argent pursed his lips, thinking. He clasped his hands behind his back and said, "She will need to leave as soon as she is able because of this."

Reacting to the sad tone that had crept into his voice, Aurelian moved to place a hand on his Strigaisha's shoulder.

"It's all happening faster than you wanted it to, but that might just work."

Argent nodded, feeling a pain in his heart at having to send Roane and Ariane away so soon.

"I'll talk to her when she rises tonight." He turned to head back into the convent. "Any delay on this will be seen poorly by the Council. It needs to be resolved as quickly as possible."

:: *Just how far down are we, anyway?* ::

Any light from above had now disappeared entirely and Jilah blinked in the cold depths of the water around them.

:: *Do you fear the darkness, little one?* ::

Jilah shook her head, unnerved, but unshaken.

:: *I've been through much worse than this.* ::

:: *Indeed you have - another point of strength to draw on. Remember this and it will serve you well.* ::

She felt a ripple around her as the Water Mother moved closer.

:: *We are not even to the midpoint of the depths of the Well.* ::

:: *The well?* :: Jilah asked, confused.

The mermaid's tone was amused as she replied, :: *It is a depth of the knowledge of oneself that you seek, and this body of water is a repository for the experiences that will show you what you most need to see.* ::

:: *It won't be unpleasant, will it?* ::

:: *Truth is rarely easy to confront, but it will not all be difficult.* ::

A cool hand wrapped around her own, pulling her downwards and Jilah steeled herself.

Suddenly, an image flared to life in her mind. Her father towered over her, his face red with anger. He seemed to be yelling something, but it sounded muddled. It was difficult to make out what he was saying.

:: *Focus, little one.* ::

Jilah blinked as the sound suddenly seemed to click into place. The man was raging.

"Why can't you be like the other girls in your school? Why do you have to be so goddamned unhappy all the time? That's what I don't understand."

A jolt shook her as she finally remembered this moment. Her sixteenth birthday was a week away. She looked over to see her younger body covered in frumpy, baggy clothes. She'd forgotten that it had been her uniform for so many years.

"We just want you to be happy, sweetheart."

Her mother had tears in her eyes. It was an old argument that just wouldn't die out.

"Remember this?"

Her own young, bitter voice sounded so savage to her ears as she watched her younger body raise up her shirt, pointing to the scar that bisected her stomach.

Her father lost a little steam and lamely replied, "It's God's gift, honey. Nothing to be ashamed of."

"Tell that to the bitches that saw it one day and told everybody in school about it," she growled, working up a fine red rage of her own. "Tell everybody else that hisses 'Frankenstein' at me whenever they pass me in the hallway!"

"Hey!" her father interjected, "Language."

"FUCK YOU and your language! You never hear me anyway! You and mom could give a shit if my life is miserable."

Jilah grimaced, not liking how petulant and petty it sounded.

Whoa, EMO train.

"I wish the doctor had let me die!"

Jilah watched as her younger self stormed from the room – witnessed her mother's shoulder slumping in defeat as her father yelled, "That's YOUR DAUGHTER, Jocelyn!"

He turned and walked towards the kitchen, hands fisted at his sides. Her mother simply sat down on the couch and placed her head in her hands, crying.

Always in between, with no way out, Jilah thought to herself, surprised to find herself sympathizing with the woman she'd never really gotten to know. Jilah hadn't really allowed herself to be known in return.

:: *Our tempers must have rubbed her raw.* ::

:: *The humans, they each have their own burdens to carry. And they are each here to help others best carry theirs. It is unfortunate that they do not always understand this.* ::

A pot clanged across the kitchen floor and her mother's shoulders began to shake. Jilah shook her head and asked, :: *What am I supposed to be learning here?* ::

:: *Self pity always hurts, and often it hurts more than one person. There is no benefit to it.* ::

:: *So, I need to pull my head out of my ass and stop feeling sorry for myself? Yeah, I get that.* :: Jilah replied, a little irritated.

:: *The point is more than this. When you were human, the repercussions were small, almost insignificant.* ::

:: *And now?* ::

:: *In many ways, you are so much larger and have more of an effect on everything around you.* ::

:: *So, 'With great power comes great responsibility', right?* ::

There was a pause before the Water Mother responded.

:: *That is a suitable way of putting it.* ::

Well, shit.

Jilah sighed, then nodded, finally hitting a point of understanding. Killing Argent was something she didn't think she'd ever truly get over. And yet, with the dark psycho in her head gone, things had changed yet again. She wouldn't be ridden anymore, forced into service to the point of breaking. She could make her own rules, somehow come to terms with what she was now, without the hindrance of something that was using her simply to erase people from existence. It was a chance to start over, with the help and guidance of her newfound family at the Synod.

It was time to get back to work.

Roane looked back at him, stunned as Ariane dropped down on the bed, staring straight ahead.

The Necromancer took a deep breath, then nodded.

"I understand. I don't like it, but... I understand."

Argent winced, wanting so badly to be able to take the words back.

"I am... sorry, little Roane. I will do all in my power to help you relocate. I spoke with Ellis earlier today and he says that there will be a place for you to lockdown for the night when you arrive. You'll be bunking with him for about a week until your new residence is ready."

Roane moved to sit beside her lover, sliding an arm around her. Ariane leaned her head against Roane's shoulder, remaining silent as tears trailed down her cheeks.

:: *It's harder for her than I thought it would be.* :: Roane sent with a tone of regret. :: *It is for me too.* ::

Argent watched them comfort each other for a moment, then sent.

:: *It is happening much sooner than I am comfortable with myself. I do not wish to see you go.* ::

He was losing members of the court far too quickly for his liking. First Jilah, and now this. He winced when he thought about how the court's cagliostro, Gigi, would react to the news.

He took a deep breath, then asked, :: *Do you wish me to tell Gigi, or is this news that you would rather share with her directly?* ::

He didn't want to take the decision out of her hands. Far too much was already being pushed upon her. She needed to retain some sense of order and control. It was the least he could offer her.

Roane gave him a pained look, swallowed and then quietly replied, :: *I'll do it. She wouldn't appreciate hearing about it any other way.* ::

Argent nodded, relieved but at a loss of what to do. There was nothing he could say or do to take the bite out of the situation.

:: *I will do all I can to ensure that this transition is as smooth as possible for you. Would that I could do more...* ::

Roane shook her head and held a hand up.

:: *Don't tear yourself up about it, boss. We'll get back up after this. We'll be fine.* ::

Argent couldn't help but smile. He hardly needed to be reassured, given what was happening, but he still appreciated the effort. Oh, he would miss her - miss them both, greatly.

Roane then looked up at him with wonder in her eyes as she asked, :: *So... what was it like?* ::

:: *I shall never be able to do justice to the experience with mere words. But it felt like... a benediction.* :: He replied, his eyes dancing as he wished that he could share it with her someday.

Roane smiled back at him. :: *In spite of everything, I'm really happy for you, boss.* ::

Aloud, she said, "Do you know if she'll be able to come back in time to say goodbye?"

A dull pain flared in his chest as Ariane looked up to meet his gaze as well. They both missed his lover very much and Roane in particular had been hounding him for answers lately about Jilah; when she would be back, why she couldn't at least take time to visit.

"I honestly don't know. If it's possible for her to do so, I'm sure she will."

Roane reached out to take his hand, her eyes full of sympathy.

"Don't think I haven't noticed you working yourself into the ground so you won't think about it."

Argent chuckled softly and squeezed her hand.

"I shall miss your sharp tongue, little Roane. You will have to find other outlets in which to exercise it, I'm afraid."

Roane grinned and hugged Ariane, who was at least smiling with them now.

"I'm sure I'll find inventive ways to give you shit from out in Kansas."

Laughing now, Argent replied, "Of that, I have little doubt."

Jilah stared at her reflection, horrified and fascinated. For the first time in weeks, she'd been able to actually get out of bed and make use of the facilities. She was not at all sorry to see the catheter go. The image in the mirror looked distorted, but some of the drastic changes she'd undergone in Africa were still present. At least her hands had changed back. Claws were handy for killing, but weren't exactly helpful when picking things up or holding them.

Trailing a finger along one of her horns, she sighed. "I started out looking so pretty in the beginning."

Zolah stood beside her, watching as Jilah then ran her fingers over the features of her own face.

"It is not conventional, true – but you are still beautiful, sister."

Jilah let out a harsh laugh.

"To another demon, maybe."

She shook her head, dismissing it.

"It doesn't matter."

She turned away from the reflection, her expression closing down.

"It's not like I'm gonna be trying to find a date anytime soon."

That part of her life was over. Now she needed to make do with what was left instead of feeling sorry for herself.

She walked back to the makeshift bedroom, stumbling a little along the way.

"How soon am I going to be ready to start working again?"

Zolah replied, "Your direction and ability must be assessed first."

"My... direction?"

"Each of us is assigned a Proctor that assesses our abilities. It is from this Proctor that we receive our assignments." Zolah explained. "They will not send you out until you are fully healed, however."

They reached the room and Jilah moved over to the bed, sitting down carefully.

"I can't stay here. Not in this room. There aren't enough distractions."

Jilah frowned, trying to shut off the natural tendency of her mind to go back to the most painful memories. With the help of Mother Water, she'd been able to meditate and find a state of tranquility in the Well, but now that she was out of it and back in the world, it was nowhere near as easy.

:: *You must find the place of no things in your mind. Go there when it becomes too difficult, little one.* ::

She remembered Mother Water's words and tried to find no-thingness within her consciousness, but like darts, her thoughts tore holes in the stillness she tried to construct. Tears brimmed at the edges of her eyes and she scooted back to lean up against the wall.

Zolah leaned forward and placed a hand on her shoulder.

"How can I help, sister?"

Jilah wiped the moisture away from her eyes, angry at herself. At her lack of control.

"Just – get me back in the game." Her voice cracked, sounding bleak.

You will not cry anymore over this, she growled at herself. *You made your decisions and now you have to suck it up and live with the consequences.*

Zolah nodded, sorrow in her eyes. "I understand. I will see what I can do."

She stood and left the room as Jilah pulled her knees up to her chest, wrapping her arms around her legs.

I just have to get through today. Every day. No big deal, right?

Jilah sighed and rested her head on her knees.

Shit.

"How'd Gigi take it?"

Argent leaned back against Aurelian as the colors of the night sky slowly faded into twilight. It had become a vigil of late, the nightly witnessing of the dying of the light. Argent still wasn't entirely sure why it fascinated him so much. He sighed and pulled the selkie's strong arms around him a little tighter.

"About as well as you'd imagine. There was a great deal of yelling."

There had been many tears as well. He'd checked in with Roane shortly afterwards. Understandably, she'd taken a few days to get herself together before sharing it with her dear friend. The cagliostro still walked around as if she'd lost something very vital and her eyes were full of pain. It still didn't interfere with her duties, and that in itself garnered a newfound respect for the woman from Argent.

Aurelian leaned into him, nuzzling his neck, his voice a low rumble as he murmured, "What do you need from me? I'll be that. Anything to help take this pain from you."

Argent watched as the first stars started to flicker against the slowly rising canopy of night.

"Tonight? Help me forget." His voice cracked, and he turned to rest his cheek against Aurelian's arm, his breathing shaky.

The selkie smiled, his tongue darting out to trace along the pulse in Argent's neck, gently biting down. The sanguine shivered and shifted in his arms, turning to capture Aurelian's lips in a fierce kiss. With a moan, Argent snaked fingers up into Aurelian's thick mane of blonde hair. An urgency thrummed through him, burning him from the inside out, and Argent pushed the selkie down, straddling him and rocking against him, drawing an answering groan from the large man.

Aurelian smiled up at him, chuckling softly.

"Should we take this inside?"

Argent shook his head, his voice thick with need.

"Fuck the neighbors."

The sanguine then dipped down to capture Aurelian's lips, cutting off any further conversation.

"Ow!"

Jilah watched as a welt rose on her thigh. Dammit! Another one! She kept getting tagged with those fucking rattan sticks. Still, it was good to be doing intense physical activity. It was remarkable how quickly a workout with the sticks cleared her head.

"You're getting better."

Her instructor, a diminutive woman with short cropped brown hair smiled back at her.

"You'll be back in the field soon."

Jilah nodded as they both dropped the sticks and began circling around the pit. Crouching, they slapped each other's palms, then tied up, pummeling.

Not soon enough, Jilah thought to herself as she feinted then took the smaller woman down, sprawling on top of her and pressing her hips down into her side to keep her from being able to buck her off. She then quickly switched the positioning of her legs, grabbing the woman's arm and pulling it into her chest. Spinning, she shoved one foot under the woman's shoulder and kicked across the woman's body with her other foot, slamming it down across her chest. Jilah then leaned back and pressed her hips up to finish the move.

The woman quickly tapped and Jilah let go as she heard somebody clapping above.

Zolah was grinning back at her, nodding.

"Your Proctor says it is time."

Jilah got to her feet. Good. She was ready.

Chapter 17
A TIME TO DEPART

"So."

Roane leaned against the doorframe to his bedroom, and Argent looked up to meet her troubled expression. He sighed and stood up. Their departure was already difficult enough without this added wrinkle.

:: *She's not going to be able to make it back in time, is she?* :: Roane asked softly.

Argent took a step towards her, shaking his head.

:: *I am afraid not.* ::

Roane frowned, and Argent could feel the first stirrings of anger roll through the necromancer. The longer Jilah stayed away, the more difficult it became to explain her absence to her friends. He still hadn't admitted to Roane that he hadn't seen her himself in several months. Aurelian alone knew the details, and that helped take some of the weight off the lie; but he was growing tired. He wasn't angry with Jilah; quite the opposite. The situation was unbearable, but there was very little that could be done about it, considering the circumstances.

Roane puffed out a breath of frustration, then sent, :: *I hope to hell what they're doing is helping.* ::

He could taste the irritation and disappointment in her words.

:: *I miss her too, little Roane. I had no idea she would have to be gone this long.* ::

Roane nodded, her brows knitting as she asked, :: *You still tell her she's missed right? When you see her?* ::

A pain flared in his chest as he forced a smile and replied, :: *Of course.* ::

:: *Shit, old man. I'm really gonna miss you.* ::

Roane walked up and pulled him into a tight hug.

Emotion threatened to overwhelm him as he circled his arms around her, returning the hug with a shaky sigh.

:: *You gonna be okay?* :: she asked, still holding him.

He thought about it for a moment, then tried to deflect the question.

:: *I can now step out into the light of the sun without coming to any harm. That in itself should be cause enough for rejoicing.* ::

Roane pulled back and looked up at him, her eyes narrowing as she snapped, :: *Don't bullshit a bullshitter.* ::

Argent forced a laugh, then gently pulled out of the embrace, taking a step back.

:: *I will endure.* ::

He paused for a moment as she nodded, understanding that this was the best answer she was going to get from him.

:: *And you, little Roane? And Ariane?* ::

Roane shook her head, frowning. :: *She's been manic all day. I wish there was some way I could leave her behind until the exhumations start up down here. Leaving her lineage behind, unprotected... it's really wrecking her.* ::

Argent nodded, knowing that it would be impossible. Ariane needed to stay close to Roane in order to get regular nightly infusions of the necromancer's blood.

:: *I will do all I can to ensure that her kin are cared for and protected as long as I hold the throne.* ::

Roane gave him a sad smile as she replied, :: *She'll appreciate that, Strigaisha.* ::

It was time. Argent stepped up to her and offered her an arm.

:: *Shall we?* ::

The necromancer grinned, and Argent could feel her doing her best to tamp down her own sadness at having to leave.

:: *Such a gentleman.* :: she crooned.

At this, Argent finally smiled and chuckled softly.

:: Don't tell anyone. It'll spoil my image. ::
Roane laughed and spoke aloud.
"Let's get this show on the road."

Roane and Ariane looked back at him, a little unsteady on their feet as Gigi walked up to them.

:: I am proud of you, little Roane. I know you'll shine in your new placement. ::

Roane nodded, wrapping her arm tighter around her mate. Argent gave a brief nod to Ariane, who was still a little too pissed about everything to be conversational with him. The mambo frowned, then nodded back, her expression neutral. Argent and Ariane hadn't really spoken since the pronouncement that the two of them would have to leave early.

Gigi looked back at him, her eyes brimming with tears; her face tight with unhappiness. Argent gave her a quick nod and Ariane blanched as the three of them disappeared. The cagliostro would ensure that the girls arrived quickly, and safely. He'd told Gigi to take a day or two for herself before returning; to make sure everybody got settled smoothly.

Argent turned and let out a sigh of relief. At least there would be fewer questions about Jilah's whereabouts to answer.

Until Gigi returned.

This would likely crank up the cagliostro's interest in the Striaga's return. Still, he would miss them a great deal.

A light presence skittered across his thoughts and he turned to find Mira standing at the edge of the throne room.

:: You have something to report? :: he asked her quietly.

Mira took a few steps toward him, then asked, *:: Is the Striaga coming back? ::*

Argent frowned as he looked back at her, trying to read her expression. True to form, it was blank and gave away nothing.

:: Why do you ask? ::

Mira paused for a few moments, then seemed to steel herself as she replied, *:: I want to know my options at this point. ::*

Argent thought about her wording for a moment, then sighed. *She thinks that I'll leave if Jilah doesn't come back. She's right to worry.*

If there had been a doubt that his lover would return to him, he would have walked away and not looked back.

:: *She will return. I do not know when.* ::

Mira took a deep breath, then nodded and turned to go. Argent caught the edge of a fleeting emotion and almost rocked back on his heels, shocked.

:: *You miss her,* :: he murmured.

Mira spun to face him, eyes narrowing as she glared back at him, her mouth tight with anger. Argent watched as her expression quickly closed down, her brow becoming placid and smooth again as she replied, :: *She kept things... interesting.* ::

Argent raised an eyebrow as Mira walked out of the room, then laughed out loud before walking back towards his office.

All of a sudden, the day didn't seem as glum as it had before.

Chapter 18
T**HE** PRO**C**TOR

"Wait, *she's* my proctor? She can't be more than sixteen years old."

Jilah looked over at the girl with the platinum blonde pixie haircut as she rolled around the room on neon green quad skates. Clad in white and black striped knee high socks, orange arm and knee pads, black jean short shorts and a tight pink babydoll t-shirt that read CARNAGE in large pink letters, the girl winked at her as she zoomed past.

"The host is sixteen, yes. The body is fairly new, but her demon? It is impossible to judge their true age." Zolah explained. "You should know by now that few things are rarely as they seem."

The girl skated up, stopping just short of colliding with them.

"Who's the new meat?" she asked.

Zolah sighed and shook her head.

"Zhara, this is the one Thea told you about."

The girl blinked and frowned. Jilah felt a warm wind blow along her skin and the girl grinned.

"Ah! There you are. Man, you look hot. Why'dya hide it? I'd ride around in that shit all day long."

Zolah snapped, "What have you been told about personal boundaries?"

The girl rolled her eyes dramatically and took off again.

"Yes, *mother*."

Jilah looked over at Zolah and blinked.

"You're kidding, right?"

The girl stopped in her tracks and Jilah watched as the color drained from her face. Zhara scrunched her features up in irritation, then rolled back over to them. Hazel eyes looked Jilah up and down, assessing.

"She's almost ready. I'll take her," she snapped. "Bring her back in a week."

Zolah breathed a sigh of relief and the girl was off again, doing elaborate turns and spins as she skated away.

How anybody can do that without breaking an ankle, I'll never know, Jilah thought to herself.

"Why a week?" she asked.

"Who can say with her?" Zolah waved her hand in irritation. "Still, she's the best one here."

"Weird." Jilah muttered. "Anyway, it'll be nice to get back to it."

They left the room, walking in companionable silence for a few moments.

"May I... ask you something?" Zolah prompted.

Jilah looked over at her and nodded.

"Sure – anything."

"I am... retiring in a month's time. I would very much like for you to be a part of the ceremony."

Jilah stopped and turned to stare at her.

"You're what?"

Zolah chuckled softly and explained, "I have been running with my companion for many years and I find that I no longer have the taste for the hunt anymore. I can feel that she is eager to dwell in a new host as well, so we are parting from each other. It is time for me to live the rest of my life, separate from this."

"Wait, you guys can do that? Separate from it without it killing you?"

Zolah replied, "It is part of the cycle, sister. We all become part of it for a time, until we are ready to age gracefully and live within the remains of a human life span."

Yeah, not so much an option for me, Jilah thought to herself. *Ah, well. It was no use dwelling on it.*

"I guess I hadn't gotten a chance to read up to that point in the books."

Zolah smiled and gently patted her arm. "You have had quite an intense distraction. It is understandable."

Jilah grinned back at her, still riding the high from her sparring session.

"I would be honored to be there for you, Zolah."

The woman surprised her by stopping and hugging her. "Thank you, my sister. My dear friend."

Jilah hugged her back, then asked, "So, you and Aaron gonna get hitched?"

Zolah blushed and pulled away.

"It is not their way, and I am not as old fashioned as all that, but I will be going to stay with his pack as his mate. It is something we have both been wanting for awhile."

Jilah grinned and replied, "I'm really happy for you. Thank you for letting me be a part of it."

Zolah smiled. "I would not have it any other way."

Jilah blinked at the sound of a foreign voice in her thoughts.

:: *Yo, new girl - you ready?* ::

Zhara's presence was light and relaxed in her mind; nothing like the sometimes oppressive feel of her previous mental roommate.

The avatar yawned, then shifted in the bed, rubbing at an eye.

:: *I just got to sleep...* :: she replied, frustrated.

:: *Cry me a river. Get up here.* ::

A location flashed in her mind and Jilah sat up. Frowning, she began moving around the room, getting dressed. Had it been a week already? She'd been pushing herself at such a frenzied pace that she often simply dropped into bed, exhausted, clothes and all. With no daylight streaming in through windows, there was no sense of time here, so the days all tended to blend together. There were so many martial arts styles to learn, so many quick and dirty ways to drop someone. All of it fascinated her. The desire to fight came from a driving need to test her limits, to see how far she could go. There was no way a human target would ever be capable of being an effective test. Too easy. Other sisters, however, that was another story. The challenge kept her going. There was sometimes a shared frustration at the nature of their work that gave them a special appreciation for being able to best somebody equally qualified in the realm of combat.

Jilah pulled her boots on, then sped off towards the room where she'd initially met the teenage proctor, wondering what she'd be wearing today. Jilah ducked into the room, wincing as she spotted her. Zhara rolled around the room in bright, lime green roller skates, purple hot pants with the word JUICY on the back and a black hoodie with a logo of a sexy red demon in a catholic school girl uniform on the back of it. The woman was winking and skating backwards, her fingertips pressed to her mouth as if getting ready to blow someone a kiss. The logo had the words Dark City Dames underneath it.

"Try not to look so excited."

The girl whooshed by with a grin.

Jilah took a step into the room and replied, "I have no idea what to expect. Hell, for all I know you could end up attacking me like Kato in those old Pink Panther movies."

The girl frowned and asked, "What?"

Jilah waved the question off.

"Nevermind. What'cha got?"

Zhara shrugged and said, "First, we need to establish the initial connection."

The girl began skating back towards her, eyes glittering.

"This will only hurt for a moment."

Jilah saw something shine in the girl's eyes and felt a hard yank that made her cry out briefly. A strange noise reverberated in her head and for a moment, it sounded as if she was standing in a very large hall that someone was moving furniture around in. The pull then stopped and she swayed on her feet.

:: You'll be able to hear me wherever you are now. Distance won't matter, :: Zhara explained.

The sound of her voice in Jilah's thoughts sounded more solid and for some reason, it was strangely reassuring.

Jilah opened her mouth to ask why and Zhara rolled away again once more.

:: Instead of receiving target information from that... thing that was in your head, you'll get it directly from me. Should be easier to understand, too. ::

The girl pulled a purple BlowPop out of the pocket of her hoodie, unwrapped it and popped it into her mouth.

So young, Jilah thought to herself as she shook her head.

:: I may be young, but I know what I'm doin'. And if I don't, my rider definitely does. Just trust that we won't put you in a situation where you're gonna be permanently damaged, and we'll get along just fine. ::

Zhara skated back towards her, then turned at the last minute, whipping past her. There was a strong scent of grape in the air as she went by.

:: Ok, next – terms. ::

The girl cracked her knuckles, placing her hands behind her head as she skated along at a maddening pace.

:: For the most part, we won't run you too far from your home base, wherever it happens to be. We're not assholes – we're adaptable. Since you're... something different than what the Synod's used to working with, we're going to need send you out on the tougher cases. Should still be a breeze for you, though. Just don't get too cocky. ::

Jilah nodded, and Zhara stopped, turning to face her, then said, *:: Ok, we're done. ::*

As the girl turned to skate away, Jilah frowned.

::Wait, that's it?::

Zhara winked back at her, then rolled away from her at a frenzied pace.

::For today, yes. Tomorrow, you go on your first run.::

Jilah nodded, glad that she was finally getting the green light. She paused for a moment, then asked, *:: Do you actually do roller derby? ::*

Zhara's answering smile was sharp, almost vicious. *:: Oh hell yes. ::*

Jilah blinked, frowning. *:: Isn't it unfair if you play against humans? ::*

Zhara laughed, skating away.

:: What, us Eventide chicks can't have fun too? ::

Startled, Jilah asked, *:: Wait, are you telling me that there's an entire league of... ::*

Zhara rolled past Jilah, shaking her head.

:: *No. There aren't enough sisters that are interested enough to form a league. Dark City Dames takes almost anybody; demons, shifters, we even have a troll or two.* ::

Jilah stood there for a moment, processing.

:: *You interested?* ::

Zhara asked, suddenly paying very sharp attention to her.

Jilah's lips curled into a slow smile.

:: *Let me think about it.* ::

Chapter 19
A BRIEF VACATION

Argent stood at the edge of the ocean in a pair of black and red board shorts, enjoying the feel of the water as it slowly softened the sand beneath his feet. With each pass, he wriggled his toes and sunk a little deeper into it. People all around him lounged in plastic beach chairs or on brightly colored towels, slathering themselves with oils and lotions that reeked of coconut, preparing themselves to be slowly roasted as they watched children cavort in the surf.

Aurelian's head bobbed above the waves, a bright blonde spot in all that turquoise and green. Argent marveled at the scenery around him, thrilled after never thinking that he would witness anything like this again in his lifetime. The sky was a clear cerulean canvas with only a few wisps of white clouds drifting across it. It still amazed him that he could stand out in the daylight, completely unharmed. The sunlight was warm, but not uncomfortably so, and he watched as other people frolicked in the surf. The water had a slight chill, but it was pleasant enough as it licked around his ankles.

Argent couldn't remember ever seeing Aurelian as happy as he was now, at home in his element. He felt a guilty that he'd pushed off the idea of going to the beach as long as he had. Aurelian had kept pressuring him to go after the discovery that he'd no longer expire in direct sunlight, obviously wanting to share the one thing the selkie loved most in the world with him. Argent could tell that it touched Aurelian deeply that he'd finally said yes. The sanguine sighed, relieved that he could still find pleasure in this.

The last report from the Synod was very positive; Jilah was progressing by leaps and bounds. He smiled, remembering how pleased Thea had looked as she had detailed the daily martial arts regimen Jilah was putting herself through. The woman was obviously very proud of his Striaga. He was as well. She was recovering quite nicely.

The other day, Thea had alluded to the possibility of him being able to sit in observation over one of her training sessions in the near future. Of course, Jilah wasn't ready to see him yet, but it was enough that he would be able to be near – to watch her. His heart leapt at the very idea. It had improved his temper immensely.

Aurelian began swimming back to shore and Argent walked in to meet him halfway.

The selkie was grinning from ear to ear as he pulled the sanguine into his arms.

"Thank you for this."

Argent blinked as a child pointed at him from the shore and asked his mother, "Mommy, why's that man so pale? And why is he hugging that other man?"

The woman quickly grabbed the boy's hand and led him away, shushing him.

"How pedestrian," Argent grumbled.

Aurelian laughed and said, "Fuck 'em" as he pulled the sanguine into a quick kiss.

Argent smiled and pushed the selkie back into the surf. Aurelian then reached out and grabbed his wrist, pulling him under. Argent spluttered as his head broke the surface of the water, looking over at Aurelian as he splashed him.

"Oh, it's like that, is it?" he asked, cocking his own hand back to return the volley.

Aurelian laughed and nodded, his voice a low rumble as he replied, "Oh yeah. Better bring your A game. I intend to kick your ass."

"Better men than you have tried, and failed."

The sanguine laughed now, splashing back before ducking beneath the waves and pulling the selkie's legs out from under him.

Chapter 20
BACK IN THE SADDLE

Jilah collided with the wall across the room, wincing before she hit the floor.

:: Ow! ::

Zolah shook her head and replied, :: *He is simply stronger than you initially suspected. Re-assess, then come at him from a different angle.* ::

Being able to communicate mentally with Zolah was a nice added bonus of the joining with the teen rollergirl from hell. It definitely made it easier than yelling at each other. This way Zolah could shadow her without Jilah giving away her mentor's location.

Jilah quickly sprang to her feet blurring out of reach of a surprisingly small, wiry man.

:: *What the hell, Zolah? Why's he so strong?* ::

:: *I believe he is currently under the influence of Phencyclidine.* ::

Jilah blinked as the man threw a television at her, blurring out of the way just in time to see it crash against the wall, the screen shattering and the frame sagging as it hit the floor. :: *Fensi what?* ::

:: *Street parleyance is PCP - it apparently brings on agitation and psychosis,* :: Zolah explained.

The man's fist went through the wall as Jilah ducked again, and she shot back, :: *Apparently. Ok, time to change tactics.* ::

Her target's overly aggressive nature had thrown her at first, and it took a minute or two to remember that she should easily be able to overpower him. Jilah blurred behind him, catching him in a sleeper hold, wrapping her legs around his waist and squeezing. Hands slapped at her and one of them caught her horns, becoming impaled on it briefly before the man's eyes rolled up into his head and he finally dropped to the floor. Jilah hit first, groaning.

:: *Fucksakes, how long does this crap take to wear off?* :: she asked, releasing him and moving quickly to tie his hands behind his back.

:: *You should be able to slide through it once he wakes and you call the memories back to him.* ::

Zolah approached her with another length of rope and helped tie his legs together.

Jilah straddled the man and frowned. Remembering something from what seemed like a lifetime ago, she tried dipping into his mind. The jumble she found there was entirely too disorienting and she struggled to find something to grab onto, anything to bring him back to awareness. She blinked as she locked onto it. The memory was sharp and visceral, a mother's punishment for spilling milk all over the counter during dinner. The sadistic woman had beaten him with a wooden spoon with a 'W' carved into the end of it, not stopping until most of his buttocks were bloody. Jilah yanked at it and the man bucked beneath her, screaming.

:: *What did you do?* :: Zolah asked, startled. :: *This is hardly an improvement.* ::

:: *Don't ask.* :: She jammed a piece of cloth into his mouth. He was snapping like a dog, and she really didn't want to get bitten. The man bucked like a bronco and Jilah couldn't help wishing she had a saddle of some kind. Trying to stay on top of him was proving to be difficult.

"Hey!" She backhanded him, careful to pull back on the strike. She didn't need him physically shattered.

"HEY ASSHOLE!"

The man looked up at her, eyes crazed and unfocused.

"Shit. I guess this is as good as it's going to get." Jilah muttered to nobody in particular as she tried to snare his mind with her gaze. If only he'd meet it.

Jilah frowned, then smiled as she thought of something. Dipping into his thoughts again, she twisted his psyche, rearranging what he was seeing until she looked like his mother, spoon in hand. The man stared straight at her, one long muffled scream almost escaping around the cloth material that forced his mouth open.

There we go.

Jilah felt a small psychic conduit open between them as she took a deep breath and called the memories to her, telling them where to go. This was the hard part – not forcing it and cracking the target's psyche immediately. She then dipped down and bit into the man's neck, drinking her fill. An odd swell of relief flowed through her as the memories came, smoothly flowing through the temporary connection.

:: What's that? I've never felt that before. ::

Zolah sat beside her and explained, *:: The memories of his victims are now being given the chance to guide their own vengeance on him instead of simply being forced into his grey matter like a knife. ::*

The man stopped screaming and Jilah sat up, wiping her mouth. His breathing became labored for a few moments, then stopped as he expired.

:: It seems... anticlimactic. :: she mused.

:: For you, it is, :: Zolah replied, then looked down at the body.

:: I do not think he would share that assessment. ::

Jilah sighed, then stood up and looked around.

:: What do I do now? Do we get rid of it? ::

:: Bring the body back with us. We'll take care of it at the Synod proper. You did good for your first run back on the job. ::

Jilah could almost feel Zhara smiling at her through the connection.

:: We'll have you back in the field within the next few days, I think. ::

Jilah nodded, sobering and feeling better than she had in a good, long while.

At least she was doing something now.

"Thea wants you in the war room in five."

Jilah lowered her weapon, nodded to her sparring partners, and headed to the door. It now took two or more of them to really put her through her paces at this point. There wasn't really time to get cleaned up, so she hoped it wasn't going to be a formal meeting. She gently placed the weapon back onto the pegs on the wall, then rushed to the war room.

She was startled to find six other sisters there; she'd shed blood with each of them on the training floor. Each was tight and toned, and they all shifted on their feet, looking at each other in silence. She looked around the room, spotting the vivid images of multiple dead women that decorated the walls. They appeared to either have been beaten beyond recognition or otherwise tortured.

Jilah's jaw dropped, and she wondered what was going on. A quiet fury echoed around the room, so thick Jilah could almost reach out and touch it.

As her eyes touched on each image, her rage began to spiral upwards. The low hum of violence barely contained seemed to spin in the center of the room and Jilah's eyes opened in startlement as her anger touched a point of familiarity. Six other points, to be exact. With the emotions of the women in the room so focused, she could almost see a swirl of their combined wrath building before them, black and purple corkscrews that danced around and entwined with each other.

"Ladies, I shall ask you to leash your tempers for the next ten minutes."

Thea walked into the room, her expression grim as she explained, "What you see before you is the collected information from two other Synods, both in eastern Europe. The violence depicted within is the aftermath of one of the largest human trafficking rings we've found so far."

Thea moved to stand before them, clasping her hands at her waist. Zolah stepped into the room, staying by the door, watching as Thea continued, "Several of you are familiar with what must now happen next. The rest of you will need to look to the direction of your seniors."

She turned and began pacing and Jilah watched as the grip of her hands tightened.

"In rare cases, we intervene in large forces to separate the wheat from the chaff, as it were. It has been at least a year since we've been tasked with an operation of such magnitude."

Thea turned and faced them.

"There are live victims still in the field, which makes this encounter all the more deadly. Your orders are clear, cripple your targets and extract the women who remain living. Once that's been completed, we'll assess the Synod's next move."

Thea's eyes met Jilah's and a sharp smile played along the edges of her lips.

"We are fortunate to have a... I believe the term is a *'ringer'*, among you on this excursion."

Several of the woman laughed softly and Jilah felt her cheeks heat.

Thea rolled her shoulders back and murmured, "You leave in an hour. Prepare yourselves. This will not be easy."

The seven of them crouched on the long horizontal jib of a tower crane overlooking a large construction site. Jilah frowned as she looked down at the area below. Jannah, the woman on point, pointed over towards three shipping containers at the edge of the yard.

:: *That's the target.* ::

Jilah watched as the last of the clients filtered out of the shipping containers. Several enormous, well armed men stepped out and pushed the container doors closed, locking the 'workers' in for the night.

Jannah looked down from their vantage point at the top of the crane, pointing towards several armed men that stood around the perimeter of the site.

:: *Ladies, you have your targets. Don't finesse it. Take them down quick and hard, then get in the yard as quickly as possible.* ::

She turned to look over at Jilah and asked, :: *You gonna be able to do this without throwing up this time?* ::

Jilah narrowed her eyes back at Jannah, her stomach already turning.

:: *Just fucking do it already. I'll meet you down there.* ::

The other sisters chuckled, knowing her penchant for nausea shortly after porting. They'd been ribbing her about it for awhile now. It had been irritating at first, but now she found it... reassuring. Like she was finally becoming a member of the family.

:: Ok, princess. MARK. ::

Jilah watched as the six of them disappeared, then steeled herself before closing her eyes. Her ears popped and the air around her rushed for a moment before she found herself on the top of one of the containers. She immediately crouched, doing her best to soundlessly lay flat against the top, grateful that they were all barefoot. Her boots would've definitely made too much noise on the metal roof. She slapped a hand over her mouth as she fought back the nausea, determined to get to a point where she stopped feeling it every damned time.

Once she felt she had it under control, Jannah's voice rang through her mind, *:: Targets at the perimeter down, stay on the roof until I tell you to go. ::*

Jilah stayed completely still, listening to the various callbacks in her thoughts from the other sisters as they started coming in. She was their heavy hitter on this first big run and was supposed to stay out of the action unless something went really wrong. Although she wanted to be in the thick of it, she supposed she understood the reasoning. Even through months of daily training, she was still green at heavy duty missions.

:: Okay, the men at the doors are down. We're going in. Stay connected and keep an eye out. ::

Jilah couldn't help but admire Jannah's confidence and ability. She'd been sparring with the woman for a month now, and she still hadn't found an easy way to take the woman down and keep her there. The sisters, rather than becoming jealous of her enhanced abilities, looked forward to sparring with her. They liked that Jilah pushed them to go all out. Adapting to life in the Synod was becoming a little easier and Jilah felt a settling in her heart that she didn't think she'd get close to again. It was something she was profoundly grateful for.

Movement in the corner of her eye caught her attention and she looked up to see a car coming down the ramp into the yard.

:: We've got company. Car's comin'. :: she sent to the sisters inside.

:: Can you handle it? :: Jannah asked.

Jilah watched as the car stopped at the edge of the yard.

:: *Shit. They see the guards down. They're radioing for backup. Finish up inside and I'll take care of the assholes in the car,* ::

Jilah blurred across the yard and jammed clawed fingers into the driver's side door. With a savage yank, she heard the groan of metal as it puckered and pulled away from the car. She tossed it behind her and let her glamour drop, laughing as the men in the car began to scream and scrabble to get away from her.

She could hear light laughter in her thoughts as her handler, Zhara, chuckled and said, :: *Now, now. Don't play with your food.* ::

Jilah hauled the driver out and smacked his head on the roof, knocking him out cold. He slumped to the ground and several loud popping sounds echoed out from inside the car, followed by a ringing sound in her ears. A dull pain blossomed in her midsection and she growled, baring her teeth.

:: *Fucker shot me,* :: she grated, picking the car up and slamming it down with a force that surprised her. The men inside were now weeping and crying out in pain. Not one of them had been wearing a seat belt. She reached out and dug through their surface thoughts, looking for helpful images. She couldn't understand a damned thing that they'd said so far, and images were always easier to figure out. The bullet wounds began itching and she balled her hands into fists against the sensation.

The man in the back had a collection of images in his thoughts that were very interesting indeed. Jilah darted in and yanked, siphoning them off and spooling them into her memory so that she could recount them later if he died from his injuries. The man's face went slack as she drew the images out, his hands clawing at the leather seats in the back of the vehicle.

:: *One of them got a call off. I couldn't stop them in time. Others are coming. How many are left inside?* ::

She reached in and grabbed the man in the passenger seat, sinking her teeth into his neck and pulling hard on the red stuff just beneath his skin. The itching quickly faded and she sighed with relief.

:: *Thirty more. We're going to need a little help in here.* ::

:: *I'll be right in.* ::

Jilah finished her meal, breaking the man's neck and dropping him to the ground. She then dipped into the minds of the three men left, twisting and wrenching their psyches effortlessly. They wouldn't be saying anything articulate to anybody about this incident, or anything else, for the rest of their lives.

She blurred over to one of the containers, wincing at the stench before ducking inside. The conditions in the small metal space were appalling. Each of the women was kept in an area that was large enough for a twin bed and a bucket. Some had pillows and blankets, some didn't. All of them were in a fevered sweat, their haunted stares looking out at nothing as they reached out to her – not for help, but for a fix. The women were in varying stages of withdrawal. They didn't even have the luxury of curtains separating them.

Jilah shuddered, both disgusted and dismayed. It was almost worse than Africa. Almost.

Stajia walked up to her and slapped something into her hand, a necklace of some sort.

"You need to start doing this on your own power at some point, and we don't have enough hands to get them all out of here. Put it on, then touch it when you're ready to bounce back to the Synod. Once you've dropped one of your packages off, touch it again and you'll come right back. It's keyed between the two places, which should make it easier."

Jilah closed her eyes and felt a cool chill rush along her skin. Something in her stomach twisted and she felt strong hands on her shoulder.

"Get past it, Jilah. Work now. These women need you."

Jilah nodded and quickly put the necklace on. She reached down to pull one of the more frail looking women into her arms, startled to realize that the girl looked only about fifteen years old.

React later. Focus now. Get it done, she told herself as she touched the small silver medallion around her neck.

After a brief popping sound, she opened her eyes, startled to find herself in a room busy with activity. Someone was rushing towards her, pulling the body out of her arms.

"Get back out there!" someone yelled.

Jilah fought a wave of nausea as she touched the medallion again and was gone.

After four more trips Jilah realized that she no longer felt the nausea that usually accompanied the jaunts. She was about to reach down again when alarm sang through her mind.

:: They're here – Jilah, take 'em out. We're almost done here. ::

She blurred outside, grateful to be out of that horrible enclosed space. Several cars were pulling up and men with guns were stepping out. She quickly pulled up her shields, blanking the minds of the men to her presence as she ran at the first car. Something in her psyche sent what felt like quicksilver through her veins and her body reacted. It was a rush bordering on erotic as she darted from target to target, dropping them quickly and efficiently before any of them could get a round off.

She then picked up the first car, lifting it up and over her head, then slamming it roof first down on top of the car behind her. The remaining car began backing up and Jilah grinned wickedly as she let her glamour drop. She jumped into the air and landed on the hood, smashing it into the top of the engine. The men inside screamed and the car began weaving back and forth. Jilah crouched and jammed the claws of her left hand into the hood to keep from sliding off, then punched her way through the windshield with her right, reaching in and slashing at the driver's neck. Dark sprays zipped in chaotic, looping patterns on the inside of the windshield and she stabbed her claws into the driver's chest, gripping behind his ribcage and pulling him out through the windshield. She leapt off the hood of the car before it collided into a cement truck with a loud metallic smack.

Three men poured out of the car, running towards a small shack and Jilah shook her head, making a tutting sound. She blurred in front of them and reached into their psyches, stopping them in their tracks and forcing them to their knees. She then dropped the driver at her feet.

:: Situation outside contained. You guys done yet? ::

:: The girls are out. Thea wants those three brought back. Stajia and I are on our way out to you. ::

Jilah nodded as she stepped up to the men and said, "Oh, are you boys in so much trouble."

They looked up at her, held immobile by the grip she had on their minds, their eyes wide and frightened.

The sound of easy laughter behind her made her smile as Stajia's voice echoed in her thoughts.

:: *Holy shit, I knew you were strong, but...damn, girl.* ::

Janna was smiling as she walked up and clapped Jilah on the shoulder

:: *A ringer indeed. Nice work. Let's get 'em home.* ::

The three women leaned down, gripped their targets by the shoulder, then disappeared.

Zolah's voice was soft and playful as she murmured, "I see that you are no longer so negatively affected by translocation."

Jilah combed her fingers through damp indigo hair as she smiled back at her friend. The shower had felt amazing after all the activity.

"I think I'm finally used to it. Thank god."

Zolah chuckled and asked, "Would you like me to help you braid it?"

Jilah smiled and nodded. Was this what having an actual sister was like? She turned in the chair and Zolah began gently working her fingers through her hair, before slowly threading it into a braid.

"So, what happens to those girls now?" Jilah asked, frowning.

Zolah explained, "There are places in this facility that you have yet to visit. Recuperation and recovery areas in which they can be weaned off the poison that's been forced into their bodies. They will be given a chance to become part of the sisterhood, if they so desire. For those who wish to leave, we will find placement for them back into the world. It is up to them what they do with their lives from there."

Jilah nodded, understanding. She had to admit that she was a little surprised. The Synod seemed geared mostly towards doling out punishment, rather than rehabilitation. She wondered how long it would take for the worst cases to recover, if they ever did. Those that made it through the process would come out a great deal stronger for having endured the punishment that had been thrust upon them, over and over. She thought it likely that a large number of them would choose to stay and fight in any way they could.

It took her to a dark place, this train of thought, and she startled herself by blurting out.

"I miss him."

Zolah's fingers froze for a moment before continuing to braid her friend's hair.

"I know," she murmured quietly. "A part of you will always miss him."

It was the first time since they'd really spoken openly about it.

"Even after everything I know he'd done.. I..."

She couldn't finish. Tears threatened, and she took a quick breath, pushing the thought away from her.

Zolah leaned forward and hugged her, silently resting a head on her shoulder. Nobody could say anything that would ever make it better, and dwelling on it would just bring her back to that miserable place she'd fought so hard to walk away from.

"Thank you, Zolah," Jilah murmured softly.

Zolah sat up, frowning. "What am I being thanked for?"

Jilah turned to look back at her.

"I wouldn't have been able to walk out of that place in my head; wouldn't have been able to get to this point without your help."

Zolah flushed, embarrassed.

"You are... family, my sister. It is what family does for each other."

Jilah turned away and Zolah began working on the braid again.

"Still. Thank you."

Zolah smiled then and the two of them sat in silence while Zolah finished up the braid.

Chapter 21
REVELATION

"Today's the day?"

Argent stepped into the kitchen and sat across from Aurelian as the selkie paused in the middle of eating a plate full of an alarming number of scrambled eggs, several types of breakfast meats and an enormous pile of hash browns.

The sanguine nodded and a little tremor shook him. The thought of seeing her again after so long... He was starting to think that the day would never actually come.

"I'm just going to watch her. They're not sure if she's ready to interact with me yet."

"It'll be good." Aurelian placed the fork on his plate, then murmured, " Just promise me something."

Argent looked up, meeting gold eyes that seemed to burn as the selkie rumbled, "Don't shut me out if it doesn't go the way you want it to. OK?"

"You have my word."

Aurelian took a deep breath, then picked the fork back up and commenced eating. Argent grimaced and looked away, chuckling.

"It is very much like watching a vacuum consume food. It's appalling. Do you even chew it?"

Aurelian grinned back at him between bites, giving him the finger before finally swallowing and snapping, "What, you want me to pass out from blood loss like last time?"

Argent rolled his eyes dramatically, then laughed before standing and walking over to the door.

"I'll call you if things go poorly."

The selkie narrowed his eyes at the sanguine and growled, "You'd better."

Shivers raced up Argent's spine as he watched his beloved spar in the pit below with several other women. Her maneuvers and reflexes had tightened up considerably.

During her time away from him, Jilah had gained an economy of movement that made the melee look like a deadly dance. The intensity in her was now more controlled; her action more relaxed and confident than he remembered.

Her appearance had also changed a great deal, which was to be expected from reading the reports, but they hadn't done her justice.

She was magnificent. It made his heart ache.

"How often did you say she does this now?" he asked, unable to take his eyes off her.

"Five hours a day, six days a week, she comes here and tests herself in a variety of different styles." Thea explained, smiling. "It has done wonders for motivation; the others push themselves harder just to keep up with her."

"That's my girl," he murmured.

S'llethe moved to stand beside him.

"She comes into her own now, brother. By her own hand, her own work."

He watched as Jilah closed with one of the women below, disarming her and twisting her arm before pushing her off to the sidelines with a well placed kick.

It was difficult to be this close to her without being able to speak to her. He ached to go to her; to hold her.

Argent sighed, then asked, "Does she... remember?"

Thea replied, "She never forgets you. It is why she pushes herself, sometimes far beyond what she is ready for."

Argent watched as Jilah faltered, distracted by something. Her opponent took advantage of the opportunity and brought her down hard, locking her leg and twisting it into what looked like a remarkably painful position. Jilah yelped out, then quickly tapped, frowning as she looked around, then up. Her eyes widened and her mouth dropped open.

Thea quickly took his hand and pulled him away from the edge of the vantage point.

"She mustn't..."

S'llethe sighed, then murmured, "It would appear that it is time. Let her come."

Argent looked over at her, stunned.

"What, just like that?"

"It will not be as easy as you think, brother."

Chapter 22
REDEMPTION

Jilah blinked, unable to believe her eyes. She shook her head, frowning.

There's no way. Can't be him, she told herself. *He's gone.*

"Hey! Get your head in the game!" the instructor yelled from the bench, irritated.

Jilah pushed her current sparring partner away from her and tried to refocus. The nagging sensation that her dead lover was watching from the balcony just above her wouldn't stop.

"Gimme a minute."

Jilah left the pit and blurred her way up to the observation overhang, her emotions a whirlwind of doubt and confusion. She had to know. Had it been a ghost? She stopped at the doorway, hesitating before drawing in a deep breath, then stepping into the room.

Argent stood alone on the platform, his expression wary.

Jilah froze, blinking as she looked over at the man she never thought she'd see again. Her eyes took in every detail, drinking him in until her heart ached. He even smelled the same. Was this a joke? Her jaw dropped, her words trapped in her throat as she stared back at him.

"You are looking well." Argent finally murmured, his eyes full of so much more left unsaid.

The sound of his voice... oh, how it cut. Jilah blinked, then took a step back. She had no idea who the fuck this was, but there was no way it could be Argent. Through her the Dark Lady had consumed him, *destroyed* him. There was no way back from that. This was some kind of sick joke.

"No. You're... *no.*"

She watched as pain flashed behind his eyes, sharp and bright. It was easy to recognize. The same pain flared in her own heart.

Her logic faltered for a moment and she frowned. Was it possible?

"But I... you're gone. *I made you gone.*" she stammered, her eyes welling up with tears. She stiffened as she waited for the sharp, cold voice of her patroness to scream for his suffering.

Argent patiently stood before her and she felt the first small traces of the connection they once shared opening back up between them. Jilah's eyes widened in shock at the sensation.

:: *She is gone, beloved,* :: he explained.

Right, she thought to herself, nodding and blinking. Seeing him had completely thrown her off, taking her back to the last time they'd been in the same room, but she remembered now.

:: *How..?* ::

Argent closed his eyes and let the event play back for her through the connection. Jilah experienced it from his perspective, felt a fraction of his agony at the assault of the memories she'd forced on him. Although she now realized that she had done this to a construct that had expired in her arms, he had definitely endured every moment of it.

Jilah shuddered, now feeling more than a little sick.

:: *Oh god,* :: she croaked, holding her stomach and taking a stumbling step back.

He was suddenly beside her, placing a gentle hand on her shoulder.

Jilah jerked away from him, wincing.

:: *I can't... Oh god, I'm so sorry...* ::

Argent's heart dropped as she raced off the platform.

S'llethe stepped out of the shadows, her tone soft and smooth.

"It was not supposed to happen this way, but we are finding that things rarely do between the two of you."

His shoulders slumped as he looked back at her.

"Was it a mistake, coming here? Have I made things worse?"

S'llethe shook her head. "No, brother. It is painful and awkward for her. You already know your own heart about the matter. She is only just now coming to terms with a reality that she thought impossible. It is no easy thing, she is doing."

Argent stiffened and nodded. "Of course."

He pulled a cellphone out of his back pocket and frowned. "I should head back. You will tell me if she...?"

"Put your mind at ease, brother. She is doing far better than even she knows."

To endure such a thing and keep living? How?

Jilah's mind spun as she ran – back to the healing room, to safety. Argent's pain echoed through the connection, very faint, but still very present. It stunned her that he was still alive. Beyond that, he still cared – she *mattered* to him, even after everything she'd done to him. Jilah had no idea how to feel about it. She had even less of an idea of what to do about it.

She slid into the bed, curling into a fetal position, feeling utterly lost.

There was a noise behind her and she turned to find Thea moving to sit beside her bed.

"Did you know?" Jilah asked, her tone harsher than she was comfortable with.

Thea nodded as Zolah walked into the room.

"We did not know how you would react to the knowledge, and feared that it would make your condition worse if you knew before you were ready."

Jilah shifted on the bed and sat up, angry.

"How the fuck is anybody supposed to be ready for something like this?"

Tears trailed down her cheeks and she clutched a pillow to her chest as her lower lip trembled. It felt as if she were flying apart.

"How long were you planning on keeping this from me?" she asked, feeling bleak and blasted.

Thea placed her hands in her lap and explained, "We had hoped that you would be well back in the rotation before you saw him again." The woman shifted in her seat uncomfortably. "That you would be able to find a small sense of familiarity and peace."

Jilah thought about it, frowning. The daily routine had indeed helped, a great deal more than she'd thought possible. It had been the first time she'd felt... comfortable in a long time.

:: *It is when you find and embrace that source of strength and support in yourself that you will be able to finally move on, little one.* ::

The words of the Water Mother echoed in her memory and she clutched the pillow tighter, her muscles cording like cables in her arms.

You can either run away, or you can finally turn and face this head on, she told herself, slowly letting go of the pillow. Running obviously wasn't working. And now that things were not at all as they had seemed...

She sighed and murmured, "I guess it's time to be an adult."

Jilah looked over at Thea and Zolah, something in her body quickening as she asked, "Is he still here?"

Argent stood staring into the night sky, watching the brilliance of the stars as they danced in pinpoints along a canopy of navy blue that faded to black. The last sliver of moon had faded, waning into a new moon.

The look of horror in her eyes as she'd fled the room; he couldn't stop seeing it. The pain cut so deeply. At sound of a footfall he turned to see Aurelian.

"I thought I'd find you up here," he murmured.

Argent turned back to the stars, sighing. The selkie moved to stand beside his Strigasha, his voice trembling slightly as he said, "You have a visitor."

Argent turned to stare back at him, utterly still.

"In your office."

He looked back out at the city, pausing for a few moments before blurring off the roof and down the stairs.

Jilah looked around the office, spotting a worn folder sitting open on Argent's desk. Her eyes scanned the text at the top of the page:

Strikezone: Democratic Republic of the Congo

As she read over the report, a chill went up her spine. She'd come very close to another run in with the Council and hadn't even known it. *Would they have been able to stop me?*, she wondered, her fingers drifting along the page. In the end, she supposed she was lucky that Argent's sister had intervened. Otherwise, things could've gotten really ugly, very quickly.

Someone cleared their throat behind her and she turned to find Argent standing in the doorway. Jilah looked down, then stepped away from his desk.

"I... I didn't mean to pry," she quickly explained.

Argent blinked and quietly replied, "There is nothing you could do that would offend me, beloved."

Jilah let out a weak laugh and began wringing her hands.

"Yeah... I, uh, I guess I've done about the worst thing I could to you already, right?"

She began to tremble as he took a step forward and she held a hand up, warding him off.

"P-please... let me say what I need to say first."

Argent stopped, then nodded.

Jilah steadied herself, then muttered, "God, I suck at this." She took a deep breath and started again, "Okay, first – I don't know how I can ever make up for what I put you through."

Argent shifted uncomfortably. She looked away from him and continued, "And then... then there are the things that the hellbitch showed me before she sent me after you... I don't know how to stop seeing them. I can't..."

Jilah took a deep breath and clasped her hands tightly at her waist.

"I don't know how to reconcile them. To let go of them."

Argent watched her carefully as she began pacing around the room. It was enough that she'd come – that she was talking to him again. She was looking back at him now, hugging her arms around herself and shivering.

His heart dropped as the first tear fell down her cheek.

"Shit, I thought... you were dead, and it was so real."

The tears fell freely now as she murmured, "Even after everything... you matter, more than I can say. And I don't know how to feel about that."

Argent took a tentative step forward.

"Be assured that I have no animosity towards you for the events that transpired between us, and my feelings for you are unchanged."

Jilah's stomach flipped at his words and her legs began to shake. She moved back to sit in a chair and Argent took another step into the room.

"I cannot erase my past; the way that you have seen me... I can only assure you that it was a lifetime ago. It died in me soon after I crossed over into this life."

Jilah looked over at him as he moved to sit across from her. A mournful sound escaped her lips and she nodded. Even after knowing the worst of his past, she still loved him. After all, when it came down to brass tacks – was she any better? Could she truly see what she'd done to her chosen targets as being any different from his actions centuries ago? It was all soulrape in the end. At least his victims left this existence able to go to the next experience, the life after this one, even after such a vicious and violent end. Hers, she simply wrenched out of the timestream entirely.

The reality was that they had both been monsters.

"You've more than paid for your past, the way I see it," she explained in hushed tones, leaning back into the chair as the tears started to abate.

Argent stilled at her words. He tentatively reached out to her through the connection.

:: Where do we go from here? :: he asked.

She could feel his overwhelming startlement at finding out that she had actually forgiven him.

She blinked, then shifted in the chair and sat forward. Answering the need he felt through the connection, he went to her, pulling her into his arms and sighing with relief as she held him tightly.

:: I missed you so much. ::

She shook as the last of her grief poured out of her.

:: And I you, beloved. ::

She pulled back to look at him, her body trembling.

:: I don't know if I can... ::

:: Be still, beloved. I will do nothing that would discomfit you. It is enough that you are here with me, truly. ::

Argent pressed his forehead against the curve of her horns and he chuckled softly.

:: This might take a little special navigating, however. ::

She smiled and his heart leapt.

:: Come - I will draw you a bath. ::

She took his hand and followed him out of the room.

:: That sounds perfect. ::

Jilah kept her head just above the bubbles, relaxing as the heat did its work, seeping into her tired muscles.

:: How long have I been gone? ::

She hadn't really been keeping track of time. There had been no reason to.

Argent sat outside the tub on a chair, looking over at her.

:: It has been about six months since we last saw each other. ::

She pondered this for a moment before asking, *:: How is everybody? ::*

Argent moved to place his arms on the side of the tub, resting his chin on his hands.

:: Except for Roane and Ariane, little has changed during your absence. ::

Jilah straightened up, frowning as she asked, *:: What happened? ::*

:: Their departure was hastened due to outside events that could not have been accounted for. ::

:: You're being oblique. ::

Jilah eyed him, wondering why he was sidestepping.

Argent shifted in the chair, sitting up now. :: *It would appear that I am no longer dormant during daylight hours.* ::

He looked uncomfortable as he continued, :: *The sun no longer holds me prisoner.* ::

Jilah blinked, then stared at him. :: *How?* ::

:: *Do you remember... when you called out to me?* ::

Yeah, that's something she wouldn't forget anytime soon.

:: *Yes...* ::

Argent sat back and explained, :: *Since that moment, I no longer experience ill effects from direct exposure to the sun's light.* ::

:: *Whoa.* ::

Argent quickly added, :: *Nobody seems to know how, but... there it is.* ::

Jilah took a moment to process this. More inexplicable weirdness. Would she ever get used to it?

She saw the sadness in his eyes and asked, :: *Have they left already?* ::

Argent nodded, frowning as he answered.

:: *It was imperative that they leave as quickly as possible. The council was already uneasy about having a Necromancer allied with the court of a prefecture. Once my condition changed, it seemed the wisest move to make.* ::

It pained her that she'd been out of touch and unable to say her goodbyes to them. Granted, there was no way she could have known, but she still felt guilty.

Curious now, she asked, :: *How much did you tell them?* ::

Argent looked down at his hands as he responded, :: *Only Aurelian knows the entire story. I couldn't bear sharing it with anybody else...* ::

His voice trailed off and he looked back up at her, his eyes wide. His expression clearly said that he hadn't meant to mention that last part. He winced as she reacted, surprised at the amount of pain that simple phrase caused.

God, they hadn't even known, she thought to herself.

Were they angry with her, because she'd stayed away so long? How often had he deflected questions about her during that time?

I tortured him, thought I'd killed him, and I was stupid enough to think that had been the worst of it, she thought to herself. She was just now beginning to understand the depths of what he'd endured, because of her.

Jilah looked away as she asked, dreading the answer, :: *Being away for this long, how did the court react?* ::

Argent leaned forward, shaking his head.

:: *No. Do not do this to yourself.* ::

:: *But...* :: she leaned forward and he pushed her back.

:: *We have endured much to get to this point. I have no wish to reflect on the past. Please, Jilah...* :: he pleaded.

Jilah nodded, reining in her emotions. He was right. They'd been through enough. She didn't need to pick at it. It would only make things worse. She chose to shift back to the previous topic.

:: *Are they OK?* ::

Argent's answering expression was grateful as he replied, :: *They seem to be settling in. They both wanted you to know that they miss you.* ::

:: *Are they..* ::

Pissed at me?, she wanted to ask, clamping her teeth down on the words before they could come out, instead saying, :: *Can I... visit them sometime?* ::

Argent smiled and nodded, his tone soft as he answered. :: *I think they'd like that.* ::

Jilah took a deep breath, then shifted in the tub. The water was starting to get a little cold and she was ready to do something else that wouldn't prune her skin up.

:: *I'm ready to get out now, can you hand me a towel?* ::

Argent reached over and collected one of the dark purple towels from the rod on the wall, passing it to her. He stood up and walked over to the door.

:: *I shall give you some privacy,* :: he sent as he opened the door and stepped out.

A part of her was relieved that he was giving her space, but she'd also wanted him to stay. She wasn't ready to deal with the confusion that this caused yet. Jilah stood up and stepped out of the tub, slowly working the towel over her damp skin as she looked toward the door, unsure of what she really wanted.

It had been an uncomfortable few minutes as Jilah wandered around the room in a black tanktop and leopard spotted underwear. He could sense her unease, the fact that she felt entirely too vulnerable in such a small amount of clothing. He remained silent as she reacquainted herself with everything in the room. The sense of disorientation coming from her was unsettling, but he remained silent as she finally looked over at him, then at the bed.

Her unease echoed through the connection between them before she finally decided to walk over to the bed. Argent scooted over as she moved to lay down beside him with her back facing him, watching her for any sign that she might bolt. He wanted to put her at ease, but was at a complete loss as how to do so. Argent watched over her as she dropped off into an uneasy sleep, still finding it hard to believe that she was here.

Back home.

Due to the size of her horns and tail his lover was now relegated to laying on her side, slightly curled up. He smiled as she twitched, dropping into deeper sleep. The tip of her tail raised the covers at their feet several times, then stopped. He wondered what she was dreaming about as he felt her tail brush against his foot. He smiled, draping a pale hand over her indigo hip. The contrast in coloring was striking and sent heat pounding through him.

Unable to help himself, he pulled her back against him, nuzzling her shoulder before falling asleep beside her.

Jilah's eyes flickered open and she turned to look over at Argent. The sanguine was pressed up against her back, sleeping deeply. She slowly got out of bed, not wanting to wake him. She then cat footed over to the bathroom, creeping slowly across the tile as she watched the reflection of her body in the mirror. Little had changed since the last time she'd looked. She kept wishing that it would tone down a little.

Was she going to stay like this?

She turned to look back at the tub and stopped. Something seemed to be pushing up from just beneath the skin of her back, which had now turned strangely opaque. She couldn't see all of it clearly with the tanktop on, so she quickly pulled it off, dropping it to the floor. She turned back to look and almost gasped.

It looked like a hump. *Two* humps.

What the hell?
She frowned and reached a hand back to touch one of the humps and almost cried out at the texture.
Oh, ick.
Her fingers sunk slightly into the skin, feeling along the ridge of the bump. It felt like a bone of some sort.
What fresh hell is this? she thought to herself, beginning to get a little scared.
Doesn't it end?
She gently squeezed the bone and almost passed out from the pain that stabbed through her shoulder muscles. She pulled her hand back quickly, slapping it on the counter to steady herself, then gave a little jump as she realized that Argent was now at her side. He looked worried.
:: *Are you injured?* :: he asked, reaching out to touch her arm.
Jilah flinched and Argent pulled back, taking a step away to give her space.
She reached out and lightly grabbed his wrist.
:: *No... I just... I'm sorry...* :: she looked back, seeing the hurt in his eyes and wanting to kick herself. Shit, hadn't she done enough?
Argent let himself be pulled closer, relaxing when she wrapped her arms around him.
:: *I'm just a little freaked out.* ::
:: *How can I help?* ::
Jilah let out a weak laugh, sagging a little in his arms.
:: *Got any idea what these things are?* ::
She pointed a thumb towards her back.
Argent gently pulled away from her, spinning her around to get a closer look. He reached out to touch one of the odd lumps and the moment his finger grazed the surface of her skin, Jilah yelped. He immediately shrank back.
:: *Did I hurt you?* ::
Jilah shivered for a moment, then turned to face him, shaking her head.
:: *No, it didn't hurt. Your finger felt like an icecube. It startled me,* :: she explained, looking chagrined.
Argent winced and said, :: *Sorry about that.* ::

He took a deep breath and simply came out with it. :: *I believe that what you're seeing is the preliminary stages of wing development.* ::

Jilah looked back at him, her expression blank.

:: *Did you say... wing development?* ::

He nodded and quietly responded, :: *I did.* ::

Jilah paused for several beats, then hung her head.

:: *What, are hooves next?* ::

Argent gently took her hand. Pulling her close, he lifted her chin, kissing her.

Startled, she pulled away.

:: *What was that for?* ::

:: *You worry that these changes make you less attractive, less desirable. I thought that perhaps proof that this was not the case was in order.* ::

He kept a hand on her waist, looking back at her as she thought about it for a moment.

Her brows knit in consternation and she shook her head. :: *It's more than that..* ::

He smiled, letting his fingers move to play in gentle circles at the base of her spine, just above her tail.

"Undoubtedly, but your biggest fear at the moment is that your appearance is becoming monstrous."

It was a very matter-of-fact statement, but the way he said it, and the fact that he'd spoken aloud made her body tremble. His tone lowered, becoming heated.

"You shine, my love. I see it, even if you do not."

Jilah shivered, her eyes fluttering as he leaned into her, tasting her scent as he gently brushed the skin of her neck with his lips.

:: *If I am incorrect in my evaluation, and you wish me to stop...* ::

Stopping was the last thing on her mind as he began trailing soft, cool kisses along her collarbone.

God, she'd missed his touch.

Jilah sighed and leaned into him, clutching at his waist. Gooseflesh raced along her skin as he nipped at her neck and she cried out. Unable to help himself, he moved to capture her lips with his own, driven by a need that shook its way through him. She matched his passion as he gripped her hips and trembled against her. Argent then hefted her into his arms and slid into her in one fluid stroke.

She cried out as they coupled, sudden and frantic. No foreplay, no professions of love, just fiery need that threatened to consume them both. Her tail thrashed around, knocking several items off the counter and into the toilet and sink. Jilah clawed at his back and Argent growled, thrusting harder as she threw her head back and screamed, her body shuddering to an almost painful climax. Argent quickly followed, roaring as he grabbed the wall and the counter, shivering with the aftershocks.

After she'd had time to recover, Jilah noticed that he was now looking back at her with a sheepish, wary expression. She immediately started laughing and Argent, still sheathed inside her, shivered at the sensation.

:: *Dear god,* :: he moaned in her thoughts. :: *If we keep this up, we will destroy the entire bathroom.* ::

Jilah looked over to see the damage they'd caused and began laughing harder. Argent leaned over to brush his tongue against her nipple and Jilah instantly quieted, murmuring, "Oh!" before again clutching at his back.

Argent chuckled darkly as he bit down, drawing blood. Jilah trembled as he fed, whimpering as he began moving inside her again.

The absurdity of it all rang through her mind as she sent, :: *I should totally kill you more often.* ::

Her blood didn't have quite the kick it used to, but it was still strong enough to make him a little loopy. They had wrecked the bathroom and a good portion of the bedroom before finally making it back to the bed itself. They lay in a twist of sheets that had pulled away from the corners of the mattress, the majority of them spilling over onto the floor. Argent began humming a sweet, meandering little song that she didn't recognize under his breath as she nuzzled his shoulder, happy to finally be home.

What had started out fiery and violent had eventually turned soft and intimate. They lay beside each other, grinning as they laced their fingers together.

He chuckled and sent, :: *Well, that was surprising.* ::

She smiled and looked down, a little embarrassed.

:: *Uh, yeah. You could say that.* ::

:: *Did I mention that I missed you?* ::

Jilah blushed and nodded. :: *Yeah, you said that already.* ::

He began kissing her fingers, one by one.

:: *I want to go to the ocean with you.* ::

Jilah blinked, finding it an odd non sequitur. :: *I... ah... well, not that I don't want to go, but... what brought that up?* ::

He smiled and opened her hand, placing a gentle kiss on her palm.

:: *I wish to see you in the sunlight. In a bikini. Indulge me.* ::

:: *A bikini?* :: She blinked. :: *You've seen the tail, right? How would that even work?* ::

:: *Details...* ::

He waved her question away, chuckling.

Argent wrapped an arm around her waist, pulling her close.

:: *How long do you think we can get away with staying in bed?* ::

Jilah grinned and kissed his forehead. :: *A couple days, at least.* ::

Argent smiled and traced a finger across her cheek, finding it hard to believe his luck. She was here; had chosen to be here again, with him. It was more than a little heady. To be able to see her smile again, after everything that had happened between them, it felt like a miracle of sorts. He opened the connection between them and was reassured by her own sense of wonder and happiness at being with him. For a while, they simply shared emotions through the link, gently touching each other, not wanting the moment to end.

He silently shared his fears and doubts with her, no longer wanting to keep anything from her.

:: *Dodging all those questions about me. Not really knowing when I'd come back.* ::

Jilah held him tightly, shivering.

:: *You are here now. It was all worth it,* :: Argent replied, trying to reassure her.

Jilah pulled back and met his gaze. :: *I was so sure that I'd destroyed you. That I'd never see you again.* ::

He could tell that she wanted to apologize for being able to move on and he quickly said, :: *I will never blame you for that. External forces pushed you to that course of action, and would not let you divert.* ::

He could feel her thoughts begin to spiral again, guilt and anger at herself for everything that had happened.

:: If I need to have continuous sex with you until you stop that particular train of thought, believe me, I will, :: he snapped, kissing her nose.

Jilah frowned and looked back at him, then slowly smiled.

:: You're right. My head needs to shut the hell up. C'mere.. ::

:: Your wish is my command, lady. ::

Devil's Gambit

Chapter 23

RECONNECTION

When Jilah tried to roll over in her sleep, she met with a little resistance.

It was enough to wake her up.

She took a deep breath, then rubbed at her eyes. There was a sudden ache in her back as she pulled her arm slowly across Argent's chest. The sanguine was still completely zonked out, and no wonder with such a vigorous homecoming. Everything ached from their various exertions, but the pain was worse in her upper back. She moved to sit up, frowning at the extra weight on her shoulders. Something brushed her lower back and she let out a little yip of fright and leapt out of the bed.

Argent was now looking over at her, bleary and curious. He looked utterly wrecked.

Jilah scanned the bed, looking for what might have brushed against her when she felt it again. She cried out and began slapping at her back, yelping as she smacked something that sent a sharp sting of pain through her.

:: *Stop. It's not what you think,* :: he sent as he tried to make his way across the covers. :: *Turn around so I can see your back.* ::

Jilah turned, her tail whacking against the bedframe. At least it didn't hurt.

:: *It is as I thought. Go look in the mirror.* ::

She looked over to find Argent slumped into the bed, face down.

:: *What's wrong with you?* ::

She moved over to him, lifting his hand and letting it drop back to the mattress.

:: *Our extracurricular activities seem to have completely exhausted me,* :: he groaned and rolled over to open an eye, looking up at her.

Jilah clapped a hand over her mouth, but not before a short bark of laughter escaped. From his position on the bed, she could see Argent's eyebrow creep up as he shifted to look up at her.

:: *I can't help it! You look so damned cute like that!* ::

Argent frowned and she started laughing.

"Ha! I *broke* you! Durable my ass..." she took a step towards the bed, then flinched when something brushed against her back again, her laughter dying out as her eyes grew wide.

Argent was now looking back at her with a secretive smile. He let out a semi-smug grunt, then rolled over.

:: *Mirror.* :: he sent, pulling a pillow into his arms and resting his chin on it.

She stuck her tongue out at him, then walked into the bathroom.

"One, two, three..." Argent murmured under his breath before Jilah started shouting.

After a few moments, when she'd been able to calm down, Jilah turned again and flexed her shoulders, startled as the wings that now sprouted from high on her back extended out to their full length. It sounded like an umbrella opening. She grabbed a cosmetic mirror, then turned to get a better look at the little buggers. They retracted and trembled against her skin, the tips hitting her just above the swell of her hips. She flexed again and the wings automatically extended, coming out to just before her wrists when she raised her arms out to her sides. They looked leathery, like bat wings. The membranes between the bones were a dark blue that bled into black at the bones. When she relaxed, the wings rustled back into their resting position. Moving a tentative finger to poke one of them, she then frowned at the texture; soft velvet lining over thin, trembling skin. She wasn't entirely sure if she liked it. They were so very soft and warm.

She gently placed a thumb and forefinger on either side of the wing membrane, marveling at the feel as she gently brushed her fingers along the surface. She relaxed and the wings closed. At least they weren't slimy. They were, however, ticklish when they brushed against her skin.

It was going to take a little getting used to.

:: *You alive in there?* :: she sent, flexing and wincing as the wings opened up again.

:: *You getting all this?* ::

Argent responded with a slurred murmur in her thoughts and Jilah wondered if she should start looking for something for him to snack on. Even the connection to him felt sluggish. Popping her head out of the bathroom to check on Argent, she found him face down in the covers again. He'd never been this ragged out before. Jilah closed her eyes and began mentally searching for Aurelian. From what Argent had said earlier, the selkie had started eating a high iron diet since he'd become a 'donor' again, and would probably be just what her lover needed to shake the lethargy out of his system.

He was apparently up and rustling around in the kitchen, finishing off the remains of what looked like a fairly big lunch.

Good. He'd need it.

She sent, :: *Ah... can you come in here?* ::

She felt his shock at the mental contact, then quickly pulled away, not wanting to seem intrusive.

The guilt didn't help, either. Would he be angry at her for what she'd done? It was something she'd tried not to think about, but she was going to have to deal with it sooner or later.

Might as well get everything lanced at the same time, she thought to herself as she sat down beside Argent, brushing her hand down along his back and over the curve of his ass.

The sanguine groaned and shifted against the bed, putting an arm around her waist and letting his thumb play along her hip. Jilah smiled and smoothed back his hair, brushing it behind his ear.

:: *You're so cute when you're so exhausted you can barely move,* :: she murmured, laughing softly.

Argent grumbled and tightened his grip on her.

Aurelian walked into the room a few minutes later, then paused for a minute to take in the aftermath of the room.

"Whoa, you guys really did a number on this place. Thank god Gigi soundproofed this room. Otherwise none of us would've gotten any sleep."

Jilah looked back at him with a sheepish grin.

"Sorry I missed it."

Aurelian took a careful step towards the bed, looking intently at her. His expression changed, softening as he murmured, "Good to have you back."

Jilah's throat clicked shut and she felt tears threaten. She knew she'd had no right to hope that he'd forgive her – that any of them would, and yet there it was. Just how bad had Argent gotten while she was gone? Another stab of guilt. Aurelian kept staring at her and Jilah looked down, then blushed, remembering now that she was naked.

It took a moment for it not to matter.

She frowned, then said, "I don't know what to say..."

Aurelian shook his head and finally smiled. "He explained everything. I'm just happy you're here. You're good for him."

Jilah blinked quickly and looked away, her voice ragged as she replied, "I'm so sorry for what you must've gone through, both of you."

She looked back at him, tears shining in her eyes. Sheer willpower was the only thing keeping them from spilling out onto her cheeks.

"I didn't think I'd see any of you again."

Aurelian took a deep breath, his voice shaky as he said, "He's not the only one who missed you."

Her cheeks were immediately wet and Aurelian was at her side then, kneeling and brushing the tears away as he looked up at her.

"Hey, don't... shit. Please don't cry," he murmured, moving to brush soft lips against her knuckles, squeezing her hand gently.

Jilah placed her other hand on his shoulder, marveling at the heat that rolled off him. Argent shifted on the bed, mumbling something she couldn't understand into the mattress, and Jilah looked down at the sanguine, hoping that he'd be okay. She tried to roll him over, but he wouldn't budge.

Suddenly, Aurelian laughed and said, "You broke him. Nicely done."

Jilah felt a flush creeping into her cheeks again, wondering if the selkie could see it. Was her skin now turning purple? She wasn't sure she wanted to ask, though.

"I didn't call you in here to show off. I think he needs to eat."

A smile gently tugged at the corners of her lips. She had forgotten how much she had missed him as well. It was really good to see him.

She began running her fingers through Argent's hair, purring, :: *Lover man, snack's here.* ::

Argent roused to see Aurelian kneeling by the side of the bed with an amused expression.

"G'way," the sanguine grumbled.

Aurelian quickly nicked himself and offered his wrist to Argent.

Jilah didn't see him move; the selkie's wrist was just suddenly in Argent's mouth. Her lover groaned as he drank, shifting against the bed.

"Ow." Aurelian winced, then his lips curled into a slow, heated smile. He pushed Argent over and climbed over Jilah to straddle him.

She watched transfixed as Aurelian shivered, his voice dreamy as he whispered, "Yeah, that's the good stuff."

The selkie's eyes slid closed and she reached out to run tentative fingers through his long blonde locks. Aurelian moaned at her touch, eyes snapping open as he quickly caught her wrist and pulled her to him, kissing her. His mouth was so insistent, it was as if he was trying to devour her. And god, he was so *warm.*

This is going too fast.

Jilah shook and pulled away, putting a hand to his chest. "Wait..."

Aurelian released her, his eyes fluttering. "Shit, sorry... I..."

Argent opened the connection between them and let her see all that had transpired between the two of them during her absence. The bond between the two men had changed, becoming a great deal deeper, if not a little broken, while she'd been away. She could feel him growing stronger as he fed and she relaxed, reassured that he'd be alright.

Her voice broke as she murmured, "Thank you for everything you did for him, while..." she looked away, unable to finish.

Aurelian placed his hand over hers and squeezed gently.

"Hey – it wasn't the same without you. Honestly."

Jilah looked down to see Argent finishing up with Aurelian's wrist.

:: *Never the same without you,* :: the sanguine added, trailing his fingers over the outside of her thigh.

He brushed a particularly ticklish part and, as she shivered, she heard the now familiar sound of her wings snapping open.

Aurelian yelped and fell off the bed, startled.

"What the fuck?!"

The selkie looked up and pointed at her.

"Where the hell did those come from? She didn't have wings two nights ago."

Jilah winced and explained, "They're a... *new* development."

Aurelian stood up, then moved to sit on the bed beside Argent. He then leaned forward, fascinated.

"Can I touch them?" he asked.

Jilah slowly turned around. "Just... be gentle."

Aurelian brushed one of the wings with a tentative finger. The sensation sent a hot rush through her, surprising her.

"Whoa. They're fuzzy. Nice."

Another zing zipped through her as Aurelian brushed soft fingers against her wings again. She then cried out as he moved forward and blew gently on them.

God, who knew wings would be an erogenous zone?

She felt a cool hand on her thigh, squeezing. Her lips now easing into a smile, she murmured, :: *Weren't you just too tired to roll over in bed a moment ago?* ::

Argent grinned and slid his hand a little higher, bringing another cry from her lips.

:: *I am finding myself miraculously restored.* ::

Aurelian then pulled back and let out a low whistle. "You realize that you're going to have to replace most of the stuff in this room, right?"

He sounded almost envious as he looked around, again surveying the various cracks and dents in the furniture before sending another puff of air across the thin membrane of her wings.

"What, did you try every piece of furniture out before finally making it to the bed?"

Jilah blushed furiously as she turned around, swatting at Argent's hand and pulling away from the large, warm man at her back. She wouldn't be able to concentrate on what they were saying if they kept that up. She quickly turned around to face them and Argent sighed, shifted in the bed, then explained, "With her new... accoutrements, we found it imperative to experiment in order to avoid certain difficulties in maneuvering."

Aurelian paused for a moment, then replied. "I bet. Did she crack ya with the tail?"

Argent winced, nodding as he sat up and replied, "Several times." The welt on his lower legs had long since disappeared, but it'd stung like a hornet when the tail had whipped into him during a particularly frenzied moment.

"Still, trial and error."

The sanguine grinned, eyes dancing as he looked back at her.

Jilah's eyes narrowed as she snapped, "Scoot over. And stop talking about me like I'm an amusement park ride."

Both men looked at each other, silent for the space of two beats before laughing uproariously. She swatted Argent on the shoulder, which only made them laugh harder.

Aurelian was wiping tears out of his eyes as he croaked, "Blue, you have NO idea."

They moved to make room for her on the mattress, and she settled at Argent's side, feeling more than a little exposed as she saw the heat growing in the depths of their eyes. She pulled the covers up, covering herself, not entirely sure if she was ready for this to happen just yet. They stayed on their side of the bed, though, almost as if waiting for something. Argent watched her shift beneath the covers, slowly sliding a hand towards her.

Jilah quickly shook her head.

"Oh, no. You keep that up and you'll end up passed out face down on the bed again. You should at least eat more, first."

Argent's smile grew wicked as he purred, :: *As you wish.* ::

The selkie's eyes fluttered as Argent turned to pull him close, brushing Aurelian's lips with his own, kissing him slowly, but firmly. Jilah was surprised at the intimacy of it, that two men could be so soft and gentle with each other. Aurelian moved to straddle him again, shivering as the kiss between them grew stronger, heated. Jilah's heart began to thump loudly in her chest at the sight and she shifted on the bed, clutching the covers in tight fists. Alabaster fingers pulled moans from the tanned man above him as Argent slid them up into Aurelian's hair, gripping gently and pulling his head to the side as he trailed kisses along the selkie's cheek.

Argent worked his way slowly to Aurelian's neck, nipping as he went, then finally biting down. The selkie cried out and bucked against Argent, his body shuddering.

Jilah had never witnessed anything so utterly erotic in her entire life.

She felt Argent's presence in her thoughts, opening the connection between them. There was an almost overwhelming warm wash of gratitude, that Argent could finally share this with her again. Although they'd enjoyed each other while she'd been gone, the connection was electric for the two of them with her there to witness; to join in.

Aurelian flipped over, clutching at Argent's hips and grinding against him. Jilah's breathing came quicker, as she was almost overloaded with sensation. She gasped out as she felt warm, solid velvet in her hand as Argent's fist closed around Aurelian's length, and the selkie let out a ragged cry, his back bowing against the bed.

It was less disorienting this time, now that she wasn't roaming around trying to get away from the sensation. Jilah watched Aurelian's tanned body shiver, his breathing became harsh and heavy as Argent squeezed gently. The selkie's blood was rich and warm as it went down Argent's throat, and Jilah found herself wanting to taste him directly now. Wrapping a hand around Aurelian's fist, she heard him moan as his fingers readjusted, gripping the sheets tighter now. She smiled, happy with his reaction as she slowly trailed her fingers along his knuckles and up the tightly corded muscles of his arm. Aurelian looked up at her, his eyes pleading as she moved in to brush her fingers against his lips. He began gently licking and kissing them, sucking them into his mouth and she let out a shaky sigh.

She felt it when Argent licked the marks closed on Aurelian's neck, and she startled herself by growling, "Get your clothes off. Now."

Aurelian looked at her as he pushed himself to a sitting position and began pulling his shirt over his head. The selkie's movements were slow and deliberate; Jilah could tell that he was drawing it out for her, wanting her to watch him. Argent moved off Aurelian and captured her hand with his own, threading his fingers through hers as she watched Aurelian toss the shirt to the floor, his eyes full of need. Argent's lips brushed her fingers as Aurelian stood up and slowly slid his jeans down, letting them drop to his ankles and kicking them off to the side.

Of course he'd go commando, she thought to herself, smiling.

His bronzed skin looked almost hot to the touch and she knew that her fingers – her body – would soak up that heat; revel in it. Jilah held a hand out to him, enjoying this feeling of control she had over this large man who was letting her call the shots. She could tell that it wasn't easy for him to hold himself in check, but knew that by doing so he was exciting himself more, and her reaction to that surprised her.

For a moment, she felt a silent stab of guilt, that she was entranced by this man.

Argent smiled against her fingers as he sent, *:: I am not jealous, beloved. He is here for both of us, remember? ::*

Reassured that she wasn't neglecting him, she smiled up at Aurelian as he knelt down and crept towards her across the mattress, his eyes flickering back and forth between her and Argent. Argent's hand slid around her wrist as Aurelian began pushing her back to the bed, the delicious mixture of cool and hot skin making her blood race. Fire and ice – light and dark; the differences between the two men excited the hell out of her, and she shivered as Aurelian kissed her, then playfully nipped at her lower lip. The selkie was practically burning up as he slid a hand up and plucked at a nipple before moving to squeeze her breast. Argent's fingers tightened on her wrist and she heard him moan.

A twinge went through her back and she shifted, "Ow."

Aurelian immediately backed off, helping her sit up. She presented him with an apologetic grin and he smiled back at her, his voice a husky rumble.

"Wings. Forgot."

"Yeah, me too. It's okay," she murmured as she shifted and rolled him over, straddling him and letting her wings stretch a little.

Aurelian looked up at her, dazzled.

"Damn, that's hot."

Jilah stared at him, startled that anybody could find the things appealing. Sure, they were kinda neat in theory, but the reality was still a little too weird for her to be comfortable with just yet.

"Really?" she asked, her voice sounding quiet and small.

Aurelian nodded and let his hands slide up her legs, gripping her waist and letting out a sigh as he pressed that hard, hot core against her.

"Oh hell yes."

Jilah turned to look at Argent who simply raised an eyebrow and sent, :: *Told you.* ::

She smiled, but wondered why he hadn't moved towards them yet.

She heard her lover's reply in her thoughts, :: *I want to watch you. The two of you are glorious together.* ::

Words were inadequate to express what she was feeling so she simply opened the connection wide between them and dipped down to kiss Aurelian. She pressed her body against his, basking in his warmth as she slid her slickness along the hot length of him. She trailed kisses along his jaw, gently nipping at his neck.

"I don't want to hurt you," she whispered, not knowing if he would be able to deal with her drawing from him so soon after Argent had fed from him.

Aurelian bucked up against her, pressing her hips down against him, his voice shaky as he pleaded, "*Please,* Blue"

She smiled at his new nickname for her, finding that she was growing to like it. She nuzzled Aurelian's neck and his body shuddered, his fingers clutching her ass as he slid her back along his length. Jilah gripped his shoulders and bit down, letting out a moan as Aurelian slid into her. Heat blossomed into her as his life splashed onto her tongue. He tasted different from what she'd remembered, but it was still heady and delicious as Aurelian's movements quickened beneath her. Argent's presence curled around her as the flicker of pleasure at her core turned into a roaring blaze.

The three of them raced to a point of white hot release, and she was surprised to feel Aurelian in her mind now almost as strongly as

Argent. This strange shared union slammed them immediately over the edge and the rest of the world simply burned away as they roared to one of the strongest climaxes she could ever remember experiencing.

Their cries filled the room as Jilah felt herself slip into unconsciousness.

:: Rise and shine, cupcake. Or did you forget? ::

Jilah opened her eyes at the sound of Zhara's voice in her thoughts. One arm wrapped around Argent's waist, she could feel the heat rolling off of Aurelian's body as he rested beside her. He had been careful to leave enough space to keep from crushing her wings against her back. It was the first time she could remember the selkie actually sleeping with them. As she shifted in the bed, both men moved in closer to her, but remained asleep.

:: Forget what? :: Jilah tried to recall what was supposed to be happening today. The boys had effectively knocked her senseless and she was having a difficult time concentrating. What day was it? She'd be damned if she could remember.

:: Today is the day. Zolah... ::

:: Oh shit! I did forget! ::

The girl chuckled and it echoed pleasantly in Jilah's psyche.

:: How soon do I need to be there? :: she asked.

:: You have a couple hours yet - and given the bone party you've likely been having, Zolah won't be bothered if you're a little late. Just get here. ::

Bone party? Jilah sighed, and shook her head. Everybody at the Synod probably knew at this point. After all, she'd just dropped out of sight, as far as they were concerned. Jilah wondered briefly if her sparring partners missed her. She doubted they'd hold it against her, though. Jilah tried to sit up, but Aurelian's arm tightened around her waist. She tried to shift out from under it, but the selkie simply pulled her close, then kissed her shoulder.

"Guys, there's something I need to do. I need to get up," she explained, sighing.

She blinked as she heard Aurelian's voice in her mind. :: *Nope. Need to sleep.* ::

Uh, ok. That's new.

Argent shifted and turned towards her, staring over at Aurelian. "You heard him too?" she asked.

The sanguine nodded, peering at Aurelian strangely before he looked back at her.

:: *Is everything OK?* ::

Jilah nodded, but couldn't stop the small thread of sadness that escaped into the connection.

:: *Zolah's retiring today. I told her I'd be there for her.* ::

Argent pondered this for a moment, and Jilah asked, :: *Can you go with me? I mean, do you have time?* ::

Her mate smiled, then kissed her forehead. He looked over at Aurelian and the selkie shifted, placing his forehead on Jilah's shoulder.

:: *Don't wanna, Zim. Wanna sleep.* ::

Jilah blinked and looked back at Argent, who now looked irritated. Argent then lifted Aurelian's arm up enough so that Jilah could scoot out from under it and out of the bed. Aurelian immediately pulled Argent back against him, making a contented sound. Jilah heard a brief growl in her mind and Aurelian's eyes popped open as he released the sanguine.

As she began getting dressed, Argent hopped out of bed as well.

:: *You didn't have to yell.* ::

The selkie's voice radiated petulance.

"Apparently, I did." Argent replied as began getting dressed.

"So... Zim?" Jilah asked, curious.

"How did you hear that?"

Aurelian sat up quickly, blushing as he looked over at Argent with a guilty expression.

Jilah gave him a sheepish grin, then stepped into a pair of black leather pants with a blue and white stripe going down the sides, "I can hear you in my head now - when you talk to either of us, apparently."

Aurelian winced, then sat up. "Oops."

"You may as well tell her, at this point," Argent replied, pulling a white wifebeater over his head.

Looking somewhat embarrassed, Aurelian explained, "It's a, uh, surfer expression – short for Zimzala. It means somebody that finds solace with sand between their toes and the ocean stretched before them."

Following the swell of emotion she felt coming from him, Jilah followed the thought and replied, :: *He's that for you. I get it. Sorry it embarrassed you.* ::

She grinned and added, :: *It's a sweet nickname.* ::

She looked over at Argent as she pulled on a pair of Doc Martens and began lacing them up.

:: *Don't be too harsh on him.* ::

Startled, she found herself swept up in a strong, warm hug.

:: *Thank you. For sharing him.* ::

Jilah chuckled and hugged Aurelian back.

:: *As long as Mira doesn't kick my ass, I'm good.* ::

Aurelian put her down, then grinned down at her. Argent rolled his eyes at the two of them but Jilah spotted a tiny smile curving his lips.

"I must accompany my Striaga to an event. Keep an eye on things while we're gone?"

Argent walked up to the blonde, then kissed him softly.

Aurelian nodded, then quickly pulled on his jeans before giving Jilah a peck on the cheek before he darted out of the room.

She grinned, then remembered something, stopping in her tracks as she asked, :: *Can we check to see if Maslin wants to go as well? I know that he and Zolah grew close while...* :: she trailed off, looking away from Argent as her thoughts went to a darker place.

The sanguine wrapped his arms around her waist, kissing her shoulder.

:: *Of course.* ::

Jilah relaxed against him, pleased to have her thoughts distracted by less dangerous topics. She kissed him, wrapping around him for a brief moment before reaching over to collect a bra. She then spent several minutes trying to negotiate the straps around the wings, but they brushed painfully against the wing roots. The skin was still really tender back there. It would only end up chafing painfully if she wore it and she grumbled, taking it off and tossing it onto the bed.

:: *Everything's an obstacle course now.* ::

Argent chuckled and tweaked one of her nipples.

:: *I think you look just fine the way you are.* ::

Jilah swatted at his hand. :: *I'm serious. At this point, all I'm going to be able to wear are tops that tie around my neck.* ::

She moved to dig through a clothing drawer, pulling out a black, soft cotton halter top.

:: *Let's just hope I don't have to run anywhere. I'll put an eye out.* ::

Argent laughed and replied, :: *You can speak with Gigi when we return. I'm sure she'll be able to construct something that will be suitable.* ::

Jilah paused, looking back at him. :: *I keep worrying that everybody's going to be pissed at me for leaving – for not coming back to visit.* ::

He stepped up to her and gave her arm a gentle squeeze.

:: *Beloved, you need to let that go. They all think you were receiving rigorous training that you couldn't possibly be pulled away from. In a very real way, you were.* ::

Jilah nodded, pushing it to the back of her mind. She'd have to have a long talk with Gigi when they returned. Not to mention Roane and Ariane. But it could wait a little while longer. The weight at her back seemed a little heavier now, and she frowned.

:: *Gimme a minute.* ::

She walked into the bathroom and turned to the side. The peaks of the wings were now higher than her head, the tips ending just below the curve of her ass. Aside from tweaking about the fact that they were still growing at an alarming rate, Jilah had to admit that they didn't really look that bad now.

She stepped out into the bedroom and flexed, extending them fully and looking over at Argent. Her mate smiled back at her, heat in his eyes.

:: *You are magnificent,* :: he purred.

She wondered if she'd ever be able to actually fly with them.

:: *I would not be surprised.* :: Argent replied. :: *At some point, you should speak with Orlando about the finer points of riding currents of air.* ::

Jilah looked back at him.

:: *Talk? With Orlando?* ::

The sanguine grinned back at her as she retracted the wings

:: He is not exactly verbose, true, but this is something that he might share with you, should you ask about it. ::

I might just do that, she thought to herself with a smile.

Chapter 24

AN ELDER RETIRES

As Jilah walked into the room, she spotted Zolah sitting in the center of a circular cave on a thick chair that looked as if it had been fashioned out of red clay. The rocks embedded in the cave walls radiated a warmth that Jilah could feel in her bones. Thea and a young woman Jilah hadn't met yet stood behind her friend with their hands on her shoulders. The three women were dressed in white shirts and pants, patiently waiting. Aaron stood off to the side, watching Zolah with an intensity that sent a zing along Jilah's skin.

Zolah met her lover's eyes briefly, then closed her own and slowed her breathing.

Jilah watched as Maslin tentatively stepped into the room, looking over at Zolah with a fondness that was unmistakable. His eyes met Jilah's for a brief moment, before darting back to Zolah. Jilah frowned, remembering everything that she'd said to him that horrible day.

:: *He's been very worried about you,* :: Argent explained.

Jilah nodded, then looked back over at Zolah. Thea and the young woman beside her started singing, low at first, but the song slowly grew louder. The women's voices seemed to weave in and out of an aural pattern that set her heart thrumming strongly. Something inside her responded and she took a step forward, surprised when her own mouth opened and an unexpected voice joined in. The harmonics of the song changed and Jilah felt Argent's cool hand close around her own.

Tears streamed down her cheeks as the sound of demonsong echoed out of her throat. It was the most beautiful thing she'd ever heard. She felt fingers curl around her other hand, and was surprised to see Maslin standing beside her now, tears in his eyes as well.

Zolah sighed and smiled, and the peace that radiated from her was a physical presence in the room as dark smoke started issuing forth from her friend's mouth and nose. While Jilah sang, she watched as the smoke took on the shape of a nightmare. Large, scythelike claws curled at the ends of the shade's arms, its legs bending back like that of an insect. Everything about it seemed sharp, meant to cause pain and anguish. The shade stretched and nebulous wings flexed open, reaching far beyond the points of its claws as it threw its head back and opened its mouth wide.

:: Whoa. ::

Jilah wondered if her own wings would grow to that length eventually. If so, flying certainly seemed within the realm of possibility. The shadow coiled in upon itself, reforming into an amorphous mass as a tendril of smoke reached out, as if looking for something. It slowly moved towards the young woman beside Thea, trailing up her arm, then across her shoulder. It suddenly darted into her mouth and the woman's back bowed, her head snapping back as she cried out. But what started out as a cry of pain certainly didn't end that way. Jilah felt her cheeks flush as the woman's hands ran up the sides of her body, first cupping her breasts and squeezing them before moving to her face.

A low throated moan echoed out of the woman's mouth as her fingers memorized the features of her face. She smiled and laughed. "Yes, this one will do nicely."

The young woman then crumpled and Aaron darted in to catch her before she could hit the floor. He looked up to see Zolah blinking down at him. She sighed and reached over to touch his face, confusion in her eyes.

"You look different, my love," she croaked.

"There will be a period of adjustment for you both," Thea explained.

Zolah brought a shaky hand to her face, scrubbing it.

"I am in dire need of a bath."

She coughed briefly, then presented them with a shaky smile. "And some water."

Aaron's voice was a low rumble as he grinned and replied, "Anything you want, darlin'."

A large woman in a white smock entered the room and walked over to the 'new recruit'. Aaron stepped away and let her collect the young woman, then moved over to Zolah and touched her arm gently.

"Babe, can you walk?" he murmured.

Zolah shook her head. "I do not think so."

She reached out and took his offered hand. Aaron helped her up, catching her as her knees buckled, then hefted her into his arms. He chuckled at the look of embarrassment on her face and nuzzled her.

"C'mon. Let's get you in the water."

Zolah smiled, then turned to face Jilah, her voice sounding very weak as she said, "Thank you so much for being here. All of you. It means more than I can say."

Jilah smiled back, a little shaken. Her friend looked beyond exhausted. She didn't realize that losing the demon would take so much from her, but she supposed that it made sense. It was probably going to take Zolah a while to get used to being the only occupant of her body again. She squeezed Argent and Maslin's hands briefly, releasing them before walking towards Thea.

"Will she be okay?"

Thea smiled and nodded. "She will be fine. Zolah will now have to readjust to being much weaker, slower and far less agile than she is used to. She understands that this is all part of the separation process."

Argent and Maslin flanked her and Thea smiled over at the therianthrope.

"It is good to see you again, young Maslin. It was a surprise that Zolah had not expected, and is much appreciated. Thank you for coming."

Maslin ran a hand through his hair and smiled back at her.

"It was the least I could do. When is the yoking ceremony?"

Thea paused for a moment, then quietly explained, "Zolah has chosen to live the rest of her life as simply human."

Maslin rocked back on a heel, shocked. "Why on earth would she do that? Aaron could easily kill her without meaning to... "

Thea held a hand up to placate him, explaining. "They are both well aware of the risk, and have chosen this path for good or ill."

Jilah frowned and looked over at Maslin. The boy looked completely unsettled.

:: *Yoking ceremony?* :: she asked Argent, confused.

:: *When one of their lineage chooses to mate bond with a human, a portion of the therianthrope's essence is woven into that of their partner. This makes them stronger, more durable. It is not quite the same as being born a full blooded therianthrope, but it keeps sexual relations between the pair from becoming damaging, or at times fatal.* ::

Jilah blinked at him, shocked. :: *Does that mean...?* ::

Argent replied with a solemn nod. :: *It will be too dangerous for them to be physically intimate with each other. But that will not keep them from trying.* ::

Maslin shook his head, closing his eyes.

"It's madness," he murmured to himself.

Thea placed a gentle hand on his shoulder. "She has had a long, full life. It is her wish to end it as an unaltered human. We must abide by her wish."

Maslin frowned, then turned away. Not entirely understanding why Maslin seemed to be so affected by it, she looked over at Argent.

:: *What aren't you telling me?* ::

Argent explained, :: *Now that Zolah is... diminished, the likelihood of the pack accepting her as their Alpha's mate is very slim. The bitches in a given pack usually jockey for position, to see who will share the Alpha's bed – who will provide offspring for him. Since she has opted out of being yoked, this is not a possibility with Zolah. Unless Aaron chooses to cease being the Alpha of Delmarva pack, they will try to kill her.* ::

Jilah gaped at him, stunned.

:: *So much for happily ever after.* ::

Argent threaded his fingers around hers. :: *It is her choice, beloved.* ::

"Can we go now?" Maslin asked, still shaken.

"I thank you for allowing us to be present for this, Thea. You and yours will always be welcome in my city." Argent smiled and gave a small bow.

"As you are always welcome here, blood regent."

Thea looked over at Jilah and said, "I will let you know when she is ready for visitors again."

Jilah tried to smile, but it felt false. This didn't seem like something to celebrate.

"Thank you, Thea."

They arrived back at the convent and Argent squeezed her hand. *:: There is an issue that needs tending to. Will you be alright on your own for a little bit? ::*

Jilah nodded and smiled, squeezing back. *:: I'll be fine. Go do what you need to do. I'm not going anywhere. ::*

Argent looked back at her, eyes glittering, his expression unreadable as he kissed her, then darted off.

She turned to look over at Maslin. The therianthrope had been watching them, wide eyed.

"Are you going to be okay?" she asked Maslin, her voice thick with concern.

He looked back at her, wincing a little.

"I, ah, this is more than a little disorienting."

Jilah stepped back from him, a little hurt. His reaction was understandable, given what she'd said to him the last time they'd seen each other.

She frowned and replied, "I'm sorry, I didn't think."

He held up a hand, cutting her off. "No, it's okay."

Something flitted through her memory and she jerked back in realization.

"Wait. Oh god, you were there when I..." Jilah covered her mouth with her hand, eyes wide. He had witnessed the entire horror show that she'd put Argent through. She could feel his discomfort at being near her thrum in his psyche.

She turned away and quickly said, "Look, you don't have to... "

Jilah felt a warm hand on her wrist and she turned to look back at him.

"Stop. It's just weird, okay? I mean, I'm glad you're back."

Maslin stared at her, taking in all her physical changes with an immense curiosity.

"You look really different," he added lamely, not really knowing what else to say.

Jilah turned to face him, nodding. "Yeah. It's taking me a while to get used to it myself."

He slid his hands in his pockets and she watched as his lips curled into a small smile.

"I, ah, couldn't help noticing the wings, in particular. Everything else is accentuated, but the wings are new."

Feeling her cheeks grow hot, she replied, "Ah, yeah. They are."

"They suit you."

He smiled now and she felt his discomfort ebb.

"Thanks."

Yep, she was definitely blushing now.

"It's good to see *you* in there again."

Jilah nodded in agreement.

"It's good to be the only one in here, finally."

Maslin looked down at the floor for a moment, then looked up and asked, "Do you want to talk about it?"

Jilah took a shaky breath, then blurted out, "She ran me into the ground out there."

Her voice became a haunted whisper. "She was going to run me until she burned me out, or until the council sent someone to kill me."

She looked away. "The things I saw over there, the things I *did*... "

Maslin nodded, solemn. "I read the reports."

Jilah frowned back at him and he explained, "I'm... ah, an advisor to the Strigaisha now. He showed it to me while you were still down there."

She looked over at him, asking, "Did he suffer much? I mean, after... "

"He worked hard at not letting it show. It didn't always work."

She nodded, then asked, "I didn't get you in trouble with your pack, did I?"

Maslin looked away, shaking his head.

"It was nothing I couldn't handle."

'Giiiirl, don't you look *FIERCE!*"

Jilah turned to see Gigi walking towards her with a huge grin. Before she could react, the sorceress pulled her into a tight hug.

Maslin chuckled and took a step back.

"You've been missed," he explained.

Jilah replied, "So I see."

Gigi set her back down then looked her over.

"Okay – one, you *need* to tell me who got you all did up like that. Two, I see I'm gonna have to work on your wardrobe to make sure you have tops that go with those fine new wings. Three – the girls are dying to see you. You just say the word and I'll get you out to see them, okay? And four, I missed the hell out of you. Don't you *ever* go runnin' off like that again and not come visit for half a year, dammit."

Jilah's chest tightened with emotion, simply elated to see her friend again.

"Don't you look so happy at me, girl. I'm angry at you." Gigi snapped, looking serious for a moment. "You had me really worried."

"I had me really worried too," Jilah explained, sobering.

Gigi let out a huff, then snapped, "Okay, you're forgiven. *This* time. But do it again, and see what happens."

Gigi was smiling now. She turned to Maslin and fluttered her eyelashes.

"How you doin', cuteness?"

Maslin blushed, flustered.

Jilah grinned as Gigi put her arm around his shoulders and said, "Relax, honey. I'm not a chickenhawk."

Maslin chuckled and nodded his head. "I know. We've had this conversation before."

"It's just so cute the way he gets all shy when I flirt with him. Makes it hard to resist, heart breaker."

Gigi smiled and gave him a brief squeeze.

"Alright, now that I know you're back, I'll let you guys catch up. Don't do nothin' Gigi wouldn't do, darlin'."

The sorceress grinned and walked out of the room, humming to herself.

Jilah shook her head and muttered, "Start having sex with two guys regularly and everybody thinks you're easy."

Maslin blushed furiously, eager to redirect the tone of the conversation.

"Tell me about Africa," Maslin prompted.

Jilah smiled, remembering the things she had loved about the land.

"Africa was beautiful, majestic. It's a place with its own distinct rhythm, a feeling that works its way into your bones. When I was allowed to rest, I was sometimes almost overwhelmed by it all, aside from the errand she had me on. Everything smelled different; even the sky looked different."

Jilah paused, then turned to her friend, her voice shaking now.

"I don't remember the faces of my targets, just the faces of the few women and girls left alive in their wake."

Her expression became hard, angry. "I thought I'd seen monsters before, but this was so far beyond the pale. The way they treated anybody that crossed their path... Animals have more sense, more *respect*. It's better they're gone."

"There is always someone eager to take their place, though," Maslin replied quietly.

Jilah shivered, nodding. "Yeah. Why is that?"

Maslin shrugged, answering, "Could be humanity's seeming need to destroy themselves. They don't understand the cycle that they're a part of, so they fight it – doing everything they can so that they don't have to live within it."

"Argent says I need to stop thinking like a human. It isn't doing me any favors,"

Maslin shrugged. "When you live longer and have more of an effect on everything around you, you tend to see life differently. Humans are here for the blink of an eye, so they don't always see the bigger picture."

Jilah looked over at him and he quickly added, "Oh, I'm not saying there aren't some sadists in the races that live longer. Unfortunately, my father was a prime example."

Maslin looked away.

Jilah placed a hand on his shoulder and murmured, "I didn't mean to bring up something painful."

Maslin looked back at her with a grateful smile, "It's okay – I know. I guess I'm saying that longer life and higher durability isn't the key either. There are some who go mad with all that additional time on their hands. Boredom and the lack of a challenge sometimes twists people."

Jilah was very familiar with that concept. In many ways, she was very fortunate that Argent came looking for her. For a brief moment, she wondered what her life would have become without him. Would she ever have been able to break free of the dark squatter that had tormented her psyche? There was something very reassuring knowing that he'd be there for as long as she needed him. The worst had already happened. She wouldn't be leaving his side again anytime soon. Here, and now at the Synod, she had friends, a supportive family.

It was more than she'd ever had before.

"Yeah. I get that," she murmured.

Maslin took a step back, then said, "It really is good to have you back, Jilah."

She smiled as he turned to go, then walked back towards their bedroom.

A bath was very much in order.

Argent looked up to see Jilah standing in the doorway to his office with a shy smile. He grinned and leaned back in the chair as she stepped into the room.

:: Am I interrupting? ::

He chuckled and shook his head, waving her over.

:: Not in any way that isn't entirely welcome, beloved. ::

Jilah walked over and took his hand as Argent pulled her into his lap.

:: I need to talk to you about something, :: she murmured.

:: That sounds ominous. ::

Argent squeezed her gently as she leaned into him, feeling the slightest thread of uneasiness.

:: I just... :: she started, pausing for a moment before continuing. *:: I want to keep working with the Synod. ::*

Argent blew out a sigh of relief. This, he could handle.

:: I figured that you would. You've been training so hard. I couldn't see you giving it up, and wouldn't have it any other way. ::

They held each other for a few moments before Jilah said, *:: There might be times when I'm gone for as long as a week or so, but it'll be nothing like... ::* she trailed off and Argent kissed her cheek.

:: Do what you need to do to sate your soul, beloved. I will not hold it against you. Ever. ::

As long as she always returned, he'd be okay.

:: There's so much in my heart, so much I want to say, :: she murmured, her voice barely audible in his thoughts.

Argent felt the connection open between them, and in that moment, he learned all he needed to. Words weren't necessary.

He looked up at her, eyes full of emotion as he sent, *:: I have something I want to show you. ::*

Jilah's lower lip trembled as she reached a shaky hand out, trailing fingers along the body of her beloved Karmann Ghia.

She looked back at Argent and asked, *:: When did you...? ::*

He smiled as he watched her look back over at the car she loved, opening the driver's side door and getting inside. Jilah had to drop the seat back and sit forward a little to accommodate the wings.

and wondered if she could talk to Gigi at some point about how to upgrade the seat to support her back without crushing the wings while she drove.

:: Shortly after I returned. I wanted... needed something substantial of you here. Something you loved. ::

She drew a shaky breath as she placed her hands on the steering wheel, trying not to squeeze it so hard that it warped in her hands.

He continued, saying, *:: It's worth it to see the look in your eyes right now. ::*

Jilah spotted the keys in the ignition and her heart raced. It took her a few moments to wrap her head around everything she was feeling before she finally said, :: *Get in.* ::

Argent grinned and opened the passenger side door. He slid into the seat, looking over at her as he closed the door.

:: *Feel like taking a road trip up to Kansas?* :: he asked, his smile growing wider.

Jilah's jaw dropped before she smiled back at him.

:: *It's a sixteen hour drive. Wouldn't it be quicker to just have Gigi gate us up there?* ::

Argent leaned back in the seat, crooking an eyebrow as he sent, :: *True, but I have the very strong suspicion that this will be a great deal more fun.* ::

Jilah frowned for a moment, asking, :: *What about an escort? Won't the pack...?* ::

:: *For a short, informal visit, we don't need to bother Alain for an escort, and Aurelian will be able to handle things for a day or two.* ::

Jilah laughed as she turned the key in the ignition, revving the engine briefly before meeting his eyes and saying, :: *Best homecoming ever. Do they know we're coming?* ::

Argent shrugged and replied, :: *I figured we'd surprise them.* ::

:: *Did I mention that I love the way your mind works?* ::

He chuckled and let his fingers play along the surface texture of the dashboard. He had to admit, it really was a great car.

:: *I believe you've mentioned it once or twice.* ::

Jilah pulled out of the garage and onto the empty street. There were distinct advantages to starting a road trip at four in the morning.

:: *Good,* :: she murmured. :: *Just so we're clear.* ::

The sound of screeching tires echoed in the night air as they began the second part of their journey together.

ABOUT THE AUTHOR

I write erotic horror and erotica, sing, eulogize those who have crossed over, challenge popular notions and am a kinky, socially marginal, mildly felonious anarcho-shamanic Santeria Priestess.

You can follow my general and sometimes spooky misadventures online in the following places:

Facebook: https://www.facebook.com/poknats
Twitter: http://twitter.com/ninjacooter